£1·50

CANDLE IN THE WIND

Reven Forrester is a British Chief Inspector of Police whose special task is to break the vicious triad gangs who tyrannise Hong Kong. Communist rule will come soon, but still the refugees pour across the border from China. When eight-year-old refugee Kit Ling comes into his care, raped and helpless, Forrester sees in her the embodiment of all that is lovely and good. He wishes to protect her, but he has made a deadly enemy in Eddie Woo, and Kit Ling becomes the tragic victim of their feud.

Fired by anger and disgust, Reven Forrester plans a relentless and illegal campaign in pursuit of the rapist of Kit Ling. But Forrester's vendetta is hindered by an ever deepening love for Woo's beautiful sister Shen, who knows nothing of her brother's darker side. Ah Fong, Forrester's superstitious old amah, believes Shen and her brother to be two forms of a single spirit, set to void the life-essence from Only Son, Reven. To save him she must destroy the very woman he loves . . .

The action of this marvellously atmospheric novel moves from the idyllic British island of Lantau, just off the China coast, to Hong Kong itself, then to the Muslim island city of Jolo in the southern Philippines. Triad warfare, piracy, crime and corruption form the heart of a gripping story of revenge in the exotic islands of the South China Sea. Previously known for adventure fiction, Peter Essex has taken a triumphant new direction. *Candle in the Wind* is not only an exciting and sinuous thriller, but also a powerfully affecting love story.

PETER ESSEX

CANDLE IN THE WIND

COLLINS
8 Grafton Street, London W1
1989

William Collins Sons & Co. Ltd
London · Glasgow · Sydney · Auckland
Toronto · Johannesburg

First published 1989
Copyright © Peter Essex-Clark 1989

BRITISH LIBRARY CATALOGUING IN PUBLICATION DATA

Essex, Peter
Candle in the wind.
I. Title
823[F]

ISBN 0 – 00 – 223441 – 6

Photoset in Linotron Caledonia by
The Spartan Press Ltd, Lymington, Hants

Printed and bound in Great Britain by
Butler & Tanner Ltd, Frome and London

For my father, Walter

Acknowledgements

This book could not have been written without the persevering assistance, kindness and hospitality of the following people:

Chris Wynne-Potts and Jacqui Donaldson of Lantau Island.

Assistant Commissioner John McDonald and Chief Superintendent Mark Pelly of the Royal Hong Kong Police.

Eric Beare, Pat Dougherty, Kevin Sinclair and Lam Kam Leung, business people of Hong Kong.

Colonel Eduardo T. Cabanlig, Major Librado Ladia and Captain Peruji Maang of 2nd Marine Brigade, Jolo, Sulu, Philippines.

Colonel Steve Perry and Colonel Graham George, Military Attachés of the Embassy of the United States.

My brother John Essex-Clark of New South Wales, Australia.

Contents

SO HELP ME GOD

'Have you seen the way the moon falls down into the waves and breaks into a thousand pieces of glass?

'I saw it happen that night as we walked close to the sea at Tai Pan Wan. Wah! it was beautiful. I pointed at it to Elder Sister so she could watch it too. She is called Yin San, but that's just her milk name. She's fifteen years now and won't use her milk name any more. Did I tell you my name? I'm called Kit Ling.

'We had to hide that night at Tai Pan Wan, three times. Father held me tight then so that I wouldn't move: I could hardly breathe. But he didn't mean to hurt me. He never hurts me on purpose. Once he stood on my toe and that hurt, but it wasn't on purpose. That was long ago.

'We hid in the shadows while the soldiers walked by. They had guns and red stars on their caps that shone in the moonlight, and I know they wanted to catch us so I kept very still. And Father kept very still. All of us kept still until they had gone by. But they came back, and that time they nearly caught us. We were right down at the sea then, right down at the edge of Tai Pan Wan, where the moon had fallen in. I know it's not really made of glass.

'We found more people hiding there. A junk came. I think it was a big junk. Well, it must have been big because so many people climbed into it. Not just Father and Elder Sister and I; there were lots more. They gave everyone a little place to sit. Someone said, "Don't you move, hah?" I didn't move. Elder Sister didn't move. She was sitting next to me so I know.

'The engine made such a big noise that I'm sure the soldiers heard us go. Do you want me to tell you about the engine? It made so much noise and smoke that everyone began coughing. And one time it stopped and everyone began to swear. I was glad that it stopped because I could breathe then. But they soon started it. And so the smoke came again.

'The next time it stopped no one swore or tried to start it. The junk went on for a bit then it bumped a bit and stopped. Someone said, "This place you get off!" Everyone was excited-talking. We were out of Big Land, they said.

'There were houses. I could see them. I hoped this was Hong Kong, but it wasn't Hong Kong. There were no lights on so how could it be Hong Kong? . . . Someone said, "Be quick. Be quick." Wah! How quick we were. Through the village and into the hills. The moon was gone now and I thought I could get lost. But I didn't get lost. The one who had said "Be quick", now said: "Make a line. Make a line." Father was in front of me and Elder Sister behind me and we were part of the line. I think it was a long line.

'We walked in darkness. We walked up a big hill, maybe more than one hill. We walked all night long, and I fell down many times. So did Father. I held on to his coat like he told me to and Elder Sister's hand was on my back. I was very hungry, but no time for rice. We did not stop that night, just walk and walk.

'In the morning we stopped. We were high up in the hills. As it became light, the man who had said "Be quick" and "Make a line" came along: "Hide here – you here – you there." Father hid me behind some big rocks and he gave me rice. He told me he would be close. He said, "You don't cry, ah. You don't move never mind what!" Then he went away.

'I don't know where Father went. Do you know where he went? Must be looking for me. He's a big man, so strong my father.

'I think they caught Father and took him away. There was

much noise. Many people shouting. Some shouted, *"Run"*, some shouted, *"Stop"*. I did what Father told me to do – don't cry out, don't move. Soon there was no more shouting. No more noise. But I did not move. When it was dark like anything I called out. I didn't call out loudly, just a little call so Father could hear me.

"He wasn't there. Elder Sister wasn't there. No one there. I walked a long way and then I saw some lights shining and I thought it was Hong Kong, so I walked there. But it wasn't Hong Kong. It was a small place like the village that I come from . . . Did I tell you the village that I come from? It's Ku Ching Yen that's where I come from: Ku Ching Yen in Big Land.

'This place was just like that but the people there were different. I asked them where my father was and they said, "How do we know, hah?" They said the police had got him, sure. They said the police had been up the hills all week looking for runaways from Big Land, they must have taken him to Hong Kong. They asked me where I wanted to go and I told them, Hong Kong. They gave me rice, and they were kind to me. They said, "You want to work, hah? Work stay here. Not work can go!" Said, "Why go to Hong Kong? What to do in Hong Kong?" I cried so much then they didn't like me any more. Said, "Hey, you a bad child. You go to Hong Kong now."

'There was an old auntie there who was going to Hong Kong and she said that she would take me. We went together down to a road where a bus came by and both of us sat in it. It took us to Hong Kong. I knew I was at Hong Kong then. Wah! This place is as big as a thousand Ku Ching Yen. I knew this place was where Father was.

'We went to a market. This was the real big market. Old auntie held my hand, she said, "You don't run from me, little girl!" Everywhere we walked I watched out for my father, but there were so many people all over. How can I find him where there are so many people?

13

'I saw him, sure. I knew I would find him and I *did*. I didn't see his face; he was walking from me. I let go of old auntie's hand and ran. But when I got to where Father was, he wasn't there . . . I saw him again. He was still walking away, so he did not see me. I called out to him, but so much noise. How could he hear me? I ran after him. There were so many people, I couldn't find him. I looked everywhere but there were so many places to look.

'I cried a lot then and some people said, "Don't you cry, hah? Where's your Mar Mar? – Where you come from?" I told them that I come from Big Land, Mar Mar was gone to Golden Hills, Father was gone to Hong Kong. Everyone laughed a lot and I felt better.

'A man came by who said, "Hello, I know this girl's father. I better take her there!" So everyone said that he should do that. I felt happy then.

'Wah! we sit in a car. The man gave me rice and fish and bought me an orange and a comb for my hair. So I believed him. He said, "You want to see your father, that's right? Then you better come with me."

'We went in the car again to the place where he said my father was. We climbed up high stairs into a big room. The man picked me up then and carried me. He told me that Father was there . . . It was such a big room, full of tables, big tables with green tops and lights that shine down on them. Some people were leaning on a table playing a game, pushing with long sticks at many little balls. He took me to some men and they stopped playing and looked at me.

'One man walked away and we walked behind him to a room. He said, "Here is your father" . . . He was wrong. I told him that this was not my father. Father was quite different. But he just laughed at me, and said, "Don't you be stupid, better behave." I cried then, I didn't like him any more. He slapped me. Then he went away and left me with the man not my father.

'That man picked me up. He said, "You're pretty, hah?

14

What's your name? You like nice fruit, that's right?" He gave me some tangerine pieces sprinkled with sweet sugar. It was nice but after I ate I felt like falling down.

"He pushed against me, hard. It didn't hurt then. I knew that it was bad things but I felt so slow that I couldn't say, "Wah! Stop!" The room turned round and round, the way it does when I play "spin-a-spin" with friends. I couldn't feel pain. Now I feel pain . . . Will the pain go away?

'When the man with the car came back I was still sick. I cried then. He was nice to me again, but I knew he was a bad man. He said, "Don't you worry, now I know where father is," but I didn't believe him any more.

'One time when he stopped the car, I opened the door and ran away. That was when the policeman caught me. And he took me to the *big* hospital and they were nice to me. Then you came.

'Now I've said everything about how I came to Hong Kong . . . *Yes*, that's the place where big green tables are, and the man who hurt me. Please, Uncle, don't take me back there. I won't be a nuisance, hah.'

'Hush, child,' said the Chief Inspector. 'I won't take you back there. You're safe with me.'

'Will you take me to my father?'

'I will try,' said the Chief Inspector. 'I will try very hard.' He thought: how could any man be so vile, so evil as to do this to this innocent sweet soul. I will try, Kit Ling; I will try to find one lost father and one lost sister amongst ten thousand lost refugees. Then I will try to see that you are not sent back to China. Brave little Kit Ling, you have suffered enough.

'Dock Transit Centre,' he instructed his driver. It was as good a place as any to begin such a search.

As the car drew away he placed his arm lightly, so lightly upon the frail shouldered creature at his side and stroked away the shiver of lost hope. He said:

'They will be punished. So help me God.'

*

15

Lucky Billiard Club: the lettering shone, gold upon crimson, and was flanked by vigorous five-clawed dragons. The sign was imposing; something worth looking at on an otherwise ordinary expanse of wall. Beneath this heraldry was painted *Third Floor, Tsing Shan House*. An arrow pointing upwards showed the way.

The building that housed the club was old and shouldered down by the flanking blocks in narrow hustling Mody Road. The entrance steps ran, smooth trodden marble, into a foyer a dozen people would crowd. Here were the name plates of the other occupants of the building. A narrow staircase offered deeper penetration for those energetic or in a hurry. For the rest, a small lift visited, on occasions, all floors.

Lucky Billiard Club was not the biggest such club in the district of Tsim Sha Tsui. But it was the newest. It was so new that the large red flower-board well-wishers had sent to invoke good fortune was still draped upon the parapet; it read: 'GREAT PROSPERITY. SUCCESS IN ALL AFFAIRS. TEN THOUSAND ADVANTAGES.'

If only it was the truth. Success had so far bypassed the doors of Lucky Billiard Club. The chatter and snick of billiard balls stirred in with human hubbub, these sounds ran thin across the green baize tables of Lucky Billiard Club. There *was* music, but it bounced in a hollow unappreciated sulk from wall to wall.

There were those who said that the whole problem had to do with the debilitated energy of the building itself. Tsing Shan House was a pre-war dwarf of just six piddling floors. All around it loomed buildings of twice that stature, and twice as hungry for any passing flow of energy. But that was not the truth and Eddie Woo knew it.

The third floor was a good floor, halfway up and halfway down, it was ideally situated to draw upon the chi – the energy of that building, of which there was no lack. He had hired one of the most respected (and expensive) Feng Shui priests in all of Hong Kong to ascertain exactly that.

16

It had nothing to do with chi at all. There was not a square foot of space that had not been travelled by the compass of the Feng Shui priest, and all of it pronounced good. Feng Shui – Wind, Water. The language of living, breathing nature. Feng Shui, a force as potent as gravity, that governed the structure of all things, great or small, visible and invisible. Eddie Woo had gone to great lengths to ensure he was in harmony with it.

Oh he had gone to great trouble to make it right. One month previously, on the twenty-second day of the seventh lunar month, at precisely 8 p.m. – an hour that was deemed perfect according to Eddie Woo's birthdate, the birthdate of the God of Riches, and the wisdom of Respected Master T'ung – he had opened his doors to permit his first-night guests into the interior of his club. And *what* an interior they had seen. 'Wah!' Many were the compliments from those who had thronged the club that night. '*Sangyi hing lung,*' they had toasted: Business in joyful abundance, Eddie Woo. It was right that it should be so.

The salon was painted out in rich dark red, a colour which deepened most auspiciously when the lights were on, as they were now. Where beams crossed the ceiling they had been tapped for chi with flutes of brass. Where there were pillars they had been hung with cunningly angled mirrors to deflect that energy to every corner. There was not a door that was wrongly positioned, not a fixture that was not part of the life force of that place.

It did not end there. The billiard tables were covered with imported green baize – as green as the lawns of the Governor's residence. Forty-four tables in all. A few more could have been squeezed in but the principles of Feng Shui had forbidden it. 'Double four,' had said the Feng Shui priest. Double four it was. The chi was there all right, doing its best to bring good things to those who worked and those who played at Lucky Billiard Club.

Eddie Woo worked there. He sometimes played there.

He was the owner of the club and *he* knew very well the reason for his lack of success. He was being victimized by the police. Someone (he did not know who) for some reason (he did not know why) had placed the name of Eddie Woo in position number one upon his hit list. It had to be someone with either a great deal of authority or a great deal of money, perhaps both. But who? Who hated him so much that he would order his destruction?

He had pondered upon these questions for many hours, and found no answer. He had spoken at length to Hei Shui Triad Society, to which brotherhood he paid squeeze in huge amounts for the privilege of being a tenant of 'their' building. They told him it was the police who were bleeding him. He told them that he already knew that. They told him that they would try to find out whose hand it was that wielded the long knife. He told them to be quick; he was going broke, and that would do none of them any good.

Frustrated to the bone, Eddie Woo stood up from his desk. Two quick and irritable paces brought him to a window. There his movements slowed. Carefully, almost in a furtive way, he adjusted the tilt of the venetian blinds to enable him to peer down into the street. It was drizzling and the sky was dark, but the streets of Tsim Sha Tsui are never without light. He scanned the opposite kerb.

There they were: the men in the beige Nissan Crown, parked in as careless a manner as only a policeman would dare. They had a camera, a small hand-held video. It was trained towards the entrance of Tsing Shan House. That was all they were doing, but had it been a machine gun that they were pointing at his entrance the effect could not have been greater. There was not a youth in the whole of Kowloon who would voluntarily submit to such exposure. Thus there was not a youth from the whole of Kowloon inside Lucky Billiard Club. At that hour the neon-fired streets were roaring with trade; slipping and sliding with humans like whitebait in a net. But who would dare to come to Lucky Billiard Club?

18

They were killing him, those fucking cops with their video camera, and until he had discovered who had put them there, there was not a thing he could do about it. At that moment the phone rang on Eddie Woo's desk. He lifted the receiver.

'*Wai?*'

'Woo Sung-king?'

'*Hai a.*' Eddie Woo acknowledged his true given name.

'The identity of the man is Reven Forrester. He is a foreign devil – gwai lo. A Chief Inspector in the Counter Triad Unit at department 'A' HQ on Arsenal Street. Do you know this man?'

'No. Never heard of him.'

'He must know you. There must be a reason for his actions.'

'I'm clean . . . What . . . ?' He would have asked what action he should now take had the question not been preempted.

'Do *nothing*. Do not speak to anyone about this. Hei Shui will take care of this. Of course the cost will be great.'

'How great? Times are bad.'

'You will be advised, Woo Sung-king.'

The call was terminated then. Eddie Woo blew out his cheeks in a long sigh. More cost, more expense. When would it end? He had dipped into family resources so deeply that there was little left. He had borrowed against collateral that no longer existed, and if his creditors foreclosed on him tomorrow, he and his family would be ruined. The shock of that, the disgrace, the loss of face, would kill Grandfather. And for the living, for himself it would be hell on earth.

He walked back to the window. The lackeys of his tormentor, the gwai lo cop Reven Forrester, they were still there.

'*Diu lei le mo.*' He called down fornication upon the mothers of Chief Inspectors of Police.

'*Diu lei seifu.*' He invoked upon those policemen an equal curse . . . It was not enough. He raised the blinds completely and opened the window wide. He shouted down into the wet and shiny street: 'Hey, you in the car. Hey, look up here!'

19

The street noise was great. But Eddie Woo's will to be heard was greater. A group of people gathered and looked up. Someone thought to tap upon the roof of the beige Nissan and point the occupants towards the third-floor window. The faces of the policemen elevated – the video camera elevated. This was the moment that Eddie Woo had been waiting for.

In a gesture that was wide and willing of forearm and knuckle and finger, he delivered upon them the salute of Sodom.

He felt like a superman. Still exhilarated from his performance he opened the phone book upon his desk and thumbed through it to the letter F . . . Ford, Foreman, Forrester: Forrester, R. What a boon was the Hong Kong Telephone Company; what a ready and concise source of reference it provided for those who sought revenge.

Hei Shui had done an excellent job but now he did not need the triads. *Diu lei seifu* on Chief Inspector Forrester. He would pay. Yes, he would pay, that snake-hearted bastard, until he bled.

The office of the Deputy Director, Crime was spacious and carpeted and air-conditioned. A desk of mahogany, broad and wide, squatted centre floor, graced with leather-trimmed blotter and pen stand to match. At the desk edge a gilded wooden name plate gave the occupant of that fine room as Assistant Commissioner B. J. Campbell. The door stood open.

'Go in,' said the Assistant Commissioner's secretary. Reven Forrester went in.

'Can I get you some tea, coffee? The AC is delayed. He asked me to seat you in his office.'

She was Cantonese and wore spectacles of studious, round design. Her summer police uniform suited her well.

'Bit late for that. How about a beer?'

She did not smile. 'The AC won't be long, sir.'

20

Forrester sat down upon a visitor's chair, impressed by the smell of good leather that arose from it, but he did not remain seated for long. As soon as the secretary had departed he stood up and began to pace. That seemed to suit his mood. He was tall. A strong neck rose from the khaki, summer drill tunic. He had good regular features marred only by a small, jagged scar that coloured his left temple: a triad fighting chain is sharp and as quick as a whip.

Seven paces terminated Forrester's walk before a standard issue, bemedalled portrait of Her Majesty Queen Elizabeth II. Below Her Majesty stood a bookcase filled up with weighty books on criminal procedure and law and forensics and a thousand other tips for the villain who wishes to succeed. Seven paces in the opposite direction brought him to a wall on which was affixed a chart displaying in the form of rectangles and inter-connecting lines the organization of department 'A': the operational arm of the Royal Hong Kong Police.

The rectangle that encased the words Deputy Director, Crime lay at the head of all these lines and squares. At the bottom was a rectangle, designated: Counter Triad Unit. A long and much broken line separated these offices. Beyond all doubt then Brian Jonathan Campbell was a most important man, and the CTU was as the tail upon the rump of the bull – a useful appendage to stir the air. But the triads, like flies, always came back.

When the door opened to admit the Assistant Commissioner, Reven Forrester stood before the organizational chart. The AC came in. A short, plump man, bluff-faced, in his middle sixties. Forty years and four gazetted ranks separated the two men. The AC had a comfortable way of making the gap seem less.

'Sir.' Forrester braced up.

The AC acknowleged Forrester with a small wave, walked to his desk and sat down. He was perspiring. Dark patches of sweat stained the undersleeves of his safari suit and his

21

forehead shone. He mopped at his brow with a hand-kerchief.

'Bloody hell!' He sprang the locks on his briefcase and swatted down a file upon his desk. 'I'll never get used to it. You were born here, Reven, it's different for you.'

Forrester sat down again. 'It is hot,' he said.

'Your father used to suffer with the heat. As you get older you feel it more.'

Forrester said, 'Quite.'

'Damn fine chap, your old man, I don't mind telling you. I knew him well, Reven. Admired him a lot. I was just a youngster in the Civil Service. He was my OC in the Volunteers in '39. Did you know that?'

'I knew you served with him, sir. You showed me a photograph once.'

'So I did.' The AC remembered. 'D company. I've got the picture in a scrapbook at home. He was a fine OC. The Japs couldn't break him in their Sham Shui Po hell hole. God knows the swines tried. Lost everything in the war you know, Reven. We all did . . . houses, furniture, jobs. Your dad's house on the Peak was shelled to bits. Thank God your mother got out of Hong Kong in time, bonny lass, your mother. She used to stand Hong Kong upon its ear I can tell you, before the war, and when she came back afterwards. She was the one who made the money, Reven, put the Forresters back on their feet. She believed in property.'

The door opened then to admit the AC's secretary once more. 'Will you be needing me any longer, sir?'

'Is it that late already?' Brian Campbell glanced at his wristwatch. 'So it is. You can go now. It's quite all right. Good night, Joyce.'

'Good night, sir.'

Forrester turned in his chair and watched the woman depart – good, full-moon buttocks.

'The people who invested in property in those days all made a mint,' Campbell said.

'Did you invest, sir?' Forrester returned his attention to his superior.

'I did, and I sold too early. Should have listened to your mother. *She* was shrewd.'

'She was that.'

'I was surprised when you decided to join the force, Reven. I always thought you'd go into business.'

Forrester shrugged. 'This suits me fine.'

'That it does,' said the AC. 'I've had good reports about you. Difficult unit yours. No end to your work. How are you finding it, Reven?'

Now what was all this about? It was neither the place nor the hour for a detailed situation report. The Counter Triad Unit was the AC's own brainchild, created to coordinate anti-triad action within department A. Campbell thus monitored it closely.

'It's all in the monthly report,' Forrester said. 'The detection rate has improved on typical triad type crimes by three per cent. Unlawful society, convictions are up by five per cent. DD trafficking, section-seven convictions show an improvement of four per cent. Possession of offensive weapons . . . Do you want to hear this kind of stuff, sir?'

'It's difficult to tell, is it not, whether such statistics indicate a rise in crime or a rise in police efficiency. I'm pleased that the ratio between cases reported, and cases detected has narrowed. That's good. We're getting more of them. The newspapers love it. But I'm not sure that we're winning the war. What I wanted from you was your *gut* feel, Reven.'

'It was a good idea sir, the CTU. Absolutely.'

Forrester leaned back in his chair, but not in comfort. He hoped that the question, thus palliated, would be forgotten. What, after all, did it matter what the gut feel was of one Chief Inspector of Police? No policy change would result. No one in high office would slap his head and gasp, 'My God, what genius!' All he would achieve by stating his opinions

23

would be to antagonize the man who had originated the CTU programme. He didn't want that. The AC was a good boss. Why spoil things?

The AC, it seemed, was dead set on spoiling things. He said: 'I chose you to head up that unit, Reven, because I thought you were the man for the job. There are plenty of superintendents who were dying for the job. I wanted a man who was not simply a robot with three silver pips or a crown to decorate his epaulettes. Do you savvy?'

'Yes, sir.' Now there was no alternative. 'My gut feel is that the Counter Triad Unit was a good idea; *is* a good idea. We *have* improved the arrest rate, but as you said what does that really mean. Take vice, sir, as an example: the fishball stalls – the one woman brothels – are being constantly raided and the prostitutes pulled in, and convicted. That's grand for the statistics but in real terms it means very little. Those women work in shifts but we can only arrest the one on "duty" as it were, and maybe a front man. The operators, the lessors of the apartments can't be nicked unless "guilty knowledge" can be proved. So the Open for Business sign stays up. The porn-show operators are so smart now that the video isn't even on the premises. They transmit the show to the theatre through remote boosters that are more than a block away. So even when we make an arrest, it's only the front men that are convicted.

'Drug pushers are getting more difficult to nick. They don't carry the stuff on them any more. They take the money then send the users elsewhere to pick up the stuff. We're arresting them all the time and making it hard for them to operate. The price of No. 3 heroin has gone up by thirty dollars a gram, which means that there's less of it around. But it is still around. So the users have to pay more, so street crime goes up. And our arrest rate goes up. But the bigger syndicates are still doing a turnover of around a quarter-million dollars a day. So what have we achieved?

'It's the old, old story. The front men are being arrested and convicted, and being paid very well for their pains. The triad bosses are not being touched . . . I'm sure I'm not telling you anything you don't know, sir.'

'No you're not.'

'Our laws are archaic. The sentences provided are so light that they're a joke; they're no deterrent at all.

'We're doing a better job, sir, but we haven't got the power to do what should be done. The triad bosses stay untouchable; the triad organization grows strong. It's fashionable to join a triad gang because it's easy, and it pays. It's nice to be on the winning side, it's glamorous, so there's no shortage of young recruits. Do you want me to go on, sir?'

'Not really.' Campbell rubbed his face in his hands in a tired way. 'You see, I know all these things, and I know what legislative remedies are required too. What I wanted to establish was the degree of frustration felt at your level. Now I have.'

'We live with it.' Forrester shrugged.

The AC stood up and Forrester thought the interview was over. It was not. The book cabinet beneath Her Majesty proved more worthy than it appeared. Campbell withdrew from it an old, pint-bottle of Dimple Haig, then feigned a rich Scots burr:

'Can I tempt you then, laddie?'

'Thank you, sir.'

Two cut-glass tumblers came from his drawer. He polished them with the same handkerchief he had used to mop his brow, placed them upon the desk and poured.

'Your dad and I had many a drink together. He was a Scotch drinker.'

'You thought a lot of him, sir.'

'I respected him. He was older than me, and my superior, but he never made me feel it. I've always thought that that is how an officer should be. That's how you should be, Reven, when you become a senior officer.'

25

'I'll remember that, sir.'

'You'll get there. If you keep your nose clean . . . What's this about a video-camera team outside Lucky Billiard Club, Reven?'

Of course he had expected this question from his superior sooner or later. The answer was obvious, and not altogether a fabrication.

'Triad connections, sir. Just routine.'

'A routine bit of harassment.'

'Harassment?' God forbid.

'Well it seems that that is how a certain group of influential Chinese businessmen feel about it. Came up on the Kowloon district Fight Crime Committee agenda today. They reckon that we could be more properly employed.'

'The FCC said *that*? I thought they were on our side.'

'You thought they were on our side? Well, they are. The FCC's pushing for legislation to curtail triad activity: to place a curfew on known triad members; to forbid them access to certain premises. Now, the Legislative Council on the other hand maintains that we don't need any more power; that we abuse our existing powers. Your kind of action doesn't help.'

'I think you should know the whole story, sir . . . On your instruction all violent crime is reported directly to my unit. A month back, almost to the day, I received a report from Kowloon Region CID of a rape on an underaged girl. Normally I wouldn't have investigated this personally, but the Prince of Wales Hospital is practically on my way home, so I called in . . . What I saw there . . . Christ she was only eight by my reckoning, if that. She looked at me and she was terrified . . . I once shot a deer; I dropped it at a hundred yards, but didn't kill it outright. When I came up to it to put a final shot through its skull it lay there and looked up at me with these soft brown eyes. *She* had those eyes; submissive, wounded eyes. She was an illegal immigrant, sir. She had been separated from her father during a sweep for IIs in the Nam Shan hills. She'd come to Hong Kong to search for him.

26

Some bastard, some unspeakable filth had raped the kid – drugged her and then raped her. But all that her eyes showed was resignation, total resignation. It wasn't difficult to find out who was responsible. It was a snooker club owner called Woo Sung-king, he calls himself Eddie Woo. I found out a few things about him. He's not an uneducated man, he's a graduate of the University of Hong Kong, commerce. His grandfather owns a motorized harbour lighter and a few long-line fishing junks of the Ha Yue Teng or Toh Mong Suen type. So there's money there and he's got access to it. He dipped in the till heavily in order to open his billiard club. Lucky Billiard Club is his place, and that's where he raped the kid. I knew I wouldn't be able to gain a conviction on the single testimony of an eight-year-old girl, so I decided to break Eddie Woo in another way.'

'The video crew.'

'That's what I did, sir. Well, it's backfired on me. I'm sorry. If I've caused you any inconvenience I'm sorry for that.'

The AC was quiet. He had sat through the entire narrative peering down at steepled fingers: an attitude of pious authority that irked Forrester. He wondered if the Dimple Haig and the celebration of the good old days had not been just a ploy to lull him into confession. Well, if it had been a ploy, it had worked. He had admitted to the commission of a disciplinary offence, and Assistant Commissioner Campbell was now in a position to impose a reprimand; even to go so far as to reduce him in rank to senior inspector. ACs had that sort of power.

Campbell looked up at last. 'Did it work?'

'Did what work, sir?'

'Did you manage to disrupt Woo's business?'

'There isn't a Cantonese in the whole of Hong Kong who wants to feature on a police video . . . yes it worked.'

'Good. But you must call off the hounds now.'

'I'll see to it.'

'You let your emotions govern your actions, Reven. You did what you did because you were angry and you wanted a quick-fix solution: revenge. That's not particularly good police practice, you know. And your reprisal action wasn't half as subtle as you imagine. It was a knee-jerk reaction to your anger. That's not good. You must learn to be patient . . . *patient*. That will make you a better policeman. You're poised to become a superintendent, Reven. Don't bugger it up.'

Forrester nodded.

'Did you find the kid's father?'

'Not yet.'

'Hand the case to Child Protective Services. That's what they're there for. They'll find the kid's father if he's in Hong Kong. It's not your business, Reven.'

Forrester said, 'I know . . . if you had seen the kid, sir.'

'Well, finish your drink, lad. Got things to do, haven't you?'

But Forrester had already swallowed the last drop of whisky in his glass. He set it down. The AC offered one final piece of advice:

'I've always found it a mistake to needle villains with petty actions. The more you swipe at them the deeper they dig; the more immune they become. The harder you make it for them, the harder they make it for you. Set them up, then hit hard. Make the first time you strike the last time . . . you savvy? That's the way I'd handle the likes of Eddie Woo.'

Did he savvy? He thought he did. Brian Jonathan Campbell had exercised authority in a masterful way. He had disciplined his subordinate with the lightest of strokes. He had provided Forrester with the wisdom of a decade in the time it took to appreciate a single glass of fine whisky.

Forrester could not help but admire the style of the man, and his counsel was sound. He *had* let his anger drive him into ill-considered action, and that was stupid. From now

28

on he would be happy to follow the AC's advice when it came to the likes of Eddie Woo.

To work with the submerged emotions of the crocodile; that was the requirement. To wait like that reptile waits, with eyes alone exposed and teeth below the muddy water with not a ripple to give away its presence. Yes, it was good advice for the taking of Eddie Woo, for retribution need not be hurried to be effective; the only criterion was that it should be certain.

Forrester thought these thoughts as the lift doors closed upon him and he descended to the ground floor of the Arsenal Street HQ; as he crossed the foyer and walked into the street. It was hot. It was drizzling and he was in uniform – no umbrella.

Now he had to decide where he should spend the night. There was a choice of two destinations. One close at hand: a luxury apartment on Victoria Peak. A short taxi ride was all it would take for him to reach that place of rest and air-conditioned luxury. Maria the Filipino amah would greet him there – sweet-voiced and shining smile. And soon a meal fit for a Tai Pan would be ready.

The alternative destination was distant: a traditional, brick and tile two-storey house on the slopes of Butterfly Hill, on Lantau Island.

That trip would require more patience. Rush-hour – a taxi ride to the Outlying Islands Ferry Pier, there to stand and queue with patience and fortitude and five hundred shouting, shoving Chinese who knew that the devil might take the hindmost but the 6.30 ferry to Lantau would not. This journey would cost two hours of his time. He would arrive at his house tired and short-tempered and disillusioned of all things Cantonese. He would open his front door to be confronted by a testy, vociferous Chinese amah who would complain that he had interrupted her meal and berate him for not having advised her that morning that he would be arriving tonight. Dear Ah Fong's complaints would be more numerous and diverse than that, but those two arguments he could be sure he would be tested with.

He chose to go to Lantau. Not because he did not feel the need for the kid-leatherette upholstery, soft music and Maria's good food but because there was someone upon Lantau Island whom he *had* to see. Her name was Kit Ling. He tried not to think about the orders that the AC had given regarding the little girl. Child Protective Services was an overworked unit. They would do all they could, but that would not amount to much.

He had placed Ah Fong in charge of the child. Ah Fong had been told that Kit Ling was an illegal immigrant, an II, and under no circumstances was the child to be allowed to leave the house. The police would arrest her if they found her, and send her back to China. This information had intrigued Ah Fong, because as she knew, and the neighbours knew, and everyone else on Lantau Island knew – Reven Forrester *was* the police. Nevertheless she had promised that Kit Ling would not as much as set her nose beyond the door gods who guarded the entrance to his house.

He had no reason to believe that his instruction had not been acted upon. He trusted the old amah totally. Ah Fong adored children, she ruled them like a Manchu warlord, but that was because she loved them so. She lived in constant fear that some evil would attend a child left in her care, and was ever prepared to defend against demons and vampires and other bad-minded spirits of the night. Ah Fong carried upon her person at all times a needle with which to prick her middle finger if any such terror should approach. For all ghosts hate the sight of blood. They turn from it in terror and immediately flee.

He knew all these things about the amah Ah Fong because Ah Fong had been his amah when he had been a child. He had taken his first steps hand in hand with Ah Fong. He had hauled himself upright on the fabric of her

30

sam fu trousers and soldiered off on to life's young adventures ever seconded by his defender in the black silk pyjamas.

She had taught him the dialect of the river folk. She had shown him the customs and ways of the people of Guangxi – her people. She had told him the story of her life.

She had been born in Southern Guangxi province, she was not sure of the exact village, the only daughter of a cormorant fisherman. This was unfortunate, for the only creature that is not forever hungry upon a cormorant fishing raft is the bird which does all the diving and retrieving of the fish. For at the night's end the ring is removed from its throat to allow the passage of a single fish past its gullet. Girl children were clearly of less value than these fisher-birds as the passage of food past their gullets occurred with far less regularity. Ah Fong remembered that she was forever hungry. In her sixteenth year, during a bleak cold winter when even the cormorants had gone hungry, she was taken by her father, alone, on a long, long journey to a place called Macau. There she had been offered for auction with several Guangdong province girls. She was pretty. She had been snapped up by a coir-rope trader of a speculative bent, with an eye for a bargain. This entrepreneur had taken her to that market place of all market places, the Fragrant Harbour – Hong Kong.

Ah Fong had then been very lucky. Instead of ending up as a two-dollar whore in the stinking, open sewer alleyways of Hong Kong's 'Walled City', she had come under the protection of the Po Leung Kuk, the institution for the protection of virtue. Po Leung Kuk, after having fattened her skinny ribs and filled out her equally neglected mind with good thoughts of Confucius, had given her into the custody of Victoria Forrester, Reven's mother. Victoria had given Ah Fong the task of attending to the everyday needs of the infant Reven. Ah Fong, the hungry, the discarded daughter who had thought herself to be empty of all things, had found that inside existed a fine and uplifting emotion. It was love. She took up the baby as though it was her own. She scratched into his silver spoon the symbol of long life. In his pocket she placed a jade marble and beneath his pillow a paper spell guarded while Ah Fong slept. She watched young Reven's good strong limbs mature in the certainty that it was she who had brought about this state of rosy health. Ah Fong had pledged herself never to marry and have children of her own. She had staked herself to the supple little tree of 'Only Son' and as it grew she had trained it and trimmed it in her subtle Chinese way.

So Reven Forrester had grown into his teens greatly loved by two mothers. One, a Guangxi river girl who taught him about all things Chinese – about dragons and phoenixes and joss-sticks and Feng Shui and the eight immortal fairies and the tricks they liked to play. The other, his mother of the womb, did not teach him very much personally, but saw to his education in a remote yet interested way. Victoria Forrester made arrangements for her son to go to Australia, there to attend Geelong Grammar School, an institution of learning that made of princes gentlemen, or so the prospectus read. It would do Reven good to board at a grammar establishment with such a reputation. Reven had gone to Geelong, but Victoria Forrester had not lived to see the result.

The Bentley of the family Forrester had taken itself and its chauffeur and its owners on a brakeless, tragic ride down precipitous Jardines Corner. It had crashed into an oncoming goods truck and not an occupant had survived from either vehicle.

One Mother had remained. Ah Fong had coveted only one thing from the estate of that tragic household – a picture of Only Son, Reven, in a carved peachwood frame. This, the executors had allowed her to have. Around it she had folded a mighty charm that invoked the responsible stars and gods to see to Only Son's return. She had waited for the return of her 'son' to Hong Kong, certain that it *would* happen. He would come back from distant Australia and seek her out. Her patience, her loyalty and her faith had been rewarded. The spell had worked, Reven Forrester had come back to Hong Kong, as a man . . .

Reven Forrester slipped the key of the front door into the lock. Music was playing loudly within, he could hear it through the panelling. Ah Fong's joy was her television set; she had paid for it with her hard-earned money, and so she used the volume control in a way that gave it worth. Forrester did not think that she would hear him enter, but he was wrong.

Ah Fong was standing in the hallway as he came in with Kit Ling. The child's hair was combed and ribboned into ponytails that dangled over each ear. Her face shone clean. Her clothes were new – a red pleated skirt with a white embroidered blouse. Ah Fong of course wore what she always wore: a black high collar sam fu trouser-suit.

Kit Ling pointed at him and said: *'Bong paan.'* She came forward and bowed.

The words meant 'help man'. It was the only polite Cantonese term for an Inspector of Police. He wondered what else Ah Fong had taught her. He greeted them both and said to Ah Fong, 'No need for food, Mother. I ate on the ferry.'

'So many hours in the day, why you choose this one when poor tired Mother is with her rice bowl? And you choose to eat that vomit that they serve up on the ferry instead of the good food of my kitchen . . .'

It was just as he had expected – dear, irascible, intransigent Ah Fong. He tapped his peak cap dry, and hung it upon the hall rack. By this time Ah Fong was in full stride.

'. . . and no word to Mother to inform her of Only Son's coming, *aieya!*'

He said, 'Has the child been tiring you, Mother?' He picked up Kit Ling. Her body went stiff for a moment, then relaxed warmly against him. Anger against Eddie Woo was

33

sudden in him. He stroked the silken black hair, it was damp and smelt of shampoo. In his pocket lay a bright set of plastic bangles that he had thought would delight her. He would give them to her later. He carried Kit Ling through the circular, arched, moon gate that led to his sitting room and sat her and himself upon a couch. To Kit Ling he said, 'After you have eaten come back to me here.' To Ah Fong he said, 'Apologies for the disturbance of your meal, Mother. Both of you must continue with your dinner now.'

Then he chased Kit Ling from him in a mock-serious boggle-eyed way that drew a giggle from her. So he did it again, and she laughed again. It was the first time he had heard her laugh and he loved it. Then he thought about what he would have to tell her and the sport came to an end.

Kit Ling ran off shouting, 'Dragon, angry dragon,' and did not see the sadness that changed his face.

Ah Fong saw it.

She stood at the archway holding steaming bowls of food as Kit Ling sped past her noisily. Ah Fong set the bowls down upon a small rosewood tea table, then lifted both table and bowls to the couch where he sat. Rice and sugar-peas, fish in oyster sauce and sprouts, yes, the food of Ah Fong's kitchen was good.

'When the day comes that Old Mother is not able to provide for her son, and the son is forced to eat food from the kitchens of strangers, then look for her on Golden Hill.'

She laid down a pair of chopsticks next to the rice bowl. Reven Forrester wondered if he would ever understand the enigma of the Guangxi mind.

'Good rice, Mother.'

'*Houwah, houwah.*' She waved away the flattery. She went back to the kitchen and when she returned she bore a pot of tea. And lest his thirst was greater than that, she also held a dewy-cold bottle of San Miguel beer. These things she set down upon the table. Then she too sat upon a chair, and, with great concentration, set her gaze upon the empty space

34

of wall above him. She would have preferred to be before her TV set in the kitchen; Forrester knew that. Both of them knew that. She had attended to his needs more than adequately. There was no need for her to linger. The stratagem was designed to make her discomfort obvious but not blatant, visible yet deniable. Ah Fong wished to discuss something that *he* might not wish to discuss. He could confront the subject or endure her pained presence for evermore, it was up to him. Of course the subject she wished to discuss was Kit Ling. He didn't mind. He led into it:

'Where's Kit Ling?'

Ah Fong allowed Forrester's query to drag her attention from the rapture of the wall. Kit Ling, he was told, was in the kitchen watching TV. 'One small girl – is it possible that she can make such a big change?'

'What do you mean?'

'Just like a man! What do I mean? I mean that your eyes are only good for outward looking, for inward looking they are no good. Not to worry. *My* eyes are not so dull.'

'I haven't found her father yet.'

'The sadness of it. Yet I wonder how well you look with those eyes of yours.'

'I've been to the transit centres at Dock Side and Lo Wu and Sha Tau Kok. Do you know how many refugees are in Hong Kong? Thousands are in the transit camps, and God knows how many others are out there, living with the sky as their roof and eating kitchen refuse. It's a mess, Old Mother. Most of them lie about their names, and which of them would admit to a lost *girl* child? I've looked. Believe me.'

'No, no, no.' Ah Fong waved all this effort aside. 'Inside you is a wall that will hide Father of Kit Ling from you.'

'That's ridiculous, Ah Fong.'

'Not ridiculous – true.'

A shriek of laughter came from the kitchen. Both of them turned towards the sound. Ah Fong pointed. 'That little

35

minnow, you think you have her in your net? It is not so. It is the other way around.'

'Nonsense.'

'True.'

'Absolute nonsense.'

'True . . . I see it. That girl is in your eyes. It makes me sad. Makes me happy too. Sad, because you must lose her. Happy, because I see time has come for you to have wife. Make one such little girl for yourself.'

'Aah,' said Forrester, as one does to whom all things are suddenly clear. This was Ah Fong's parrot cry: Find wife; settle down; make children. '*Aah,*' once more, that Ah Fong should know that he was not yesterday's child.

'You want children, Ah Fong? *You* make your own.'

'And who would marry this old six-toed, river woman, ah? It's quite different for me. I will be amah for your little girl . . . maybe boy. Better you make a boy. Who will get all your money when you die? Rich man, I say not. No child; no heir; *no* rich.'

Again the ripple of laughter from the kitchen. Again the happy sound drew them.

'I do like *some* children,' Forrester conceded. 'But that doesn't mean I want one of my own – or that I want to get married.'

'Why not?' Ah Fong harped on. 'What is wrong with the big busted blonde one who stays high on the Peak? *She* has child-bearing hips . . . Or the one who owns the fat jung dang yacht. The one with burning fire hair that sets the whole of Hong Kong alight. She would pass water with joy if you chose her. She'd make good strong children – boys, many boys.'

Forrester spoke sternly. 'No more about marriage, hear?'

'*Aieya!*' Ah Fong threw up her hands. How dull-headed this son: 'An ox-skinned lantern!'

Kit Ling arrived, smile creased from the exploits of the squabble-voiced duck and his three impish nephews who had entertained her: 'Very funny people.'

36

She sat down in the centre of the carpet and observed Forrester in a most interested way, her eyes following the movements of his hands from bowl to mouth as he consumed his food and sipped his tea. He watched her too. She smiled at him; she looked happy. She seemed to be confident that what should be happening to her was indeed happening. She had opened her arms to fate and was now content. It was amazing: as a bird of the nest spreads out its wings one day and offers itself to the invisible air, so this young soul was certain of the latent, unseen power of fate. It was the Chinese way. Ah Fong would shrug and give him that answer were he to enquire of this mystery.

And tomorrow he would ride with Kit Ling upon the ferry that would return them to Hong Kong. He would tell her that all things had changed. She was to be given into the care of the officers of the Child Protective Services unit. And she would spread out her little wings once more.

'Is it not past her bedtime?' Forrester wished to be beyond the trusting gaze and the happy little smile.

Ah Fong claimed Kit Ling's hand and led her away. It was not her bedtime. Chinese children did not sleep according to convention – they slept when they were tired. As soon as the little girl was gone, Forrester wished her back.

But he did not call for her. He listened to the giggle of Kit Ling that flowed now and then from the kitchen. It added a brightness, like freshly painted walls, and fresh cut flowers. The house had benefited from the ambience of this little girl.

Reven Forrester loosened the buttons of his tunic. He disliked the overtight summer dress of the RHKP and only wore it when it was essential. It looked smart, but that was probably because it was too tight to prevent any movement that might wrinkle it. He thought of changing then but was too lazy. Anyway he would retire soon. He carried his beer towards the covered porch that opened from his lounge. He thought he would prefer the darkness, it would be restful in the darkness, dry and comfortable while a few paces away the wind swirled and the rain drove down. The woodwork had expanded since the rains, and a shoulder-hard shove was required in order to open the door. He would get Ah Sau, the village handyman, to come up and attend to it in the morning.

There was a comfortable chair upon the balcony, with fat, kapok-stuffed cushions that he could flop upon and wide wooden arms that would keep his beer within effortless reach.

It began to rain quite heavily. He could hear the hiss of raindrops on foliage and the gurgle of the gutters as they drained the roof water away. From his place of shelter it came as a pleasant, most soothing sound. The sensuous perfume of round-spurred and cymbidium orchids hung in the humid air. He breathed and sighed and agreed with the Chinese who called that scent the Fragrance of Kings.

The chair was as comfortable as he remembered it to be but an unfamiliar pressure within his hip pocket kept him from rest – the bangles he had bought for Kit Ling. He would give them to her when she came to wish him good night.

Eddie Woo cursed the rain. He cursed the cheap rainproof jacket that was so incompletely rainproof that he was soaked. But more than anything he cursed the person who was the cause of his suffering – that egg of a turtle, gwai lo cop. There was no one that he hated more than Mr R. Forrester.

Eddie stood absolutely still. He had found that movement encouraged the passage of rain water past his collar and down his spine in a most irritating way. But more importantly, he kept still because he did not want to be seen.

His position was close enough to the house of Reven Forrester to have hawked and spat upon wall or window, had that been his desire. It was not. Mere gestures would not satisfy at all, his desire was to retaliate in a way that the world would see; in a way that would cause real hurt.

He was close enough to see clearly into the room beyond the tight-shut window facing him. And there was the man who had cost him such loss, eating from a rice bowl, sipping tea. He studied him . . . long strong fingers, a face upon which the cheekbones caught light, the eyes were sheltered and private. The mouth was full, bowed up at the edges. He searched for weakness and saw none. It was a face, in truth, that the mirror of destiny would record as being without great fault, and that made him hate the man all the more. He noted a small kinked scar upon the man's temple – the jab of a broken bottle perhaps. He wore the khaki twill tunic of the police; his shoulders were studded with the three silver pips of a chief inspector.

Sitting opposite him was a woman whose face he could not see. She was Chinese, dressed in an old style sam fu. Her hair, grey-streaked, was pulled back in a tight bun. They were talking, but he could overhear nothing of the conversation. He could hear the sound of a radio or television set, and the rumble of air-conditioning motors, but nothing else beyond the drubbing rain. Forrester took both food and conversation at a leisurely rate. Eddie felt sure of his concealment; so sure that he moved a pace closer.

Forrester looked up directly towards the window. His eyebrows frowned in puzzled concentration, and Eddie knew that he'd been seen. In a second the man would grope for his revolver and rush to the window, and he would be shot. Run, his mind said, *run*, then robbed him of the power to move his legs. The ligature of fright bound sinew, breath and heart and his stomach plunged in a violent way . . . Then Forrester looked to his rice bowl once more and raised some food with his chopsticks to his mouth.

The limbs of a weak man carried Eddie a pace, two paces in retreat. He was not a coward, he had stood his ground in vicious fights in his time. But that moment had been different – so fraught with dilemma. He drew the collar of

39

his raincoat tighter about his neck and waited, and watched, a wary distance now from his adversary.

A child came through a moon-gate into the room; a girl. She wore a red skirt and a white blouse and had ribbons in her hair. She walked towards the centre of the room, and there she sat down, the height of the window lintel hiding her from his view. The clothes that she wore were new, the blouse and the skirt he had not seen before. Nor had she worn ribbons in her hair the last time he had seen her. But Eddie Woo knew instantly who this little girl was: Kit Ying, no Kit Ling. He remembered the child so well.

Forrester gazed down upon the girl, and his whole face seemed to soften as a father's face softens when he watches his most loved child. He understood now exactly why Forrester had done what he had done and he hated him for it. This man saw himself as some avenging angel. He was being persecuted because of this shrimp of a child. Unfair! He could not change his carnal needs. He could not abide the thought of sexual entry into a woman, a grown woman. He had tried and it was no good; just a limp and hardly manageable affair of thrusting hips, cold lips that sucked their way like slugs upon his skin. He hated that. He hated the stench of mouth and crotch of the filthy female. They were rotten like garbage drowned in perfume. To penetrate them was to immerse himself in foulness. He could not do it . . . Flawless was the mouth of the child-woman; as sweet as sugared pomelo. Perfect was the girl-body unmarred by mature growth. Ecstasy was to take these untouched, ungrown things and break them on the hard rock of his yang. That was his *need*. That was his right.

And there sat his detractor, his persecutor, smiling nobly down in the certainty that all he did, he did in the name of British righteousness and white-wigged jurisprudence. There sat the guardian of it all on the soft cushion of self satisfaction, while outside like a kicked dog in the rain stood the 'sinner', cold with hatred and bitterness. And then

Eddie did spit upon the wall before him. '*Diu lei le mo*' – may you lie down with your own mother, may life's most awful degradation befall you. A curse as common as backstreet litter in Hong Kong. But never before had he uttered it with more hope of fulfilment.

As he waited in the wet it came to Eddie Woo that to injure this man in a deep and satisfying way would not be a difficult matter. No night-assassin or chopper-wielding street gang would be needed, no triad bosses paid out. The girl, Kit Ling, presented the perfect instrument for the punishment of Forrester. The kicked dog had teeth, had it not?

Reven Forrester had brought Kit Ling to his house in order to cage his little sparrow for her protection. Kit Ling had to be severed from his custody in such a way that the blame for it sat square upon the policeman's shoulders. He had to be made to look careless, foolish and unworthy, a clod of a policeman. His loss of face would have to be absolute and so complete that superior and subordinate and all and sundry would mock him, and there would be nowhere to hide, for even in his own mind he would know that it was his incompetence that caused the sparrow to vanish. That knowledge would kill him as surely as a cancer in his gut . . . Yes, Eddie Woo decided, *that* would kill him in a slow and tortuous way, and his pain would never end.

Eddie Woo drew himself from the window where he had stood all this time and began to explore the other windows of the house . . . The kitchen.

Kit Ling came there with the Chinese amah. They settled down to watch television. The room was darkened but Eddie could see them well because the screen of the TV set lit them in ever-changing bursts of colour. He studied the little girl. She was a pretty creature, red skirted and quick limbed, and fresh, so fresh. He watched her for a while, and remembered. Then he moved on.

There was a porch with steps that led into the garden.

Light from the lounge spilled through french windows casting wide squares of yellow upon the polished tiles. There were some chairs there; out-of-doors furniture of painted wood with wide canvas cushions. Around the walls were tiers of pot plants, some large, some minute. The smell of flowers leaked into the night. He could see the interior of the lounge. Forrester was still there. He sat upon his chair with his eyes cast towards the kitchen. Eddie contemplated the shelter of the porch – it was wide and long, mercifully dry, and there were great areas of shadow to absorb him. He looked carefully to see if there was a dog there. House dogs invariably sought out such places of shelter when it rained. There was no dog upon this porch and Eddie was about to swing his leg across the balustrade when Reven Forrester stood up and began to walk towards him.

He knew he had not been seen this time. The man carried a bottle of beer and a glass and his gait was relaxed. Eddie had to decide upon a course of action – to flee, yes there *was* time to do that, or to remain where he was and hide. He decided to remain. He sank down so that he was hidden below the balustrade. There were gaps between the pillars that provided a good view. The door creaked in a stubborn way then Forrester came out, and with a sigh that was audible stretched out upon a lounger. He was so close that Eddie could have reached out and touched him.

It was a fine position to observe from provided that he did not make a sound. The problem was that he was bent forward at an angle that severely taxed the muscles of his thighs and back. Within a short while his spine and legs began to ache, still he kept absolutely rigid. It got worse. His back was wet and cold and becoming more painful with every second that passed, and his rear thighs were threatening to shoot off into a cramp that would buckle him. He could not stand the agony. He contemplated moving, and to hell with the consequences. He was about

42

to risk it when the amah came out on to the porch with Kit Ling at her side.

'*Jo tau, Ah baak.*' Kit Ling's voice.

'*Jo tau, sai lo nui.*' Rest well, little daughter. He went on in Cantonese. 'A little present for you, Kit Ling.'

She opened the packet and screamed with delight. She thrust her wrist through the bangles and held them up. 'Oh pretty. So pretty. I am so lucky.'

'It's nothing . . . you must go to bed now, Kit Ling. Off you go now, off you go.'

'Will we look for Father again tomorrow?'

'Yes, we will . . . Of course. We'll get up early tomorrow and look for him. Bedtime now.'

She jangled the bangles on her arm as she skipped back into the house. 'Look how they shine . . . look how they shine.'

'Ah Fong!' Forrester called the amah back to him. He waited until Kit Ling was inside the house before he continued. 'I'm taking the girl with me back to Hong Kong tomorrow morning.'

'To look for her father?'

'In a way.' Forrester sat up and faced the woman. 'She won't be coming back here, Mother. I can't keep her any longer. She has to be given to the Child Protective Services. I'm taking her there tomorrow . . . I'm sorry. I've no choice.'

'No need to be sorry for me.' Ah Fong turned away. 'Be sorry for you. I see the girl is in your eyes.'

'Nonsense,' said Forrester. But the truth was obvious to the kicked dog in the rain.

New energy flowed through the muscle of Eddie Woo; new strength that pillared his limbs and his spine. For here was his plan, offered to him on a plate by the gwai lo, Forrester himself. The turtle was in the jar!

He would need helpers, a man and a woman he thought. No more than that. Force would not be required, simple

43

resourcefulness would do it, and good timing: the quickness of the swooping hawk on this little bird.

The slow killing of Mr R. Forrester could soon begin.

When Uncle had taken her to the house on Lantau Island it had been dark. They had stood upon the open deck and watched the churn of the big ship as it shivered and shoved at the sea. A place of miraculous brightness; that was her memory of Hong Kong. A place so bright that the sea was soaked with its colour in a way that the lonely pale moon could not imitate. And the wake of the ferry had ploughed and tumbled the colours, red, gold, blue, as though to mix them to water. But the colours were too strong. They had floated back and separated and stayed until the shoulder of the island had reached out to hide that place of lights.

Now it was daylight and Hong Kong was a different place. The harbour was filled with ships, big ships at restful anchor; ships so fast that they skimmed like flat, thrown pebbles across the water; sampans and junks and motorboats of every sort. The land was different too. Where there had been lights, there were great buildings that rose up so high that their tops were lost in mist.

As they came closer she could see people, many, many people.

'How many people in Hong Kong, Uncle?'

'Not as many as in China.'

'There seem to be more. There are many more cars than there are in China.'

The ferry groaned and slowed and began to slew itself around with the sluggishness of a pig on a cold winter's morning. It had to fit into a very small space, it seemed.

Hong Kong was bustling with people. Like straws in a riverflow they joined them and were swept from the ferry and along a grey passageway that spat them into a street. Here the confusion grew greater. For here no one seemed to

44

wish to travel in the same direction or at an equal speed. Some paused to buy food or newspapers from a train of small stalls that were spread along the road. Some walked and some ran and some shouted, *'Way!'* as they thrust barrows at fearsome speed at anyone who defied them.

It was quick here, then quick there, but Uncle kept a firm grip on her hand and she held tightly too, and she was not afraid.

'How far, Uncle?'

Kit Ling felt the need to go to a toilet. On the ferry she had breakfasted on cola drinks and milk and all this fluid had worked its way down and now was aching to be released.

Kit Ling's question did not reach Reven Forrester. One small voice, one fragile sentence; it shattered under the growl and sweat and wrestle that was Pier Road. Kit Ling would have tugged at his hand but felt that such an action might be thought impolite.

They walked up steps to a girdered bridge that shook from the roar of traffic beneath it. This view seemed worthy of attention for Uncle stopped there and crouched next to her.

'See, Kit Ling, how big that ferry is. Look how wide its mouth is, and how it takes in all the trucks and cars. It's going to carry them across the bay.'

She nodded. It was fine for him to have such a loud voice, but she needed to be heard too. She gestured for him to come even closer, and when he complied she cupped her hands to his ear: 'How far to go?'

'Not far,' he said in his good loud voice. 'We'll get a taxi at the terminus.'

She had no idea what terminus he was speaking of or how long she would still have to endure her 'little need'. It did not seem polite to say any more.

So they crossed the noisy bridge that led back on to the noisier pavement and they walked towards the terminus, wherever, whatever that was. They walked until they came to a place with gates that spun and clanked as people shoved through.

There Kit Ling saw what she was looking for. A sign that pictured a little painted woman with the characters WOMEN'S LAVATORY. She stopped firmly. She tugged at Uncle's hand, and when he looked down she pointed determinedly.

He said, 'I can't go there with you. You will have to go all on your own. Can you do that?'

Could he not see she was a big girl? She nodded. She released his hand and walked quickly into the lavatory.

Kit Ling had never visited such a place as this. It was so big and white-tiled and the smell of it burned her nose. Along one wall a row of cubicles waited, some closed, some open-doored, some fitted with elevated bowls and some recessed into the floor. A woman with grey hair, grey face and overalls stood ready to welcome her guests. She did not care much for little girls who came unaccompanied, Kit Ling guessed, because she frowned and put her hands upon her hips in a forbidding way. But that all changed when a kind lady, wearing a black sam fu trouser-suit like Ah Fong's, came in and smiled at the grey lady and said to Kit Ling, 'Go in there, Daughter.'

And then she entered the cubicle with Kit Ling and said, 'Uncle sent me to look after you.'

'But I'm the big girl now.'

'Of course you are, but Uncle said that I should take you by the hand. No more to be said.'

'Are you his friend?'

'Yes. I'm his very good friend.'

'Then I will go with you.'

Kit Ling flushed the toilet. It roared with water in a most satisfying way.

They left together, pausing at the entrance until the kind lady said: 'Come on! Be quick!'

She was as quick as she could be, but that did not seem to

46

satisfy the kind lady. She took hold of her wrist in a most painful grip and dragged her so fast that she almost fell down.

Kit Ling knew at once that here was another bad person; she was not kind; she was not a friend of Uncle, and she did not intend to take her to Uncle. For there was Uncle helping a man who had fallen badly down some steps, and she was being dragged in quite the opposite direction. Before Kit Ling could cry out they had turned a corner and Uncle was no longer in sight.

'Stop,' she cried. 'Let me go.'

'Bad talk!' The woman did not stop and did not release her. She tightened her grip. She clawed her fingers around Kit Ling's thin wrist and quickened the pace.

Escape: that was her thought. Escape from this bad woman then run back to Uncle. But she did not know if she could. The woman was so strong, and every few paces she would wrench her hand so hard that she cried from the pain.

'Stop. Please stop!'

There were so many people. She turned her face up to them but no one looked down. She began to sob, but no one heard.

'Help me. Help me.'

No one helped her. They passed by – a thousand deaf people. They had legs that marched and arms that swung; they had eyes that watched everywhere but her. They had ears but they could not hear. People everywhere she looked, quick-walking people who could not hear.

They ran on to a covered pier. Big junks were tied up there. Some with people on them and some with empty decks. She did not call out to those around her any more. It was no use. They were all deaf.

She could hear. There was a slap and hiss of waves there. A big wind was pushing inshore and the junks were riding, dropping and rising, creaking on their ropes, the gang planks see-sawing up and down.

Slanting rain began to reach under the shelter and wet her

legs and her new white socks and nice shiny shoes. She tried to dodge the puddles. They slowed at last. Perhaps the woman was too tired to run any further. Kit Ling looked at her and saw that she was tired, her mouth hung open and her breathing was quick. Still, she did not loosen her grip. She looked this way and that as if searching for someone or something. Then she saw what she was looking for and waved.

It was a green-painted sampan. It was not tied up at the pier amongst the big junks but rode the harbour waves a short distance out. Kit Ling saw the man who held the tiller wave back. He turned the sampan and it bobbed like a cork as a big ship passed it by. Then it came towards the pier.

Then Kit Ling saw Uncle. He too had reached the pier. He was running, pushing people from his path as he came on. She shouted, 'Uncle. Here. *Here Uncle!*'

He was too far away to hear her. She wrenched with her free hand at the grip of the woman and jerked away. She was free. She ran towards Uncle but the concrete was slick with oil and rain and she slipped and fell down to her knees and got her skirt all dirty. The woman was upon her before she could get up. She grasped her by the waist and picked her up. Kit Ling bit through the bad woman's tunic sleeve as hard as she could.

The sampan had arrived, lifting and falling – now it was level, now it had dropped far below. Its tyre-cushioned nose bumped the pier side. The grip upon her tightened. The woman jumped and stumbled down upon the deck and Kit Ling struggled from her grasp and sprang across the deck.

'Get her quick,' shouted the sampan driver. '*Diu lei!* She's going to jump. Don't let her jump!'

The engine sound quickened. Sluggishly the sampan drew back from the pier and began to turn. Kit Ling was not boat-wise, yet she knew that the moment the next wave lifted them was the moment to jump for the pier. She steadied herself . . . She sensed the nearness of the woman

48

behind her, she dared not look for now the sampan was rising, rising, *she jumped.*

She felt the pluck of an outstretched hand on the waistband of her new red skirt. Just a small grip, a fingerhold, no more. It slowed her momentum. Her jump did not take her far enough. Instead of landing with her feet upon the pier, she struck the concrete with her chest. There was no handhold. The concrete was wet and slick and gave her nothing. She shouted, just once.

'Uncle!'

Then she slipped into the scummy green water.

A Water Tours ferry was preparing to pull away from the pier, filled with eager tourists, its stern rope sprung and its engines full ahead. The frail little human was caught up in the turbulence and churned like flotsam into the race water.

She screamed; a bubble lifted from her, unheard. She gasped, but there was no air for Kit Ling in that liquid green world.

In a minute she had drowned.

2

AN EYE FOR AN EYE

Reven Forrester mourned Kit Ling's death in a tearless, bitter way that did not show his pain. The agony of recrimination was his to bear. He had taken her to Lantau; if only he had not. If only he had not left her alone at the public convenience. He should have been more alert; she was in his charge. God, if only he had reached the pier-end before she had been finally swept under that canopy of sludge. The barbs of self-censure were sharp and painful, and every one of them deserved. Dear God, what had she thought in those final seconds in that place of choking green muck? . . . Ah Fong, who knew him well, and had eyes that were good for inward looking, saw the dark and empty place within her son. And she mourned as much for him as she did for Little Daughter.

As the true father of Kit Ling had not yet been located, Reven Forrester took it upon himself to arrange for a proper funeral. He had the body brought from the Police Medico-Laboratories to Lantau Island, then summoned an astrologer from the monastery at Ngong Ping to divine the exact moment when the little spirit would emerge from its earthly shell. A good chorus of priests was instructed to be on hand to ensure the passage of that spirit directly to the Western Heaven. He secured a grave site with fine Feng Shui properties on a slope overlooking the sea. And that was where they took the earthly remains of poor Kit Ling.

A brass band crashed shrilly and he and Ah Fong burned paper flowers as the small coffin was lowered to rest.

It was an affair that the gods could not ignore. Many people were on hand to give face to the 'father' of Kit Ling. And in conclusion, each honoured mourner was invited to a picnic feast. They all came and what they could not eat there, they carried away, together with a small gift of money. Kit Ling was sent upon her spirit journey washed by a thousand tears, raised by a thousand prayers, and with a fortune in incinerated dollars bought from the Bank of Hell. Everybody agreed: it was a splendid funeral. It was more than a small girl's due, by far. Kit Ling, by Chinese reckoning, had died at ten years of age – just old enough to be vested with a soul. Kit Ling's soul would be proud and happy, and not in the least inclined to malice. That was what they said.

It had not been Forrester's intention to buy face through all this expenditure, but that is what happened, at least amongst the islanders. The Cantonese admire prodigality. Any man who saw fit to spend so much to ensure the comfort of the spirit of one little girl (not even his own little girl) deserved face. They gave him face.

The smiles of the islanders of Lantau did not warm Reven Forrester. The lavishness of the funeral had not been intended as a sap to his conscience; an attempt at the procurement of soul-deep forgiveness. He did not give a damn for forgiveness. He did not give a damn for the expansion of face. In the matter of the death of Kit Ling all he wanted was justice, biblical justice – an eye for an eye. He who had brought about the death of this innocent little child should suffer an equal fate. And that person was Eddie Woo, Reven Forrester was sure of it.

He did not have proof, not the sort of proof that a jury of twelve would accept in order to return a verdict of guilty. He doubted whether such proof existed.

He had in his possession a photograph taken by a tourist aboard the Water Tours junk that had been departing from the pier when Kit Ling drowned. The photograph showed a green-painted sampan, about eighteen feet in length with a small deckhouse of plank and canvas. It showed a young girl in a red pleated skirt and white blouse, poised to jump from the deck of the sampan to the pier; it showed a middle-aged Cantonese woman reaching out to prevent this from happening. It did not show the licence number of the sampan, for that had been painted out. Nor did it clearly show the face of the woman, or the driver of the sampan who was hidden beneath the deckhouse. But this did not discourage Forrester.

Every vessel, bar the smallest of yuloh-dinghies that plied the waters of Hong Kong, was required to be licensed at the Marine Department in Kowloon. So it was to the offices of the shipping division of the Marine Department that Forrester took the photograph. The building was pure Civil Service drab, inside and out. It was staffed with uninterested clerks who resented the break in routine that the visit of this gwai lo cop forced upon them.

It took Forrester time and patience to locate the man who was in charge of the register of shipping. Pimply-faced and with bad breath, his name was Lau. The green-painted sampan, Forrester guessed, would be classified as a vessel not exceeding 150 piculs – a class-one sampan. Mr Lau agreed:

'This is class-one vessel, Mr Forrester.'

'I want to try and trace this vessel.'

'Not possible without licence number.' He tapped the photograph. 'No number here you see.'

'Yes I know that. What I want to find out is if a certain person has such a vessel registered in his name.'

'Name of person?'

'Woo Sung-king, or Woo Yin-wah. It could be either.'

'One moment.'

A register was brought to the desk by one of Mr Lau's assistants. It was heavy, thick and bound together with steel hoops. It did not contain the name Woo Sung-king.

'Woo Yin-wah,' said Forrester. 'That's his grandfather.'

'Woo Yin-wah.' Mr Lau hunted with his index finger through a list of Woos that occupied five pages, and then some.

'Woo Yin-wah.' The finger came to rest. 'Yes, this man owns three class-one vessels. He also owns a class-two harbour lighter currently syndicated to Flourishing Harbour Lighter Company, and two class-six vessels – mechanically propelled fishing junks. Probably a matched pair of trawlers. They are Cheung Chau registered.'

'Cheung Chau island,' Forrester said.

'That's right. He probably fishes the waters south of Lantau Island. An excellent trawling ground for garoupa and bream, I assure you.'

Mr Lau became more genial now that the questioning was over; more curious too.

'You think the sampan in the photo belongs to Woo Yin-wah? Why would he paint out the number? It's an offence to do that, you know.'

Forrester said, 'I'm most grateful to you, Mr Lau. All I need now is a list of licence numbers of all Woo Yin-wah's vessels . . . Thank you, Mr Lau . . . Yes that is exactly what I need.'

'You're welcome.' Lau wrote down the numbers. 'One sampan registered at Yau Ma Tei, two registered at Cheung Chau. Two class-six junks registered at Cheung Chau. There you are, Mr Forrester. Our licensing department can go into this matter if you like.'

Forrester did not want that. 'Better not, Mr Lau, police business you know.'

To be exact, it was *Marine* Police business. All crime that occurred on the waterfront or at sea, or upon the outlying islands, was the business of the Marine Police.

It was to the Headquarters of Marine Police that Forrester now directed his steps; a twenty-minute walk to the waterfront at Tsim Sha Tsui, then a short climb up the tree-shaded path that led to the gracious old Headquarters.

Forrester had known this building since childhood, and then it had seemed old. The huge fig trees had always been that generous with their shade, the building had always stood solid, bulldog-British, in dominance of the harbour it watched over.

The expatriate officers who staffed the Marine Police region were more British than other Hong Kong police officers. It had to do with their job, Forrester thought, their daily dosage of sea breeze and salt water kept them true to pedigree.

Forrester had business with one such officer: Superintendent Wilson. 'Tubby' Wilson's office was wide and roomy and creaky-floored. A map of Victoria harbour, Hong Kong's main harbour, covered one entire wall. It showed all moorings and buoys, and the fairways that the big ships were confined to whilst under power. It showed wharves and terminals and typhoon shelters and dockyards and under-water cables. In fact it showed all things of maritime interest upon the expanse of water that lay between Hong Kong island and the mainland. For this was the area policed by Harbour Division, Tubby Wilson's division. Tubby Wilson was not at home so Forrester wrote him a note:

Tubby,
Thought you should know. Woo Sung-king has access to three class one sampans. As you'll see from the licence prefixes, one is registered at Yau Ma Tei and two at Cheung Chau. I think the green sampan in the pic must have come from Yau Ma Tei anchorage. It's close to the point where the crime was committed.
Have you got someone you can put on to it? I would dearly love to find that sampan before it gets 'lost'.

Forrester underlined the word 'dearly', then pinned Lau's list of licence numbers to the note. He concluded:

54

I'm giving you this list because it's more than likely
that the licence number will have been painted back on
the vessel by now.

Regards
R. F.

He placed the note inside an envelope, sealed it and
marked it: 'Confidential. SP Wilson.' He left it on Tubby
Wilson's desk, weighted down by a miniature brass ship's
bell.

The note was in fact *very* confidential, but not in any
official sense, for Forrester's involvement in this case was
most unofficial, and discovery of his actions could bring
censure, swift and consummate. Inter-departmental line-
crossing was deeply frowned upon in the RHKP. This
investigation was in the hands of the Regional Crime Unit
of the Marine Police. They had entered a docket of Assault,
Kidnapping and Manslaughter. They had thickened that
file with many eyewitness statements, including that of CI
Reven Forrester. And that was all. That was as far as they
had got. Reven Forrester had seen to that; he had deliberately blocked their progress.

Forrester had been first to board the Water Tours ferry
after the ferrymaster had aborted its departure. He had
questioned all those who had witnessed the incident. And,
but for one passenger, their offerings had proved to be
quite useless. The exception was an Australian tourist who
had been standing on the rear deck of the ferry, who
believed that she might have photographed the incident;
she was not sure. Would the Chief Inspector like to have
that film on the off-chance? The Chief Inspector had said
that he would very much like to have that film.

'They could have saved her,' said the Australian. 'There
were hundreds of them watching. I don't know why someone didn't try . . . such bloody apathy.'

'They're like that.' Forrester did not try and explain the Chinese mind to the tourist. He thanked her for the film and left.

The green sampan had emerged from that roll of Kodacolor. A picture of excellent definition and composition considering that it had been taken with an autofocus camera with a lens of limited capability.

Forrester had not given over that photograph to the investigating officer from the Crime Unit as he rightfully should have. Nor had he provided that officer with the reasons for his belief in the culpability of Woo Sung-king, or Eddie Woo as he preferred to be called.

He ought to have done these things but he had not, because he believed that the investigation of this crime would not lead to the conviction of its author. Eddie Woo was separated from the deed of crime by too long and twisted a line of technicalities for it to be connected to him. Even if the identity of the kidnappers was established, and it was proved that the green sampan was the property of the family Woo, the case against Eddie would still be too remote and tenuous for justice to be done. The Shui Seung Yahn boat people would go to prison with a smile before they would 'break the rice-bowl' to testify against their employer. And that was exactly what would happen in this case.

Kit Ling was dead. Who was there now to testify that Woo Sung-king had raped her, and therefore had good cause to have abducted her and taken her to the green sampan? Who was there to say that she had not simply been taken by the notion that the green sampan would transport her to her father?

Kit Ling was dead, and that was partly due to the good intentions of a Chief Inspector of Police who had, quite illegally, taken custody of her, and sheltered her, and gone on to provoke her rapist into further action that had brought about her death.

Now that Chief Inspector of Police was bitter and very angry. And he felt tied to this crime in a way that left him with an uncomfortable feeling of failure and liability. Those were the reasons why Forrester had hampered the investigation of the Crime Unit of the Marine Police, and had shared his evidence and his beliefs with no one but Tubby Wilson of Harbour Division, who wore the same old school tie as he, and played cricket in the same eleven, and would therefore go in to bat for Reven Forrester.

SP Wilson had the advancement of his own career to think of, though. He would give Forrester a discreet measure of aid and an accordant measure of time, then he would retire to the pavilion. He would suggest politely that the case be given over to the proper authority – the Crime Unit, Marine Police.

That was the way that the gentlemen officers of the Royal Hong Kong Police played the game. And it was with those limitations in mind that Forrester trotted quickly down the steps that led from the old parade ground to the street.

It was well past lunchtime. He called up a mental picture of the state of his desk top at that hour. He saw paper, much white paper: purple-stamped – *urgent*; red-stamped – *most urgent*. His phone was ringing and his teleprinter was printing, more and more paper. He winced mentally, flagged down a taxi which flew past him, cursed. The next taxi drew up. He flopped into its air-conditioned interior. Thank God he did not have to get by on a Chief Inspector's pay.

His desk, in reality, was not the nightmare he had envisaged. Interpol needed information on possible Chiu Chow Triad Society links between Hong Kong, Bangkok and Amsterdam. It took him half an hour to piece together an answer for them that might be helpful. There were two teleprint requests. One required all available information on Wo Yuet Shing Triad Society in Western area. The other and more interesting request was accompanied by a crime sheet which set out in brief the CV of a girl who had wanted to be a movie star, and became instead a gorgon monstrosity on a police video.

The complainant's name was Lee Ah-my and her age was estimated to be fifteen. She said she had come from China and had been picked up by a man whose name was Chan Kai-charm, or Chan Bing, or Yee-kim. Different people knew him by different names. Chan Kai-charm (his most used name) had met young Lee Ah-my at a disco. He had said he was a movie talent scout and promised to make of her a *big* movie star. She had gone with him and had found that the audition room contained but a bed, and had a single window that did not open. A procession of movie directors had come and tested her out upon the bed. This she had not liked and she had said as much. Chan had beaten her up and locked her in that room without food or water for a few days, after which she told him she was ready to be a good and obedient girl. But she had not been so; she had escaped. Inevitably she had been caught and brought back to Chan. As a lesson to her, and presumably the rest of his stable, he had splashed a bottle of vitriol upon her face. She was ugly and she was blind, but still she had managed to get to the police. Chan had been arrested. Poor Lee Ah-my had gained her revenge by committing ji saat – suicide – by drinking a full litre of Lysol.

The question to CTU was, did the names Chan Kai-charm or Chan Bing or Yee-kim ring a bell within the memory cells of the CTU computer? The answer was yes. Chan Kai-charm was a Grass Sandal elder brother of Yuet Tung Triad Society of Mong Kok area. He had one previous conviction of assault with a deadly weapon, one conviction for aggravated burglary, one theft from person. A mixed bag of violence. At the time of arrest Chan was out on parole. Now, in addition to a charge of serious assault he could be charged with membership of an unlawful society. Moreover, he would have poor Ah-my's spiteful ghost to contend with.

58

Life was about to become that much harder for Chan Kai-charm.

As Forrester typed his reply into the teletypewriter he could not help but think that this could have been Kit Ling.

Better to drown, he judged; far better to drown. Then he saw the sick green water of the harbour that had swilled into the lungs of the sweet child and smothered her, and kept her until she was limp and filthy and dead . . . He knew that that judgement was just soft soap for a stained conscience.

For the rest of the afternoon Forrester worked upon the update of records that related to Hei Shui Society. The triad group had an octopus-limbed ability to regenerate and reorganize. It had recently come to life in the form of Sap Saam Tai Po in the Sham Shi Po area, and there it had wrested from a weaker triad group its prostitution business. Police action against the leadership of Sap Saam Tai Po had been effective. Sap Saam Tai Po had disappeared and out had come Sing Yee and Lee Kwan, which societies' office bearers were known as the Ten Tiger Generals. These triad bosses were reaching out to advance their narcotic operation into the Castle Peak area and some vicious fights had occurred there. They were also known as Wo On Lok in other areas, but with office bearers as yet unidentified . . .

By the time Forrester had given some structure to the amorphous enemy, and cleared his desk, it was very late. He was hungry and his mind lay dull and unco-operative. He leaned back in his chair and deposited his feet upon the desk top. The phone rang and he remembered Tubby Wilson. But it was not Wilson. It was Caroline O'Shea; an annoyed Caroline O'Shea.

'We were supposed to meet at seven o'clock, Reven. Where the hell are you?'

This was the girl Ah Fong had described as 'the one who owns the fat jung dang yacht', who would pee pure joy if Forrester chose her. They had made an arrangement to meet, Forrester remembered now, for cocktails and then dinner. Where?

'Are you there, Reven?'

'Yes. Sorry, Caroline.' He really was sorry. 'Where are you now?'

'I'm where I'm supposed to be now, where *you're* supposed to be now. You've forgotten, haven't you?'

Inspiration came. He said, 'Of course not. The Chin Chin. I'll be there in five minutes.'

'You'd better be, boyo.'

Her alliteration stumbled a bit. She'd been seated too long at the Chin Chin bar, and it was happy hour.

It took him fifteen minutes to get there, but Caroline seemed to have cheered up in the interim. It *was* happy hour, after all. She raised her whole arm and waved as it is recommended one waves when in trouble in the surf. Tall, Caroline liked big gestures, and big handbags and bright dresses with wide belts. Olive-green eyes and a torch of red hair made of her a talking point in a city of little dark people.

Caroline's parents were Dubliners who had met in Malaya at the end of the Second World War, where Sean O'Shea had gone with the sole purpose of becoming rich – he had become rich. He and three like-minded partners had bought up a war-scorched Johore rubber estate. Malaria had killed one partner; a Min Yuen-inspired bullet another. The third partner had died of natural causes – cirrhosis of the liver. Sean O'Shea, who had an instinct for danger, a liver as absorbent as a peat bog, and took his quinine daily, had gone on to become sole owner of the Johore estate, and a pound-sterling millionaire.

Caroline was the product of this durable man and the widow of the ambushed partner. She had seen out her nursery education in an open-sided nipa hut, being mis-taught the oral values of *r*s and *l*s ('Maly had a rittew ram') by a Chinese-Malaccan Sister of the Oblates of Mary Immaculate. Things had improved when she had been sent to board in Singapore. But education *ne plus ultra* had had to await the new-era demand for all things elastic. Then she had been sent to Cambridge to read English. Now she was a columnist with the *South China Morning Post*. Which employment was, to Forrester's mind, the ultimate waste of talent.

The air in the Chin Chin bar was crisply conditioned and the lighting subdued. It was crowded of course but Forrester spotted Caroline immediately. Who could miss her; that hair, that open-hearted wave. She was seated at a table and not at the counter where she preferred to sit.

''Bout time, boyo.'

Forrester sat down and looked around for a hostess.

'I was propositioned,' said Caroline.

'I would have been surprised if you weren't.'

'Twice. But I told them you were on the way, and you were a weight-lifter and as mean as a mad turtle, and you hated Americans.' She probably *had* said that.

A hostess named Stephanie who wore a 'Suzie Wong' split cheong sam came to take his order: 'San Mig.'

'Do you like her?' Caroline asked. 'You wouldn't look at her if she was naked. She's got no boobs.'

Caroline believed in total honesty, provided it was she who answered her own questions. She felt absolutely certain of the provision of truth that way. She was into astrology and karma and life after death, thus felt qualified to provide genuine and worthwhile advice to those for whom she cared. That advice was likely to be forthcoming at any moment, and to be on any subject. Stephanie's lack of boobs, and thus lack of appeal to a mammary-ravishing Scorpio such as Forrester, was a prime example.

'I like her,' said Forrester the heretic. But Caroline smiled, serene in the knowledge that he didn't, and never would, and felt no threat.

She said, 'So why *were* you late?'

Stephanie arrived with his beers. 'Happy hour.' She set

61

them down. Forrester had a good look at her and perceived that Caroline was right. It was surprising how often she was.

Caroline said, 'You had a lousy day.'

Forrester shook his head – worse than lousy. He took from his beer glass a very substantial pull and then set it down upon the table.

'Do you want to talk about it, Reven?'

He did not mind if they spoke about it, as long as it was not in a forgiving sense. Caroline would try to administer the healing touch and he wasn't in the mood for that. He didn't mind hating Eddie Woo one bit. It didn't upset him. It was a fine and exploitable state of health and he would hang on to it. What he would love to have discussed was methods to inflict equal pain on the killer of Kit Ling but Caroline was not into that sort of thing.

'Nothing to talk about,' he said. Both of them knew that was a lie.

He finished his first beer and then tackled his freebie. That was what he really wanted to do: to get drunk. Not stumble-tongued, legless drunk, just sufficiently, transiently numb to be able to bridge the day and go on to enjoy the evening the way a man and a woman should enjoy it. Stephanie came again with more liquor.

They drank together in the Chin Chin and ate salted peanuts and cheese sticks, enough to spoil the appetite. They listened to a singer, a Cantonese girl who did a fair Jennifer Rush imitation. They chatted about Caroline's assignment to the People's Republic next month to cover the festival – 44 Glorious and Heroic Years of New China! The People's Liberation Army was to put on a grand parade of troops and weaponry in Tian An Men Square in Beijing – the march-past would be a splendid and frightening sight. The unisoned tread of those marching companies would carry like an earth tremor from Beijing all the way to little Hong Kong. And the speech of Senior General Zhau from the Tian An Men podium would be especially relevant on that

62

militant anniversary. The people of Hong Kong would be waiting, listening, hoping for a balmy breeze but fearing a typhoon.

From the Hokklo boat people in their leaky keel homes to the Tai Pans, forty floors above the peasant earth, they would feel the current.

'When China farts, Hong Kong shits itself.'

Latrine humour from Forrester, but both of them thought it very funny, which proved that, by then, they were very well lit up. It was time to depart from the Chin Chin bar.

In the taxi Reven Forrester kissed Caroline immediately, and she, in her belief in honesty in words and actions, smoothed her hand over the material of his trousers across his thigh and upwards. Massaging each other then into a state of high prurience they rode to Forrester's flat.

Caroline loved Reven Forrester. She said she would not make love to him were that not so, but if she loved a man she would do anything for him – and that was what made their sex so good. And it *was* good. Creatures of pleasure, they knew how to give, how to receive, and how to indulge. And she would take the lead as often as not. If she wanted Forrester on his back she would turn him on to his back; she had strong arms, that girl, and tireless hips. There were no unfulfilled sexual longings in her life, no nagging hang-ups. What she wanted she took. When orgasm was impending she would stop, rigid, as though shocked by the fierceness of the thrill – wide-eyed, gasping, she would beg him to stop too and share the rippling spasm of her womb: 'Don't move, don't move. Feel me coming, *feel* me.'

She wanted that so badly.

That night, though, Forrester was venal in his wants. And she sensed that this was not just simple lust. This was the catharsis of a man who did not know how to talk out the rage that was in him. So she was gentle in return, and skilful. With the love of her body she tried to milk him of his great anger. His orgasm made him cry out. When he went limp she gathered him to her breasts like a baby.

'I went off like a Neanderthal man.'

'I loved it.'

'I'll make it up to you.'

'What's eating you, Reven?'

It was a long time before he spoke about it.

'There was a child, an illegal immigrant called Kit Ling. I was becoming fond of her. Then a man killed her.'

'That's awful. Oh Reven. I knew there was something . . . You must be hurting terribly. When did it happen? Please tell me.'

'As helpless as a little bird, and just as cute. She'd lost her father, and all she could think about was trying to find him . . . Well, I tried to help her do that. She touched me, that little kid. I bent the rules and had her stay with Ah Fong. She was a joy to have around. I took her down to Mui Wo beach and we made sand castles. Can you believe it, *me* making sand castles and splashing around in the waves, and pulling goofy faces because they made the kid laugh?'

'I can imagine.'

'It made me feel good. A few days of having her, and I was plotting how to keep her permanently. I was hoping that her father would never turn up, so that I could adopt her . . . Then she was murdered. There is a man who hates me with such savagery that he took his revenge on *her* in order to get at me . . . So that's what happened. She was drowned in the harbour.'

'I remember. Yes, I read about that . . . Why didn't you tell me about this before?'

'I didn't want to.'

'If you're feeling such grief then I want to share it.'

'I'm going to get the bastard that did it, Caroline, so help me.'

'Oh.'

'You sound disapproving.'

'No . . . No, not disapproving. Afraid.'

'It amounts to the same thing.' Her response annoyed him. 'You always shade your disapproval with words like that. "I'm afraid." What does that mean? Don't do it, it doesn't suit my ego to be privy to that sort of thing.'

'You assume wrongly, Reven. I meant I'm afraid of where your vengeance will take you. I'm not asking you to forgive, *never*. But I think you might hunt him down and destroy him without a care about the consequences, and that's what frightens me. Don't you think I can't feel the anger in you? I know you so well.'

'What, then, if he went unpunished through lack of evidence? You did your stint as a court reporter, didn't you? You know that the detection rate for this sort of thing barely tops fifty per cent. Tell me, how would you feel if Eddie Woo walked away scot-free?'

'Eddie Woo. So that's his name? Are you sure of your facts? Are you dead certain that Eddie Woo did it?'

'I'm satisfied that he organized the whole thing.'

'Then surely a judge could be convinced on the same evidence.'

'You're not serious.'

'I'll say it again: I'm afraid you'll make a vendetta of this. You'll go after this man, and destroy him . . . and probably destroy yourself too. I think that could happen.'

'Why don't you answer my question?'

'How would I feel if he walked away, scot-free . . . I would hate it. You know that.'

'I've never wanted justice more than now.'

'Justice? . . . A question for you, Reven: do you hate Eddie Woo?'

'You know I do, so why ask. Do you think I'm a robo-cop . . . Sure I hate him.'

'You have the Scorpio's unquenchable thirst for venge-ance: *Lex talionis* . . .'

'The law of vengeance – don't tell me that it's not in everyone's blood.'

'It will drive *you* too far one day.'

'So you think I should stand back from this and view it as just another murder docket? Caroline, I held this little kid in my arms; played with her. I tucked her into bed . . . And you ask me if I hate him. By God I hate him.'

'All I ask is one thing: will you promise me that if you turn up evidence that would convict him in a court of law you will have him brought to trial?'

'Irrefutable evidence.'

'Yes.'

'It won't happen . . .'

'But if it does?'

'Then I promise that I will do that.'

She kissed him and stroked lightly at the hair of his chest. He lay still and relaxed and after a while his thoughts began to drift in that lazy limp haze that is the alchemy of sleep. But he did not sleep. She whispered it away:

'Reven I love you . . . I love you. Make love to me, Reven.'

Near his mouth lay a nipple. He nuzzled it, kissed it, tongued it until it had grown marvellously, and she began to lift and twist. She freed herself, crouched down, brushed his hips with a curtain of flame hair and drew him into her mouth until he was hard. Then she mounted him. This time their climax built slowly.

'Feel me, Reven, oh feel me.'

He felt the trembling grasp of her womb, and she the kick of his embedded penis as it flooded her . . . Coupled, mouth to mouth they fell asleep.

He dreamed that he was in his office, and the teleprinter was spewing paper at such a rate that desktop and floor were carpeted white. The phone was ringing, ringing. He searched for it, but could not find it. It rang in an incessant angry way.

'Reven.' Caroline's voice. Now what was she doing in his office? 'Reven.' She shook him until he awakened. 'Reven.'

The bedside light was on. She held the handpiece of the telephone. My God, it was 3 a.m.

'Who is it?' he asked of the mouthpiece.

It was Charlie Lam. Inspector Charlie Lam of Kowloon Regional CID. Forrester was fully awake in an instant.

'Charlie. What have you got?'

Charlie spoke English: 'Just what doctor ordered, Mr Forrester.' He added, 'I'm sure.' Which meant he probably wasn't sure.

'Give it to me,' Forrester said.

'His name is Chang, Chang San, better known as Sin Chui, 'Eel-eyes', Chang. His name is on the list you gave me . . . number twenty-two.'

The list that Forrester had given Inspector Lam and a few other police officers with whom Forrester had a 'special' understanding, comprised fifty-six names, all of them office bearers of Kowloon triad societies. Forrester did not have a duplicate list with him. He told Charlie Lam that.

'Which group is Chang with, Charlie?'

'Wong Cheung Boxing Club, sub-branch of Luen Ying. Chang San is incense master of Luen Ying Society. A real big balls.'

'Incense master, *very* good, Charlie. You've made my day.'

Incense master or Heung Chu was a high official in charge of lodge ceremonial affairs. The Heung Chu it was who accepted the poems of obeisance of all triad recruits before the West Altar – the arch priest of the lodge of the 'City of Willows'.

Forrester was pleased.

'Make more your day, Mr Forrester. Same Eel-eyes Chang is owner of Bright Golden Orchid Trading Company. Same Eel-eyes Chang is owner of race horse War Lord, favourite to win next Saturday. Seven to two, good bet, Mr Forrester. Put on a thousand.'

'Did he tell you all that, Charlie?'

'Sure thing. He offer me squeeze too, to go blind.'

'I can't believe he'd be such a fool. What charge have you got him on, Charlie?'

'No charge yet, Mr Forrester. Remember?'

'Of course.'

His instructions: the fifty-six office bearers, in the event of their arrest, were to be held without charge until CI Forrester had interviewed them.

'Of course,' he said again. 'I meant, what *would* the charge be, if one were laid?'

'DD, Mr Forrester: heroin. At his *tsip*'s flat; his concubine's flat,' Charlie interpreted needlessly. 'Sin Shaang House, Fuk Wah Street, Sham Shui Po. Do you know it?'

'Heroin, fine, fine,' Forrester said. 'Yes, I know it, I'll be there in half an hour, Charlie.'

Caroline appeared with a tray, upon it coffee and cheesecake. She placed it on the bed.

'It was all that you had in the fridge.' Forrester realized how hungry he was. 'I'll cook you an omelette if you've got the time.'

Omelette sounded wonderful but cheesecake it would have to be. He ate it while dressing.

'I suppose', said Caroline, 'that if I asked you why you were getting up at 3 a.m. you'd tell me I sounded disapproving, and to mind my own damned business.'

'No I wouldn't.' Forrester slid open his balcony door, went outside and stuck his hand beyond the railings. As he suspected, it was drizzling.

'Well then, where *are* you going?'

'Ask me *why* I'm going.'

'Well then?'

'I'm going because I set a trap, and into that trap has this instant walked a very fat rat. He is going to do something for me, this fat rat. He's a king rat you see. He bosses up lots and lots of lesser rodents. To save his miserable neck, he's likely to do anything I ask of him, and I intend to ask quite a lot. That is why I'm eating cheesecake . . . Is there any more of this stuff? And putting on my raincoat at 3 a.m. in the morning when all sane citizens are safely abed.'

Caroline shook her head. 'Has this fat rat got anything to do with the murder of Kit Ling?'

'That is one reason why I like to be near you.'

Forrester kissed Caroline hard upon the mouth. 'You are so bloody intuitive maybe some of it will rub off. This fat rat *is* going to help me screw a certain man called Eddie Woo.'

'The king rat is going to turn his rodents upon Eddie Woo in order that he be pardoned for a Dangerous Drugs offence?'

'That is the precise offer he will be made.'

'And then what?' Caroline followed Reven Forrester to the door of his flat, still naked as sin. 'Will that be the end of it? Will that satisfy you?'

He stood at the door. He held her and the warm musky bed-odour of her body made him heady.

'Will it?' she said. 'Will that end it?'

'Perhaps.' Forrester kissed her and it was an effort to draw away. 'Go back and sleep now.'

'Be careful,' Caroline said. 'Please.' She closed the door and stood listening for a while. She heard the hum of the arriving elevator, the rumble of the doors as they opened, then closed.

She did not go straight back to bed. She went to the bathroom instead. With a hot flannel she wiped her belly, her groin and her buttocks. Had she wished to do so she could have bathed or made use of the bidet to cleanse herself internally. She did not.

The sperm of Reven Forrester reposed deep in her and that was exactly where she wanted it to be. She stood before the big bathroom mirror and examined herself; first frontally and then in silhouette. She stroked her palms over her smooth pale belly, then she mimed a new, much swollen shape. She pulled a wry face. 'Are you sure?' she said to the fat lady in the mirror. 'Are you dead certain that this is what you want, babe?'

It's what I want.

Then she did return to bed. She plumped the pillows, straightened the duvet and covered herself. She curled up like a warm, well-licked cat, expectant of the arrival of good sleep. It did not arrive.

Every time that she began to drowse, a quiver of excitement would rise up and twist her stomach. It was apprehension and it was hope, those opposite emotions were see-sawing inside her in an irrational unbalanced way and keeping her from peace. She had been so certain that what she was doing was right, so who then had called in this upstart, teasing rogue of doubt. Away with you!

It did not go away.

She switched on a pedestal light, sat up and stretched her body languidly. She placed her hand upon the copper-red triangle below her navel, beneath which, at a rough guess, her ovum must now lie, towards which a million or so scrimmaging, wriggling spermatozoa were blindly and ir-revocably headed. One, just one, would survive the journey, perhaps to knock upon the door of life. The drama of it! It was a stupendous business, and it was happening right there . . . *there*!

And if the ardours of those fervent little cells were not enough to keep her from sleep, then there was the consequence of it all to consider. She had thought about it at length prior to her decision not to take her pills, and not to hose his sperm down in a jet of cold bidet water. For she wanted a baby. Not just any baby; she wanted a baby that carried the genetic imprint of the man she loved. She had made all these decisions weeks ago. Consciously and deliberately she had thought the matter through and had arrived at her conclusions. She would become pregnant. She would tell no one who the father was, not her own parents or

70

friends, *no one*. It was no one's business but her own. With sealed lips she would bring into this world a baby of her own. And if Reven Forrester loved her then, and if he loved the child, then she would share it with him.

He would surely love the child. After all that she had heard tonight she felt certain he would love the child. Dear God, let him love the child as he had loved poor little Kit Ling.

Inspector Charlie Lam stood waiting for Forrester in the street at the entrance to Sin Shaang House, quite a modern looking building of eight floors. He was smoking a cigarette which he extinguished upon Forrester's arrival.

'Penthouse, Mr Forrester.' He directed Forrester to the lift. 'Only the best for *tsip* of Eel-eyes Chang. Very nice pad . . . Man, you should have seen his face when we nicked him. *Wah!* That was worth seeing.'

Forrester followed Charlie Lam into the elevator cab. 'We better talk, Charlie, before I interview Chang. OK?'

Charlie lit another cigarette. 'Sure thing, Mr Forrester.' He probably had guessed what it was that his gwai lo friend wished to know: had Eel-eyes Chang been set up?

The truth of the matter, however, would not be a straightforward thing to arrive at. Part of the difficulty was that the family Lam, of which Charlie was a member, owed a deep debt of gratitude to the family Forrester, of which Reven was the sole heir. It had to do with a grant that Reven's father had made in order that most studious Second Uncle might attend the University of Hong Kong.

In order to show that gratitude was as high as heaven and as everlasting, Charlie might insinuate that Chang had been set up by him. This would be considered as a most proper and acceptable lie because it would open the way for Forrester to apply squeeze and get whatever he wanted from the man without feeling obliged to see him prosecuted for a serious offence.

Forrester knew all of this, but he did not want Charlie to lie to him on account of it.

'We're men who understand each other,' Forrester said.

Charlie smiled a subtle, deep smile that allowed that this was so.

'The point is, Charlie, that sometimes the best way to do a thing is not the prescribed way. I would like to use Chang to do something for me. Something that I can't do myself.'

'Oh sure,' Charlie agreed cheerfully. 'I know what you mean, Mr Forrester. Chang is a bastard egg-of-a-turtle triad, but even such a man has his uses.'

'That's right, Charlie. You've done me a big favour. I can't tell you how big without involving you further. You're going to take me in there and you're going to show me where you found the heroin, then you and your boys are going to leave me to get on with it.'

Charlie deprecated his actions with a shrug. 'Sure thing. Anything you say, Mr Forrester.'

'Yes, but before I can use Chang, I need to know how deep he is into trafficking. I need to know the truth about the man.'

The elevator stopped on floor eight and both men stepped out. Charlie Lam faced Forrester for a moment and drew deeply on his cigarette, contemplating this request, then he shrugged.

'He's guilty. He's in deep. You still want to use him, Mr Forrester?'

'Let's go in.'

'OK by me,' Lam said. 'This way.'

The corridor was tiled, the floor polished. A wrought iron gate protected the entrance to flat number 88.

Charlie Lam opened it.

'Double Prosperity.' Charlie pointed to the number. 'But not for Eel-eyes Chang. His luck just ran out, hah?'

Eel-eyes Chang's apartment spoke of great wealth. Embroidered silks hung upon the walls. Deeply carved rosewood tables held vases and intricate jade carvings, and bronze

72

libation-cups and cauldrons of dynasties long past. Islands of hand-woven mats lay over a carpet of deep-sea blue. The air smelt of sandalwood – rich.

'This way,' Lam directed. 'First I'll show you where the heroin was hidden.'

A many-mirrored bedroom. Here the wall silks were inventively erotic – of pallid swan-necked lovers, all bent to impossible poses, their robes artistically unfastened to reveal lubricious little private parts. All very anaemic really. Not the stuff that hairy foreign-devil gwai los got turned on by.

'Here.' Lam opened the drawer of a lacquered chest. 'Ten grams, I reckon. What do you think, Mr Forrester?'

Ten grams was Forrester's assessment too, made up into ten small plastic 'street' packets: sufficient heroin to earn Chang a conviction as a trafficker of DD – sufficient heroin to put Forrester in a very good frame of mind.

'Perfect,' Forrester said. 'Quite perfect.' Which statement meant that the haul was of ideal magnitude: large enough to incriminate, small enough to remain their secret – thank you, Charlie Lam.

Charlie Lam chuckled his pleasure. He walked lightly ahead of Forrester to the lounge, where Chang San and his *tsip* were sunk into opposite ends of a wide, white, very modern settee. 'Eel-eyes' – there could be no nickname more apt than that. Chang was a small, thin man, bespectacled with thick-lensed glasses that made his eyes look staringly grotesque. Little hands protruded from expensive Swiss voile cuffs, fingers twisting apprehensively over the handle of a malacca cane he held between his knees.

Concubine of Chang, at the other end of the couch, did not seem nervous at all. She sat up, straight-backed, long-necked, hands folded one upon the other. She was lovely in a ceramic sort of way, like the delicately painted ornaments at the entrance: stilted and precious, yet beautiful. He wondered how she would be in bed – 'imaginative' was the adjective that sprang to mind. Whatever could be construed from Chang's taste in erotica, let it be known that his taste in women was good.

Charlie Lam nodded to Forrester, beckoned to a young detective who had been standing there and they both departed. Forrester smiled a most deliberately false smile towards the occupants of the couch and was pleased to observe Chang's fingers writhe then like a nest of snakes. Forrester placed a chair facing the couch and sat down. When it looked as if Chang was at his lowest ebb, Forrester began to talk.

'Well, Chang, it seems as though you and your lady friend here are in serious trouble. Seven, yes *seven* years in Shek Pik, that is what that haul of heroin would cost you. It's a hell of a place, ugly people, strict routine, bad food, bad smells. You'd go out of your mind there, believe me. I've seen it . . . No, no; I'll do the talking Mr Chang. I want you to listen. I want you to pay *very* close attention to what I'm going to tell you. I'm going to explain to you how to avoid going to prison. You would like to know how to avoid prison? . . . Yes, I thought you'd be interested; the more so when you realize that you'll be advancing the interests of Luen Ying Society at the same time. I'm talking about Mody Road, Mr Chang, Mody Road Tsim Sha Tsui, where the Hei Shui Society have had it all their own way for so, so long . . . Interested, Mr Chang? . . . I thought you might be. It works like this . . .'

Eddie Woo could hardly believe how swiftly and dramatically his luck had changed. It had happened that afternoon, he could even put a time to it. At 5 p.m. a trickle of customers had begun to enter Lucky Billiard Club, teenagers most of them. He could see that they knew the game, they were playing their shots most professionally. This was just the type of clientele that he wished to attract.

At 5.30 the trickle became a stream, and then, as though the floodgates of good fortune had been thrown wide, a spate of customers trod up the stairs and through the main doors. Soon there was not a table in the hall that was not occupied. The few regulars who came in later were forced to stand and wait their turn. Ah, but could he help that? They would simply have to realize that things had changed at Lucky Billiard Club – 'Be patient,' he told them, 'be understanding.' He busied himself. He rushed around in a fine mood, chivvying staff, cracking jokes and giving of himself in a way that he thought he had forgotten.

At 6 p.m. Eddie Woo noticed something strange about his new customers: they did not eat, they did not drink. His fast-food kitchen had done no turnover, his beer stewards stood scratching arse. His clientele clung to their games in a 'dead-shot', inconclusive way that kept them in occupation of the tables for an inordinate length of time. His regulars could not get a game so they left. In short, though his club was full of people, his cash registers were full of nothing. Something was amiss. He smelt a set-up.

He endured this situation for a further hour, then he retired to his office to telephone his protectors – Hei Shui Society. He was given a number to phone where such matters were dealt with. He phoned that number and was given a further number. At last he spoke to member 426 Hung Kwan – Red Pole – who was in charge of the administration force. Woo explained his predicament. He asked for help and was told that such aid lay beyond the scope of his current contract. Simply put: he would have to pay a lot more for such a problem to be resolved – would he pay? *Aieya!* Had he any option but to pay?

Help, he was told by the enforcer, was just around the corner.

It arrived in the form of thirty or so members of Hei Shui street gang. They stormed up the stairs yelling like madmen. They swarmed into Lucky Billiard Club waving meat cleavers and chains and all manner of sharp and deadly instruments and descended upon the 'customers' at the tables.

Eddie Woo had not known what to expect when he had requested of Red Pole that Hei Shui relieve the siege of Lucky Billiard Club. Something of great threat and little violence, he had thought, might rid the club of these pestilent, pimple-faced louts. He had not expected this furious and immediate onslaught.

As for the 'customers' at the tables, he had expected them to vacate the premises in a frightened but orderly way once it became evident that Hei Shui did not want them there. Quite the opposite occurred. In an instant they too had produced weapons of equally destructive power, they had formed up and were raging into battle. Chains flailed, choppers and knives, feet and fists, all lashing and lunging and seething with battle-lust. At first it appeared that Hei Shui would prevail. The suddenness and shock of their attack carried the bloody battle into the heart of the saloon, and several 'customers' went down: slashed, chopped, screaming and clutching at their wounds. But far from running in terror from the protectors of Lucky Billiard Club, they re-formed and counter-attacked in a most determined and organized manner.

Eddie Woo fled to his office. He slammed and locked the door. His hands were trembling so badly that he could hardly control them. The telephone receiver jumped from his hands like a live fish, he clutched at it, gathered it and began to dial. The telephone was dead. *Diu!* He looked up in time to observe a speeding snooker ball meeting the two-way mirror that separated him from the mayhem – *Crash!* Another ball came through the gap. Eight hundred dollars, he remembered, that piece of glass had cost him. That really hurt.

Through his improved view he could now see far more destructive and costly things occurring. He watched a young lout in the act of slicing from end to end the 2,000-dollar baize playing surface of a billiard table, smiling as he did so. Now the tide of battle had changed, the 'customers' definitely had the upper hand. A number of their contingent were free to concentrate their destructive efforts upon things inanimate: like his cigarette vending machines. (They at least were on lease.) And his beautiful wall mirrors at over 1,000 dollars a fixture – *crash – crash – crash.*

Eddie Woo looked aghast at the havoc. The snooker balls, red and pink, which had destroyed his office window lay amongst the shattered glass upon his carpet. He clutched one, and with a sudden roar of rage he threw it, he did not care whom it hit. Then he bounded from his office wielding his personal billiard cue. The strength of the tiger was his. He smacked the cue down hard upon the head of the table slasher and saw blood spray. The table slasher collapsed.

Blood, more blood. He broke his cue across the cranium of a lout who was engaged in slashing up his 5,000-dollar-apiece curtains, but he hardly thought of the money. *Blood!* He whacked his shortened (and thus improved) weapon down upon any skull within range. The madness of battle was upon him. He was a war lord, a Tsao Tsao, a Sun Tzu of the invincible sword. He suffered wounds but that did not slow him.

However hyper-adrenalized his state, the odds were against him. A leaded pipe swung violently through ninety degrees proved more than a match for the temporal plane of Eddie's skull. He felt as though his head had exploded into debris – a shocking bright pain, then blackness, emptiness.

The return of consciousness for Eddie coincided approximately with the arrival of a Police Emergency Unit squad, all plastic visored helmets and batons. He did not comprehend what he was seeing at first. He could not remember a thing. Faces, beak-like beneath their opened visors, stared down upon him. Then pain and memory and desperation came as one. His eyes tracked slowly back and forth across the wreckage of his club. Torn things, broken, splintered and shattered things, were all that remained to him. He was ruined. He moved to raise himself but was crushed back by the weight of his agony. He tried to speak but his tongue was not part of him. *They* were speaking; words that bounced and chased around his head in a illusive way. 'Hurt . . . Look . . . Finger . . . Off . . . Relax . . . Why . . . Ambulance . . . We . . . Don't move . . . Soon.'

So it came to him.

Then he focused on a face that he recognized: a gwai lo face. The man knelt next to him. There was a small zigzag scar upon his temple. He focused upon that as the face came close to him, close enough for a whisper to be heard:

'Remember Kit Ling,' came the whisper. 'I . . . never, never . . . forgive. This is just the beginning . . . the beginning.'

He remembered Kit Ling. And he remembered this unforgiving gwai lo. A man holding a camera bent over him, a flashbulb exploded white light. Then blackness flooded him again, and in it he floated from this horror.

If, for Chief Inspector Forrester, there was to be an enduring memory of the destruction he had brought about, then that picture would certainly be of Eddie Woo flat on his back, contused and bleeding amongst the shambled remains of his palace, his creation, his joy. How appropriate that at the end of it Woo should have lain there as part of the debris.

An ambulance had arrived and Woo had been carried to it, and thence to hospital. More joy for Forrester: the good surgeons there had decided that the second finger of Woo's right hand, which had been almost severed by a Luen Ying chopper, would have to be completely severed, to the knuckle. Was he right-handed, he had enquired? Yes, came the answer, Woo was. And how fitting that was too: at the end of Woo's best hand, *in absentia*, a reminder that would go with him to the grave, of the worst day of his life . . .

Well, the worst day of his life *to date*. He did not judge the loss of one single digit, albeit a most essential digit, as counting for much in the totality of Woo's sentence. An eye for an eye, he had promised, and that was the only arithmetic he would accept.

Immersed then in these thoughts, Forrester speculated not a bit upon the purpose of a meeting to which he had been summoned by the boss: the Assistant Commissioner of department 'A'. In fact it was not until he reached the AC's door that he realized he was five minutes late. It didn't really matter, Campbell would be late, he always was . . . but Campbell was not late.

Campbell was at his desk, he was addressing the telephone receiver on traffic co-ordination matters when Forrester arrived. His door was open and he made towards his subordinate an abstract sort of gesture which Forrester read as an invitation to come in and sit. So he came in and sat, and while the AC carried on his conversation, he gave thought to the possible reasons for this, his second meeting with his commanding officer within a month. He did not seriously consider that it might have to do with his manipulation of triad gang warfare. This was more likely to have to do with a cheeky postscript he had submitted a week previously on the idiocy of a law that forbade the Chinese national sport – gambling, other than that organized by the Royal Hong Kong Jockey Club. For gamble the Chinese would, on the horses, legally, or illegally on fifteens or pai-gau dominoes, on mahjong or two roaches crossing a tabletop, or two locusts screwing on a twig, or any other thing that moved in any way and in any direction at any time. But mainly they gambled on the triad-run games where they could get credit and the payoffs were high. And that was a major source of income for the gangs, and a major source of frustration for those trying to beat them. That was what his thesis had been all about, and it had upset some people (for one, the CSO Commercial Crime) on whose desks the memo had come to rest.

He primed himself half-heartedly to defend his views. But there was no need for that. The AC set down the telephone handpiece and stared absently at Forrester for as long as it took him to light a cigarette.

'Shouldn't,' he said. 'Gave it up for six months. It's a drug, d'you know. Did you ever smoke, Reven?'

Forrester said that he had once. 'Have an occasional puff.'

'Filthy habit,' said the AC on a puff of smoke. 'Well, let's see . . .'

He shifted some papers to expose a file, a bulging cardboard file; the kind of file that contains within its cardboard hide a record of all things rightly and wrongly, indifferently done, or not done at all in the course of a nine-year career. The kind of file that one of senior rank calls upon Personnel and Training department to deliver up, in order that one of junior rank may be discomforted in a rational, scientific and, of course, compassionate sort of way. Reven Forrester had an uneasy feeling that this file had to do with him, and he was right.

'I've got bad news for you, Reven . . .'

Forrester's stomach tightened. But of course Campbell was joking.

'Seems your promotion is at hand. In fact is due to be published in this month's gazette. How the devil you managed it with a record as bad as this, I'll never know.'

The AC began to leaf through the papers at a prodigious rate, a single comment accompanied each turned page: 'Good . . . I see . . . Hmph . . . Good . . .' So it went, until he reached a sheet near the bottom of the file, which to Forrester's reckoning meant that the earliest days of his career were now being studied, and with some care too.

'Hm'm . . . *Aha.*'

Was this the pub brawl in Wan Chai; the brutality charge that the 400 lb ex-sumo wrestler had levelled against him? Or was this the case of the motorbike ridden off Blake Pier, flat out into Hong Kong harbour after 'Nobby' Clark's

80

bachelor do? Other insidious deeds sprang to mind. Forrester craned his neck until it creaked but still he could not see what it was that the AC was nodding over in such a rational, scientific and, yes, compassionate sort of way.

It was in fact a record of his service with the Royal Australian Navy.

'Four years' cadetship at Jervis Bay,' Campbell said. 'Then on to patrol boats in Northern Australian waters. Executive Officer on HMAS *Cessnock*. Joint exercises in Celebes area with Australian, Indonesian and Philippine naval elements. I'd forgotten all this stuff about you, Reven. Seems you're quite the old salt.'

'I wouldn't say that, sir.'

'Hmph . . . Attached to RN Hong Kong station. Exec Officer, once more, on County-class destroyers. Those are guided missile destroyers, are they not?'

'Seacat,' Forrester said, 'anti-aircraft, and Seaslug long-range surface to surface. Pretty obsolete now, I'm afraid.'

'That's the nature of these things. Was a time when there was no such thing as radar. You plotted out your enemy's position with compass and protractor then let him have it – *bam!*' The AC did not say whether he favoured or disfavoured technology that enabled man to kill man in such a remote and unthinking way. He shuffled Forrester's papers back into order and closed the file. 'I suppose I should be pleased for you,' he said. 'Fact is that I'll be losing a good officer, and that galls. You're being posted to Marine Region.'

'*Marine* Region?'

'Don't look so surprised. You're a natural for it.'

Now Forrester understood why Campbell had wanted the pink file at hand for this interview. He wanted to be able to point to its contents and say, 'There you are, my boy, don't say we don't try and fit every good square peg into a good square hole.' Forrester wondered whether a protest at this stage would carry any weight. It was worth a try.

'I was on destroyers,' he said, 'vessels of over six thousand tons. I'd be totally lost if you put me in command of a squadron of Damen-class launchers . . . I would prefer to stay in A department if possible. There's an SP's post available in Intelligence.'

'Filled,' said Campbell.

'There's one in Special Investigations.'

'There is,' Campbell acknowledged. 'And I must say you were considered for it. But Don Sutherland at Marine had just claim on you. He needs an ADC urgently to work with Tim Bevan at Cheung Sha.'

'Cheung Sha?' Forrester's face soured with disbelief. 'Cheung Sha is Islands district.'

'That's right.'

'That's not even one of Marine's sea-going divisions. I wouldn't have to set foot on a launch more than a few times a month.'

'You just said you'd be lost if you were put in command of a sea-going division. *Totally* lost, I think your actual words were.'

'But what's the point then, sir? You were the one who said I was perfectly suited. With respect, sir, perfectly suited to do what?'

'Well, in the first place you have a house on Lantau – Cheung Sha is on Lantau, is it not? So the move would be quite convenient for you. And you know the island and the locals, and they know you. You've got face there and that's good for Marine. Secondly, Don Sutherland likes *all* his officers to have had naval experience. *Most* importantly, I think the job will be good for your career.'

Forrester would have liked to remind the AC of the fact that there upon Hong Kong island he had an apartment of perfect convenience. He would have been pleased to receive a sensible answer to the question: 'Good for my career, how?' He could have named half a dozen superintendents of Police who would have sold their grandmothers for a ticket to that quaint, green, dreamy mountain island called Lantau. He did not name those names nor ask those questions. He did not protest.

He had had his question and it had been answered. Assistant Commissioners, even friendly Assistant Commissioners, do not like to be cross-examined by those at Inspectorate level, not even those about to be advanced to Superintendent level. Not even when such questions were so obvious and begging for an answer . . . So he was to be transferred to Marine division.

'When,' Forrester said, 'does this happen?'

It was due to happen at the end of that month. 'I want you there by the first of October,' Campbell said. He sat and regarded Forrester thoughtfully for a moment. Then he answered the question that was begging for an answer.

'I want you to take this job, Reven, because you are a brilliant police officer who is about to wreck his career. You're *too* good at your job, I think. It's too easy for you. You developed CTU into a superb unit, it's everything that I hoped it would be. The information available from the CTU computer is amazing, quite amazing. The problem, Reven, is that you went on to use that amazing information and ability to serve your own ends . . . your own most manipulative and adventurous ends. That was wrong. No matter what your motive was, it was wrong. You weren't listening to me last time I spoke to you, and that's a pity. Understand, Reven, I too am very good at my job. If it were not so then you would not be hearing this from me. You would receive the posting that seemed best to suit your ability, then you would probably go on to destroy your career. I don't want to see that happen. You see I have more than an average interest in you, laddie. I think you know that, and I'm sure you know why. So I want you to go to Lantau. It's only a ferry ride from Hong Kong but it's a different world there. I don't need to tell *you* that, though. What I *do* want you to understand is that between the pink covers of this file lies the record of a near-perfect career. It's as good as I've seen. You could get a top posting in almost any country on the strength of what's written in here. Don't spoil it now, Reven. And don't look so bloody pained. You're not being banished, you know. Lantau is a plum posting in its own way. You know the island, and the island people know you. You've got lots of face there. You're in a unique position to handle the administrative problems of an ADC. There is no one better qualified for the job.'

Campbell stood then and came around to Forrester's side of the desk. His smile was wide. He extended his hand, which Forrester rose up and took. He had the fierce quick grip that short men sometimes surprise with.

'Well done on your promotion, Reven. Your father would have been proud of you. I certainly am.'

They walked together from Campbell's office into the main office. As they passed her, the AC's secretary took up her boss's smile, as did a young probationary inspector. Campbell left him at the lift station.

'I know I can count on you . . . Give my regards to Tim Bevan.'

A lift arrived and Forrester rode it to the fifth floor. He travelled along the busy passageway that led to CTU. Already he felt remote from this environment; a stranger amongst these people, this unit that he had built up from a few dusty and untrustworthy files. While all around him his department lived in a chattering clattering pulse of human and electronic endeavour, he felt like a dead thing amongst it. He had malfunctioned and he was to be cut away, like a microchip that had burned out.

There were those who would say: 'Lucky Reven Forrester, what a great break, what a haven of peace.' Those were people who did not know him.

He did not feel unfairly treated. He did not feel angry. He did feel bitter that someone whom he trusted had betrayed him to his superior. He did feel disappointment – dolorous, colourless, it weakened him.

He sat very still for a long time. His face remained expressionless, his head cocked slightly in meditation. He thought: this must not stop me. This is just a minor hindrance, a time for testing, and I must go on. To stop and turn away is to offer pardon and forgiveness for the unpardonable, the unforgivable, and I cannot do that. It would make me a worthless man, my efforts irrelevant and absurd.

I will go on, because I am tied to this by the lost life of a little girl. I will go on because, God knows, it is beyond me to stop.

The telephone was ringing. Mechanically he reached for it: 'CTU, Forrester.'

'Reven.' The voice belonged to Tubby Wilson. 'I've been trying to get you all day. Aren't you ever at your desk?'

'What is it, Tubby?'

'Jesus, have you forgotten? Your note, Sport, you asked me to trace the sampan in the picture.'

'Did you trace it?'

'No, but you can eliminate one of those class-one vessels: the Yau Ma Tei registered vessel. I found that sampan and it's not that one. *That* vessel is out of the water, it's in a boat yard at Aberdeen. It's been there for two weeks.'

'One down, two to go.'

'This might interest you,' Wilson went on. 'The yard owner says that Woo can't come up with the cash to pay for the repairs, and he won't release the vessel until he does.'

'That *is* interesting. Do you know how much it is that he owes?'

Wilson did not know that. He did know that the sampan had been brought in to have its prop shaft re-aligned, and new bearings fitted. Wilson said, 'I won't be able to help you any further. Got a helluva lot on my plate. Anyway, Cheung Chau is out of my area.'

'Cheung Chau?' Forrester said absently.

'Cheung Chau – where the other two sampans are registered.'

'Of course.'

'Quite a separate division. Sorry, Reven.'

'I knew it was. I'd forgotten . . . Don't apologize. You've done me a huge favour, Tubby.'

It was not a huge favour, both men knew that. It was a favour in proportion to the type of favour that Wilson might one day expect to be granted in return. Just the type of courtesy that came clothed in the colours of the old school blazer, nothing more. What pleased Forrester was the timeliness of Tubby Wilson's call. It had lifted him at the time of a hard fall. It had pointed him once more in the direction of the hunt.

3

A FADING GOD

October came, the ninth month of that lunar calendar. To Hong Kong it brought the gift of autumn weather. The hot, wet south-westerlies that had blown all summer began to waver. From the cold Asian hinterland a dry wind lifted and came rushing to take their place.

The first days of this moon are good days for a visit to ancestral graves, as a prayer to the departed during this time is sure to be answered. Requests from the other side will flow readily through the mouths of the medium during these days, for the dead have needs too. Money? Burn some Hell money, brother. Warm clothing? Well burn some paper coals, for the winter is at hand and the departed must not shiver.

On the ninth of the ninth it is wise to climb to a high place to avoid disaster. Nobody *really* believes that, but everyone does what everyone else does, so we Cantonese all climb the highest hill available.

In the People's Republic, October is marked by a celebration of a less feudal, capitalist, revisionist nature. Here, in lieu of all this superstition, we have a march-past of a hundred thousand soldiers, sailors and airmen, God knows how many SSMs and SAMs, and tanks, and other assorted fighting vehicles through Tian An Men Square, Beijing.

Here we have fine oratory from the podium before the great hall of the people.

Part of the speech gave rise to the dictum of the Field of the Thousand Flowers, 990 more flowers than Chairman

Mao cropped in 1956 in his betrayal of the intellectuals, mark!

It took the form of a parable about a farmer who had let a vacant corner of his vast rice field to a neighbour only to see that neighbour misuse this portion of land and allow it to become trampled and weed-choked. Of course the good farmer demanded an end to this damaging occupation. He had ejected the tenant.

The vast rice field was of course China. The unwanted tenants were the British imperialists, and the little corner of earth – Hong Kong.

The responsible farmer had gone about restoring his field by ploughing under all the weeds, then reseeding the black earth with a Thousand Flowers.

The Flowers – that was easy. The faces of the future, the children of Hong Kong. There ended the parable, and began the lesson.

To professional China Watchers the warning was obvious: old methods of education must cease at once. The lies and distortions of the imperialist doctrine had brought forth generations of Chinese who thought themselves to be of a different race – Cantonese; who did not wish to speak their mother tongue, Putonghua; who spoke only Cantonese dialect and English. These Cantonese knew only what had been taught them by the British, who looked through a microscope at their own faults; who had glorified Gunboat Diplomacy, the Opium Wars and the unequal treaties. Now the children must be shown a new view – a global view through the eyes of Marx; a local view through the eyes of the Central Committee of the Communist Party. For the children were the future.

It was clear that the Central Committee held little or no hope for the chances of rehabilitation of much of the adult Cantonese population. They were yesterday's weeds.

These words did not come as a shock to all those who fell into that category. That they were to be ploughed under did not surprise or disturb them unduly. It would not happen tomorrow, and what man lives for ever? Why else had the Government of the People's Republic allowed the clause: 'Hong Kong's previous capitalist system and lifestyle shall remain unchanged for 50 years', to be written into the joint declaration? That was how long they thought it would take to plough under the old ways, and fifty years is a long field to furrow.

So it was futile to worry about things so far ahead. Now, today they were dismayed to discover the outstretched arms of the Central Committee upon the shoulders of their sons and daughters. For what other colour would the Thousand Flowers blossom but deep, deep red? *Aieya!* And how would this affect the old customs, the family traditions and observance of worship in the near future?

Not in a good way, most Cantonese thought. Those who trembled at the dictum of the Field of the Thousand Flowers were those who did not have the means to send their children away. Their fears were real and potent, but they were as ants upon the cooking pot lid. What to do? Where to run? Who was there who cared about their plight?

Caroline O'Shea thought she might know how it felt to be in this predicament. She wrote about it in her column. She pointed to the plight of the millions who feared the discrimination of the Beijing Government, who did not want to unite with the comrades from the mainland and did not want to be considered 'patriots of the Motherland', as they had only just escaped the rigours of such patriotism. No one had forgotten the Grand Fishing Game of 1967 when thousands of corpses had been taken from the Pearl River waters with Red Guard bullets in the backs of their heads. What of these trapped people? she asked. Were they expected to applaud the thought of First Son being fitted for the uniform of the People's Liberation Army?

Good question. The Xinhua Communist Press must have thought that too, because they answered it, not directly of course, but in a way that left no doubt as to the direction in which the pen was pointed:

> Foreign journalists, even those so-called experienced China Watchers, find extreme difficulty in comprehending the true meaning of Chinese patriotism, which goes beyond family ties and country of adoption. The Chinese patriot stands unique in his total devotion to Mother China, alone.

Reven Forrester smiled when he read the rebuke. Caroline had had her mischievous, rumour-mongering-foreigner fingers rapped.

He lifted his phone and dialled Caroline's number for the second time that day. At the first try she had not been there, this time she was.

He spoke in Mandarin. 'This is Zhou Guangxiu of people's newspaper, *Wen Hui Bao*. Would like to gain interview with honourable China Watcher regarding filthy, twisted, imperialist lies.'

'Comrade Zhou,' she giggled. 'You can kiss my azalea.'

'Oh! Oh!' Forrester grunted in pleasure. 'You have any other shockingly lovely, decadent, Western ideas?'

'You're a pig, Reven,' Caroline said. 'What do you want?'

'I wanted to find out if you were back from China.'

'I've been back for days. And I'm sure you knew that.'

'Well it's four o'clock,' said Forrester. 'And I've got bugger-all to do.'

'You have an irresistible charm about you, Reven. So it's four o'clock on your island paradise, and the world has closed down. You're bored and you want me to come to Lantau and share in your sorrows. Is that it?'

'I thought you might like to take in a dinner at Charlies. They've got cuttle fish on with sliced beans and chili.'

'Can't make it, Reven – deadlines to meet. But if your offer stands, I can make it to Lantau tomorrow morning.'

90

'Saturday,' Forrester said. 'I've arranged to visit Tai O police station with the DC in the morning. I could change that I suppose.'

'Don't,' said Caroline. 'I'll meet you at Tai O. I'll come across in *Dolphin*. We can sail out to one of your deserted islands if the weather holds.'

The view from Forrester's office window gave of green lawn and acacia trees that were nodding to the genial east breeze. A distant, soundless helicopter walked like an ant across a blue canopy sky.

'It will hold,' he predicted of Saturday. 'I'll be finished by noon. I'll meet you at Tai O jetty.'

Saturday arrived with all the crisp promise that Forrester had expected. As the sun lit his room he woke to it and went out to his veranda. Yesterday's dry easterly was still fanning Lantau. Winter was waiting behind it. The first vagrant, cold-loving thrushes were ahop upon his lawn, quick beaks amongst the leaf trash of autumn . . . Yes, a picnic upon the islands would be a fine thing; Tung Wan beach upon lonely Tai A Chau island would be beautifully sheltered on a day like this.

A tickle of good nature spread through Forrester. It made him grin at the face in the shaving mirror, and select from his wardrobe a jaunty pair of rope-soled yacht shoes to go with blue slacks and a Filipino embroidered shirt. He threw a pair of shorts, a vest and some toiletries into a floppy gym bag. He came downstairs (two at a time) whistling, and tapped upon the glass of his barometer. He read it carefully but that was just habit; had the needle spun to the storm warning mark he would have laughed at it. Today was to be a fine day, he had decreed it. He said as much to Ah Fong.

'You needn't pack an umbrella with you, Mother. The skies will stay bright today.'

Of course she knew that already. Had she not consulted the red-covered almanac of T'ung Shu, wherein (amongst ten thousand other wise hints) lay the peasants' calendar? And had not the calendar given this day as falling between points 17 and 18 – cold dew and descent of frost. Of course it would not rain on such a day. It was, on the other hand, an inopportune day to go abroad, to start new building projects and to visit the barber.

'I'm going to Tai O,' Forrester said. 'I'll be gone all day. Don't expect me for dinner.'

The moment she had seen the packed sports bag she had known not to expect him for dinner, and probably not for tomorrow's breakfast either. She was curious to know what it was about Tai O that he found so demanding of his time. Perhaps it was a woman. But what sort of woman would Only Son find in Tai O other than one smelling of fish and diesel fumes?

'Should pack food?' sly Ah Fong said. 'Or *wine*?'

'Not necessary,' said Forrester. 'It's all arranged.'

What was arranged? He drove her mad, this son of hers. And, she suspected, he did it on purpose. Back in the kitchen, she watched the breakfast bacon curl up and smoulder. He did not deserve fine treatment. Still, she hoped for a reprimand . . . None came. A black glance at least . . . Not even that. He munched through his breakfast, burned bacon and all, then drank his coffee in silence upon the porch amongst his beloved orchids. He went to the garage and climbed upon his huge silver motorbike, then smiled and waved to her and drove off, singing. *Singing!*

She would phone Tai O and speak to a most bribable station sergeant whom she knew. The man would tell her *everything* that happened that day to do with Only Son's visit to Tai O village. *Aieya!* It was hard to be the mother of one who sang as she sufffered, alone.

Reven Forrester sang, not very well, and not for very far down the road. Singing aloud whilst riding at speed upon a quicksilver Suzuki 650 is unsatisfying in that words are distorted by the blast of oncoming air, lips slobber and saliva tends to dribble across the cheek. Forrester confined the song to the back of his throat until he reached Islands District HQ about twenty minutes later. There he ceased to sing altogether. Chief Superintendent Bevan was a good sort but he did not approve of any sort of behaviour that smacked of unorthodoxy. If one wanted to sing one should do it in the pub, preferably drunk and in the pub – there was nothing wrong with that. People who sang in other circumstances were infinitely suspect. Forrester's uniform, clean and pressed, was hanging in his change room. Winter dress was the order now: navy-blue jersey with arm and shoulder patches; navy serge trousers and web belt. His headdress was a felt beret. He folded his civilian clothes into his gym bag, then went to look for Bevan.

Timothy Bevan's office was Civil Service grey with carpet of regulation size and veneer desk. The walls were brightened by silk pennants of saffron and red, bestowed by various associations to give face to people of such seniority as he. His desk had an in-tray that was empty, and an out-tray that was empty, and a top that was littered with forms and documents through which jutted a blue plastic nameplate engraved both in English and Cantonese. Bevan sat at his desk. He had a telephone, which he had just used. As Forrester entered his office he replaced the handpiece.

'Good, you're here. That was Marine HQ. Got to go in I'm afraid – meeting, City District Committees. Damn nuisance. Look, old boy, would you take these down to Tai O with you.'

He handed Forrester a brown-paper parcel.

'They're young Potter's new rugby boots. Size thirteen I believe – amazing. Well, got to go now.'

And he went.

Forrester watched Bevan's police-blue Rover glide out of the driveway and turn east. He stood there for a moment holding the rugby boots of the amazing-footed Potter that he was to deliver. Then laughter came to him, copious and belly-deep. In a lesser form his mirth rode with him all the way to Tai O village.

Tai O was a favourite place for Reven Forrester, a bay of magic memories. It was into that harbour that his father used to cut the yacht *Marie*, skimming like a dandelion wisp on the noon breeze, while all around the ponderous, batwing-sailed junks of the island traders crept in their serious slow way. Pirates? Oh yes, there had been pirates then, they sailed in the night to count their loot, unseen, at the village of stilt houses in the throat of the bay. There was a creek there, a smelly little dog-leg channel that opened at both ends to admit a trickle of seawater when the tide allowed it. That was where the pirates went on those dark nights. And in the daylight he had gone there too, piggy-back upon the broad invincible shoulders of his father, safe to look down upon the hustle of pigtailed coolies and Hokklo fishwives who spread their offerings still wriggling wet upon the cobbles. And thus they'd walked, his father and he, through the village and on to the long praya walkway that circled the bay. The police station on the hill above the bay, that was their usual destination. His father knew people, no matter where he went. Here there was a chubby inspector whose name he could no longer remember. The inspector and his father drank beer, while he drank orange cordial and looked down across the bay to the gliding sampans and junks and the distant *Marie*. It was easy to remember this place.

Tai O had not changed as Kowloon and Hong Kong had. It was still largely a village of stilt houses. The Hokklo and Cantonese fishermen still brought their craft into the bay. The island traders still sailed in from China to sell bargain sweet-melons and oranges and squeaking, basketed Szechuan pigs. And the old police station stood as patronizing and solid as ever upon Fu Shan Hill.

Of course there were more buildings of brick and mortar now: houses and banks and schools, many little shops and a

94

modern clinic too. Most alleyways ran concrete underfoot and the praya had been widened and tipped with a fine modern pier. But these things did not really alter Tai O any more than a new hat alters the features of the wearer. It was a slightly taller, more mature Tai O than Forrester had first known, that was all.

What had brought change, radical change, to little Tai O was something quite invisible to the eye. It was a quite amazing discovery to do with the creek, or rather, what the creek really represented. For this creek was not simply an insanitary little passage of water that looped into Lantau, and scooped from it a small island. This creek, it became apparent, was an international boundary; the boundary between Crown land and the People's Republic of China. The British had been in illegal occupation since 1898, mark you, of a little chunk of China.

Aieya! What a state of affairs!

And how had all this come about?

It was the British who had boobed. For it was they who had drafted the Convention of 1898 – that piece of Gunboat Diplomacy that had left them as 'tenants' of the new territories of Hong Kong for 99 years . . . To be more specific: to attach blame in a just and proper way, one would have to look to the signatory of that lease, Sir Claude MacDonald. Certainly the clerk who had penned the boundary line upon the somewhat erroneous map had erred too. For the western tip of Lantau was the corner of the British claim, and he should have seen to it that no little creeks cut through it in such an erosive, sly and problematical way. But the late Sir Claude was really the fellow who would, posthumously, have to carry the can for the fuss and bother that occurred almost a century later.

Beijing did not quite know how to handle the matter of the lease that wasn't. Imperialism is still imperialism, even if its infamy is only discovered some ninety years later. Even if they didn't really want the imperialized little island, the

Chinese had to do *something*. So they insisted that the British *un*-make some costly sewerage improvements that they had just made upon the island. This gained them some face at British expense.

The ever-cunning British put it out that it was a Chinese company which had manufactured the sewerage system that was sub-standard, and not at all what they had ordered, and would have to come up anyway. This gained them some face at Chinese expense.

Both sides then allowed each other face by not disturbing the status quo of Tai O island any further. The bone was too small and devoid of meat for two great nations to contest. The British were told that they could continue to administer both island and islanders if they so wished – *but* no changes, please, of any sort, without prior consultation with the Government of the People's Republic. High-souled and dutiful to the end, the British agreed. For the end of it – 1997 – was but a short walk ahead upon the path of posterity. The Chinese would have their island soon, with good sewerage or without.

Superintendent of Police Reven Forrester was content to play his part in this administration, especially if in so doing the cause of his vendetta could be advanced. And he had discovered that this might be possible. He too had been active in the early days of October. He had not visited ancestral graves, nor had he climbed Lantau peak on the double ninth. He had worked his way into his new job with diligence and commitment. He had attacked the obese administrative ogre that was dumped upon his desk and deblubbered it and deboned it and parcelled it into digestible proportions. He had taken his seat upon all the mandatory committees and societies – Po Lin Tse Golden Buddha Committee, the Islands District Advisory Board, the Lantau Area Committee. He had attended meetings; listened seriously to long and tedious discussions, and advised, when called upon to advise, with Confucian self-

96

effacement and dialectic, which indirectness the Cantonese found delightfully paradoxical and commendably un-British. In police matters, of course, he was efficient and quick, and not in any way ambivalent. He became the model of a model Assistant Divisional Commander – a Ging Si who was a credit to the RHKP. And only one person knew otherwise.

Forrester was constantly aware that he was living a pretence. Beneath the shining armour there moved a champion of another sort; a crusader in a most private and illegal war. Every step he took, he took in the hope that it would show him something of his enemy. But though he probed and he watched and he was ever alert, he did not find the evidence he required to further prosecute Eddie Woo. Frustratingly elusive were the fishing vessels and sampans registered in the name of Woo Yin-wah.

The two fishing junks did not call at their place of registration. The two class-one sampans that were likewise registered at Cheung Chau were nowhere to be found in that busy harbour. Cheung Chau Island lay close off the south-east tip of Lantau, with a sea gap of but a few miles separating the islands. Even so, it was not a simple matter for Forrester to get there. Islands District did not possess sea-going transport, so he had had to requisition a launch from South Division in order to reach Cheung Chau. This he had done twice since his new appointment.

He had taken the big Damen MKI patrol launch into Cheung Chau Harbour, transferred to a shallow draught patrol boat, and from the deck of that small boat had searched every corner and pier of the harbour. He had ordered the Police coxwain to take him alongside every junk anchored there. None of the vessels bore the registration number he was searching for. It was possible that the junks were at sea; but where were the two sampans?

That was a question that Forrester dared not ask of the junkmen of Cheung Chau. If the reason for his search became known then word would undoubtedly get to Eddie

Woo and the green sampan would disappear beneath fifty metres of water, for ever.

At the completion of his second unfruitful visit to Cheung Chau, Forrester felt compelled to seek help. He took his query to the man he regarded as least loved by the fishing community – and thus least loving in return – the licensing inspector, the official whose duty it was to collect the annual tax, then personally to paint the licence numbers on to the vessels, stern and bow, and be vilified for his efforts. Shek had a much-vilified, forbearing kind of face. He had a small office at Fire Station Pier whence he sallied forth upon his sampan with brush and paint in his war against reluctant licencees. Forrester spoke to him on his sampan. 'Where are they, Mr Shek? Two junks and two sampans, class one? Of course, I realize how *hard* things are on the islands, and here is a little tea money, Mr Shek, that your day may be brighter.'

Mr Shek did his best to brighten Forrester's day in return. Seven hundred fishing junks were registered at Cheung Chau, he informed, many of which were seen only when the number eight storm warning went up. *Then* they came running in, the rascals, the typhoon shelter was packed to the walls with them then. Old Woo was one such fisherman.

'His base is Tai O, Mr Forrester, I'm quite sure of that. His junks are long-liners, both of them. So his fishing grounds will be the deep-water shelves south of us, during the summer. In the winter the best grounds for the long-line junks are off Hai Nan Island, a hundred miles to the south-west. If you want him that's where you'll find him now . . . Somewhere there.' Shek waved vaguely towards the south-west. 'That's where he will be, trading with the Red maybe.' Shek spat. 'Got to pay; got to trade with the Red to fish those waters. Still, not so bad these days as before, *ma ma ti*. You know what I mean?'

Shek had brewed tea, a tangy Fukien blend that Forrester did not enjoy. Nevertheless he made all the right noises as he sipped. Shek said he was unsure about the whereabouts of the two sampans, but suggested that Forrester look for them at

Tai O. 'Such sampans are as common as flies in that bay. Gill-netters, Mr Forrester, a paltry living but they survive. They grow fat. I don't know how.'

Forrester agreed; it was incredible. he had one more question for Mr Shek:

'The shore address of Woo Yin-wah . . .'

Mr Shek, it seemed, thought Forrester was joking. 'Ah! Ha! Ha!' he interrupted his comical gwai lo friend. 'And why should he have such an address, Mr Forrester, hah? His junk is his home. Find his junk and you have found him. I've told you his address, it's the South China Sea.'

You had to be Chinese to appreciate Shek's humour.

There was a notice at the bottom of the flight of steps that led to Tai O police station that Reven Forrester had always been intrigued by:

ANY PERSON WISHING TO MAKE A REPORT
SHOULD CLIMB THE STEPS AND RING THE BELL.

Forrester climbed the steps. He did not ring the bell at the top gate, he had never done that, but had often been tempted to do so. He wondered what would happen if he did; what miracle of police efficiency would that bell inspire?

Inspector Potter of the size thirteen rugby boots was in the report room. He braced up as Forrester entered, as did the Duty Sergeant. It was a small room; a desk, a few telephones, a VHF radio unit and behind all that, two silver-painted grille doors that led to an armoury. Three people in that room made it seem full. Potter was checking the report book which he offered to Forrester: 'One drunk, one assault. Nothing exciting, sir.' Forrester did not even pretend to examine the entries. He knew what he was looking for; it could not possibly lie between those unexciting pages.

'These are for you, Potter.'

'My rugby boots, sir.' The man had a boyish smile. 'You've no idea how hard it is to get proper sized boots in Hong Kong, sir.'

'Do you have a pair of binoculars?' Forrester asked of Potter.

'Binoculars, sir?' This was going to be a station inspection with a difference, Potter could see that. 'Yes, sir, in the safe.'

'Well then . . .'

Potter dashed into an adjoining room, there was a clash of keys, the clank of a heavy metal mortice being drawn, then the same sounds in reverse sequence. He appeared with the binoculars.

'May I ask if you're looking for anything special, sir?'

Now that was a question that qualified Potter as dumb. Perhaps it had to do with all the head-butting in the front row. 'You do play front row, Potter?'

'Oh yes, sir.'

'For the police fifteen?'

'Tight head, sir.'

That explained it. 'I want to have a look around the bay,' Forrester said. 'Are any of your staff native to Tai O?'

'*Native*, sir?'

'Tai O born and bred, Inspector.'

'PC Kwong is your man, sir.'

PC Kwong was walking a beat in the village. Potter had him brought in.

'This is PC Kwong, sir.'

Kwong saluted. He looked nervous.

'Kwong, the Ging Si wants to look around the bay.'

He was a short man, even by Chinese standards. He was smartly turned out and wore the English language proficiency tab. Forrester invited the PC to walk with him. They took to the praya in the direction of the village.

Kwong was intelligent; that became clear to Forrester as they chatted. Kwong had written his sergeant's exam, and was expecting promotion – an ambitious man. He took a

100

decision to invest in Kwong – a limited investment, a small amount of trust. He told the constable of his search for the vessels of Woo Yin-wah. He described the green sampan.

'There are hundreds of those around,' Kwong commented. 'If it's based in Tai O we'll find it . . . It would be better not to ask the fishermen though, that's if you don't want the owner to be frightened off. They're very easily frightened, these fishermen. Anything to do with authority scares them. You'd never find this man if word got to him that the police were looking for him. It's not much help having his name either. Woo is one of the commonest of all family names. There must be thousands of them in Hong Kong and the islands. Woo Yin-wah is his "book" name, his official name. Maybe his family use it too but I doubt it. Some of them might not even know what his "book" name is, and know him only by his "milk" name. If he went to school at all, then his school friends will know him by his "school" name. Then when he got married he probably took on a few more "great" names which his wife and children would know him by. But the *most* likely name of all for the villagers to know him by would be his nickname, everyone would know him by that . . . You don't perhaps know what his nickname is, do you, sir?'

Forrester did not know what his nickname was. He said, 'I only know him as Woo Yin-wah, and his son as Woo Sung-king, or Eddie Woo.'

'Oh yes,' said Kwong. 'It's quite the fashionable thing to adopt a Western name – like Victor or Paul or Tony, or something that sounds like one of their given names. But I'm sure I've told you nothing that you don't already know, sir.'

It was true, Forrester knew of the Cantonese infatuation with names; their will to sprout, in one lifetime, a whole foliage of identities. Kwong's treatise, however, had brought home to him how hard it would be to find the stem of Woo Sung-king – Eddie Woo – the heartwood that would bring the entire tree crashing down.

Kwong's thoughts concurred with his own. 'Quite so,' Forrester said. 'We don't want Woo to hear about this. In fact the fewer people who know about this matter, the better.'

The praya led into the market which was as boisterous as ever. School was out and the pavement was a riot of children. Games of hop-scotch were on the go – jumping aeroplane they called it, and that described it well. When the two men had walked beyond this scrimmage of sound and energy, Forrester spoke again.

'It's not police business this. It's a private matter. You will be doing me a great favour.' He observed Kwong carefully as he said this.

Kwong nodded. 'There is nothing as deep as the un-spoken.'

It was a Mandarin expression. His superior need say no more. He, PC Kwong, had grasped that this was a discreet matter that words would only complicate.

The street they were on ran parallel to the creek. Here shacks of clapboard and sheet iron sprawled out on stilts across the low tide mud. Upon the muddy litter sampans lay tilted, grounded, dressed with drying nets and rope and washing. The green sampan was not amongst them. They walked on.

Less houses here, and fewer sampans. The street became a pathway that formed the wall of a tidal pond, then wandered on towards the mouth of the creek. At the mouth of the creek a wooded hillock stood. This small green hump guarded from the sea and from the typhoon winds a small old temple. It guarded it well because this temple was two centuries old, and though in places the walls were chipped and brick-bare, they were sound. The ceramic frieze that topped the roof was mostly intact – writhing with fantastic fish and dragons chasing, of course, the precious pearl of fulfilled wishes. The deity whose home was this old building was Hau Wang, who had been a garrison commander of the

102

Sung Dynasty emperor, Ti Ping. Ti had elevated Hau Wang to god status in reward for faithfulness and loyalty in defeat at the hands of the Mongol invaders in AD 1280 . . . As Forrester had done many times before, he stopped there to look.

Some old men were seated upon benches outside the temple, and he greeted them with a nod. '*Jo San.*' They nodded in return. Hau Wang's worshippers were old people. Hau Wang had always been a reasonable sort of deity, not the type to bear down with thunder and lightning upon an offending soul. He was a moderate amongst the gods, but moderates are not survivors. The fact of the matter was that with every year that passed, Hau Wang's adherents grew older in years and fewer in number and fainter of heart. And Hau Wang was dying for want of earthly sustenance. He would not last a further two centuries. PC Kwong thought so too.

'A fading god,' he gestured. 'Wasted ground.'

'What would you do with it, tear it down?' Kwong's absolute scorn rather surprised Forrester. He didn't expect an answer from the constable, and he didn't get one. Kwong grinned, embarrassed. Forrester said, 'I'm going on a bit. You go back to your beat now. Should you have information for me then phone me directly at Cheung Sha police station. I don't need to tell you how grateful I will be if you get this information.' That hint of reward did not change Kwong's expression at all; he had expected it. The back door had been opened for him, and so he had entered it – no more to be said. He saluted and Forrester watched him walk away.

Forrester sensed the eyes of the old men upon him, curious eyes. He did not look towards them again. He set off upon the path that led up Fu Shan Hill. He found a grassy knoll near some old graves where the trees were low and the view was good. From that position he was able to study all the fishing junks and gill-netters for miles around. He did not see the green sampan.

He did see *Dolphin* come into sight. *Dolphin* had been a jung dang fishing junk until an enterprising islander had converted it into a kaito, a junk licensed to carry passengers on short island hops. His enterprise had floundered. Caroline had bought the vessel; had refitted and rejuvenated it from engine-room to bridge. Across its bows she had smacked a bottle of champagne and called out, 'I christen you *Dolphin*.' A mild misnomer, for though a pair of good, new Lugger marine diesels drove the old jung dang hull quicker than ever, and the woodwork was now varnished to a gleam, no one could compare it in elegance to a dolphin. Its lineage was obvious: the bow was too blunt, the transom ponderous, and the superstructure sat as square as a garden shed upon the deck. The ex-jung dang's home mooring was the Aberdeen Marina Club, where it sided up to sleek cruisers like a gaffer at the Governor's garden party.

Forrester watched it for a while as it came around the islands to the north of Lantau. He noted the bow wave that it was pushing out and gave it twelve knots. Caroline would be early. He turned away and began the walk back to the police station. He judged that he would have time to go through the Report book, and the Occurrence book, and the Registers, and to inspect whatever else should rightfully be inspected by touring Assistant Divisional Commanders, and by then *Dolphin* would be off Tai O Pier.

His judgement was perfect.

One hour before noon he was standing on the pier and *Dolphin* was rounding the bluff. The steeringhouse of the traditional jung dang was a kennel-sized box perched aft upon the superstructure. Two ropes led from it through some tackle to a tiller blade; you tugged with your left hand to turn port, with your right to turn starboard. Caroline had done away with that. Her wheelhouse was cut into the roof of the superstructure. Her steering gear was hydraulic. It was from this cockpit that she waved to Reven Forrester.

104

Forrester saluted her – very naval, very gallant. Her laughter trickled across the divide.

The Lugger engines purled sweetly as *Dolphin* came alongside the pier. In the low water its wake was brown with churned mud. This vessel was twelve metres long, and no toy. Forrester sprang on to the foredeck, then climbed the ladder to the cockpit. Caroline reversed the engines then held the wheel down hard to starboard. *Dolphin* came around. She pointed her nose to the bay mouth.

Forrester kissed Caroline lightly on the neck. Caroline mumbled, 'M'mm.' She thrust forward the engine controls and *Dolphin*, like a rather obese but willing shire horse, set off to canter.

They drank champagne and got a bit drunk before they had as much as reached the bay mouth. A glorious heady, happy drunkenness, the kind of mood that God intended from the indulgence of the grape. They shared the moisture of their mouths which the wine had made sweet, and their minds were made as sweet as that. The alcohol reached into them in a slow burn, like a touch-paper fuse to a skyrocket. Their sex was a brazen, quick struggle for ecstasy upon the plump canvas cushions in the open-air cockpit of *Dolphin*. No words of love, no tenderness from him. He knew how to give her pleasure and he gave it without such frills. He gave it with the thrust of his hip and the depth of his maleness. And she tilted to fit him, tight, awed, white-teethed, wide-eyed. 'Feel me, Reven, feel me!'

The Lantau channel was a fine place to cruise that day. The wind was mild and the sea waves it mustered were toothless baby-like ripples that *Dolphin* tossed through, happily. The sky was china-blue and from the high cockpit of their boat they could see for many miles.

Their course took them around the western tip of Lantau, Fan Lau it was called – Division of Flows. For here the silt-stained water of China's mighty Pearl River met the even mightier flow of the Kuroshio current and was swept to the bottom. So they sailed into clean deep water, and a dozen small green islands rose hump-back all around.

There were the Soko islands of northern Lantau where he had promised they would go. But they would not go there at once. His binoculars had given him the distant shapes of some long-line junks to the south. He gave a bearing to Caroline that would bring *Dolphin* down upon them. They had their sampans out – two per mother junk; one to pay out fresh baited line, the other to haul it in, all two and a half miles of it, hopefully laden with fat wriggling fish.

Forrester watched them as they drew nearer. He wanted to see how such men worked.

'I couldn't do it.' He lowered his binoculars. 'One trip out would break my back. There's four or five thousand hooks on each line, so they say, and a lineman will draw in five hundred kilos of fish every day.'

They had come close enough to observe the long-liners without binoculars. The fishermen hardly paused at their task to look back. They perched like cormorants on the transoms of their sampans, hauling in and paying out, never stopping; tough sinewy brown arms – elbows working, working, working.

These were not Woo's men. The registrations on the bows of these junks were of Chinese origin. But there were more junks in the distant south-west, and these too appeared to be long-liners.

Caroline took Forrester close enough to make out their registrations. They were Hong Kong junks but Forrester needed to read no more than the first letter to establish that these were not Cheung Chau registered vessels.

'What are you looking for?'

Forrester had expected that question from Caroline for some time.

She went on: 'Why this extraordinary new interest in the fishing junks?'

106

'Not all junks,' Forrester said. 'For instance, I'm not interested in that junk over there.'

'You're being devious.'

'I'm interested in long-liners.'

'Jesus, there's a whole bloody ocean full of them. Are we going to cruise around the entire South China Sea? You should have warned me, I would have taken on stores. Anyway I don't believe you. Your interest is more specific than that. That's pretty obvious.'

'There's a certain fisherman I'm interested in.'

'And he fishes from a long-liner, and these are his regular grounds?'

'Yes, he fishes from a long-liner. I don't know for sure where he prefers to go at this time of the year.' He shrugged. 'Hai Nan, I think.'

'Hai Nan is three whole degrees west of our position, Reven. I'd hate to tell you how distant it is.'

'Two hundred miles,' Forrester said. 'Look, I did *not* expect to find this fisherman. I was just looking . . . on the off-chance . . . seeing we weren't doing anything.'

'We were going to have lunch on the islands.'

'And still are.'

'That's not the point.'

She did not say what the point was. Forrester guessed it might have to do with his down-grading of their lunch date. The brass all-weather chronometer in the cockpit console gave 15h00. The Soko islands lay one hour to the south.

'You really annoy me sometimes, Reven.'

'I'm sorry.' He meant it. He stood behind the coxwain's chair and kissed her on the neck.

'Beware the Scorpio who comes with kisses and flowers,' she wriggled her neck away, 'and coos into your ear like the turtle dove of peace. Look closely and you'll see that this is no dove, this is an eagle, with three-inch talons and razor-edge beak.'

He continued to kiss her. There was nowhere she could go

while seated on that chair, and he held her to make certain of her imprisonment.

'Why don't we stop engines right here,' Forrester said, 'and open another bottle of Dom Perignon, and eat our lunch on the foredeck, and get madly drunk. And then go to your cabin, in which there is a double bed and strategically placed mirrors, where I will make love to you as you have never been made love to before.'

'And then again,' said Caroline, 'they say that there is no mating more intense and no more beautiful love than that between the Scorpio and the Ram.'

'I will sting you,' said the Scorpion. And so saying he bit gently at the soft skin of her neck.

'Sting me then,' said the Ram. 'Excite me. But first, for God's sake, feed me.'

Ah Tsai, who was 'doer of all jobs' upon *Dolphin* – coxwain, cook or engineer, depending on the need of the moment – appeared at Caroline's summons. He set a table for two upon the deck then laid out food enough for twenty. All manner of small tender snacks were offered; course after course of food to warm and fill out the male yang.

They finished with coconut puffs and more champagne. Then as quietly as he had come, Ah Tsai crept away, and they were alone.

'Now you may sting me.' Caroline brushed back her hair and showed her neck. 'Here.' It was a long neck, a smooth neck, a most exquisite neck. Forrester was most happy to kiss the flesh of it.

'I promise you, Mr Scorpio, today will be a day that you will *never* forget . . . You see, I love you, little Scorp.'

'I love you too.'

'If that's true then take me to the cabin of the double bed and the many mirrors and quench my fire. I'm impatient now, Scorpio. I *want* you.'

The cabin did not have many mirrors. That was Forrester's fabrication. It had one, and they scarcely saw themselves in it, so deep was their concentration upon each other. She held him from her as he advanced. Hands pushing, massaging, neck, chest, groin. Then she yielded. She pulled herself into him. She pressed her mouth to his; her hips to his. I'll quench you, lady, he thought, *I'll* put out your fire.

It was as well that he did not verbalize that boast. For though he rode her wildly, innovatively and passionately, she matched his every move. And it was he who finally fell away, sweated, limp and exhausted. If there was to be declared a victor in this match then clearly it was Caroline, the Ram. For there was nothing left within him with which to come at her. His manhood hung like a slaughtered snake, not even a very big slaughtered snake. These were *his* musings of course; his private musings. He would not admit to them, or share them. Caroline, though she might joke immodestly sometimes, did not regard their coupling with any sort of humour. So he said nothing as she pressed upon him sweet, tender kisses; the measure of her satisfaction. She was as full of love as ever.

'I love you, Reven. I really love you.'

It was a fine time for sleep. A gentle swell was rocking *Dolphin* as kindly as a mother at the cradle. A breeze played coolly upon his sweaty skin. His mind was slow, his belly was full and his scrotum was empty. Annoyingly, Caroline did not share his need for rest – they had so little time together, why sleep it away? She was still curious about his midday activities.

'Who is this fisherman that you're looking for?'

He turned upon his stomach and muffled his face within a pillow. This did not discourage her.

'Why are you looking for him? What has he done to you, Reven?'

She traced her fingers idly upon his spine. She knew he could not resist that.

'What on earth makes you think he's done anything to me?'

'You,' Caroline said. '*You* make me think that. I know you *so* well, you see. You've been the hunter ever since you came on board; binocular to eye like a U-boat commander. I'm right, am I not?'

'It's to do with the little girl who was drowned.'

'This fisherman was involved?'

'Indirectly, yes. He owns the sampan that was used to kidnap her. He's the grandfather of Eddie Woo.'

'I see.'

'The fisherman's name is Woo Yin-wah. That's just about all that I know about him.'

'What would you have done if you'd found Woo Yin-wah today?'

'I don't know. I didn't expect to find him. I told you that.'

'But you will find him. I know that. You won't give up until you do. What will you do when you *do* find him?'

'I don't know.'

'You've already destroyed Eddie Woo. What do you want with his grandfather?'

Forrester thought deeply for a moment. Then he sat up. He said, 'How do you know about that?'

'You said that you were going after him. I don't forget midnight phone calls, especially when they drag my lover from my side. When *you* say you are going after someone I take you seriously. I read the newspapers and I look for such names as are mentioned by you in anger such as Eddie Woo, of the Lucky Billiard Club . . . I am so, so glad that I am not your enemy, Reven. If you received a splinter from a tree you would not rest until that entire forest had been razed, and the roots torn out. That is why I fear for Grandfather Woo.'

'I would not go against him without reason.'

'If you saw guilt upon him, no matter how lightly he carried it, I would fear for him.'

'We've had this argument before, I think.'

'He must be old.'

'And age has no conscience?'

110

'Vengeance has no conscience. It is a bad friend – pitiless, spiteful and monstrously strong. Where do you expect it will lead you? Not to the truth, I promise you.'

'You don't understand at all. I already know the truth.'

'You promised that you would look for evidence that would stand up in court.'

'And I haven't found it.'

'But you've already attacked Eddie Woo. He was chopped by triads and his business was wrecked. Now on to the grandfather.'

'What happened to Eddie Woo was not a punishment equal to his crime.'

'An eye for an eye.'

'Exactly right.'

'Then your search for evidence is just a sop for your conscience; the war goes on.'

'I'm trying to find the sampan that Kit Ling jumped from. My conscience is clear.'

'Vendetta is an anachronism. Leave it alone. You're destroying your career . . .' Campbell's words; he listened, he did not interrupt. 'You have a thirst for revenge that is a desert thirst. I thought it would be satisfied, but I see that it is not . . . If you could see how you are looking at me now, if that gaze was directed at you, your scalp would tingle. But I love you so I do not stay silent in the face of it. I will not keep quiet. And my hope is that if I can show you to yourself then perhaps you will see the wrongness, perhaps you will let this thing rest, as it now should rest.'

He said, 'Did you tell Campbell about that midnight phone call? Campbell is a house guest of your father, did you say *anything* to him about me?'

'Of course I spoke about you. He knows we're friends. But I never said a word about that phone call. I promise.'

'I don't know if I believe you.'

'*Reven!*'

'Somebody shopped me.'

'So turn your anger on the closest one to hand, no matter if it's your best friend. Reven, listen . . .'

'It's your turn to listen, lady. A little girl was murdered. Before she was murdered she was raped, drugged and then raped. Now the man who did all that is protected by the very laws that should see him hang. Justice is an impossibility. I know this and it makes me disillusioned and cynical. But now I hold the hand of a dead girl and inside me a loud voice cries out, and it says "Vengeance" and I must listen, or walk in shame. Therefore I'll hunt Eddie Woo, I'll chase him to his death. That's how I answer to my conscience. I don't ask for approval and I don't expect help. It doesn't upset me that others see my efforts as vindictive and wrong. It does not hurt me. What hurts is *your* betrayal of me. I took you into my confidence and you betrayed me to my superior. That was a filthy thing to do.'

'Oh God.' Two red blotches stained Caroline's cheeks like rouge on a corpse. In her nakedness she came to him and reached out. He clasped her wrists in a grip that would hurt and pushed her firmly away. She whispered, 'Reven, *please* . . . I did not do that. I *love* you.'

'You are lying and we both know it.'

'Oh God, don't say things you'll regret.'

'I will leave you to regret, Caroline. You knew how I felt about this bastard, and you knew what I intended to do. And you told Campbell . . . For that I can never, never forgive you. It's over between us. Do you understand that: it's *over*. Now get your clothes on, we're going back.'

She drew her clothes on quickly; nakedness seemed suddenly so wrong.

'Caroline.'

She lifted her face and it was full of hope. But in a voice that was winter he killed it. 'Hong Kong is a small place. But I don't expect I'll see you after today.'

'You are so blind,' she said. 'I don't think that you have ever really seen me, my love.'

112

Reven Forrester watched until the riding lights of *Dolphin* were no longer visible from the tip of the Tai O ferry pier, then he stared into the darkness. The wind had freshened and the sea was ahiss against the wall below.

'Why did I do that?' The anguish in him brought the question out loud.

'She had no right.'

'You fool. She was trying to protect you.'

That did not give her the right to do what she had done. Nothing could justify such disloyalty. He could not forgive that. 'Jesus, no!'

In this bitter, lonely quarrel with himself, Reven Forrester turned away and began the walk that would take him on to the praya. There was a shelter built upon the pier for awaiting ferry passengers. The shadows within it were intense, so he did not see the man standing there until he had stepped almost into his path. Had the man not then spoken Forrester might still not have recognized him.

'Good evening, sir.'

It was PC Kwong.

'You shouldn't do that, Kwong. Someday, someone will take you for a villain and do for you.'

'I trust your judgement, sir.'

Forrester continued his walk and Kwong fell in with him.

'So, you were waiting for me, Constable.'

'I have news for you, sir.'

'Good God, Kwong. You can't have been that quick.'

'Oh yes, sir. I know where this man Woo Yin-wah lives. I can take you to him if you like.'

'He's on Tai O?'

'That's right, sir. Quite close by in fact. He owns a house on Shek Tsa Po Street. We passed by the house this morning.'

'But he's a fisherman. I was certain he would live on board his junk.'

113

'A *retired* fisherman, sir. Woo Yin-wah is quite old, and spends little time at sea now. His granddaughter looks after him. Her name is Woo Chi-ying, or Woo Shien. She calls herself Shen. She teaches primary four at the mission school in the village.'

'I know the school well.'

'Do you want me to show you where the house is, sir?'

'Of course. Right away, Kwong.'

The houses on Shek Tsa Po Street lay on the verge of the praya, overlooking the bay. A short walk for the two men.

'There,' Kwong pointed. 'That one.'

Square, like the shoe-box houses children make, a modestly sloped roof, flat walled, with four little windows on each side, Woo's house stood between several similar dwellings. They were made of lumber, clad with sheet iron that glowed dull silver in the early risen moon.

'There it is,' Kwong said again, as though awaiting some response from his senior officer. 'I was watching it earlier. I think that the granddaughter sleeps upstairs and old Woo below. I saw her several times at the upper window, earlier . . . that window.'

Forrester followed Kwong's up-raised arm. They watched the window for a while, but no one came to it. He thought, they must be eating. He pictured the interior of the little house and gave it four rooms, two below and two above. The upper floor, where the granddaughter slept, would be something of a loft with a ladder-like staircase leading to it.

'Shen,' Forrester said. 'You say she calls herself Shen.'

'That's right, sir.'

'You've done well, Kwong.'

The constable made small modest noises: '*Houwah houwah*. It was nothing, really nothing.'

'Perhaps I should decide that, Kwong . . . So, how did you come to trace Woo so quickly?'

'I was fortunate, sir. A junk came in today with a good

114

catch of pomfret and yellow croaker in their hold; too good for that type of junk, and the short time they had been at sea. The junk master's name is Chan. They call him One-Arm because he lost an arm in a fish dynamiting accident when he was young.'

'And he's still at it to this day?'

'In a big way, sir. He had on board more than twenty sticks of amon-dynamite already tarred and fused . . . One-Arm Chan and I spoke for a while about the two thousand dollars and two months' imprisonment that all that dynamite could earn him.' Kwong gestured to the shoe box dwelling: 'The house of Woo Yin-wah.'

He had a fine sense of theatre this clever constable – Behold: the address you asked of me; the man you seek.

'Did One-Arm know of the green sampan?'

Kwong, in his Chinese way, hated to disappoint. His answer was eloquent but empty of testimony. The green sampan 'regretfully' remained as elusive as ever.

'Thank you, Kwong,' Forrester said. 'You can go now. I am most grateful to you.'

'It was nothing. I am not worthy of your gratitude,' Kwong said. But of course he did not really believe that.

Kwong went away and there was good reason for Forrester to do so too. The wind had veered and was now coming in from the north, from China's cold heartland – the breath of Siberia. It whipped through his thin cotton shirt and made him shiver. A question that Caroline had asked earlier occurred to him: 'But you will find him, and what will you do then?'

Well, he had now found old Woo; there was the house of Woo Yin-wah, the owner of the green sampan, the grandfather of Eddie Woo. His enemy's soft underbelly lay open. So what was to be done? Of course the answer was: nothing yet. Not a thing would he do until he had found out more about this old fisherman; until he had established how deep the stain of guilt had worked within

115

that family. Now he was weary and miserable and cold. It was time to go home.

He had taken but three paces when the front door of Woo's house opened and a woman came out. She stood for a moment within the spill of light from the open door, then she closed it softly and walked away in the direction of the creek.

Forrester followed her. His coldness, his tiredness, the acrimony of spirit; all this vanished as he walked behind the woman called Chi-ying – Shen.

He had seen her for a few seconds only and he wanted to see more. Long hair had hidden her face, but he thought she was pretty. An anorak bulked her upper body but jean-sheathed legs had shown beneath – and he thought they were good. He wanted to see her better. He wondered where she would lead him.

Her course took her through the market which was quiet at that hour. The stalls were closed, the barrows vacant, the awnings flapping idly in the night breeze. Here, streetlamps were lit and he glimpsed her often as she turned to greet a villager, or a child. She was pretty and she walked with grace. She passed through the market and walked on towards the creek. The ferry was crossing towards her and she waited for it at the steps. Someone called her and she turned to wave, and it was in Forrester's direction that she looked. He came on towards her as Dark-boy Poon, the ferryman, hauled his vessel in. He came on until he too stood upon the steps at the creek, and now she was but a single pace from him and he saw that she was exquisitely beautiful. The pull of her beauty was so strong he felt compelled to stare; to absorb all he could of this perfect being that he could see but not touch. In modesty she could not look back and so the advantage was his. He could stare, unrationed and unchallenged, and so he did.

The ferry came and he rode it with her to the east bank. He studied her for those minutes while she looked up river, aware of him, he was sure, but too constrained to show it.

The incredible thing was that he could see her brother's features here, and yet her face revealed her to be everything that he was not. There was joy and lightness in her eyes, where his were hung with dark cruelty. Her mouth looked ready at any moment to curve into laughter. His mouth was moulded and set with hostility. Eddie Woo was a perversion of this beautiful creature, a forgery. That nature could be allowed to perpetrate such a travesty was a wonderment.

Then, just before the ferry docked, she turned her head and glanced at him, and her eyebrows arched quizzically. He smiled and she turned away, but he thought it was to shelter her own amusement – an exposure as quick as a camera click past the façade and into the truth of Shen Woo. The woman hid a humour that transcended the dreary limits of her beaten-iron walled shack. She was as unrelated to the shriek-mouthed, wide-faced, thick-thumbed fishermen's daughters of Tai O as it was possible to be.

Once the creek had been travelled and the ferry had stopped, he could pursue her no further without it being obvious. He guessed that she was on her way to the mission school – Our Lady of Perpetual Help, perhaps, for some extra-curricular activity. Her pathway led off to the left, his to the right. He had to cease following her, so he stood and he watched until the shadows of the alleyway took her from sight.

He had found Woo Yin-wah. He had seen the sister of Eddie Woo. And the question 'What should be done now?' was as alive as ever.

The motorbike ride back to his house in eastern Lantau was not the exhilarating affair of the morning. The cold was acute, but more uncomfortable than that was the confusion that was building in him. Shen Woo had a face of innocence, and haunting beauty. He had come close enough to touch her, and had in fact wondered how gentle that contact would feel . . . And yet she looked so like her brother.

And he hated her brother.

4

THE DRAGONS OF HAU WANG

Woo Yin-wah was old enough to remember when the fishing junks of Hong Kong steered to a compass card marked with the twelve earthly branches and the ten heavenly stems; when sails were made of matting and bamboo battens bound with hand-wrung hemp. He remembered when time was kept by burning down marked tallow candles; when time was not so scarce that it needed to be portioned by the second, as it was today. Woo had nothing against modern things, he acknowledged the superiority of a north-pointing compass, and a clock that ticked on through the wildest gale. He had been the first man in Tai O to use such devices, and install diesel motors in the bowels of his junks, so they could navigate in any weather. He was ready to admit that these things had made him much richer than the less progressive junk masters of his time . . . And yet he remembered the early days with a wistful longing.

Perhaps it was because he had been young then, hard-muscled and bursting with energy. Everything is easy when you are young. There is no pain to youth, or if there is it is soon forgotten, for he could remember none. Hardship, yes, he could remember hardship, typhoons and torn sails, and cowering crews that had left him alone to reef and gather the sails and drive on the tiller to bring them about. But he'd laughed at those things then, as he'd laughed at the Japanese who had tried to starve them all to death in their war.

Now he was an old man, and content to let others sail his junks, while he played mahjong in the teahouse, or let the balm of the good sun melt the winter from his knees. His favourite spot was no longer at the tiller of his Toh Mong Suen long-liner, it was before the temple of Hau Wang. His favourite companion was his sworn friend, Au Wai, who, in the absence of a full-time priest, performed the role of fortune-stick reader, and keeper of the temple.

He loved that temple. It was a place of harmony of all elements, a place of absolute Feng Shui. When visiting that spot a quietness settled upon him that reached down to his soul. It was a place where, if you listened, you could hear the breath of nature. He did listen, and he watched. He observed before him the north entrance to the creek that bisected Tai O Island. He observed the mountain peak – Cheung Shan, that was the head of the dragon that inhabited Lantau Island. And the little island of Tai O, was that not the pearl at the dragon's mouth? There were those who did not understand these things, but he did, and Au Wai the temple keeper did. The two friends discussed it often.

They also spoke about the god Hau Wang. They agreed that their deity had declined in repute; but his power was still amazing, and the day would surely arrive when his popularity became great once more. Something would happen, they reassured each other, some wonderful event that would bring the worshippers in droves to fill the temple coffers and enrich the spirit of the noble Hau Wang. The two old devotees debated at great length on the form that this wonder might take. They wanted to be sure to recognize it when it did arrive so that they could proclaim it throughout Hong Kong. But on that matter no consensus could be reached. It *would* come, that was the only certainty.

'I am not a prophet,' said Woo Yin-wah.

'And I am neither a prophet nor the friend of one,' said the sage temple keeper, Au Wai.

In the light of events, both statements were mutually retracted . . . It happens in life that such roles may be thrust upon one, willy-nilly. Thus it was, that, like the flower-pot

120

that falls from a height upon the unsuspecting passer-by, this bright and painful vision came whizzing down to stun poor Woo Yin-wah.

It happened one day when old Woo was sitting alone in the late morning sunshine upon the bench in front of the temple. He was, as usual, contemplating the high peak of Cheung Shan, noticing how the clouds that passed behind it caused it to move in a most lifelike way. A sampan came up the creek – a gill-netter on his way to market. The man who held the yulo blade swayed gracefully at his slow task. Woo watched the intriguing mingle of elements – heaven and earth, the high almighty and the low born. He was pleased simply to be there, a small but natural part of it; as small and natural as the fallen pine twig lying there in the dust at his feet. He touched the little dry branch with the toe of his sandal and rolled it closer to him. He picked it up and examined it idly . . . The bark had fallen away excepting at the joints and these he pared with his fingernail until it was bare. Then he dangled the stick between his legs so that its tip once more rested in the dust. He held it but paid no further attention to it . . . Another sampan approached the creek, its master flicking the yulo blade, in imitation of the tail of a lazy fish . . . And beyond him the sea, and beyond that the clouds, and beyond that . . .

Au Wai came out of the temple then, chatting to two sensible city people who had come to the house of Hau Wang to have their fortunes read. Woo had heard the rattle of the tsim fung sticks being shaken. They must have fallen well for this couple, for they were laughing as they emerged. Au Wai was a gifted man, given to a good understanding of tsim fung.

He dispensed with the couple, bade them a good journey, then came to sit with his old friend Woo Yin-wah. In his black baggy trousers and tunic and cloth-button cap he stretched out his legs and yawned.

'They are going to America.' He nodded his head towards the departing couple. 'The tsim fell well for them . . . Ten

121

dollars they gave me. The worth of it was ten thousand dollars, hah?'

Woo did not comment.

'They'd pay a hundred dollars to get the same answers at the monastery at Ngong Ping.'

Woo did not so much as nod. In fact he appeared to be asleep, so rhythmical was his breathing and so peaceful his expression. It was difficult to tell if he was merely squinting against the shimmer of the low winter sun on the creek, or if his eyes were closed in sleep. Age had hooded old Woo's eyes, and they were well hidden.

Then Au Wai saw that his companion was not as at peace as he had seemed. Occasional trembles were rocking him; little starts that jolted him, chest, shoulder and arm. A dribble of saliva ran upon his chin. Au Wai was alarmed. He shook his friend, gently, and when that did not serve to cure him, he tugged in a vigorous way. He said into Woo's ear, 'Are you all right? Are you all right?'

That did it. Woo Yin-wah gave a great snoring sigh and opened his eyes.

'You were dreaming a troubled dream,' Au Wai suggested, 'so I gently woke you.'

'I was neither dreaming nor was I asleep,' Woo said. 'And I would prefer it if you did not shout in my ear again. My hearing is perfect.'

'Forgive me,' Au Wai said. 'I thought it best to wake you.'

'I was watching the mountain. I was watching that sampan come up the creek,'

'So where is the sampan, old friend?'

Au Wai gestured towards the shiny water. Woo had to admit that there was no sampan to be seen. He remembered his stick, the pine twig he had pared. It was no longer in his hand.

'I held that stick.' Woo pointed and both men looked down to where it lay in the dirt at his feet. 'And I made that scribble.'

It was obvious that he had held it because in the soft dust had been traced a pattern of some complexity.

'So how could I have been asleep?'

For Woo's part this counterstroke was decisive. He was about to reach forward to claim the evidence when Ah Wai commanded, 'Don't touch!' He leaned across his companion's lap the better to observe Woo's scribble. Then he said, 'Old friend, would you stand up.'

There was a gravity of tone in that request that made Woo raise himself without argument. Au Wai took the place that his friend had vacated. He bent forward and examined the ground Woo's stick had decorated. He seemed excited.

'Yes,' he said, 'yes. Look there.'

Woo looked, but he could see nothing of any interest. Just some interconnecting lines, some curved and some straight, none in the least artistic. His friend, however, was now on his knees, tracing with his finger upon an adjacent patch of dirt a similar design to Woo's, not exact in every respect yet in essence the same.

'Hm.' He drew. '*Mcho!*' He darted his finger with great energy this way and that, stopping occasionally to erase with his palm a section of the composition that was not quite right until at last it met with his approval.

'Look,' he said. 'Just look, old friend. Look what we have here.'

Woo looked. He said, 'I can't see why you're so stirred up, Mr Au. It's just some lines and curves that I thoughtlessly drew while *you* said I was sleeping.'

'Exactly!' Au Wai was now in a ferment of excitement. 'Thoughtlessly, but not without thought, you drew them but you did not draw . . . Have you heard of mystic writing, my friend – Fu Kei as it is called?'

'Who hasn't heard of it . . . Fu Kei . . . this?'

'Without doubt.'

'You must be wrong, for you know I can't write, so I could not have done it.'

123

'But you have done it! You see, no one ever knows that this ability is in them until it comes out, just like this . . . here.'

Au Wai handed his friend a cigarette, his hands shaking. He placed one in his own mouth and needed both hands to hold a lighted match to it.

'Fu Kei,' Au Wei said, 'is a message from a god, written in the most ancient of scripts, usually in answer to an important question. In this case, because we are right before his temple, it's obvious that this is Hau Wang's message. Don't you see, hah? This is certainly Hau Wang's message.'

Woo nodded thoughtfully. He was no longer averse to his friend's theory. After all, Au Wai was a scholar. He had served, had he not, a brief apprenticeship in a Taoist monastery? He could beat a drum and blow a tune on the siu-nut flute. He could chant long passages of poetry and read with understanding the most cryptic passages of the Almanac of T'ung Shu. If Au Wai saw this scribbling in the dust as the word of the god Hau Wang, then who was *he* to argue? In fact Woo felt quite good about it, for after all, it was not everyone who could do such things. In the voice of a believer, he said, 'What is his message, Mr Au?'

'*Aieya!* I should never have distracted you from your art . . . We have been given half a message. That's all. Just half a message from Hau Wang.'

Woo thought that half a message was better than no message, and said as much. But Au Wai was not to be consoled on that matter: 'Break the pot and sink the boat, *aieya!*'

'But what is this half message?'

'It's in the form of a warning.' Au Wai pointed. 'This character means "Beware". This character "Destroy" or "Enemy", and this "House".'

'That's all?'

Woo Yin-wah could now see why his friend was so upset. In fact, he felt more than a little annoyed with him himself. But perhaps there was a way of completing this most curious and enigmatic inscription.

'What if I tried again, hah? Let me sit there and close my eyes and hold the pine stick. Perhaps *then* the rest will come. We'll never know if we don't try.'

And so they tried. They went into the temple and there Au Wai made *kau tau* and begged forgiveness for his stupidity, and entreated Hau Wang to return and complete the interrupted dispatch. Then Woo Yin-wah took his place upon the bench outside, and, coached by the temple keeper, he opened his mind and readied his arm, and waited, and waited. It was a failure. Hau Wang was not the type of God who did things twice. The stick remained stationary; the full message unsaid. At midday they broke for lunch. Neither man said it, but both of them had come to realize that the revelation they had anticipated so keenly had indeed come, and gone. And all they had for their years of faithful waiting was an obscure three-word message that could mean anything. If it was a warning, then to whom was it a warning? Warnings were the stuff that the reputations of gods were built on. But the prophets of Hau Wang would not get far on this publication. *Beware, Enemy, House* was simply not awesome enough to impress anyone. Something more directly prescient was required to get the villagers going.

'Are you *sure*, Mr Au, that that is all? What about these other marks over here? Don't they mean anything?'

'Hmmm?' Au Wai got down upon his knees again.

'They must mean *something*,' Woo complained. 'Look at all those lines, ah.'

Au Wai was as aggrieved as Woo at the limited nature of Hau Wang's communication, perhaps he was even more upset. He felt that a little advance notice from Hau Wang to his devoted temple keeper might have saved the day. How was he to know that Woo Yin-wah was capable of such amazing feats? That the god should now sulk, and refuse to complete the message was bitterly hard to take.

'Look at this stroke here,' Woo encouraged. 'Don't you see how it grows up like a young stem of bamboo, hah?'

125

'Yes,' Au Wai said. 'But there's no meaning in it. No meaning.' He continued to stare at the picture in the dust. 'But if this line here were a little more slanting and a little more centred then it would give life to the character "They come".'

'Beware. They come. Enemy, Destroy, House.' That was more like it. 'Perhaps when you shook me it went wrong.'

'I was thinking that,' said Au Wai.

He was also thinking that if *that* line had gone wrong due to him, then any of the lines could have gone wrong. He bent himself to the ground again; eager to discover more, but in honesty it would need greater poetic imagination than he was prepared to allow to take it further. He was even tempted to retract the 'They come' bit.

'It's not exact enough.'

'It *would* have been.' Woo weighted his words with innuendo. '*I know.*'

'*Aieya!*' moaned Au Wai. The hurt of it!

They went into the village, the two old friends with their heads bent together in secret talk. Their destination was the teahouse of the Lotus Moon. But they had a most important decision to make before they arrived there. Should it be made known that Hau Wang had come with a message to Woo Yin-wah?

Well, there were some good reasons for, and some equally good against. The message itself was the crux of the matter. It was short and it was cryptic. But as every good Taoist knows: from chaos there came creation, and from emptiness, fullness. So they worked on it.

'"Beware",' said Au Wai, 'is a word of great significance, especially when uttered by one as good and just as Hau Wang. It must mean that badness and injustice are afoot – guard against it.'

'Be vigilant,' added Woo. '"They come" means that the badness is not yet here. That it is outsiders who have yet to arrive.'

126

'"Destroy" means that something that is material and capable of being broken, may be broken.'

'Something that lives in a house,' suggested Woo.

'Or a brotherhood, or a family,' said Au Wai. 'But the most important thing is to remember that this destruction can be avoided. Or what would be the point of such a warning?'

'The more people who are aware then, the better. We shall need many dragons to help guard the temple gate.'

'It is a good name,' said Au Wai. 'Yes, "*Dragons*", that is what we shall be called.'

There was the teahouse of the Lotus Moon, and it was bursting with people and noise. Mahjong games were being fought, the warriors of the walls were in full-throated battle. Woo and Au Wai too had come to play mahjong. They had their regular partners, their regular table. And Yung Ping, the proprietor, held a reserve of the best *shansi*, triple distilled, in all of Hong Kong.

There was no better place and no better time to begin the recruitment of the Dragons of Hau Wang.

Au Wai tried many times in the weeks that followed to tap the psychic wellspring of Woo Yin-wah. Nothing came of it. Hau Wang remained indifferent to his disciple's pleas. The newly recruited Dragons (they numbered eleven) were left to base their faith on the original writings of Woo, the evidence of which was now preserved in the form of a chalk sketch upon the bell wall of the temple.

Eleven is not a lot of dragons, especially in the face of such a dire threat. It hurt Woo, but did not surprise him, when Lai Po the snake-wine merchant slithered out and they were left with ten. When Wong Hou the barber cut his affiliation, Woo Yin-wah knew that something had to be done. But what?

'Another Fu Kei session,' suggested Au Wai the temple keeper. 'We *must* try.'

They brought offerings of fruit and (watered down) Sheung Ching 60 proof, and burned incense at the altar of the intransigent god. The eight remaining Dragons bent the knee in respectful *ta him* before the main altar, while Woo sat on his bench by the creek, with the pine stick trailing, waiting for the divine impulse that never came. More incense, more offerings, more hours of fruitless devotion. Hau Wang stayed mute.

The Dragons became seven, and a day later, six. They might not have survived for another week had not the prophecy of Woo Yin-wah begun to come true.

It was a fine November evening, a few degrees too warm for the joggers on Upper Albert Road who sweated past the gate-lodge at the front of Government House, but comfortable for the policemen who patrolled the Governor's scented gardens at leisurely pace. And for those inside the old building, seated at the banquet tables beneath the regal gaze of the gold-framed portrait of Her Majesty Queen Elizabeth II, the temperature was cool. His Excellency the Governor, Sir William Thompson, liked it that way. His principal guest, the Guandong Provincial Governor, Mr Lin Yuchi, who was recovering from a bout of influenza, did not, and was glad when the last course had been cleared away and they could retire to the drawing room for liqueurs and coffee.

Lin smiled a smile that was wider than his mood and downed a brandy. He looked around the huge, white-pillared room and mentally redesigned it to his own taste. The insipid pale-blue curtains and carpeting would be the first things to go. Sir William approached. Hard to talk to someone so tall, even though the Englishman's Mandarin was near perfect.

'A fine meal, Your Excellency.'

'The sweet and sour garoupa is my chef's speciality, Mr Lin.'

The chef would go with the curtains and the carpet. Lin set his empty glass down. 'Your Excellency, you and I must talk . . . in private.'

Sir William allowed the slightest of raised eyebrows. 'Of course. My study.'

The study had once been the library of Government House with free access to any member of staff. The bookshelves were still there, from plinth to ceiling, laden with gilded-leather volumes. But now the door was closed to all but those few who knew the code to its electronic lock.

Lin approved of such secrecy. The Governor punched in the code, the lock clicked and the two men entered. Lin rested his elbows on the long oak table and said what he had come to say. 'No change in our position. I have consulted with my committee. Our views are firm.'

Sir William frowned critically. 'The Foreign Office believe, as I personally do too, that such a course of action will be destabilizing and will further erode the political confidence of the people of Hong Kong. I advise against it.'

'Your Excellency's, and the British Foreign Office's, recommendations were considered most carefully. On the balance however the weight of our requirements tipped the scale.'

'Tai O is such a small, abject island, a fishing community, that's all. Excuse the bluntness, Mr Lin, but its appropriation by China might be perceived as an unworthy move.'

'Your bluntness is welcome, Your Excellency. And let me be equally as straight. China will not be appropriating anything. Tai O never did form part of the agreements, ancient or modern, between your government and mine. And so we invite you to cease your administration of that "small, abject" island without delay.'

'It would be appropriate if I consulted with my Executive Council before the Guandong position is announced.'

'Indeed, Your Excellency. But please appreciate it is not

129

only the Guandong Government that is involved. Beijing have given their unequivocal approval.'

Now that statement Sir William found hard to believe. Some kind of a deal had been struck between central government and the Guandong provincials, that was certain. Special Branch had warned him about this event weeks ago.

SB's opinion was that the essential interests of several factions would be served by such a move. Both the provincial military establishment and the provincial government were unhappy with the slice they had been offered of the Hong Kong cake. They were southerners, and southern interests were not sufficiently protected by the 'Joint Declaration'. They saw the wealth of Hong Kong being dissipated in the north, and it did not belong in the north. But the thought that probably horrified the southerners more than any other, was that of northern troops being sent to garrison Hong Kong. So the southerners saw Tai O as the toehold to Hong Kong harbour.

'And what is Hong Kong without its harbour?'

'I beg your pardon, Your Excellency?'

'Musing,' said Sir William, and mused further as to why Beijing had allowed the southerners this advantage. He did not voice that question though . . . 'Well then, I have given you our point of view, and best advice.'

'And we have appreciated your courtesy.'

'Shall we return to the drawing room?'

So Tai O was to revert to the Chinese. There was nothing to be done really, except to advise the small contingent of Marine Police upon the island to withdraw, and to placate those Executive Council members who thought they should have been consulted. The newspapers would probably play the thing down. It was too close to 'Ninety-Seven' to tread on any Communist corns.

'My office will conclude the business.' Sir William held open the door for the Guandong Governor. 'They'll need to know your time schedule as soon as possible.'

Seventy-two hours. That was all the time the Chinese were to allow. Thereafter a task force of the People's Armed Police and the People's Liberation Army, Guandong Military Region, would land in Tai O Bay.

Mind you, if it was to happen this way it was better that it should be quick. There were the feelings of the Tai O islanders to be considered; and the less time for such consideration, the better.

If the Tai O islanders had something to say about the matter, they certainly would not have time to say it to the British. They were, after all, citizens of the People's Republic, they always had been. It was up to their rightful masters to 'persuade' them that all was well.

As Task Force Commander Fang Hung Lik put it: 'Nothing will change, and everything will change.'

Major Fang addressed the village elders with these words within the grounds of the Tai O primary school, the largest piece of open ground upon that little island. 'The junks will go out, and the junks will return. And the market will still operate, and the school, and the hand-drawn ferry at the creek. In fact, Comrade Islanders, you will live exactly as before, provided you do not break the law. Of course *that* is the law of the People's Republic of China.'

'Hm,' murmured the elders.

'A most just system of law,' Fang added. 'The people's courts are renowned for their justice. There is only one *new* law to be remembered. Just one. That is that Po Chue Tam . . .' Major Fang pointed to Po Chue Tam Hill. 'Po Chue Tam is *out of bounds*. The old and disused temple of Hau Wang is *out of bounds*. The north entrance to the creek is *out of bounds*. This ground is required for a most patriotic purpose and only members of the People's Liberation Army will be allowed to go there.'

A murmur of incredulity rose from the elders.

131

'Guards of the People's Liberation Army are now posted at the south end of the walkway that leads to the disused temple. No one from the village must go there. If you are stopped by such a guard you must obey. *That is the law.*'

The elders hoped that in the fullness of time all this would become clear to them. Comrade Fang spoke Cantonese with a Hakka accent that was as leaden as a basket of sinkers. He also had a habit of pursing his lips as he spoke, to suck upon a cigarette, thus further distorting his vowel sounds. There was a most appropriate name for this braggard: *Sihk jo syun tauh* – Great Mouth Odour. This was adopted quickly and unanimously. Comrade Great Mouth Odour noticed the rising good humour of his audience and was pleased by it.

'So you, Comrade Fishermen, and I will get on like the bamboo and the plum blossom.'

Later on that day they learned that Comrade Great Mouth Odour was not the funny man they had taken him for. Old Woo and Au Wai were stopped on their way to the temple of Hau Wang by a PLA sentry brandishing a bayoneted rifle. The soldier had been instructed to make the attitude of the new administration absolutely clear. This he did by bayoneting Au Wai in the buttocks when he was slow to turn away.

The meeting of the Dragons which was then called was attended by the full membership of eleven. As they could no longer hold meetings at the temple, they met at Woo's house. And so Shen Woo was witness to all that was said.

'The enemy I warned about has come,' Woo said. He was basking in face. All doubts about his bona fides as the spokesman of the god Hau Wang were gone. When he spoke there settled a simpering silence. 'Some of you did not believe me. Well, what do you think now, hah?'

Well, of course, the less faithful hung their heads. The faithful six made noises of solidarity. Au Wai, who also had great face since punctured by the PLA bayonet, said, 'We must not recriminate. The point is that we have received a message from Hau Wang.'

'Through me,' Woo reminded.

'From the god Hau Wang, through you, Professor Woo,' Au Wai acknowledged. 'We have been called to his protection.'

'To stop them from destroying his house,' Woo said.

'Yes, disaster will come to us all if we don't prevent that.'

'*Aieya!*' was the somewhat cowering response of the Dragons. 'Disaster; *all* of us . . . are you sure, Mr Woo?'

'Sure,' said Woo. That got them going.

'*Aieya!* Then we *must* do something.'

The point was: what?

They debated well into the afternoon. They spoke of every possible option, from mobilizing the entire village to march upon the temple: 'Let's see them bayonet each one of us!' 'Does the bayonet wound hurt, Mr Au?' To guerilla tactics in the night: 'Remember how we tricked the fornicating little Japs, and flavoured their rice store with bucket-loads of "night fragrance", hah? Remember the time . . .'

But all of this chatter left them with their basic problem unsolved: 'How are we to protect the temple? Where will this get us at the day's end?'

Where indeed? Shen Woo, who had listened to the conspiracy of the Dragons of Hau Wang all afternoon, was pleased that they had finally arrived at this dilemma. For these were dragons without fire – there was not a man amongst them who was under sixty years of age. Even assuming divine power was with them, they were no match for the bayonet-wielding PLA. That had been proved. But they were angry, angry enough to try some wooden-headed adventure that might get one of them killed.

She too had been thinking. She had a plan. It was as shaky as a green bamboo ladder but she was ready to give it a try. Of course Grandfather would not approve, so she would not tell him.

133

The Dragons were tired now, and one by one they departed from the home of Woo Yin-wah. She served the old man his meal, and she stroked his bristly white scalp and hoped he would listen.

'Grandpa. You must not be impatient. Something will happen to save Hau Wang. You will see.'

'You're just a girl.' He drew her hand away. 'You don't know anything. This is a sad day for me; a sad day for all of us.'

'Don't fear,' she said, and she thought about the words that she would use to convince the gwai lo police officer to help Grandpa. She would tell him that Grandfather had known King George as 'his King'. She would tell him how Grandfather had tricked the Japanese during the war and smuggled food to the defenders of Hong Kong, all shut up and starving in dismal prison camps. She would tell him of the old man's devotion to the god Hau Wang and she would ask that he intervene to restore the temple to its disciples. He was a Ging Si – a Superintendent of Police. He could do it.

She thought about the gwai lo Ging Si. She remembered his face as she had seen it that night as they had crossed the creek . . . She hoped that in the light of day those eyes might not cut with such intensity.

'A dangerous one,' Dark-boy Poon, the ferry man, had told her. 'That mark upon his temple, they say it cost several lives to put it there. He's a real Ah Tau – a big balls in the police.' Dark-boy Poon knew everything about everyone on Lantau.

She was frightened. She admitted that to herself and to her guardian goddess in the god-box in the corner of her bedroom. She bowed her head; she steepled her fingers and said:

'Kuan Yin on your pink lotus throne,
It is respectful Shen.

134

Here is an orange and three incense sticks.
There are devils loose in the village.
We need help.
So I earnestly call your name; I ask this:
Take away any fear.
Save from suffering,
Bring success to good endeavours . . .'

When she had finished her prayer, she lay down upon her bed and worried so constantly that sleep stayed distant from her all through the night.

Or so it seemed, but she must have slept, she realized the next morning while attending to her toilet, for she remembered a dream she had had. The gwai lo had been in it, but his face had been black. He had reached out to touch her hair in a gentle way but instead of gentleness he had tugged it. He had pulled some loose . . . There was more to the dream but that was all she could clearly remember.

Of course it was a good omen. There was nothing in this world that a demon found more distressing than a blackened face turned towards it. But what of the hair?

She knew she had beautiful hair. It was not stringy like some Chinese girls'. It was long and lustrous, especially when she had washed it. 'Cloud-hair' the Chinese called it. She thought she would wash it now. 'Important to look your best.'

So she scented and soaped and creamed and used blusher and black pencil. She put on her red dress with brass buttons, and a jersey of white angora.

Grandfather was still asleep when she left the house.

'Morning prayers' at Cheung Sha police station was not the usual laid-back affair that day. The twenty-four-hour reports were in from all the stations in the district, excepting Tai O.

135

Their work had been taken over by a temporary post on the British side of the creek.

Things weren't working well there because the villagers on the People's Republic side were still reporting crime to the Hong Kong police. To complicate matters, there were still houses at the mouth of the creek that were built beyond the halfway mark. These houses had been built up around old unseaworthy junks that had been grounded there, never to sail again. Now these old rotted hulks were totally clad and hidden behind plank and sheet-iron – walled and windowed and roofed. Some of these houses no doubt straddled the halfway mark. Access to them was by sampan.

'Who the hell do those residents report to?' said DC Bevan to those assembled in his office. 'Which country are they citizens of?'

'It's a problem,' Forrester agreed. 'Why don't you put it to Marine HQ?'

'I did. They said, "You're on the spot; you're District Commander, you deal with it." Personally I think our people want to play this thing down and keep negotiations at as low a level as possible. Don't give them any more face than we have to . . . So we will have to sort things out with the PLA.'

'The PLA cadres won't have a clue about who stays where,' Forrester said. 'Why don't we make the decisions for them? Later on, when they've settled down, we can all sit down and shuffle the boundary around.'

'No, no.' Bevan shook his head emphatically. 'Got to be done now. Anything else will lead to conflict. The Commies have got a totally different criminal code . . . Do you know their law, Reven?'

'A bit . . . Enough not to like it.'

'Exactly. I was reading up on it last night. Maximum punishment for hooligan behaviour – death. For pimping – death. For trade in explosives – death. Membership of a reactionary sect – death . . . smuggling, speculating, and so it goes on. We can't allow them to try one of our citizens.

There'd be a public outcry. You read the Criminal Law and Criminal Procedure Law of China, Reven. It'll make your toes curl!'

A young inspector who had said nothing so far, said, 'Death by firing squad – *bam*.'

'Exactly,' said Bevan. 'We've got to get things straightened out at once.'

Tea was brought in then, and set down upon Bevan's desk. While they were drinking it a station sergeant came into the room carrying further dispatches from Tai O. He handed them to Bevan then turned to Forrester.

'There's a lady waiting for you in the report room, sir . . .'

Bevan interrupted. 'We've got to get down to Tai O, Reven, to sort this thing out. The sooner the better.'

From the way Bevan was looking at him Forrester understood that statement to mean – *you've* got to get down there, Ging Si, to sort this thing out. He was to be all the negotiating face that the British would allow. He said, 'I can leave now if you like.'

'The sooner the better,' Bevan said again. 'Do whatever has to be done. Set up some kind of a liaison committee. Keep me informed . . . Now, Inspector . . .'

Forrester had already reached his Land Rover when the station sergeant came running out.

'The lady, Ging Si. What shall I tell her?'

'What does she want, Sergeant?'

'Don't know, sir. Won't talk to anyone but you. Her name is Woo, Woo Chi-ying. Shall I say you're too busy?'

'No.' Shen Woo . . . He felt intrigued and vaguely excited. He remembered her perfect beauty; the quick, quizzical glance she had given him as they rode Dark-boy Poon's leaky old ferry. But that had been in the deep of night. Would her beauty be diluted in the cold light of day?

'I'll see her in my office then.'

She was exquisite; more beautiful than before.

'Thank you for seeing me,' she said.

'Sit down.' He waved towards a chair. 'What can I do for you, Miss Woo?'

A hint of perfume wafted by the big ceiling fan reached him then, like spring jasmine. He liked it. He had forgotten how similar this woman's features were to those of her brother, yet how contradictory. He had forgotten how deep and unsettling were the emotions that this false duplication evoked.

'I have come to ask for your help, Ah Sir.'

'How can I help you?'

He saw that she was wary of him and that pleased him. She had come to ask for help and that dignified him. He pushed some files to one side and leaned his arms upon his desk. This demonstrated vast superintendency, it also brought him as close to her as he could get from his side of the desk. He saw that she had applied make-up, delicately and with care. She kept her eyes low, which showed her eyelashes to be very long and dark. In that position she began to speak.

'I have come to you because you are a big officer in the police. I hope you are not offended by this impertinence. The problem I have come to you with, Ah Sir, is serious, I think, and one that will require the wielding of great authority in solving it.'

She spoke so well, so sincerely – how could he be offended? She began her story by telling him of her grandfather; of his faith in the British; of his loyalty during the war: a simple, kind man who had never walked an evil step. Then she told him of the temple at Po Chue Tam, and old Woo's devotion to the god Hau Wang.

Forrester said he knew the temple well. He did not tell her he had been there a few weeks previously. There had been some old men outside the temple then, it was possible that one of them had been Shen Woo's grandfather . . . He'd been looking for the green sampan, and perhaps the owner of it had been but a few paces from him. That made

138

Forrester smile. Shen Woo saw his grin and her shoulders unstiffened slightly.

'Grandpa believes that Hau Wang spoke through him. Have you ever heard of Fu Kei writing, Ging Si?'

'I've *heard* of it, yes.' A sceptic, let that be clear.

She began to tell him about Grandfather's Fu Kei experience, and the effect it had had on old Au Wai, the temple keeper, and some of the villagers.

'Au Wai is Grandpa's *kit pai* friend, a sworn friendship that makes them as close as brothers. Au is an educated man, he was an apprentice monk until the Japanese came and destroyed the Taoists. He never became a monk but he resisted the Japanese and he has face. The villagers listen to him.'

'Do you listen to him, Miss Woo? Do you believe him?'

The question was not answered.

The door to his office opened at that moment and Bevan came in. He looked at Shen Woo and his eyebrows arched in approval. He said to Forrester: 'Glad you haven't gone . . . Need to speak to you.' He gestured with his head: 'My office.'

The door closed and Shen Woo was left alone in the office. It *was* big, and very tidy, just as she had expected it would be. He was not as she expected. Frequently when she had been speaking, she had looked up and found him staring at her – not an arrogant stare, no, the look in his eyes had been intense, but not oppressive, and not unkind. It had all been much easier for her than she had imagined. She had been right to respect the omen of her dream. If anything could be done, then this man would do it. Absently, Shen Woo traced her fingers across the desk top, touching the things he touched. The varnished wood name plate with his name in gold letters on it, the trays and files, a floppy blue beret with a silver police badge – a very intimate feeling came from handling that cloth. This was his armour and she had felt it, and found it agreeable. He would wear it and never know that she had pressed it to her cheek . . . like that . . . A delightful secret, was it not?

Footsteps approaching the office door caused her to sit straight-spined in her chair, as a respectful visitor should sit, and face the desk. But the footsteps passed, and the door remained closed, and her thoughts returned to the owner of that office and the symbolism of the dream. He had reached out for her hair; he had tugged at it.

Shen Woo touched her long hair where it lay upon her shoulders, she twined a lock between her fingers and tugged it as it had been tugged in the dream. And she thought: how nice if he would touch my hair. He would find it to be lovely hair. He would like it.

The sound of approaching footsteps came again. Forrester was back. He opened the door and stood there. 'I'm afraid I have to leave for Tai O immediately. If you like you can ride with me, I'll take you home and you can talk to me as we drive. Then I'll tell you if I can help you, Miss Woo . . . or not.'

But she was *sure* now that he would help her. She walked with him to the blue Land Rover with the white roof and the police-badged doors, and she sat next to him on the front seat. There was a radio set in the dashboard that constantly crackled and issued messages, some of which he responded to – he held a small microphone in his fist and spoke into it in Cantonese. They had spoken only in English until then. Now, without remarking on the change, they spoke Cantonese. It seemed to bring her closer to this man. Sometimes he would look away from the road to question her, or just to look at her while she spoke, and told him of her fears and hopes.

When they reached the bus terminus east of Tai O, he drew the Land Rover into a single police garage, which was low-roofed and scraped the high radio-aerial noisily. From there they walked.

He said: 'I don't know whether I'll be in a position to do much for you, Miss Woo. Tai O, as you know, has been turned on its head. On the other side of that creek the Hong Kong police don't have any power at all, it is another country, with other laws. I can tell you that by starting his Society of Dragons, no matter how harmless it is, your grandfather and his friends are already on the wrong side of that law . . . So you see, even if they do nothing further, they could be arrested and severely dealt with. They must disband their little temple society at once, and I will do what I can. There *may* be someone on that side I can talk sense to . . . Now you must go home.'

He walked away from her then.

Forrester walked onwards on the pathway on the east side of the creek. Police E Department engineers were setting up a prefabricated complex at Yim Tin just outside Tai O village. A small jib-crane was hoisting prefab walls and concrete was being led from clanking mixers to form the floors. Several buildings stood complete. Potter of the size 13 rugby boots came out of a finished hut, saw Forrester and came over to him.

'Sir.' He saluted.

Potter was pleased with his new HQ. He showed Forrester around the site.

'In some ways we're better off than we were before. The old building was bloody cold in the winter, sir. The quarters that they've built for us are comfortable. And the report room has got more space.'

'Are you operational?'

'We've set up the radio. The technicians tell me that the radio will be on net by this afternoon.'

'How are the villagers responding?'

'They turned out in their hundreds to help with the move. We stripped the old station to the bones. Took the bloody lot.'

'Probably couldn't wait to get rid of you.'

'We're popular here, sir. This new site has got good Feng Shui, I'm told. And the Fishermen's Association has laid on a Lion Dance team to make sure we have good joss . . . Did you hear about Kwong, sir?'

'Yes, just before I left. I'm amazed he's the only defector, if that's the right word.'

'Damn right, sir. Bloody ankle-biter! Just when his stripes came through. If I could lay my hands on him.'

'Can't blame him, Potter. Just a few more years and the whole place is theirs. Then all of them will be working for the People's Armed Police.'

'Bloody Commie, sir. Did you know that he's second-in-command of the PAP contingent? That didn't just happen by accident. I wonder how long he's been working for them.'

'Years, maybe. It doesn't matter does it? We're all supposed to be cooperating. In fact that's one of the reasons why I'm here today . . . boundaries. Comrade Kwong sounds like the ideal man to sit down with on that subject.'

'He probably worked them out a year ago.'

'I hope so. That would save us all time. Don't look so bloody murderous, Potter. Time may come when you'll be working for the PAP too.'

'*Never*, sir. I'm on contract. I won't be staying on after '97.'

'So how do we get hold of Comrade Kwong, Potter?'

The procedure was to cross the creek by ferry and to call at the PAP post that had been set up on the Chinese side. They had a runner there who would, hopefully, summon whoever it was who was required.

Kwong came within fifteen minutes of Forrester's request. He was dressed in a white over-shirt and slacks, and appeared to be unarmed. He seemed pleased to see Forrester. What could he do to help?

'Let's walk,' Forrester said, and without giving Kwong the chance to choose a direction, he stepped off on the village lane that led towards the temple.

Kwong said, 'I didn't have a chance to thank you for getting my promotion through, Mr Forrester.'

'It was a small thing.'

'This time let me be the judge.'

142

There was a new air of authority about the man. Forrester wondered how deep it ran.

'We can all use help sometimes . . . Why I'm here is because the DC is worried about boundaries. There are a lot of houses that more or less straddle the midline of the access channel to the creek. The DC felt we should be clear about who falls under which jurisdiction.'

'Very wise,' Kwong said. 'Very sensible that we talk about this and avoid any conflict.'

'I'm glad you see it that way.'

'I don't think that it would be satisfactory to attempt this using a map. It will have to be worked out on the ground.'

Kwong spoke on and Forrester did not interrupt him. They reached the edge of the village and did not stop. Now the temple was in sight. Upon the walkway a barbed-wire barrier had been erected. The PLA guard braced up with his assault rifle when he saw Kwong. Kwong stopped there, and gestured Forrester to do likewise.

'I hear you had some trouble here,' Forrester said.

'Where there are laws there are law-breakers.' Kwong shrugged. 'It was a minor thing.'

'I hear that the temple keeper was bayoneted by a PLA guard.'

'Temple keeper is a misnomer,' Kwong said. 'You know that place. Would *you* call it a temple?'

'I would if I was a Taoist and I believed in Hau Wang. Why don't you let them go there? What is the harm in it?'

'Difficult . . . Difficult.'

'Why not?' Forrester persisted. 'They're no danger to you.'

'They are not as innocuous as you may think. They are rumour-mongers and propagators of feudal superstitions. They are members of a secret sect.'

'They're old. They're candles in the wind.'

'New China takes the line that such people are an obstruction to the socialist revolution.'

143

'They didn't commit a major crime. You know that as well as I do.'

'I do know that. And that is why I'm lenient with them. The law of the People's Republic has as its guiding ideology the thought of Mao Zedong. Leniency is as much a part of our law as is punishment. But then they must cease to undermine the social order . . . But tell me, Mr Forrester, what is your interest in this?'

'The granddaughter of one of these old men is concerned for him.'

'Would that be Shen Woo?'

'Yes.' Forrester saw no point in lying to Kwong. 'Shen Woo came to me . . . Old Woo is convinced that the god Hau Wang spoke through him. She's concerned about her grandfather's reaction to your area restrictions.'

'I know all about Woo Yin-wah's supposed Fu Kei writings: such superstitious reactionary nonsense was the curse of old China. I will not tolerate it here. The grand-daughter was right to be concerned. I will take the strongest action to stamp this thing out. As for the restrictions . . .' Kwong looked towards the temple, then to Forrester. He stroked his chin in thought. Then he said, 'Come.'

Once past the barrier gate they walked on in silence for a while. It was Kwong who spoke first:

'I have no interest in punishing old Woo for his misguided beliefs. I recall the story of the origin of Pa Kua Secret Society. The man who originated it was a peasant. It became the most powerful secret society of all time. I do not wish to see these "candles in the wind", as you term them, rise up to become a roaring bonfire. But they must stop what they are doing at once . . . Look, here is the temple. Come inside with me. I will show you the scribblings of old Woo and you can judge for yourself whether they are divinely inspired.'

The big red doors were shut, the painted guardians frowning upon the planks, but they were impotent. The new guard wore olive-drab fatigues and a smart peaked cap with a red star badge, his hands held an assault rifle, and it was he who permitted or denied entry now. So they entered. They bypassed the screen that blocked evil spirits and came into the house of Hau Wang. A cheerless emptiness hung there. The fragrance of incense, the rattle of tsim fung brass, the chatter of old Au Wai, these things were gone . . . Beyond the altars the gods stared, deadpan, melancholic, spiritless. Hau Wang and his attendant figures, Pak Tai, the spirit of the north, and his two celestial advisers seemed to have wilted since last he'd seen them, shrunk like old men in a hospice.

'Dolls. All of them.' Kwong gestured. 'Look at them. Did you ever see such a feeble, moribund sight? Come, look at this.'

Beyond the wooden cradle of an old brass temple bell some chalk marks had been scratched upon the wall.

'Are these the revelations of a god? The story is that Woo Yin-wah, while sitting on a bench out there, fell into a trance and drew some lines upon the sand. This is a copy of it. See here . . . this is the twig that he had in his hand.'

Kwong smashed the stick upon the big brass bell, which murmured in a dead dull way. The broken stick he threw to the ground as they walked outside.

'That's where he sat.' Kwong pointed.

The tide was out, the creek was just a trickle; too low even for the shallow-draught sampans to navigate. Upon the opposite bank stood a group of men. They had not been there when he and Kwong had arrived at the temple. A Hong Kong policeman was standing close by them.

'They came yesterday too,' Kwong said. 'They stood there for a while, then they went away.'

These people did not look as though they were about to depart. Some of them were seated on the verge of the retaining wall that edged the creek, and more were coming from the direction of the village. Forrester had spent time with the Police Tactical Unit, he was experienced enough to know that this little crowd had a purpose in mind . . .

Forrester turned once more to face the temple. 'I've got an idea that might suit everyone. It's been done before by the Hong Kong Government when they needed ground to develop the Mass Transit Railway. A temple stood on the exact spot required for a station entrance. Well, the people weren't happy about that, as you can guess, so the PWD disassembled that temple brick by brick, and re-erected it on another site. With your resources you could easily do that here. The state wants the ground and the people want the temple. We'd do everything we could to help. It's the perfect solution.'

Kwong did not agree. 'This ground belongs to the People's Republic. Those old men must learn that their loyalty is to the state, not to an altar full of idols . . . *That* is the perfect solution.'

The citizens lining the opposite bank had grown in number and resolve. It seemed as if they too had decided upon a solution. As Forrester and Kwong watched a banner of white calico was unfurled. Two men of quite advanced age stretched it aloft. Black lettering read:

TEN THOUSAND YEARS MINISTRY
FOR NOBLE HAU WANG

Now in single file a group of equally old men walked down the steps that led to the creek bed. Stone and mud – one old gent slipped and fell but was quickly helped up. Now the standard-bearers were coming on. They too were negotiating the steps, holding their message up high.

Kwong watched their progress. Forrester saw that he was silently counting their numbers. There were eleven of them upon the creek bed, a small crowd remained lining the wall. A police Land Rover was speeding across the open ground behind them, rocking and swaying on the rough terrain. Potter was at the wheel.

'You must go now.' Kwong's voice was quick with agitation.

Forrester did not go. He did not move from that spot. He had seen that the girl Shen Woo was amongst those lining the bank. He guessed that Grandfather Woo was one of the walkers on the creek bed – which one?

'Tell them to stop, to turn back.' Kwong flung this order at Forrester. Kwong was pacing nervously this way and that, obviously afraid of losing face before the soldiers should the villagers not obey him.

Forrester said quietly, 'I cannot give orders while standing on Chinese territory. You must take command. But I will tell you what *I* would do. I would march your detachment down from the gate, not in a hurried way, your men must not think you are in the least bit worried. Then I would form your men up where those people can see them. Then in a very calm way I would call upon them to turn back. Give them all the time in the world. Everyone must see that you are totally in command. Do not do anything rash. Do not use force. Just line up your men, that will be enough.'

Perhaps Kwong heard him, perhaps he did not. He did not react as he had been advised. He rushed off and Forrester heard him shouting at the guard to turn out. This they did. A section of men came running towards the temple with Kwong at their head, shouting and pointing. There came the rattle of metal as weapons were cocked, and raised . . . Dear God they were going to shoot.

'*No!*' Forrester shouted. 'Don't shoot. They're not on your territory.'

In surprise they responded to the order.

Kwong's mouth was working, but no sound came. The eleven Dragons had reached the centre of the creek now. There they halted and formed into a line facing the temple.

The loudhailer on the police Land Rover scratched into life, a command echoed across the divide: '*Mo Yuk! Fan Lei!* – Stop! Come back!'

147

Potter and two PCs came running towards the creek. *Don't run.* Forrester's telepathy must have worked. *Nice and easy.* They came on down the steps at an even pace.

Everything was going to be all right.

From the group of eleven, one man detached himself. He looked towards the approaching policemen, then he looked towards the temple. And Forrester knew exactly what his intention was. The old man (could it be Woo?) stepped off towards the temple.

The Hong Kong policemen broke into a run again, but they were yards too late to haul him in. He was now clearly past the dividing line, and upon PRC territory. He came on in that slow and deliberate way of the very old – one foot firmly set before he lifted the other, with total concentration on every step. Now he was wading through the shallow water, his head bent down to observe his path . . . Now he had cleared the stream.

'Go back!' Forrester did not care about protocol any longer. He filled his lungs and shouted: '*Go back!*'

'No! *No!*' Kwong pushed his face within inches of Forrester's. Angrily: '*You* say no more!'

Forrester said, 'I'm going to walk down there and I'm going to stop that old man. That is what you asked me to do, and now I'm going to do it.'

'*No!*'

Forrester noticed for the first time that Kwong held a pistol – a little black Makarov. The Communist had lost face badly now and this had enraged him. His reliance was on the potency of the weapon to restore his authority. He did not point it at Forrester but the threat was implicit.

'*No!*'

Woo, if it was he, had now reached the boat launching ramp at the temple. He wore a black tunic and black trousers rolled up to the knees. He held a pair of silk slippers in one hand so that they should not become soiled.

Kwong backed away from Forrester, glancing over his

148

shoulder at the old man. A knot of soldiers stood at the head of the ramp. Some held their rifles levelled, some held them at the trail. They looked very young, too young to hold such deadly weapons. Yet they would use them if they were ordered to. They were children of China, obedience was life's purpose. If Kwong said shoot, they would do it.

'*Go back*, old man!' Forrester shouted.

The old man looked up. He was grinning with fear. The muscles at his eyes were aflinch. He came up the ramp and walked past the guards. They looked bewildered. They turned their faces to Kwong.

A ragged cheer broke out from across the creek; the patter of clapping.

Forrester saw Kwong take a pace towards the old man. His face was flushed, his jaw locked. He was trembling with fury. He lifted his pistol. Forrester said, '*Don't.*' All the authority he could muster he lent to that command. But Kwong was beyond authority, his anger drove him now. The pistol lashed down. The old man fell forward into the dirt. His cloth-button cap rolled across the sand. The stubby grey-haired skull leaked red.

Forrester knew that the old man was too frail to survive such a blow.

So the prophecy that had been written in the sand by the hand of Woo Yin-wah that day was written into history. The enemy had come; they had destroyed; they had killed old Au Wai.

It was not the way of these 'little people' to confront officialdom. And though they posthumously admired Au Wai and gave him a grand send-off, no one was prepared to copy his style. So they went about their lives much as before. As Comrade Great Mouth Odour Fang had promised: the junks went out and the junks came in, the market opened and the market closed, and the children went to school, and the hand-drawn ferry plied the creek . . . As it was in the People's Republic, mahjong was officially banned upon Tai O Island, and that took some of the zest out of life. But it was like trying to ban prickly heat, the itch of mahjong was endemic, and it simply had to be scratched. In back rooms, behind closed doors, the addicts played on.

The denial of access to the temple of Hau Wang was deeply resented by the villagers. Hau Wang's popularity had resurrected since the death of Au Wai. People had come to realize that this god was capable of marvellous predictions. He had predicted the downfall of his own house and death of his own temple keeper. How much more simple for him to foretell the numbers of the winning horses of the Double Quinella, or to offer up the lucky character in a game of tsz fa. That he could not be visited to provide such information simply meant that Hau Wang could never disappoint. His unavailability thus became his strength, and he gained a profusion of new fans.

Woo Yin-wah, for his part, did not go without credit. Here was the man who had done the Fu Kei writing; whose wrist had moved in the power of Hau Wang. So he was watched wherever he went, and spoken of with respect. He found he had more friends than before; more people were keen to walk his path, and smilingly greet and enquire of him about this and that, and what direction should one sail, and how deep to lower the nets, and of course, what horses did he fancy for the next meet.

An old lady swore that at the exact instant Woo passed her door one day, the precise location of a long-lost bauble of precious jade came to her in a vision. A gambler down on his luck told how he had observed old Woo sneeze thrice. Number three on the third race had come in that day at 20 to 1, and he had made a killing. Thus the actions of old Woo were observed with a reverence deserving of his celestial fellowship. Woo, himself, made no claim to divine association, but that did not matter one bit to the villagers. They saw in this hapless, bereaved old man the scratching post of good fortune.

If one wanted to find the old fisherman, without that intention being too obvious, then that was easy. Every day Woo would go down to the creek, to the position on the bank opposite the temple where the Dragons had forgathered that dreadful day. There he would sit and gaze broodingly at the forbidden temple, and the site of his friend's tragic end.

One simply had to station oneself there and wait, and sooner or later old Woo would arrive. Sometimes he would be in the company of a friend or his granddaughter, sometimes he would go there alone. On the day that Reven Forrester sought him out he was in the company of Granddaughter Shen. It was a sunny winter Sunday afternoon.

'I remember you.' Woo peered at Forrester, putting face to circumstance. 'Saw you at the temple . . . you were there when Au Wai was killed.'

'Yes,' Forrester said. 'Excuse the interruption, but if possible I'd like to talk to you, Mr Woo.'

This was of course possible, but it was equally possible that Woo had no desire to be 'talked to' by this man – his eyes were good and his memory was acute. He had seen this Cantonese speaking gwai lo on two occasions in the company of Kwong, the one-time Hong Kong policeman who had battered poor Au Wai down. What could such a white ghost devil bring to him other than the worst of bad luck? The old man contemplated denying that he was who he was.

'Which man you say you wanted to speak to?'

'You,' said the gwai lo, 'Woo Yin-wah.'

'You, Grandpa,' said Shen. 'Please listen to him.'

'Perhaps you don't trust me,' Forrester said. 'That is of no consequence. I've got something to tell you. Your granddaughter spoke to me, Woo Yin-wah. From her I gained an understanding of the meaning, to you, of the temple of Hau Wang . . . I don't have good news.'

151

It was the worst news possible. The People's Liberation Army were about to tear down the temple. The ground was to be used for a camp for the soldiers of the PLA. Fu Shan Hill was to be utilized by the PLA as a radar site; an installation that would watch over the eastern approaches to Hong Kong harbour.

'Do you know what radar is, Woo Yin-wah?'

Stupid man, what fisherman today had not heard of that most incredible device? Woo did not reply.

'Well,' said the gwai lo, 'there is nothing we, that is the Hong Kong Government, can do to prevent this happening. But what we have arranged is that the temple will be rebuilt, brick by brick, exactly as it was before. The new site has good Feng Shui, it's on the hillside at Tik Tak Shue, just a mile from here.'

Woo nodded again. Shen Woo said, 'All of it, as it was?'

'That's right,' Forrester said. 'Exactly as it was, overlooking the sea. You'll be able to walk there whenever you wish.'

For how long? That was the unasked question in Woo's eyes. Until the Communists take over Lantau tip to tip. And then what? What purpose would all that labour serve?

Woo said, 'They should not do that.'

'The Hong Kong Government has arranged it.'

'The Hong Kong Government is a brown leaf on a winter's tree. What happens when it has fallen?'

'It would help if people such as you were to guard their traditions. Is that not what Au Wai's bravery was all about?' Forrester was sorry immediately he'd said that. It was a rude, presumptive statement.

Woo clearly thought so too. He rumbled angrily: 'Hm!'

He turned away from this most meddlesome gwai lo. 'Now we go home,' he said to his granddaughter. As he walked off towards the village, an admonishing finger wagged at the girl who had thrust this awful foreign devil-man upon him. She held her back straight and her chin tilted up, in defiance of his mood.

152

Forrester watched this and shook his head and thought: You think you understand them but you don't, and you probably never will. Then he too turned away. His direction took him towards the grassy slopes of the mountain called Cheung Shan. Once he looked back and saw that Shen Woo was standing at the edge of the village, watching him. He turned and walked on and did not look back again. But he found he was no longer travelling in the direction of his choice. His thighs burned and his lungs expanded, but the exercise had lost its appeal. Cheung Shan summit gave a wide view of Tai O village and the bay; the creek and the temple of Hau Wang. If he looked north he could see clear across the Pearl River estuary into the grey-blue Chinese hinterland. The view was boundless but his thoughts were turned inwards, and this vast amphitheatre appeared as no more than a painted backdrop to the players of his mind.

There they were: Reven Forrester, the beautiful Shen Woo, and her brother, the man who raped and murdered little Kit Ling.

Shen Woo would be his lover if he permitted it. That was obvious. And he did wish it. When they had met at the creek that day, his ardent wish had been to run a fingertip caress over her hair, and to kiss her mouth and discover if it was as sweet and tender as it pretended . . . And he knew that if he did these things, he would be weaker for it. He could not hold out one hand, in love, while the other concealed a dagger. He could not mate with Sister while poised to maim Brother. His inclination was to do just that, but he *could* not.

The man upon the hilltop tightened his forearm and clenched his fist. He walked on a little as though another place might show him a different perspective, but it was all the same, sister and brother: lovely Sister, hated Brother.

He called himself a fool. He told himself he really had no choice: Eddie Woo's ugly guilt must not be diluted by the beauty of his sister. How could he love the person who loved his enemy? What sort of man could do that?

153

The kind of man, perhaps, who in the full knowledge of his weakness had spoken softly and invitingly to the woman he should have coldly rejected. For she had phoned him at Cheung Sha just yesterday. He should have been stone, he had been water. She had told him how grateful she was for what he had tried to do. And he in return had trickled and purled honey-sweet hints into her ear – 'Any time I can help, don't hesitate, Shen.'

'I might see you again then?'

'In fact,' he lied, 'I *have* to go to Tai O in the morning. If you have the time.'

Their meeting that day had been no accident. If she was waiting now on the path down Cheung Shan Hill, that too would be an act of will. She must *not* be waiting.

A dying orange sun was topping the blue Tai Shan hills of distant China when Reven Forrester began his downhill walk towards Tai O. By now she certainly would have tired of waiting and have gone. And that would be the end of it.

In the greyness of the dusk he reached the footpath that skirted the creek. Some kids were walking there, one of them held a portable radio upon his shoulders – its volume shattered the quiet dusk. He was angered by their intrusion but did not stop them. Noise was the joy of the Chinese. He was the foreigner. He waited until they and their dreadful music had passed into the shadows and was about to walk on when he thought he saw Shen Woo.

A woman stood upon the bank of the creek, quite still, staring at the water. Long black hair fell past her shoulders – Shen's hair. He came on until he was close enough to detect her jasmine scent – Shen's scent. Now he was directly behind her and, as quiet as he was, he knew that she was aware of him. She did not stir. She stared down at the water, as still as a statue, watching the little moon that shimmered there . . . And now he was beyond her; away from her, and striding towards the village. He had kept his covenant and he hated what he had done.

She had waited for him. She *was* waiting for him. Walking from her was miserable; it was all wrong; it was crazy. He stopped. Reason and emotion clashed; there could be no compromise choice. He knew what he should do, and he did the opposite.

He walked quickly back down the path towards Shen Woo. He touched her upon the shoulder and she turned. He drew her in, their lips touched.

Reven Forrester had not thought possible that in him there existed such a rage of love.

5

RIDING THE TIGER

Reven Forrester made the compromise that he had thought impossible . . . and found that it was possible. He could love the person who loved his enemy. He could wage his war against Shen's brother without her even knowing it. He could caress with one hand while the other held the secret dagger, and not be limited in love or in hate.

That was what he believed, and it seemed to be the truth. For when he was with Shen he was immersed in love, and when she was not there he emerged to hunt . . . But there were night times that were less than restive. When he was alone, and needing sleep, his thoughts became an unguarded rabble who crowded him with hard questions.

What happens when you do locate him? Will he then shout out for all the world to hear: you used my sister, gwai lo, to trap me? Will Shen's love endure it?

I will never use her in such a way, he told himself. Eddie must not be allowed the space to offer up one single shout. And when that time comes, I will tell her the truth. I will then tell her everything and hope that she believes me.

And so he went on.

The courtship of Shen was a delicate sport. A high kite on the autumn winds, it rose up splendid with colour to glide on paper-thin wings; to swoop and swing and sometimes fall; to plunge to seeming destruction. But never was it crushed. For Shen, the mercurial, and Reven Forrester, the compulsive, like kite and gusting wind, were well matched to a degree. They had to have each other, but in different ways.

She, withholding, loving, restrained in the giving of affection. He, bold and voracious: frustrated by his lack of purchase on this elusive woman. They loved each other.

They tramped the footpaths of Lantau, mountaintop and valley, grasslands and woods. Hand in hand they wandered and watched the butterflies as they drifted in the chill, and chased the whirring grasshoppers through the dry grass. Children's games, and yet the passions of adulthood were but a touch away . . . But Shen was not brought to earth. Shen danced away with last-breath fear of the 'secret things'.

Reven Forrester had never been so treated by any woman, neither had he wanted any woman more than this. So it went on, he never totally in control of her, never satisfied with what she gave. He brought her to his house on Butterfly Hill. As proud as an emperor, he opened the doors of the veranda and showed off his orchids.

'They're lovely.' She clapped her hands in delight. She tilted her head and sniffed the heady air.

'This is the one.' Forrester introduced her to his Slender Calanthe. 'This is the one that's giving such a strong scent.'

'So delicate,' Shen said. 'Like little ballet dancers in their white tutus. Which is your favourite?'

'I'm their father. I'm not allowed to have any favourites.'

He took her hand and led her to the edge of the veranda. A bamboo orchid was in flower there. She bent down to examine it. Her fingers brushed its pale rose petals as delicately as a hovering insect. She peered into its deep yellow throat.

'Your children,' she said absently. 'Well they're very pretty children. But they're very quiet.'

Forrester still held her hand. He walked her further.

'Some of these orchids belonged to my mother. When she died, a collector in Hong Kong bought them. After I came back to Hong Kong the man contacted me and told me he had them. He said he thought I might like to have them back . . . When I went to see him this one was in bloom.'

In a recess of the veranda a mottled-leaf plant grew in splendid isolation. A most exquisite flower of white and purple lifted from its foliage. He pointed. 'I saw this orchid, and pictures that had been dormant in my mind for ten years came back to me in an instant. I remembered this plant; even this pot that it grew in. I remembered how my mother used to tend to this orchid. So I bought it and all these others back.'

'He was a considerate man, the orchid seller.'

'He was old,' Forrester said. 'He really loved these plants. He came over with them on the ferry and positioned them all, then he used to visit them every month or so . . . He's dead now.'

'Oh,' Shen said sadly.

'So you see, I have a special responsibility.'

'Little green children . . .'

Ah Fong came on to the veranda then. She held a tea tray which she set down with a clash of porcelain and brass, then walked away quickly. Forrester thought: 'Bad mood.'

Shen's thoughts were darker. 'I don't think your amah approves of me.'

He laughed.

'I mean it, I don't think she likes you to be seeing a Chinese girl.'

'She's old,' Forrester said. 'She goes back further than these orchids in my family history. Ah Fong has been my amah since I was in nappies. She gets ratty but she gets over it soon enough.'

Shen lifted the teapot lid and wrinkled her nose at the aroma. She pouted her lips approvingly.

'Hi Chun,' he said.

'Good tea. Are you a tea connoisseur, hah?'

'Maybe.'

'Maybe.' She shrugged her shoulders as he had done. 'You surprise me, Mr Forrester: orchids, Hi Chun tea. What else are you a professor of?'

158

She poured and they drank the mature brew, slowly, and with appreciation.

'She wants better for you than a fisherman's daughter.' Shen set down her cup and nodded as one does who has thought a subject to its conclusion. 'She will never like me.'

'Ah Fong not like you? Nonsense.'

'You can't see it. You're not Chinese. She's very angry, Reven.'

'Don't be silly.'

But Shen was very quiet thereafter, and when Ah Fong came to take the tray away Shen would not look up. Forrester watched his old servant, and wondered; her face was impassive but her movements were quick and severe and the cups trembled upon the tray.

They rode upon Forrester's big silver Suzuki to Chi Ma Wan beach. Forrester pushed the machine hard, to thrill Shen and shake loose the pall of Ah Fong from her. It seemed he did neither. The sands of Chi Ma Wan were deserted. They walked to the water's edge and sat there, their long shadows lapped by the waves, and he held her by the waist and kissed her, but her response was faint and deferent and her kisses came more upon his cheek than upon his lips. This angered him.

'What is it?' He felt her whole body jolt at the sharpness of his tone.

'Oh no!' She closed her hand on her mouth in distress.

This didn't make him repent. It irked him further. It had him say, 'For God's sake, Shen, don't act the oriental wife with me.' And as fast as the words came he moved to retract them: 'I didn't mean that . . . You mustn't let other people's opinions come between us.'

'I'm sorry,' she said.

'I'm sorry too. I'll take you home.'

'Don't do that, Reven. Try to understand. We won't survive like this. We are so different.'

159

'No, no,' Forrester said quickly. 'We'll do more than survive.'

'I love you,' she said. 'I really love you . . . but we *are* different. I was not acting the oriental wife, I was upset that I had caused you hurt. That's the way I am.'

'I know,' Forrester said. 'I'm impatient. That's the way *I* am. But I don't want to lose you, Shen. I want to marry you.'

'Ah Fong would not approve.'

'Ah Fong will cherish you when she knows you.'

'I doubt it, she has made up her mind about me. She disapproves of me but I can't fault her for that, and neither should you. She's trying to protect you from something she sees as being wrong for you. And perhaps she's wiser than both of us. Perhaps we should look at our relationship through her eyes.'

'It's got nothing to do with Ah Fong. Shen, she's a servant in my household, no more than that.'

'That's not quite true. She's more than just a servant, and she sees you as more than just an employer. But she's a simple woman and doesn't want anything for herself so we must accept her opinion at least as being honest. And I think her opinion is that a marriage between us would burn up to a cinder, leaving us nothing but a string of half-and-half children to remind us that once there was a great flame.'

'It sounds as though you share Ah Fong's opinion. Do you?'

'What if that was to be our terrible fate?'

'We won't let that happen.'

'Can we control it? No two people could be more different than you and I: two different cultures; two unrelated beliefs. We're weighted like brick against each other, don't you see? And all that bonds us now is the cement of good love. What happens if that erodes? . . . And don't say "We won't let it". We can only be masters of the present, not of the future.'

'Then let's take the present and fill it out. If that's all that we're masters of then let's master it in a grand way. Let's make memories right now . . . unforgettable memories that will last a lifetime.'

'I'm a fisherman's daughter, Reven. You're the son of a Tai Pan. I was born on a long-line fishing junk and walked bare-footed on those boards until I was seven. I didn't know what a flush toilet was until I was double that age. When I went to stay on shore all my friends envied me because I was going to such luxury – a board partition cubicle four foot by six foot in a building honeycombed with these "rooms". Yes, that *was* luxury . . . I tell you these things not because I am ashamed of them but because our pasts are so at variance.'

'You haven't let this "fisherman's daughter" complex stand in the way of your life so far. You don't squat on a pavement in the fish market. You're a teacher, in a school. You don't wear a black sam fu and straw hat. You dress beautifully. Your hands are soft and you make up your face. I, on the other hand, the son of a Tai Pan, am now a calloused-handed cop. So what is there so different between us?'

Shen laughed. She said, 'It's not the same and you know it . . . Before you ask me to marry you, allow me to tell you about some of the people who would show up at the wedding. My mother and father are dead, they were common fisher-folk. Both of them were killed in 1972 when a killer typhoon called Rose brought up an army of twenty-foot waves to smash their junk and drown them. Grandfather, who owns some fishing junks and a harbour lighter, would come. Don't ask him to sign the register, though, he cannot write so he would die from loss of face. I have two uncles – both of them fishermen who work Grandpa's long-liners. One is married and to his dismay has daughters, but no sons. The other uncle never married, he is what you might kindly call, not very bright. There are some aunts, most of whom live on board junks and sampans, and smell of fish bait in a way that no soap could

161

expunge. No need to ask them. I have one brother. He is probably the most "acceptable" member of the clan. He stays in Hong Kong . . . You're suddenly very quiet, Mr Forrester. Does this list of guests disturb you?'

Behind the Lantau hills a dusk of gold was settling. Forrester stood up and brushed the damp sand from his trousers seat. He said, 'Nothing you have told me disturbs me, Shen,' and cringed from the lie. 'Come.' He lifted her to her feet and kissed her. 'I love you, Shen. Please remember that whatever I do, I do not wish that to end.'

She said, 'No one could ever convince me otherwise.'

She hugged her body close into his back on the ride back to Tai O. He could feel the soft warmth of her and he loved it. But hard memory partnered him on that ride too. Hate for 'acceptable' Brother Eddie tightened on him with a harsh grip.

Once there had existed upon Eddie Woo's right hand a fine and capable second finger. Now, from the knuckle down, there was nothing – a blank and useless space. At the knuckle of Eddie's first finger a purple scar ran like a centipede around the joint; the stitches that had recently been removed had given the centipede its legs, and there it lay curled. This finger did not work very well; it had no feeling to it, and was as stiff as a stick. But at least it was there in its proper place, doing what it could when called upon to write, or hold a cigarette, or dial a telephone number. From a cosmetic point of view, he was indifferent to the mutilation of his right hand. In fact, it might have been a source of pride to him in different circumstances. The truth was, that every time he looked down upon that hand he was reminded of the evening of his ruin, and no man could be proud of such a monument.

But he was a man of resilience, of optimism and infinite self-forgiveness. He had been hurt and shamed and brought down. But as surely as his physical wounds would repair, he

162

told himself, so the scars of ill fortune would heal too. On the day of his discharge from hospital, bandaged into a body that pained from head to toe, he had limped into his wrecked club to see what could be made of it; what could be salvaged. What a dismal sight to see: not a mirror unshattered, not a tabletop intact. The lovely velvet curtains lay slashed and torn. The kitchen was a jagged mess of glass and chrome. And everything was wrapped in the foetid sickening smell of decaying food.

He went into his office and tilted his chair to rid it of glass slivers and then sat down. He knew that the circling sharks would soon close in. The first of them was his landlord. Lamenting, commiserating, *reminding*: rent was due, in fact overdue. *When* could he expect his rent?

'I'm working on it,' he told the landlord.

But the bank had regretfully advised that his overdraft was well beyond the prescribed limit. More collateral support was required before more funds could be provided. Could he provide more collateral?

'I'm working on it,' he told the bank manager.

But there was no more collateral. From the ruin of his office he phoned his failed protectors, the Hei Shui Triad Society. He then registered, in the strongest terms, his complaint concerning the ineptitude of their fighters. He had requested compensation: 'They provoked the whole thing. I need money to repair the damage that they brought about.' Hei Shui had not only laughed off his claim, but served him with a bill for 50 'Big Reds', 5,000 Hong Kong dollars, immediately due. They told him that they suspected him of arranging the whole thing in order to spark conflict with a rival triad society. Their patience was strained. He had better pay up.

Eddie Woo had never been in such a fix. For where was he to turn for money or support? His family . . . no, no. He could not face that. He had spent all the money and traded the resources of the family Woo. And though he was not to

163

blame for this, and had only tried to improve their fortune, the fact was he had failed to do so, and now there was not even sufficient money left to send to Grandfather the small monthly sum upon which he depended.

Exiled then from all succour and aid, his body in gasping pain, he began to sweep and clean. His optimism bent low beneath this hardship. He worked for days, until the debris was gone and the floor was clean, and he could do no more, but wait and hope and pray. So he waited and he hoped. He visited the Tin Hau temple in Market Street and bought 'Hell money' from the temple keeper and placated his Birth god with it. He brought offerings and burned incense bundles and petitioned of Tin Hau that he intercede in the business of his debts without delay, or see his faithful devotee come to a precipitous end.

He moved to 'old' Yau Ma Tei; to a squalid, stark, single-room flat on the top floor of a five-floor tenement that reeked of rotten food and rat droppings. No water on tap, a squat-bucket in which to excrete, a broken cot, a folding chair and table – a man's mind worked in radical ways after such an iniquitous tumble. And he feared he had not hit bottom yet.

Eddie took to staying indoors at night. He added a new bolt to his front door, and even thus protected, awoke at every noise with the jolt and sweat of fear upon him. He did not respond to anyone who knocked upon his door. He had nothing to offer anyone – no money and no prospects. In the daytime, if he went out, he was a mimic of the street rat: quick scurrying paces took him from corner to corner. On some days his apprehension was so massive that he did not leave his little flat, which deepened his gloom. He would mope upon his bed or go to his pigeon-loft balcony and peer down through the hung-out washing of his neighbours to the street five floors below. Five floors; was that a sufficient drop to break his neck and end this misery?

The wounded hand of Eddie Woo healed up, but the

wounds of ill fortune still festered and ran, and did not look like clearing.

All the blame could be laid at the feet of that black-hearted policeman, of course. Eddie would have been rich, were it not for that interfering gwai-dan bastard. *Diu lei* on Forrester! What had he ever done to deserve such a vicious enemy?

Eddie Woo smoothed his hand across his troubled features and thought about that, and other questions . . . Revenge. How then was that to be achieved? For revenge there must be. The thought of it was his sustenance, his strength, it swirled in him, exciting him with pictures of slow retribution; Forrester bleeding; Forrester crying; Forrester dying, while *he* laid on the punishment, cut by cut. It was such thoughts that helped him bear the load of his misfortune and kept him from the balcony ledge.

Eddie, of course, realized that survival came before revenge. Hei Shui would come calling soon, and they would chop him if he could not pay them their 5,000 dollars on the nose. So he took his precautions: he came down to the street less often, and when hunger drove him out, he kept away from Hei Shui-controlled areas. Time; he needed time to get things right.

But time passed by and in its passage it left nothing good for Eddie Woo. His seed of hope stayed dormant; his persevering faith in the goddess of mercy and Tin Hau went unrewarded . . . So it came to him that time did not represent hope; Hei Shui would get him, no matter how he dodged.

And they did.

In Yau Ma Tei near the typhoon shelter there are narrow streets and shops where fishball stalls flourish. These are not places to eat; these are cheap brothels where a man can empty his litchis into an oily whore's hand, or belly, or wherever, for a dollar or less. Eddie Woo was not there for such sordid recreation, he would have vomited had such a woman touched him. He was on his way home after buying food. When his name was called he stopped; limp.

'*Wai*! Woo Sung-king.'

The man was young with the fine build of a kung-fu fighter. On his right arm a writhing dragon tattoo ascended into the sleeve of his T-shirt.

'Here, come here.' He gestured with the decorated arm.

Eddie's muscle power had failed at the first call. He had no strength to disobey. He came to the man.

'You are Woo Sung-king?'

Eddie nodded. He looked around him, certain that he would see more men like this. There they were, coming towards him from both ends of the street; as lithe as cats. Eddie lied: 'I've got the money.'

The man extended his hand, palm up: 'Fifty Big Red.'

'I don't have it with me . . . It's at my flat.'

Eddie watched the hand curl into a fist, then reverse, then fly at him and the pain of its strike was shocking. He raised his arms in defence but one fist had become a hundred that whirled and struck, raked and pierced and stunned from groin to skull. Helpless as a child he groped against the assault. Mercilessly it crashed on, hit after hit, so quick, so hard.

Then it was over. The numbness of shock lifted away and in its place savage pain rushed in. On his knees, then on his face, he curled up like a foetus and vomited and writhed against the pain. Crippled, he lay upon the pavement while around him legs strode by and faces looked down, but not a hand was lowered in aid . . . Let someone help him, *please* let someone help him.

She was a whore, a 'fishball' stall operator. Her face was lined and puffy and it sagged as she bent down to him. But her eyes were round with concern and her scarlet mouth was bitter against the triads:

'Bastards.' She spat. She leaned her skinny frame until her body was against him and her arms gained a purchase beneath him, then she hauled. He groaned and pushed against the pain. Together they rose up. She said, 'You come home.'

Home was in the adjacent building upon the second floor. A green-lettered sign that hung there read:

HIBISCUS CURTAIN.
PLACE OF WARMTH AND SOFTNESS.

They rode an old elevator to that place. Dark, one bare lightbulb to illuminate its curtained cubicles and dens; a radio turned up high to drown the guttural sounds of sex. That was all it was.

They went into a cubicle that smelt of sour, spilt semen and he lay down on a matted velvet couch.

'You stay here,' she said. 'Don't worry.'

The curtains swished shut and he was alone. As he lay in that muck of spent passion, many thoughts marched impassively past his pain. He closed his eyes and rested back his head and thought about the woman who had helped him: a broken down 'chicken-whore'. He wondered what had moved her to come to his aid . . . He thought about the beating he had just taken. That had just been a sample of things to come, the next time it would not be fists wielded against him, but choppers. They would kill him when they came again.

The curtains parted; the 'chicken' was back. For the first time he noticed that she wore a cheong sam; bright red with a side-slit from ankle to hip. In her arms she held a steaming bowl. Another woman came in, this one older and even uglier. They began to undress him. Swift-fingered from their trade they stripped off trousers and shirt and vest. He did not utter a word. They dipped towels into the hot water and pressed them on to his bruises, and the aromatic odour of Tiger Balm filled his nostrils. Head, neck, chest and hips, they bathed him and their herbs chased at his pain. The pain was *very* deep, but they knew how to reach *very* deep; they brought him a pipe with a red clay bowl as big as an apple, and a long thick bamboo stem. The mouthpiece was brass-ferruled and wet with saliva and a trickle of smoke lifted from it.

'Suck in,' they said. 'Be quick. Don't let it die.'

He sucked the sticky, pungent smoke from the opium 'flag'.

'Again,' they said. 'Hold it down.'

He sucked in again, and slowly exhaled. They took the flag away. Slow languid warmth spread through him, massaging its glow into his hurt body. He felt fine; at peace. The ugliness around him dissolved, as though it had never been.

'Why they hurt you like that?'

He was alone with his whore now. 'I owed money,' he said. 'What's your name?'

'Sugar, Mama-San.'

'Thank you, Sugar.'

'You got no money.'

'I had a lot once. Now I don't have much.'

Sugar giggled at that. She said, 'I got money.' She reached out and lifted his penis. She inspected it in a most clinical way. He let her do it. 'Those guys are bad,' she said. '"Mr Dragon" chopped a man dead here last month.'

'Kung-fu fighters. I had no chance.'

She shrugged and let loose his organ. She sat back upon her chair and lit a cigarette.

'You better go,' Sugar said. 'You better get back home before more pain, ah.'

At that moment it seemed as though the pain would never return, but of course it would. He rose up from the couch feeling light and wonderful.

'Wait,' Sugar said. She plugged her cigarette into his mouth. 'Wait,' she said again. Then she slipped past the curtains and was gone.

168

Eddie slowly began to get dressed. He had clothed himself in shirt and trousers and was about to lace his shoes upon his feet when Sugar returned.

'Here. You take this.'

A handful of grubby, creased ten-dollar notes and some silver; she held her treasure out to him. 'One hundred Ngan chi,' she said. 'OK you pay "Mr Dragon" now.'

One hundred Ngan chi – one hundred Hong Kong dollars. It was not a lot of money. It was not enough to buy a restaurant meal for two, or a pair of leather sandals. It was not enough to restore as much as a single square metre of the fabric upon his ruined snooker tables, and it certainly would not pacify Hei Shui Triad Society.

He took this paltry sum of money from the hand of the whore called Sugar because it would have been an insult to refuse her, and for no other reason. He knew that for Sugar the fishball stall operator, one hundred dollars was a large sum. Her kindness puzzled him and disturbed him too . . . She walked with him to the rickety elevator and pulled closed the expanding trellis gates. With the grid dividing them he had looked hard at the whore. In that light the caked make-up and dye, like lime-wash upon a crumbling wall, did a shoddy job of hiding the decay: the opium-sick eyes, the foraged, used-up skin. Her cheong sam was old and shoddy – a relic of the Wan Chai waterfront of the fifties, and so was Sugar, Mama-San. She called out: 'You come back, ah.'

'Yes.' He wondered if he would.

She was ugly; hatefully ugly, that was plain to see. But beneath that repulsive exterior there lived the soul of the Queen of Heaven, and he could see that too. And though he was bathed in the benevolence of opium he was vexed by the contradiction. When the elevator jerked into descent and she turned away he was glad.

It was not until Eddie woke late that night that the whole truth of his experience was delivered to him. In terrible pain he moved to sit up upon his mattress. He observed the

169

crumpled, dirty ten-dollar notes on the folding table and it came to him: there at his side was more wealth than an ordinary man could gain in a lifetime. No, this was not simply money, this was an emblem, and a promise. This was the call that he had awaited so long, for lying beneath those hundred dirty dollars lay the form sheet for the tenth fixture of the racing season; due to take place that very afternoon on the grass track at Sha Tin. He was not conscious of having placed the money upon the table when he had gone to bed. In fact he never did leave money unhidden like that. So here was the message: Go to Sha Tin; take the one hundred dollars to Sha Tin. Your days of misfortune are over, Eddie Woo.

For though a hundred dollars cannot buy a pair of leather sandals or a metre-square of baize, it can buy ten 10-dollar stakes in the quinella at Sha Tin race course, and he knew that today a greater hand than his would plot his betting card.

There was no one in the queue that wound through the turnstiles at Sha Tin that afternoon who moved with a lighter tread than Eddie Woo. His confidence was boundless. The skies were clear and the eyes of heaven were unhindered. The betting hall where he took himself lay beneath the main grandstand; a great concrete concourse edged with betting windows in their hundreds, where quick-fingered clerks took in money from the punters like pollen brought by worker bees. And in they swarmed, those punters, in their thousands and their tens of thousands to chose their permutations – six-up, quinella, tierce or quartet. It's your money, Brother, place it where you will.

With 10 dollars in his hand, Eddie Woo stood before a quinella window awaiting his turn to bet. There was no doubt in his mind upon which two runners to stake his money in the first race. The first two horses to cross the line would be number 6 – Silver Bullet – and number 3 – Jet Stream; in the quinella their order did not matter. Eddie did not leave the betting hall after he had placed his bet. He was not excited, the horses he had bet on were favourites and the quinella pay-out would be small. Anyway, the race could be watched on any of the hundred or so course television screens that grew everywhere from walls and centre pillars.

So he stood there with a paper cup of Coca-Cola in one hand, and his card in the other, with a pencil behind one ear, and he watched the quinella-board monitor as it followed the money. Big money, every fifteen seconds the lights changed, and every change added a million dollars to the total. Another screen showed the horses being led into their stalls. The faintest twinge of suspense grasped Eddie then, like a shot of morphine, and the pain of yesterday's beating ebbed away.

With the ring of the starter's bell, his excitement leapt – dare he have doubts? A bad start for Silver Bullet, boxed in early, but Jet Stream had broken from the bunch . . . no change at the halfway mark. 'Diu!' swore Eddie Woo and a thousand other voices, and the drone of the betting hall grew louder. 'Sam luk, sam luk, three six, three six.' It seemed that everyone had bet on those horses. Now look at that idiot jockey, he must have been paid to pull it. 'Diu! . . . But look again, it's the run to the post and number 6 has broken loose: 'Luk! Luk! Aieya!' It's a win: luk sam, sam luk: Silver Bullet and Jet Stream.

A human tide rushed to the pay windows, like starving men. They wanted more, and the betting clerks gave them more; another ticket, Brother, another chance. But the dividend was small: 90 dollars for Eddie Woo.

Ninety dollars was small change in monetary terms. It was the invincible truth the win represented that warmed Eddie.

Without hesitation he took his winnings back to the quinella window. He bought five tickets on his next combination: Moving Mountains and Diamond Eyes. Then he moved on to the tierce window and forecast the first three horses to the post: Moving Mountains, Diamond Eyes and Sun Spot. At that window he laid down a further 50 dollars. When he had done that Eddie went out into the sunlight with his Coke, his race card and his pencil and sat down upon a bench before the massive grandstand. In front of him now, on the infield border a 100-metre-long tote board surged with dot lights as it kept track of the mood of the stake money. A television screen as big as a tennis court showed pictures of the horses and the jockeys, their form and their handicaps. And the punters watched, and diagnosed, and chased up the odds by millions . . . Eddie just sat there quietly; he sipped from his paper cup, and smoked a cigarette, and waited. But beneath this tranquil camouflage a storm of tension now roared.

Race number two was run, and as the horses reached the main straight it was clear what the result would be: Moving Mountains, Diamond Eyes and Sun Spot. Eddie Woo's chest felt so tight that he had consciously to move his girth muscles in order to breathe. At the pay windows that time he collected more than 2,000 dollars. His hands were shaking as they took the big orange-coloured bills.

He was steady, however, by the time he had next reached the quinella betting window. He placed 1,000 dollars on a single pairing, then he proceeded to bet a further 1,000 dollars on the six-up. Eddie went once more to his seat and watched the big board as it twinkled out multi-million digits. Everything is fine he told himself. Just stay steady, Eddie Woo. Keep faith and keep betting.

These and other sanguine thoughts hid the real issue of the moment. Eddie Woo was quite sure that his celestial tipster was on the ball, what bothered him was the vagueness of communication: no numbers were coming to him, no names or symbols or colours, in fact, no revelations of any sort. Of course, he knew he was being inspired in some way to do what he was doing. But how? In his oblivion he feared he might make a horrible mistake.

Keep faith, he told himself again. Today is the day you become a rich man – a millionaire. Think of it; a real *yau chin lo*!

He thought of it all the time that race number three was in progress. He bit down so hard as the horses came into the home straight that there was the taste of blood in his mouth at the end of the race. How silly of me, he told himself; why, there is nothing to worry about – no risk at all. That time his dividend came to 12,000 dollars, *twelve thousand* dollars! Enough to settle his account with Hei Shui and begin life afresh.

He looked down at his race card, his pencil poised. Which horses to bet upon? Of course his six-up placement was still good and rolling, but how to pair that horse in the quinella and companion it in the tierce? Eddie's pencil did a lively dance upon the card before coming to rest against the names: Royal Arrow and Fai Tung.

That was how he bet, and with his anchor horse in the six-up to lead them in, that was how they passed the post. Eddie Woo held 75,000 dollars in his hands when he came to bet upon the fifth race of the day: 75 big orange notes, and he laid them down, every one, at the betting clerk's window. The fifth race was the main race of the day, only class-one runners in this race – each horse handicapped to the ounce. A tricky affair to forecast.

But Eddie did it.

Now he was a rich man – a real *yau chin lo*. In various pockets of Eddie's jacket were stuffed over two hundred thousand-dollar bills . . . The variety of bets available to the punters on the sixth race was mind-boggling – doubles, trebles, tierces, quartets and of course, his favourite, the quinella. Given all these options, and all that money, a lesser man might have made a hash of things and found himself with the 'off' bell sounded and a fat wad of dollars still to spend. Not so Eddie Woo; his system was so unintellectual and simple that he had bet all of his money with five minutes to spare.

173

The sixth race was for class-three horses over 1,600 metres, a close one that had them on their feet, but when it was over Eddie was halfway to being a millionaire, and there were two races yet to be run.

Eddie kept his face impassive and his pencil steady so that his divine guide should notice his absolute equanimity, his total faith. But inside him the plunge and surge of his visceral parts was half killing him.

The gods were not the only ones taking a keen interest in Eddie Woo at this stage. The Jockey Club security staff had had Eddie under surveillance for the past two races. What bothered these guardians of the turf was not the enormity of Eddie's winnings, but his consistent ability to defeat the laws of chance. They believed he was cheating, but they could not work out how. They noted his lack of overt excitement and put it down to syndicate money. They noted his disregard of form and put that down to race fixing. But *how*? They watched him on closed-circuit TV. They watched him through binoculars. They assigned a squad of men to cover him on the ground. All they could report was that here was an unknown man who drank Coke and chain-smoked Camel cigarettes, a man with a bruised, beaten face, and one finger fewer than is normal. For all this he was neatly dressed in slacks and sports coat with open collar.

He did not pick his nose, or scratch his rectum, or ears, or gesture in any other suspicious manner. He did not watch out for signals from trainers or jockeys or *mafoos*, or any other obvious accomplice. He bore no radio, no earphones were plugged into his ears. Now and then (this seemed a bit odd) he would range his gaze heavenwards before pencilling his card. But all in all his general demeanour was innocent. *Which of course it could not be!*

The band of the Royal Hong Kong Police was on the final bar of the 'Grand March' from *Aida* by the time that Eddie Woo had concluded his betting for the seventh race of the day. He did not take his customary seat then, but waited in the betting hall near the pay windows in order to be quicker off the mark.

Race seven was a sprint over 1,100 metres and Eddie's chosen horses led from start to finish. He had won on the double and on the quinella, on the treble and on straight bets all down the line. His six-up was still rolling but the Jockey Club stewards did not know that then. What they did know was that manipulation on a grand scale was occurring: big money was causing the odds to shorten dramatically on horses whose form did not warrant such betting extravagance. What they did know was that they were facing the most diabolically clever swindle in the history of the Jockey Club. The bastard was now camped next to the pay windows; that was how certain was the fix. This could *not* go on.

Eddie was now every bit a millionaire, and had every intention of becoming even richer. Just one more race would do it. He carried with him a plastic bag stuffed with thousand-dollar bills, and his pockets were bulging too. He was in a fever of excitement. And his betting action had not gone unnoticed by his fellow racegoers. They wanted to be near to this professor of all punters, to gain by any dispensation of good fortune that his aura might permit. No one dared to say a word to him lest it interrupt his luck. They simply stood around him, to be touched by his shadow, to touch the things he touched: a discarded paper cup, the seat that he had warmed. Eddie could not help but be aware of his new disciples, but he refused to notice them overtly. He tipped a Coke stand attendant 500 Ngan chi, 'lucky money', and that caused a sensation: *Wah!* But Eddie did not smile, or show joy, or expectation, or fear. Within him these emotions raged volcanically, but on the surface of the mountain there was ice.

On the eighth and final race of the day he took his million to the betting windows and laid it down. The onlookers gasped, and the betting clerks trembled, and the odds on

Woo's chosen horses plunged in a twinkle of the tote board lights. But it did not end there.

Eddie Woo did not fully realize the influence that his strange betting pattern, and the weight of his money were now having, not just on the track punters, but on the 'Telebet' punters too. Two thousand telephone lines lead into Sha Tin's 'Telebet' centre. A half a million bets per race meet are taken in this way. The tote board is their final chronicle of light; where the big money goes, there they go too. Eddie's millions rocked the tote board and a tidal wave of dollars surged behind it.

Unaware of the repercussions of his actions, Eddie Woo stood at the betting windows, and though his head was spinning he had no trouble in the selection of his horses. That was because he could not break faith now. His earlier doubles and trebles were still riding forward, his six-up was still good. The horses for the tierce and the quinella in this, the ultimate race, were therefore practically pre-chosen. They were: Perfection, Royal Crown, Dragon Fire.

That was how Woo placed his final stake; with Dragon Fire as his anchor, straddling each leg of every bet. These horses, 5 to 1, 6 to 1 runners in normal terms, became outright short-price favourites in the moments that followed.

The stewards were outraged. The Chief Stipendiary Steward called together his course officials: his stewards, the Clerk of the Course, the Starter and the Clerk of the Scales.

'We cannot allow this,' said Sir Percy White, the Chief Steward. 'I don't know who's behind it but I will find out. Have no doubt ICAC will be called in to investigate, but in the meantime these people must be brought to book.'

'It's diabolical,' said the Clerk of the Course. 'One man, I hear it's one man, placing *millions* on rank outsiders, and his horses are romping in.'

'Not always outsiders,' said a steward. 'He backed some favourites too.'

'They're carrying fair weight,' said the Clerk of the Scales.

'I've checked all the winners.'

'Check them all. Not just the winners,' someone advised.

'The losers could be overloading.'

'Or passing weights before the Off.'

The Clerk of the Scales looked acidly at the meddlers and his colour rose. He shouted, *'Nonsense!'* Sir Percy gavelled the tabletop with his knuckles until there was silence. 'Gentlemen,' he said. 'There is no time for conjecture. A race is due to be run ten minutes from now, the outcome of which has been interfered with in some way. What I propose to do is something that I have only done once before during my career as a steward . . . Gentlemen, I am going to go down to the start to call out the jockeys of those three horses and warn them in advance of the race that we suspect them of cheating.'

And that was what Sir Percy did.

He rode with the starter in his station wagon to the 1,200-metre mark. The jockeys were walking their mounts behind the starting stalls. They all knew that something was in the air.

Sir Percy took the assistant starter's megaphone and held it to his mouth: 'A'hem.' He cleared his throat. 'I think you have all noticed how incredibly the odds came off on three horses in this race. Jockeys Lee, Koo and Mo. I think you three might like to pay special attention to my words.'

Jockey Lee turned his mount Dragon Fire to face the Chief Stipe. He *had* noticed how the odds had shortened on his horse, and it had surprised him. Dragon Fire was a good horse over a short distance and had a few wins to her credit. But recently a string of losses had spoiled her form. She didn't deserve to be favourite on form. And yet Dragon Fire could win this race. He knew it, and Dragon Fire's trainer knew it too. She had been wrongly ridden on her past few outings. Dragon Fire had a devastating 200 metres in her, but she was not a stayer. She had been ridden from the front in the past and had used herself up too early. The filly had a good feminine temperament and did what was asked of her, but she could be a tearaway if she wasn't controlled. The secret with Dragon Fire was to ride her from behind, to come slowly through the field up to the 200-metre mark, and then let her go: these tactics, both jockey and trainer had decided, were the right tactics for this horse. Sir Percy's words chilled jockey Lee.

'So don't do anything stupid, boys. I myself will be here at the break to see that there's no interference. You'll run your race as you always have in the past. We'll be watching you like hawks. Is that clear, Koo?'

'Yes, sir.'

'Is that clear, Mo?'

'Yes, sir.'

'Is that clear, Lee?'

Jockey Lee felt the game heartbeat of Dragon Fire beneath his saddle. She was keen to enter the starting stalls and go, and he knew he could win this race. Then he looked into the rain-grey eyes of the Chief Stipe and he knew his career would be on the line if he did win. He had already been warned once that season for striking a challenger on the snout.

'Yes, sir,' he said. 'But . . .'

'No "buts", Lee. Just a straight "yes" or "no". Understand?'

'I understand,' said Lee. 'Yes.'

What he understood was that Dragon Fire would race true to form, and Dragon Fire would not place.

Sir Percy gave the megaphone back to the assistant starter who began to call them into the stalls. The starter stood upon his platform, his finger on the gate trigger. With a clash the gates sprang open. With a great shout the jocks incited their mounts on. With a leap Dragon Fire jumped out and into the race.

'*Paau! Paau!*' Lee bellowed. '*Go! Go!*'

Two hundred metres went by in a flash. Running sweet, Dragon Fire stayed four lengths off the pace. A perfect place for her. He should have kept her there but he did not. At 400 metres he gathered her up and tapped her with the whip. At the turn he lashed her hard and Dragon Fire leapt forward. At 600 metres Dragon Fire was in front and eager to stay there. The straight opened before Lee and Dragon Fire bolted into it.

'*Paau! Paau!*' Lee screamed.

He could not help himself. This horse was so game. High in the saddle, body and mind, he willed the win. *Diu lei* on the stipes. They could not fault him now. He saw nothing but the winning post. He heard nothing. He sensed the stallion Hoi Pai at his shoulder; another horse on his inside. Still Dragon Fire held on.

A hundred metres to go and *Dragon Fire had the lead.* Horses were challenging on both sides and he lashed Dragon Fire again and again, and shouted into her ear.

Locked to Hoi Pai with the winning post dead ahead, Dragon Fire gave up.

Eddie Woo's mind was blank with despair. The bruises of yesterday were throbbing cruelly again, and his legs could hardly bear him from the heights of the stand to the ground. The crowd surged past him, still crackling with the voltage of high excitement, their voices keyed up, modest about wins, laughing about losses: a game of face.

How could he laugh about what *he* had lost. At five minutes past five he had been a millionaire. One minute and eight seconds later the trapdoor of poverty had dropped open beneath him. *Yau sam*! he had crashed low; so deep, so dark . . . He walked obliquely through the homegoing crush; certain that all who passed knew of his leprous misfortune – as indeed most did. He did not want to be near them. He had no face. He went to stand next to the railings that guarded the track and leaned there, staring at the hoof-scarred turf, alone. Misery in its misty, time-defeating way closed around him – an hour passed before he moved, startled.

'You, go now!'

A man in a white shirt with a Jockey Club ID card clipped to his shirt pocket stood next to him. In the distance two uniformed policemen stood watching.

'We don't want you back here,' the official said. 'Is that clear?'

Eddie Woo said, 'Yes.' It was not clear but he didn't care. Fallen millionaires were probably very bad luck. He began to walk towards the public transport terminus.

The man called after him: 'If you set foot on Jockey Club ground again we'll deal with you.'

Eddie Woo ignored the harsh words and walked on.

At the terminus he caught the bus that would take him to Kowloon, he climbed to its upper deck and took a forward seat. There he sat in leaden unthinking misery once more. He did not notice another thing until they had left the race course and the skyscrapers of new Sha Tin well behind, and were climbing towards the dual carriageway tunnels that cut through the hills there to give access to Kowloon: Lion Rock tunnel it was called. It wasn't really one tunnel but two, adjacent to each other, one to carry Sha Tin bound traffic; the other to carry traffic southwards to Kowloon. And at the tollgate plaza that led into the tunnels, Eddie Woo became once more alert.

As the double-decker drew up at the toll it was overtaken by an armoured security vehicle: a big boxy thing all rivets and gun-ports, with thick, dark glass for the crew to peer through. It was painted black and the lettering on the side read: 'Hoh Kaau Security Services'. Two police motorcycle escorts rode before it, and two at its rear. They did not pause at the toll booths. With a revving of engines and a flashing of lights they raced through. It was all well arranged. By the time his bus had lurched into motion once more, the armoured convoy had reached the tunnels. He watched them disappear through the half-oval portals. There went the millions from the Sha Tin races: there went *his* money. And there went his thoughts.

180

What wonderful fiction he dreamed up as they drove into the mountain depths. He saw the police escorts spinning this way and that, slipping and sliding – yes, on a road slick with oil. Now the armoured van, out of control, side-swiped the tunnel wall – crash – over it went. The back doors burst open and crates full of money spewed out . . . So simple to take it: like fallen fruit in the ripe of summer.

Now they were well into the tunnel, the engine noise rose thunderously, the amber strip lights whizzed by, but Eddie was not distracted: he was still picking the fruits of fantasy. But was it such a wild dream? It was obvious that any vehicle that entered this tunnel had only one way to leave it: forwards. But what if, by some means, that forward movement could be prevented – cut off or blocked? Of course that vehicle would have to stop. If that convoy could be stopped within the narrow confines of the tunnel, its defences would be considerably weakened. With only four outriders to protect it, would it not be possible then to take on that armoured car and crack it open like a tortoise on its back? He thought that the answer to that question was: *yes*. If it was properly planned, and resolutely executed, such an operation could succeed.

By the time the bus had exited into the bright sunshine on the Kowloon side of the tunnel, an embryo of a plan had formed in the mind of Eddie Woo. The resolve to see it through followed immediately. And who could be surprised at that?

Eddie Woo defied the ban imposed on him by the Jockey Club official. The following Wednesday he returned to Sha Tin, not as a punter this time. This was an evening event, the eleventh fixture of the season, and Eddie arrived during the running of the seventh race. This time he remained on the periphery of the course; he walked around the public transport terminus. He stood upon the fly-over crossing that overlooked the clubhouse and took note of the events that occurred when the racing was over. Especially he observed the courtyard and the circular, flat-roofed buildings below the clubhouse, for here was the security centre. Wire-mesh gates guarded this area. In the courtyard a bauhenia tree grew, and opposite that, the reason for all this security: a steel-shutter gate set into a concrete wall that led to the safe area beneath the grandstands, where all the money went. It was brightly lit, a high metal standard clustered with floodlights threw shadows that were midday stark, and he could see perfectly.

He saw Rolls-Royces and Bentleys and Jaguars pass by, but he was not interested in those. He saw police vehicles come and go, and those he watched with greater attention. But he had to wait for over an hour before he saw what he had come to see. Four motorcycle patrolmen arrived before the wire-mesh gates, which swung open to accept them. In the courtyard they dismounted; they drew their cycles on to their stands then stood about. They did not have long to wait.

At some signal they all started their bikes and once more mounted up. Eddie could hear the low growl of their engines, and the crackle of their radios. He could also hear the rumble of metal as the shuttered security gate began to rise.

The headlights of the armoured vehicle peered out. The cycles came up to it and stationed themselves fore and aft. Then off they drove. Eddie stood there for a moment longer, deep in thought. Then the cold of the night reached him and reminded that his work there was done.

Now he knew how the Sha Tin takings were brought out on to the road. He knew what happened thereafter; he had travelled the Sha Tin–Kowloon highway through the Lion Rock tunnel so many times during the previous few days that he knew every crack and kerbstone. He had drawn a map, and upon it marked calculations and timings. He had obtained full-colour pamphlets from the PWD that proudly gave the workings of the innards of their 1,400-metre-long-tunnel. *Aieya!* they were complicated. There were huge fans to extract bad air and more fans to push fresh air in. There were TV monitors throughout the length of the tunnel and radar traps too. There were gauges to measure carbon monoxide and visible pollution, and alarm bells to trip if all was not well. In the northbound tunnel was set a towngas detection system, because beneath that tunnel ran a huge towngas feeder pipe: 'The tunnels would be closed off at the hint of a leak,' read the pamphlet, 'be assured.'

Eddie studied all these facts and put together his plan: a good plan, he thought. And now he was ready to take the next step. It would be a step that once taken could never be retracted. He would be riding the tiger; it would be impossible to get off. He would go to Hei Shui with his plan for the robbery of the Sha Tin convoy. It was that or nothing, for only a powerful triad gang could take on such an operation. They could accept his plan, or reject it. They could forgive him his debts or they could chop him. It would be out of his hands then.

The last Sunday in November was the day on which the Centenary Cup was run, and seventy thousand people were there to cheer on the runners of that event. A rank outsider called Highwayman flew past the winning post with a head to spare . . . Perhaps the name was prophetic. Over one hundred million Hong Kong dollars, bundled and packed into sealed metal cases, rode in the back of the armoured security van when it drew away from the course that evening and turned south towards Kowloon.

At the same time as this convoy left the racecourse, a light, open-backed delivery van pulled away from a sidestreet in Kowloon Tong. Its cargo was a clanking, rattling load of LP towngas cylinders, its course northwards towards Sha Tin.

Its job was to run the length of the tunnel with every cylinder valve wide open; to spew towngas into the tunnel and set off the detectors – panic in the tunnel control room was the objective. Next to the driver sat a man who held a small but powerful two-way radio. It was important for this vehicle to arrive at the portal of the north tunnel at precisely the right moment – the moment that the armoured convoy approached the tollgates at the southern end, the Sha Tin end.

Another event that would occur at that exact moment was the sudden repair and restoration to life of a troublesome engine of a heavy reticulated horse and trailer rig that had been sidelined in the facility area lateral to the portals at the Sha Tin end. The crew would then drive this rig immediately into the tunnel; *200 metres exactly* ahead of the convoy. This phase of the operation had to be co-ordinated to the second.

Eddie Woo was part of this team. It was his job to deactivate the cut-off switch that had been installed beneath the fuse panel of the horse and thus restore power to the 'dead' engine. Unfortunately when the moment arrived for the switch to be activated he was unable to reach it, and that was because an officious PWD mechanic had wormed his way, unwanted, beneath the tilt cab and now lay flopped across the panel that hid the vital switch.

'I know what your trouble is,' said the mechanic.

'No you don't,' Eddie said. '*You must get out of there!*'

'One minute and I'll have you started.'

One minute and the operation would be a shambles: the convoy would have swept into the tunnel and be gone. From his position Woo could see the approach of the outriders; then the big black armoured vehicle. The rig, at this stage, should have been mobile.

'*Get out!*' he screamed at the mechanic.

He held the man by his overalls and pulled, but the fellow was heavy and slow to move. A triad fighter called Big-squid Yin saw what was happening. Big-squid grasped the mechanic and hauled him clear. Then he hit the man hard and he crumpled at once. Woo fumbled with the switch, his hands were shaking, his mutilated fingers disobedient. Then he got it right. The starter motor grated – cold, the engine was slow to life . . . The convoy had reached the toll.

The operation was dependent on the position of that rig. A lead distance of 200 metres on the convoy was critical, for that lead would mean that the rig would be deep inside the tunnel before the traffic that separated them had passed by. He could, by adjustment of his speed, thus select the exact spot to swing into the path of the convoy. That was how it had been planned.

It didn't work out that way. The rig drove on to the approach road less than 70 metres ahead of the convoy. They worked the engine of that horse until it screamed and they hung on to their lead. Near the big, grey rock portal six cars and a fruit van separated them from the convoy; all in the passing lane . . . In the slow lane, then, they drove into the amber-lit gloom.

'Go! Go! Faster!'

One car passed, then, quickly, another two. The fruit van had reached them; 'Fortunate Transport', read the sign on the driver's door.

'Go! Go!' shouted Eddie Woo.

The van passed them by. Blank-faced coolies upon the back stared into their headlights. Another car came up – a white Honda.

'Slow down now,' Eddie shouted.

The Honda slipped by. The lights of the convoy were bright in the side mirror. The last car to divide them arrived at their side, a red sports car, a gwai lo at the wheel.

'Be ready.' Eddie leaned as far out of the cab window as he dared, the better to judge the exact moment:

'Slower . . . Slower . . . *Now!*'

A scream of rubber – the cab slewed right, the tunnel wall came up, and they struck it. He was flung forward. He saw the windshield coming up and he knew he would smash clean through it. Impact brought a stunning blackness to Eddie Woo – a jumble of sounds; a spiral of lights. When Eddie's senses read true again, he saw an awful sight. The driver of the rig lay heavily against him, he didn't look human any more. His face was crushed on one side, yet he was alive. One eye was open and working and his lips and cheeks were blowing frothy saliva like a baby. Eddie shoved the monster away; in a panic of legs and arms he fought free. The cab lay on its side. He levered himself through the upmost window. Now he could hear the crash of gunfire; hollowed by the tunnel it sprang at him. He clambered from the cab and ducked low.

He saw a motorcycle lying upon its side, its front wheel still spinning slowly. A policeman lay unmoving next to it. He saw the armoured car – flashes leaping from its gun ports.

Crash-boom, crash-boom.

He heard the cry 'Blow it up, blow it up!'

He fell to the ground and covered his ears. The repercussion was not as great as he had expected. Still the road beneath him trembled and debris pelted about. The effect on the armoured car was devastating. The explosion ripped its steel doors from their hinges and silenced its aggression. They had beaten it.

It took them minutes to unload it. Twenty-six sealed black metal cases they took from its smoky interior; dragged them, pulled and shoved them along the narrow tunnel walkways. 'Hurry, Brother, hurry!'

The fruit van stood waiting beyond the wreckage of the rig. They hid the black steel cases beneath wooden crates of melons and winter-squash. Then they boarded the van and drove out of the tunnel.

Eddie Woo's ears were ringing and his eyes would not focus well. His voice was tenuously connected to him as he said, 'We did it, Brothers, we did it.'

'Fortunate Transport' joined the innocent southbound traffic of Kowloon Tong and was swallowed in the crush.

'*Diu lei* on the Jockey Club tai pans. *Diu lei* on the police . . . *Diu lei* on you, Mr Forrester!'

Ah Fong the amah was wrinkled with the wisdom of old China, and she carried this lore before her like a spiked shield into the battle against the myriad demons, ghosts and vampires that infested every hole and crack in the pavement of life. She could write charms that would frighten away the most pestilent spirit. She had a vocabulary of secret words of immense power that when inked down, and pasted to door or staircase, protected all who passed. She was versed in the use of mirrors to reflect back the power of evil to its source. Ah Fong kept house on Butterfly Hill and had furnished it and decorated it in accordance with the principles of Feng Shui. When Only Son came there she fed him with food in harmony with his needs, and when he was not there, though he did not know it, her good influence still prevailed, for Maria the Filipino who kept his Hong Kong flat was terrified of her. There was nothing that happened at the Victoria Peak apartment that Ah Fong was not told about, immediately.

Ah Fong knew about Caroline. She knew her full name, her birthdate, her preferences in food and drink. She knew her residential address, and that of her place of work. She knew exactly how often Caroline visited Only Son, and the consequent sexual events. Maria was required to assess the state of the love-bed: each nest of creases, and each stain of 'jade juice', it was all reported to Ah Fong. Caroline had a willing lotus gate; a healthy appetite for the *yang-tsat* of Only Son, that was clear. Ah Fong approved of her.

She did more than simply approve of Caroline. She had made up an invincible spell using writing of great power sealed in a red envelope, tied with a red ribbon. She had taken this charm with her to a little coved island called Kat O, to a place where an old banyan tree lay fallen with its roots exposed in a most intimate human-like twisting and

187

twining. A place in obvious sympathy in matters of sexuality; a place of pilgrimage for the matchmakers of Hong Kong. Upon this open-air altar of roots, then, Ah Fong had burned her spell, and implored that her son should marry the copper-headed Caroline, and that they should have boy-children, a full quiver of boy-children (though girl-children would be acceptable too).

Ah Fong could not understand how things could have gone so drastically wrong. For within the month her son had discarded Caroline and was on the scent of the fisherman's granddaughter like a dog after a bitch on heat. How had this woman Shen managed to overmaster so potent a spell?

Ah Fong called upon all her powers and all her knowledge in the pursuit of that answer. She thought that a devastating counter-spell must have been cast by Woo Chi-ying, or Shen, as she called herself. Night magic was in the air, Ah Fong could smell it. She would protect her son from it resolutely. But she would have to be very cunning and very quick.

She began by searching the house on Butterfly Hill from ceiling to cellar. Perhaps the charm had been secreted there. She thrust her hands down the sides of the chairs and lifted the carpets. She peered into cupboards and lamp-shades and toilet cisterns and flower-pots and found nothing sinister.

She searched through the drawers of Only Son's carved blackwood desk, and beneath the drawers too. She paged through his desk diary and discovered Shen Woo's birthday – she was born in the Year of the Cat. She riffled through the pages of a scrapbook, and several pieces of paper fluttered loose . . . There was a colour photograph of a sampan and upon the deck of that sampan a little girl ran – it was Kit Ling, there was no doubt about it: Kit Ling in her new, red pleated skirt and white blouse. Behind the little girl a woman dressed in a black sam fu reached out. Ah Fong had not seen this photograph before and it distressed her. But it was not what she was looking for so she inserted it once more between the pages of the book. Two more photographs and a newspaper cutting had been expelled. One picture was of Only Son dressed in leg pads and waving a big wooden cricket bat in the air. The other photograph was harsh black and white and showed a man lying beaten upon a floor, looking up through a mist of semi-consciousness. His hair was matted with blood and more blood had seeped on to the floor. The newspaper cutting was clipped to this photograph with a wire paperclip. The cutting came from a Cantonese daily and it told a lurid story of a triad gang fight that had taken place. The owner of a billiard club had been badly beaten up in the battle – his name was Woo Sung-king. Ah Fong returned both cutting and picture to the book and went on with her search.

She looked into every shadow and felt into every niche that the hand of Shen Woo might have entered – no demons jumped out, no packaged spells lay hidden.

That afternoon Only Son brought Shen Woo to the house for tea. Ah Fong sealed herself in the kitchen and spied on the lovers through a chink in the door planks, and hated Shen Woo through that small, obscure view. The woman was undeniably beautiful, her features were fine and lightly touched with make-up. Her eyes sparked with the bright-ness of a sharp mind. Her hair tumbled down upon her shoulders, and it shone with cleanliness. She did not look evil, but looks proved nothing. The deadliest of all man's enemies was the enchantress, *fox fairy*: a beast of the graveyards, nine hundred years old, that could change its decayed looks into that of a beautiful woman, and then emerge from the cold ground to seduce and kill. So good looks and such charm as Shen Woo presented were no guarantee of goodness . . . Ah Fong watched the laughing couple and she saw them kiss passionately and long, and as she watched, a tingling, horrifying thought came to her.

She observed carefully for a while longer then withdrew

from the chink and went to her room. She paced for a while and thought very deeply. She waited until she heard the motorbike engine of Only Son start up some hours later then she went back to the sitting room, there straight to the carved blackwood desk. She took out the scrapbook and lifted from its pages the black and white picture with the newspaper cutting clipped on. Her excitement grew and her heart quickened. She took a plastic shopper from the kitchen and dropped the photograph into it. Then she locked up the house and walked down the lane that led from Butterfly Hill to Mui Wo village. At the ferry terminal she joined in the queue with the daytrippers who were now returning to Hong Kong. Several times as she stood waiting her hand dipped into the plastic bag to withdraw the photograph of the man called Woo Sung-king. And every time she looked at it she became more convinced: here there is night magic at work. On the trip to Hong Kong she thought about little else.

Why would Only Son keep that picture, and the cutting? She thought that there was only one person who might be able to answer that question – the flame-haired Caroline. Caroline was a newspaper reporter; Caroline was clever. Caroline loved Only Son and she could therefore be relied upon to come to his aid if night magic was at work. Ah Fong needed her help.

From the Outlying Islands ferry terminus at Hong Kong, Ah Fong took a taxi and gave Caroline's address to the taxi-man. Let her be home, she willed as they moved through the sluggish evening traffic; let her be there when I arrive.

She was home. She came to the door at Ah Fong's insistent ring, tying up the sash of a long, silk gown. With the lethargy of the just-awakened she regarded the amah.

'Why it's you, Ah Fong,' she yawned. 'Come in, come in. What is it, Ah Fong?'

'Most humbly apologize for disturbing you.'

'Hang on, I'll make some tea.'

Ah Fong was grateful for those minutes alone. The words that she had prepared for this moment had flown like startled sparrows, but in Caroline's absence they came to her once more. When Caroline returned, with hair freshly brushed, bearing a tray and steaming pot, Ah Fong was ready.

'I've come about Only Son.'

'Reven?' Caroline's eyes wrinkled, concerned. 'Is something wrong?'

'Something wrong – yes, Missy.'

'What's happened, Ah Fong?'

'Bad that you and Only Son are not together.' She frowned: '*So* sorry.'

'I am too, Ah Fong. I'm sure you know that I love Reven. But I can't make him do what he doesn't want to do. No one can do that.'

'Is possible to do that.'

'No it's not.'

'Is possible.' Ah Fong would prove her statement. She dipped into the plastic bag: 'Look this picture from his desk.'

She handed the photograph to Caroline, who examined it critically, then said, 'Looks like a police pic.'

'Is photo of Woo Sung-king.'

Caroline looked thoughtful, said, 'Oh,' then re-examined the picture.

Ah Fong leaned closer to Caroline. She judged the moment to be right to tell this woman about her fears and her discoveries; to tell Caroline about fox fairies and their amazing and frightening ability to transform their horrid features so as to become immortal. And as they sipped their tea Ah Fong drew piece by piece from her dark box of beliefs until she had said all that was on her mind. And Caroline was horrified. Her teacup rattled in its saucer as she set it down.

'You're telling me, Ah Fong, that there is a woman called Shen Woo, and she is a great beauty . . . and she is a fox fairy?'

'Fox fairy.' Ah Fong nodded.

191

'And Reven is in love with this fox fairy?'

'You must help him. Only you can help him.'

'Ah Fong, this is *crazy*.'

'You don't know, Missy . . . Look at the picture.'

'This man and Shen Woo are the same person?'

'Same fox fairy. Change, day, night, whenever it wants. I've seen it, sure, sure.'

'Ah Fong, the only Woo that Reven came up against is, as far as I know, named Eddie. Perhaps it is this man in the photograph. I don't know. I do know that he is very real, and very alive, and Reven would give anything to find him.'

'A great hate, hah?'

'Yes.'

'*See!*'

'It's nonsense. I don't want to hear this.'

'She'll kill him, Missy.'

'Ah Fong, *stop it*.'

'He's blinded by her. He can't see what we can see. Truth. She'll suck him dry. I saw her doing it. *Aieya!* You'll see, he will get sick soon. You must help him.'

'No more about it, Ah Fong.'

'Must fight her.'

'*No!*'

'Yes, yes, Missy, you must get him back. You love him. You right woman for him.'

'But he doesn't love me, you see, Ah Fong. So there is nothing I can do . . . I wish he did love me, but he doesn't.'

'Does love you,' Ah Fong insisted. 'It's the fox fairy. She's sucked out his mind with night magic.'

Caroline shook her head. 'Dear Ah Fong, what do you want from me?'

'Help me.'

'I would if I knew how. I don't know how. I'm sorry.'

Both women sat observing each other then. No words came to either of them. Ah Fong had told her story, she did not know what more to say. She had expected more from

Caroline: anger, spiteful resentment and a zeal for revenge. These were the passions that would have heated the blood of a Chinese lover. But this woman was not Chinese; this woman's brow was calm, her eyes unfurnaced by emotion. She refused even to believe in the existence of such demons as fox fairies . . . Yet there was something in the deportment of Caroline that caused Ah Fong to study deeper than the smoothness of the brow, and she saw that there were thoughts at work inside this girl's mind that were as lively as a lightning storm. She was hiding something. *She was pregnant!*

Ah Fong wondered why it had taken her so long to read such obvious signs: the gentle brush of hand to stomach; the glow of secret pride. The full-bloomed look of the woman with child. All these things Ah Fong saw now.

She said: 'You carrying Only Son's child, hah?'

Caroline's answer came in the scalding blush that reddened her to her red hair roots.

'Does *he* know?' Ah Fong asked.

'No,' Caroline said. 'No, he doesn't.'

'Will you tell him?'

'No.'

'He will leave the fox fairy if you tell him that.'

'*No.*' Caroline spoke in that straight-spined, starched way that British women stiffen to when authority is the thing: 'If you tell him, Ah Fong, I will deny it, and I will *never* forgive you.'

Ah Fong gave in: 'Yes, Missy.'

Caroline softened. 'I'm sadder than you are that he's in love with someone else. I've known it for a while, of course, Hong Kong is a small place . . . Today is the first time I have been told her name: Shen Woo. Ah Fong, don't do anything to hurt this girl. It's *not* her fault. I hate what's happened too, but it's not her fault. People fall in love and they fall out of love, and spells and charms have got nothing to do with it. Get those dangerous superstitions out of your mind, Ah Fong. Do you hear?'

'You'll lose him, Missy. Child won't have a father.'

'But, Ah Fong, don't you see, I would not want Reven unless he came to me out of love.'

'No love for you, Missy, while fox fairy is alive.'

'Dear God! you *mustn't* talk like that.'

'Tell him about child, Missy.'

'*No.*'

'You can't hide it for all time. Soon he must see it.'

Tight-lipped, Caroline said, 'No.' Her face saddened then and her eyes shone. She said, 'I am going to have his baby because *I want* to have his baby, that is all.'

Ah Fong was sad too, but it was an angry bitter sadness and it was directed at this woman; this stupid, disbelieving foreigner who would see no reason, and would do nothing to defend what was rightfully hers.

Ah Fong left Caroline's flat then. She caught the late ferry back to Lantau. She was cold and hungry and her whole body was atremble with fatigue by the time she reached the house on Butterfly Hill. But her mind was clear by then and it danced with new hope. For now she had a weapon with which to fight the fox fairy of Tai O. It lay safe in the womb of Caroline; growing in strength by the day.

Her prayers at the banyan tree had been answered.

┤ 6 ├

ONE HORSE,
ONE SINGLE SPEAR

The flickering film reminded Reven Forrester of the old black and white gangster movies that were sometimes re-run on late-night TV – deep character villains with hat brims pulled down low and flashing pistols, and no great respect for reality. But this was not late at night, this was midday and the movie was not 'B' grade fiction. It was a factual recording, on VCR tape, of the robbery in the Lion Rock tunnel. The tape was quite clear, it came from the cameras that were set to detect traffic offenders, lane swoppers and speedsters.

This was the second time that Forrester had seen that video. On the first occasion he had been seated amongst his colleagues at Marine Police Headquarters at Tsim Sha Tsui. Now, he was seated in the office of Mr Yip, the supervisor of the tunnel; an excitable little man, who preferred to practise his English on Forrester than to speak Cantonese. Mr Yip's fly was undone . . .

'Jesa' Cris'!' Mr Yip yelled. 'Look a' that.'

The tape had reached the part where the horse and trailer slewed across the road in the path of the armoured van.

'Jesa' Cris'!' Mr Yip shot up from his chair, then sat down, then pounded the replay button of his recorder. 'Look a' *that!*'

Whoever had been driving the rig had been either fearless or ignorant of the characteristics of a horse and trailer when thrown into such a wild manoeuvre. That he had died at his task was not surprising.

'Mad,' said Yip. 'Fucking crazy-dog mad!'

That summed it up. The horse came into the right-hand lane in the path of the motorcycle escorts and the armoured car.

'*Wah!*' Mr Yip slapped his forehead.

The rig jack-knifed as its brakes came on hard – sparks and smoke and a heaving of metal – the rig crashed on to its side, the escorts crashed into the rig, the armoured car crashed into men and machine and whatever else lay in its path.

'*Wah!*' shouted Mr Yip.

From a car men came running. No rescuers these. They had guns; several pistols and an assault rifle. On they came, crouching, firing as they ran. Their guns were puny things with which to take on the armoured car, but that they knew. They had brought with them explosives and a man who was versed in their usage. While the guns fired on he fixed a charge on to the rear doors of the van then scrambled away. A bright flash – a judder of the TV image – and in they swarmed for the spoils. Forrester watched closely for a few moments longer.

'OK,' he said.

Yip switched off the VCR, his face flushed. 'Same time they do all that, they run another truck through number two tunnel,' he said. 'They spray towngas into the tunnel and set off the alarms. Jesa' Cris', every fucking man in control room in fucking panic.'

'I can believe it,' Forrester said. With Yip as the fucking panicker-in-chief.

'We closed the tunnels off,' Yip said. 'What else could we do?'

Well they could have watched the closed-circuit monitors in the southbound tunnel, and seen that a robbery was in progress. Then they could have notified the police of that discovery, immediately. But it wasn't for Forrester to tell Yip these things, and besides that, he liked the little man.

Mr Yip had been helpful. Mr Yip (with his fly in its present state) had taken him on a tour of the tunnel, and had arranged for him to interview a certain engineer, Pig-boy Ho. Pig-boy had yesterday given a most ambiguous statement to the Serious Crime Bureau concerning the crew of the crashed rig.

'Is Pig-boy back yet?' Forrester said.

Yip bellowed into his telephone. Forrester gathered that Ho had done whatever it was that required doing in the air-conditioning plant, and was now on his way back to the tunnel control centre. Mr Yip looked up from his telephone and confirmed this: 'Pig-boy coming now.' He gathered some papers from his desk and left the office. 'I come back when you finish him off.'

Forrester did not have it in him to point Yip to his delinquent zip.

Pig-boy Ho's face was a mess. His nose was taped and both eyes were blackened. He spoke with the minimum of jaw action and the minimum of words, but what came out, came out readily. Unfortunately it was a hash of lies.

'Sure I like to help you, Ging Si . . . no problem.'

'Just a few questions, Pig-boy.'

'No problem.'

'I read your statement, Pig-boy. I don't believe a word of it.'

Pig-boy's bruised eyes widened. '*Wah*! Why not?'

'Your description of the men who rode the rig was hopeless . . . useless . . . shit.'

'Shit? I told the police all I could remember. It all happened so quickly. I was speaking to one man; trying to help him start the engine of the horse. Then this big guy came up and hit me. *Diu lei* – it felt like a door had been slammed on me . . . They wore peak caps and dark glasses, those *laan Tsai*. That's all I remember about them. I told your guys that yesterday. That's the best I can do.'

Forrester believed that it was not the best Pig-boy could

197

do. He told the engineer that. But he understood the reason for Pig-boy's poor memory, and he told him that too: 'You're scared that the triads will chop you if you talk, aren't you, Pig-boy?'

Pig-boy was so scared that he paled at that thought. Forrester knew how to palliate this fever of cold fear. He had brought with him quite a large sum of money. He opened his briefcase that Pig-boy might see it.

'Pig-boy,' he said, 'I've brought with me some photographs. You've seen them before. They were lifted from the closed-circuit tape shot in the tunnel. I want you to look at them again.'

Pig-boy Ho looked earnestly at the photographs laid before him. He also looked at the ten-dollar bills still stacked within the case.

'Here,' said Forrester, 'we have a picture of a man climbing from the upended cab . . . Here we have the same man standing beside the rig.'

Pig-boy squinted at the photographs. He said, 'They're not good, Ging Si: too grainy. The cops who came here yesterday had these pics too; they didn't think much of them. These CTV cameras are designed to record high-contrast number plates, not features. These guys knew that, they didn't even bother to wear masks.'

'Yes.' Forrester pointed to another photograph. 'This is the picture that interested me most. It's a blow-up of the man as he climbs from the cab. See his hands as they grip the body work; quite a good bit of contrast there. Look carefully. Do you notice something strange about his hand?'

'His hand?'

'Yes, look at it.'

Pig-boy looked raptly at the picture, but it was clear to Forrester that the attention of the engineer was elsewhere. His dilemma was one of values: was the risk worth the money on the table? Apparently it was. He looked up.

'Could be one finger missing from his hand . . . Yes, I

remember the man who was working on the broken-down rig had only three fingers on his right hand. This must be the same man.'

'It's not just a camera illusion, a trick of the light?'

'No. I *do* remember now. He did have only three fingers on his right hand. *Wah*! How I forget that?'

'You saw him closely, you'd remember him well?'

'Yes.'

'This money is almost yours, Pig-boy. Don't lie to me, there's no need.'

'Won't lie now, Ging Si.'

'Now I'm going to show you one more photograph, Pig-boy. This one is in perfect focus. See if you remember this man's face . . . the truth.'

The photograph, glossy black and white, showed Eddie Woo lying beaten upon the floor of his snooker salon. His eyes were slitted in semi-consciousness, and his hair matted with blood. Forrester laid the picture in front of Pig-boy.

'That's him.' Ho tapped the picture. 'That's the man I saw . . . Is he dead?'

'No, he's not dead,' Forrester said. 'Which brings us to the matter of *your* safety. If it should ever become known that you identified this man you would be chopped. Do you understand that? You would not have a chance.'

Forrester took the wads of dollars from his case and set them down upon the desk. Pig-boy Ho descended on the cash.

'Listen to me,' Forrester warned. 'You made your statement to the police, stick to it, Pig-boy. That *this* policeman knows the whole truth is enough. I will handle this thing *my* way, but I will not be able to protect you from being chopped if the triads should come after you.'

'No problem.' Pig-boy Ho smiled through his pain as the dollars filled out his pockets.

May you live to enjoy it, thought Reven Forrester.

Forrester did not return to Lantau Island that night. There were things to be done in Kowloon; people to be spoken to. 'Twenty-five' boys they were known as; informers who emerged at night to thrive on the periphery of crime. He knew how to get to them and how to work them, he took with him the expert – Inspector Charlie Lam. The coat of arms of the Royal Hong Kong Police said it all: a junk and a clipper, a Chinese and a European man shaking hands over six bundles of opium.

So he and Charlie Lam walked the shadows of Yau Ma Tei and Sham Shui Po that night and sought out the untouchables who survived there – maggots. But who else other than the maggot has the knowledge of the rotten core?

Forrester sent in his human worms. He told them to bore deep, as deep as the hidden man, Eddie Woo. He promised favours.

When the dawn came he went back to his Hong Kong flat. He felt tired; more tired than was warranted by the forfeit of one single night's sleep. At midnight he had felt the arrival of a dragging fatigue. While seated in a taxi he had bent his face forward into his hands, and despite the hooting traffic, the jolt-stop-start driving of his taxi-man and the chatting of Charlie Lam, he had fallen blackly into sleep. It had taken such an effort to carry on; to lift himself from the soft upholstery and into the night.

But now in the dim of the early sun there were the peaks of Hong Kong where the roads wound through leafy green woods, and birds sang their morning song and grew fat on the purple beauty-berries and orange morindas. These heights had been deep gouged to accommodate fine buildings – houses and apartments with balconied, distant blue views. This was where Forrester's taxi deposited him.

By now he had realized that his lassitude was unnatural.

Once before he had felt like this; while an Executive Officer with the RAN on exercises in the Celebes Sea. He remembered how the tiredness had flamed into fever; days of sweating and days of arctic chill. Of course after all those years it could not be malaria. Perhaps a touch of the flu.

Forrester refused breakfast. He wanted nothing more than to lie down; to close his eyes and stretch out full length, just for an hour then he would bathe and shave and eat all that was put before him.

He lay down, he curled up beneath his duvet and waited for the return of his strength. It did not come. What came was a spasm of raw coldness that shuddered through him, wave after wave.

Maria, the amah, brought tea to the bedroom at the appointed time and saw the shivering, duvet-wrapped body of her employer. She rushed off to phone Ah Fong.

Ah Fong brought all the right remedies: paper charms and amulets, dried Chu Ku leaves and cicada-shell tea. She knew exactly what to do, and the imposition of her rule was absolute. When Only Son next drew back the duvet it was to the tinkle of spoon on porcelain, a sound he remembered from the sickbed of childhood. Ah Fong was at hand, and the air was bitter with the smell of steaming herbs. He said, 'I feel so weak and cold.'

Ah Fong held out the medicine cup.

'It's like the malaria I had once.'

'Not malaria,' said Ah Fong. 'Worse than malaria.'

The medicine tasted like ink. Forrester drank it and settled back upon his pillow.

'Can be cured,' said Ah Fong. 'But you must listen to Old Mother.'

Forrester did not have the energy to speak. Ah Fong went on.

'So evil is the fox fairy . . . Hair like black silk and skin soft like moss, when they make "come here" with their long fingers men run to them . . . Strong men go weak. Look at

201

you with your male essence all gone. Where do you think it's gone? Hah? Sucked away so she can live for another nine hundred years.'

From somewhere deep in him a chill burgeoned outwards and he began to shiver. '*Aieyaa!*' Ah Fong keened in sympathy. On the duvet she laid blankets but nothing could give him heat. She cried for her son. She burned charms for him. And she cursed his tormentor, the fox fairy of Tai O.

Forrester heard all her accusations and all her curses but the wracking chills were all he could cope with. He did not answer her until they had passed. Then he said, 'Don't talk like that, do you hear? I won't have it.'

'*Aieya! . . . Aieyaa! . . . Aieyaa!*'

'*Stop* that!'

Ah Fong stopped.

'Shen Woo is a good person, and she would do nothing to hurt me.'

Ah Fong sulked out of the room, and that did not distress him one bit. He was tired of the amah and her keening accusations. He knew that the rigors would return soon and he needed all his strength. Ah Fong's nostrum would help, he was sure, but more than that was needed to combat this fierce disease: a bit of Western magic.

Dr Yuen, who was Oxford trained, thought so too. He came within the hour and diagnosed possible malaria.

'Can't be sure without a blood test.'

'Can it return after so many years?'

'Oh yes,' said Dr Yuen. 'Some strains of symbiont parasites lurk within the red blood cells for years; break out occasionally and you feel a bit off . . . then something like this: a transient episode, severe, but short-lived. You think you won't survive it, it's that bad, but it passes soon enough. Had any stress lately?'

He prodded steel fingers along Forrester's rib line. 'Does that hurt?'

'I keep fit,' Forrester said. 'I take vitamins.'

'No accounting for it,' said Dr Yuen. With a huge hypodermic syringe he robbed him of blood.

'No accounting for it,' he said again. 'I'll get this to the lab and we'll see. In the meantime, bed rest and analgesics. You are strong, Reven. You will recover quickly.'

Bed rest and analgesics and Ah Fong's potions and prayers, something helped, for the rigors diminished in severity and frequency and Forrester slept a deep healing sleep. The next morning he felt better. Dr Yuen called again, and his news was that the blood tests were negative.

'But we should do more. A single negative finding does not exclude malaria. When you're on your feet I want you to call at the lab and let them do another smear.'

'I feel better,' said Forrester.

'Still, get the tests done.' Dr Yuen frowned with one eyebrow. 'It's possible that you have a tolerance for malaria. If you were exposed to the disease as a kid you will have developed a certain immunity, but that's lost in later years. The episodes could get worse. We don't want that, do we?'

They both agreed: they did not want that.

Ah Fong showed Dr Yuen out then returned to Forrester's bedside. She hovered there, looking concerned yet smug. '*No* malaria,' she said.

'Can't be sure.'

'Know for sure: *no* malaria.'

'Something I ate.'

'No, nothing you ate. Old Mother know for sure.'

Forrester knew exactly what Ah Fong knew 'for sure', and what she was leading up to. He did not want to hear any more such rubbish. He toned his voice sternly. 'Ah Fong. I will be angry if you accuse Shen of trying to harm me, or of any such nonsense. I don't know why you don't like her, I wish you did. I think she would make me a good wife.'

'Love Caroline. You belong Caroline.'

'It's over with Caroline.'

'Not over with Caroline.'

'You've gone too far, Ah Fong. I don't want to talk about this. It's really none of your damn business.'

'*Not* over with Caroline.'

Ah Fong marched from the bedroom, strutting her little elbows like a drummer boy on parade. At the doorway she paused. She said, 'Caroline have *your* baby.' Then she turned quickly away and left.

Forrester heard her, shrill-voiced, as she berated Maria in the kitchen; then the rattle of crockery. Then the front door slammed and peace returned to the apartment.

'Maria,' Forrester called.

She came in an instant.

'What did Ah Fong say to you?'

'She told me: bring the Ging Si everything he wants, even before he calls out for it.'

'Bring me my uniform.'

Maria did not like *that* instruction, that was obvious. Her eyes widened and she turned away. She knew that street clothes, though not embargoed specifically by Ah Fong, were not what the terrible amah had had in mind. If the Ging Si left the flat before Ah Fong returned who would get the blame? Maria would dawdle in the provision of the clothes, Forrester knew, in the hope that Ah Fong would return in time to relieve her of that responsibility.

Forrester prepared to get dressed. He showered and let the hot jet pummel his shoulders and back and work at the residue of his headache. It was vague now, a forgivable pain, and he could think clearly. He thought about his most recent conversation with Ah Fong; most specifically her statement 'Caroline have your baby'. What had moved her to say such a thing? Ah Fong was old, quick to anger and slow to retract. But Ah Fong had, to his knowledge, never lied to him.

'Caroline have your baby.'

He tested the words in the tone and manner in which they had been addressed to him.

'Caroline have *your* baby.'

Dear God, it couldn't be so. Caroline took precautions. She had told him that. Could women fall pregnant whilst on the Pill? Surely not. He splashed some cologne on to his freshly shaved cheeks. It stung and the aroma of camphor wood rose up in the steamy air; Caroline's gift to him. Caroline loved that aroma. He had a drawer full of soaps and talcs and deodorants presented by her . . . Caroline pregnant, pregnant with *his* child? He would look very foolish if he asked her that and it was not so.

The event that Maria had hoped would occur, did occur. Ah Fong the Terrible returned before the deadline arrived for the provision of the Ging Si's uniform. Forrester, clothed only in a towel, came into his bedroom. His shrill-voiced amah was somewhere in the flat. He exchanged the towel for a silk gown and went in search of her.

Ah Fong was in the lounge with Maria, who slipped away, when Forrester, in his dragon-embroidered gown, marched in. Forrester called after her:

'My uniform, at once Maria.'

It was a clear day. The broad, wide windows of the lounge were open. A bonny breeze played at the curtains and the view ran clear across Victoria Harbour. The perfect view for Ah Fong to observe when being questioned.

'The truth: is Caroline pregnant with my child?'

'Prayed that you would give her a child,' Ah Fong said. 'At banyan tree on Kat O Island, prayed to Great Aunt – Bo Po . . .'

'Never mind that. Is she, or is she not pregnant?'

'Bad you be angry with me.'

'Just *tell* me!'

'Is it not right that Mother likes to pray for the happiness of her son, whom she loves more than life; whose joy and prosperity and good fortune are her great concern.'

'Look at me!'

Ah Fong turned reluctantly from the view. 'Remember Kit Ling,' she said. 'That child was in your eyes . . . Remember how you loved that girl? . . . Now, Caroline give you your own child.'

Forrester felt compelled to sit.

'Promised Missy Caroline that I would not tell you. Would not have told you, but you *made* me. It's bad you be cross with Old Mother.'

The enormity of it reached Forrester. Caroline pregnant. He a father!

'Are you certain of this?' he said to Ah Fong. 'How can you be so sure?'

'Sure,' said Ah Fong.

He still could not believe it. He changed into his uniform and left the flat. His intention had been to go to Dr Yuen's lab, and from there on to Lantau Island. He did not do that. He waved down a taxi and instructed: 'Tong Chong Street – Quarry Bay.'

His destination was the offices of the *South China Morning Post*. Caroline was usually at her desk at that time of the morning.

A clatter of word processor keyboards; a purr of conversation, a trill of telephones. These were the sounds that met him at the portal of the news room. Caroline was at her desk, her lips moving silently as the words in her fingertips came to life upon the screen before her. He watched her at her work for a while. He had carried a mind picture of her over the months of bold features and big gestures; of copper-flame hair and floppy wide hats ever in danger of ignition. This woman looked less sulphurous and more staidly groomed. Her face was as beautiful as he remembered it. He came on towards her desk and she looked up and saw him. Her hand went to her neck – a protective gesture that hurt him by implication. He stood in front of her.

'Ah Fong told you,' she said.

'It's true then.'

'Yes it's true . . . I thought of denying it but what would have been the point? Ah Fong found out. I knew it was only a matter of time before she told Only Son. So there you are.'

'I don't know what to do.'

'Good gracious me!' Caroline laughed. 'Just look at you. Like a little boy who's broken the cookie jar. Why should *you* do anything? I won't tell if you don't.'

A copy boy dumped a hash of printouts on Caroline's desk. Forrester waited until he had passed on before he spoke again.

'But it's *my* baby.'

'*Oh* no.' No, it was *not* his baby. Caroline left no room for misunderstanding on that point: 'I expect nothing from you, Reven. I want nothing and I will give nothing. This is my life; *my* baby. You can sleep easily on that point.'

'I see.' He really did not see.

'That's good, Reven . . . Look I'm nearly finished here. I've got an assignment, but that can wait. There *is* something I should talk to you about, that is if you've got the time. Have you?'

Had he not had the time he would have lied about it, for there was so much that he wished to talk about to this woman who was carrying his child. They drove in a pool car with one window that would not wind and every ashtray crammed to the brim. Caroline drove well, but impatiently. Hong Kong's drivers were tolerant of lane dodgers but he found himself with the thought: a pregnant woman should not drive so fast. He said: 'Will you give up your job?'

She turned and looked at him for too long. 'You know I get the impression that you think you owe me something – forget it.'

'You amaze me. You're carrying a life inside you that's part of me and you ask me simply to fade out of the picture.'

'It was your choice, Reven, remember?'

'But the baby isn't just yours. It's part of me too.'

207

'You put it there. Is that it, it's your fault that I'm pregnant.'

'Weren't you on the Pill?'

'No.'

'But that was asking for trouble.'

'There, you've said it, Reven. That is the exact response that I expected and the exact difference between your attitude and mine. I don't see my pregnancy as "trouble". I'm thrilled that I'm pregnant. I *wanted* to be pregnant. I *tried* to become pregnant. You see it's not your responsibility at all.'

'You trapped me into saying that, Caroline, you're using the word "trouble" in a sense that was not intended . . . I don't know what's going on. I *do* feel responsible – what the hell do you expect? I'm a bit confused. I'm a lot confused. You're telling me *you* planned to have my baby? Is that right?'

'I don't want it to affect you in any way, Reven.'

'Jesus! Of course it does. It changes things. No matter what *you* planned or how *you* planned it, I'm involved. I'm amazed you can think otherwise.'

'I didn't expect us to break up.'

'I'm not a stud bull, Caroline. You had no right to do this. It's unbelievable.'

Caroline threw the car hard and without warning into a left-hand curve. Hooters sounded. Caroline tossed her head in a defiant way; her words were defiant: 'I have a right to decide what happens inside me. And that is what I did. I've told you, I don't expect anything from you. If you're labouring with old-fashioned ideas of paternal responsibility, then you're off the hook. I *didn't* expect us to break up but even if we hadn't, my sentiments would be the same. If you can't accept that, Reven, then I can't help it.'

They drove without speaking for a while, and the silence bred more silence. They arrived at the central district without a further word having been exchanged. Caroline drew up. She turned to face him, and a deep breath escaped her.

'That's how I feel too,' he said.

'I'm sorry. Can we be friends?'

'Yes, I'd like that . . . Let's get out of this bloody car. There's good food at that restaurant . . . there.'

'Lead on, friend,' she said.

They ate shrimp patties and rice flour rolls and finished with coconut pastries and *ma chai*, all very good. They spoke as 'friends' would speak, but their spines were stiff and their gestures too fitful, and the tension was obvious. She told him he looked drawn, and asked if he had been ill.

'A touch of the flu.'

'It's going round,' said Caroline. She smiled a short-lived, transient smile. 'Ah Fong told me about Shen Woo.'

'Is that so?'

'Is she the sister of Eddie Woo?'

'Is that *really* your business, Caroline? I'm not using her to get to her brother, if that's what you're thinking.'

'I wasn't thinking that . . . Others might.'

'She's a lovely girl, Caroline. You'd like her.'

'Mm . . . Do you really love her?'

'I think I do.'

A waiter brought fresh tea and set it down.

'So the great Ging Si has fallen in love at last.' She saluted him with the handleless teacup. '*Yambui!* . . . Ah Fong does not approve of Shen. Did you know that?'

'I've said all I want to say about Shen.'

'I thought you should know.'

He stopped her with a sharp gesture. 'I'll handle the situation between Ah Fong and Shen, OK?'

'Be careful.'

'I will be careful.'

'You have a way of "handling" things that can hurt more than you can imagine. In a way I envy your Shen, but I pity her too. Try not to hurt her too much.'

'I never wanted to hurt you, Caroline.'

'Oh yes you did. That day on *Dolphin* . . . but it doesn't matter now.' She lit a cigarette, then immediately stubbed it in an ashtray. 'Got to stop that now, with the baby on the way . . . Oh I suppose you were just retaliating that day, in your bloody-minded Scorpio way. I never really believed that you loved me, but I was hoping that I was more than just a "good lay". Was I good, Reven?'

'That's not funny.'

'Humble apologies, Ging Si.'

'I don't want to hear that kind of crap.'

'I don't care so much any more about what you want to hear or don't want to hear. If you're bruised by my attitude, if you feel taken advantage of – well that's too bad. You'll have to live with it. I never thought of you as a stud bull. Nor did I try to trap you.'

'You had no way of knowing how I would react to this. I think what you did was wrong, totally wrong.'

'I'm sorry you think that. I did think things would work out well, I really did.'

'That we would get married?'

'I thought that if you loved the child . . .'

'It's a mess, Caroline.'

'I don't see it as that. I'm content, I told you that, Reven.'

'You can handle it? Is that it?'

'I'm not ashamed of my state. Can't you get that into your thick head? I don't give a damn about wagging tongues . . . But this I will promise you, Reven: never, *never* will I disclose the identity of the father of my child. That will be my secret, and yours. They can guess as much as they want, but they will never *know*.'

'I think that *that* appeals to you. I suppose you will have the baby right here in Hong Kong?'

'I wouldn't like to leave. You know that. But if you feel that *you* can't handle it; if you feel it would be easier for *you* then I will go away.'

'I don't want that.'

'No, give yourself time to think about it, then tell me what you want.'

'Where would you go?'

'Oh! I've good friends in Australia, in Sydney, and in Melbourne . . . And in Singapore. I like Singapore.'

'Singapore . . .' he said abstractedly. In fact he was not thinking of that destination at all. He was thinking how frightened she looked, and full of doubt. All this panache and bravado was just dazzle. Nor did he want her to leave Hong Kong.

He said, 'Don't leave Hong Kong, Caroline. This is your home. I said I would be your friend and I meant it. I'll be the best friend you and your kid could have, you'll see. This is where you stay.'

She laughed then; sobbed and laughed all at once. She turned her face so that her copper-bright hair curtained her eyes. Then she glanced at her watch. 'Good Lord, how time flies when you're with friends.'

Before he could stand she was on her feet. She bent towards him. He looked up and she kissed him on the mouth.

'For old times . . . my love.'

Then she walked quickly away.

In the days when the fishing junks of Hong Kong were driven by bat-wing sails of matting and bamboo and the rigging was of hand-wrung hemp, the junk of the father of Woo Yin-wah had sailed on the winter monsoon winds to a distant place, many days to the south. A place of green islands and handsome brown people who loved to dance and sing. The seas there were blessed, typhoon free, flat, deep blue and swarming with fat fish that fairly tore into the baited hook. They sailed back to Hong Kong, low in the water from the weight of their salted fish cargo. Those were the memories of old Woo Yin-wah. That was how he would describe it to anyone who cared to listen to him talk as he sat in the Lotus Moon teahouse, and gazed across Tai O bay.

The story was not new. He'd told it many times, but always there were listeners: some believers, some sceptics, but all of them attentive.

'What a fine place,' said the believers. 'No typhoons, ever, just think of it.'

'Youth is a liar to the old mind,' said the sceptics. 'There is no such paradise in the East.'

'Did *you* dance too?' asked the believers. 'Were the women *that* willing, ah?'

There were more believers than detractors these days. It had to do, of course, with Woo Yin-wah's amazing Fu Kei prophecy regarding the arrival of the soldiers from the Big Land and the destruction of the temple of Hau Wang. Beyond doubt this old man had marvellous divinatory powers that might emerge at any time, like a summer mountain spring of crystal clear water. Proximity with this psychic source at the time when it bubbled up had to be the surest way to collect. So they shuffled their chairs in the teahouse of the Lotus Moon, and drew near to the teller of the stories of mat sails and distant places, and waited.

When Woo Yin-wah was not at home, or in the teahouse, he was most likely to be found on the bank of the creek opposite the temple, watching the PLA soldiers demolish the house of his god. An observer upon this pathway might have noticed that the mouth of the old man moved in a bitter, silent mutter as he watched the soldiers at their work. But whatever his thoughts were, they remained unsaid. He never visited the reconstruction site at Tik Tak Shue where the rubble of the temple was being taken, and indexed, and arranged in orderly heaps within a mat-walled godown, in the hope that one day it might rise again to house the homeless god.

The winter solstice came – the sun was at its stingiest and the moon cold white. The nature gods who shaped the rocks and trees received due worship on these chilly days. At the entrance to the house of Woo, a little shrine existed; a red-painted cement arch in which bright niche there lived a small crouched rock. Woo set down offerings there of rice and wine and planted smoking incense in the sand before it. Woo did not have much to say to this divinity of the earth as he was a seaman at heart. But as he was now old in body, and landbound, he paid his respects to the little To Tei rock. He reported on the death of Au Wai and of the sorrow that had attended since that day. He said he would like to be able to share more with To Tei but all he felt these days in his heart was emptiness. And how did one share something that was not? With Granddaughter Shen at his side, he asked that To Tei should protect the house that sheltered his shrine until the next winter solstice came by.

Then Shen Woo with her long hair trailing, and her pretty red dress billowing in the winter wind, went away, to Hong Kong, so she said. She was young and her pulse was quick and her face was aglow. She was seeing the gwai lo Ging Si. Woo knew this and he was against it. A good Chinese man was needed for her. Someone of her own kind; someone schooled and cultured in the Chinese way. Not a hairy, ignorant, sweaty foreign devil, *Aieya*! But she would not listen. The gwai lo would use her, he had warned: like a flower she would be plucked and coarsely held, then tossed away. That was how the gwai los were. Everyone knew that; everyone but his little Lui Lui. In his day young girls were obedient to the wishes of their elders; not so today. Look at her now as she strode down the village street, head tossing like a race horse at the start. Could he hold such a creature from its course? He did not have such strength.

The wind reached, cold-fingered, beneath the quilted jacket that covered him and speared into his bones. He'd greased his joints with Tiger Balm and eaten heating foods, yet he felt as cold as stone. His walk to the teahouse of the Lotus Moon was hard going that day. He thought the gusting north-easterly might blow him from his feet and sweep him like a paper kite into the bay. But he did arrive; he took his seat and immediately drank a cup of Shansi triple-distilled, and that worked some summer into his stomach and knees, and his mind, so he ordered another cup, and some food. He lit a cigarette.

Woo's view from his seat in the teahouse was of the length of Tai O bay to the ferry pier where Shen had just gone. A Chinese gunboat was tied up there, its red pennant stiff in the cold blow. In the central channel some Toh Mong Suen long-liners, similar to his own fishing junks, were anchored. The wind had turned them to face bow on and white-fringed bay waves broke meekly at their stems. It was a sight that begged an old seaman's eyes and Woo watched for a long while. His own two Toh Mong Suen would be returning home soon from the fishing grounds off Hai Nan Island . . . Perhaps he would go with them on their next voyage. How fine it would be to go with them on their next voyage; to *lead* them on their next voyage.

The thought of going to sea again was not new to Woo Yin-wah, but never had it seemed more attractive than on that winter's morning. To the south; that was where they would go, to the warm, distant, green islands, to the south; to the flat, blue seas to the south. They would fish there and fill up their holds and then let them say such a place did not exist. Yes, that was where he would go.

'To the south.'

Those words came as an old man's mutter. They were part of a dream and no one should have noticed them, yet they did. 'What did you say, Mr Woo?' He was immediately asked. 'Did something of importance come to mind?'

'Of importance?' Woo Yin-wah looked absently towards his questioner. 'Of importance?'

'You said something . . . something "south".'

214

'I was thinking aloud. No more than that.'

'It would be most considerate if you shared your thoughts with your friends.'

All eyes turned towards Woo – heads poised, ears spooned to scoop up every last syllable. How disappointing that he could not give them something of moment. Some great divination that would set them rigid in their chairs, wide-faced with wonder. But he was not Au Wai, and truly this time he had simply been day-dreaming.

'Just an old man's dream; nothing . . . really nothing.'

Foolish men, what did they want; that he should sell them the wind? He turned from them and gazed once more towards the anchored junks, then plunged into the warm seas of his memories . . . the good smell of oiled camphor wood, and hemp rope wetted by the rain. Someone called him softly:

'Woo, Lo Baak.'

He looked at the old woman who had come to stand at his table.

'Woo, Lo Baak, so ashamed to disturb.'

Her face was lined and her eyelids puckered. Her whitening hair was clean and combed into a strict bun.

'No trouble,' he said. 'Sit down, old woman. Tell me your respected name.'

She sat down. She said: 'My humble name is Fong.'

'And what affair brings you, Ah Fong, out on such a harsh day?'

When Reven Forrester had asked her to spend Christmas Eve with him on Hong Kong, Shen had been delighted. Christmas Day was a special day for Christians, a day of presents and celebrations, much like the Chinese Shou Sui celebration, but not as exuberant. She felt honoured. She felt excited. Neither of them said a word about what would happen when Christmas Eve ran on to become Christmas Day. But Victoria Peak was a long way from home.

215

On Christmas Eve she had risen very early and bathed and washed her hair, then brushed it until it shone like the feathers of a raven. She had scented her body then dressed it in most exquisite sheer lace, a bra and pantie set that clung and showed everything it touched in a most provocative way. She drew on her red woollen dress with the mandarin collar and full sleeves, the dress she had worn when first she had visited Reven Forrester at Cheung Sha. She felt pretty in that dress, the bodice hugged her tightly, shoulder to bust; the skirt, if she walked quickly, billowed royally around her.

She had gone with Grandfather to the little To Tei stone that dwelt at the front of their house and helped him in the deliverance of offerings and prayers. He did not approve of her destination that day, she knew it. She did not want to debate it so she did not linger when they were done. She had secret, intimate thoughts with her, as secret and intimate as the new underwear she wore. Exciting thoughts – not to be touched by an old man's cold disapproval. If Reven wanted her that Christmas, she would open herself to him. Yes, she would do it. The time had come for trust, and reality.

So Shen walked quickly along the praya towards the pier, not looking back, high-headed with excitement at the prospects that lay ahead.

The ferry toiled against the wind, a slow and lumbering thing while her desire was the speed of a swallow. From Tai O to Tuen Mun it creaked and laboured. At Tuen Mun a European and his Chinese wife came to sit near her. They had children, a boy and girl of about the same age. Brown wide-eyed children, well dressed and as pretty as they could be. Shen watched them play all the way to Hong Kong; rushing up and down the aisle between the seats, laughing till they were weak from it. They came to look at her, she smiled, and they smiled at her. 'Lovely kids,' she said to the parents. 'So lucky.' If she could give Reven such children then their marriage would endure; it would be as firm as a

216

rock. She would pray at the temple of Tin Hau – the Queen of Heaven – the giver of children, for such a blessing.

Reven was at the Kowloon terminus to meet her, standing tall above the bustle and noise of the Chinese crowd. She was hidden amongst that bustle and noise and he did not see her until she was almost upon him. Then he gathered her in and turned and they walked with the clamorous human tide.

'See the children,' she pointed. 'Look.' The little Eurasian kids were there, holding tight to their mother's hands. 'Aren't they cute?' she said. She wanted him to see them; their little legs quick-stepping in the rush. She wanted him to observe how pretty they were. A squeeze of the hand told her he had seen them. He led her quickly through the crowd.

A gleaming red Porsche graced the kerbside in Wing Lok Street, a policeman saluted. How fine it felt to be stared at – a 'rich bitch' for a day. 'Banana', the Cantonese would label her – yellow on the outside, white on the inside. She didn't care what they thought. The Porsche leapt forward. *Aieya*! What a thrill!

Shopping! Reven wanted to buy for her every dress and handbag and gold trinket in the windows of Tsim Sha Tsui. She had not known what to expect that day, but *this* excitement, never. She loved it, but forbade him to spend more on her than she could spend on him, so their purchases were small but their fun was immense. He had face in many of those shops and always it was the proprietor who stepped forward to serve them. '*Hou saangyi la!*' Reven bade them prosper as they departed. No wonder they gave him such face.

Then in the red Porsche again to Repulse Bay to have dinner there in a most magnificent, Western-style restaurant – a table upon the veranda, of course, overlooking the bay; bowed to in their seats by obsequious waiters in white coats. Handled as though she were made of precious jade, Shen Woo walked unsurely into this new world.

'I'm going to pinch myself,' she told Reven. 'If I wake up and find that I'm not here, will you come after me?'

'Wherever you may be.' He kissed her and the waiters smiled and pretended not to see.

They drank ice-cold champagne that chased a pathway straight to her head. She felt so happy, so buoyant. There was a simple red rose in a vase upon the white linen cloth, and that was the standard of her spirit – that was how singly beautiful she felt at that moment. Then Reven took her hand and wove his fingers with hers, and her pleasure expanded and welled up in her until she thought she would burst with it.

'Dear Reven . . .' What words were fine enough to disclose her state of happiness? 'I love you . . . I *do* love you.'

Their fingers loved each other, then regretfully parted. The food arrived; European portions that needed dissecting before they could be transferred from plate to mouth. Chinese cooking was more sensible by far. The kitchen was the place for cutting; the table was the place for eating. And nimble chopsticks were superior in every way to these cumbersome knives and forks. Still, it was a fine meal, punctuated often by the toast: '*Yam bui!*' Drink a cup of wine! They finished one bottle of champagne in that way and then he called for another.

'We're going to see the lights,' he said. 'Tsim Sha Tsui is a wonderland this Christmas. You won't believe what you see tonight. Hurry now, let's finish here.'

To the beautiful Porsche and the envious stares. She looked back sublimely. 'This is my everyday motorcar, can't you see?'

Tsim Sha Tsui *was* a wonderland. There was not a building of note whose owner had not vied for face in the decoration of his structure. There were Christmas trees and snow blizzards, red-coated Santas and reindeer springing to the moon. All Chinese love a celebration – the bigger and showier it is, the better. There was not a family in the whole of the territory that was not out walking upon the streets of Tsim Sha Tsui that night. They parked the Porsche and joined the crush. The police had closed off the roads to make safe their enjoyment, and how they enjoyed it.

'Don't ask me why the Chinese get so excited about a Christian festival,' Reven said. 'I've never been able to fathom it.'

'We just love to make a fuss,' she told him. 'That's why we've hijacked your holiday. Oh, Reven, Reven, *look*!'

At the turn of a corner a giant's castle glowing pale-blue and silver loomed up. Six storeys high and a whole block wide, it was a wonderful sight.

'Beautiful!'

Shen stood in front of him, her face up-tilted and he bent to her and kissed her there. He said, 'Shen, both of us know that it's too late for you to go home?'

It was a question that required no more response than she gave him at that moment. She held him tightly and opened her mouth upon his and kissed him as she had never kissed anyone before. Then they walked on. He was so tall, he towered over her, their dynamics were so different that it made no sense to walk wrapped to each other thus. But good sense was not the criterion in fairyland that night. She judged her joy by the pressure of his surface against her. She wanted all of him against her, and he, it seemed, wanted that too. So they clung together in walking, and embraced tightly in the car and in the lift that whizzed them upwards to his heaven-high apartment.

They undressed slowly, watching, watching . . .

'Teach me,' she said. 'I feel so small against you. Don't break me, my love.'

His male-thing rose proud. She was frightened that this would hurt. All things must change, she reassured herself; be glad, Shen, that your time has come.

'Change me,' she whispered.

From girl to woman. She stepped from her dress, and came to him.

'Perfect,' he said. 'Dear God, so perfect.'

Hands warm upon her breasts. He kneeled and kissed her stomach, her navel . . . down. Gentle lips pressed on her garden of love, as soft as mist . . . down. She began to tremble and little moans made their way up to her mouth: *'Oh . . . Oh!'*

Fire, water. Creative, receptive. Her sex parted for him and heaven smiled down as they thrust in instinct in the act of creation. From pain came perfect wholeness and harmony, and raw, raw rapture, as deep as death.

She was changed.

Closed windows and shut doors and the thick acrid dullness of many, many cigarettes. Grandfather was waiting in the dim of the room, his chair turned towards the door, frowning down like the Guardian of Hell. He stared at her for a long time, unmoving upon his seat. When sternness was called for, no one could produce it better than this old man. She had known he would be angry because of her absence for a whole night. She was prepared for it.

She wished him good morning, then walked past him to the kitchen.

'You spent the night with him, not so? Did you do . . . "secret things" with him?'

'*Wah!* Wrong to ask such a question. I'm not a child. I'm a modern woman. Must choose my own husband.'

'As for that, we will see. I warned you that this stinking gwai lo would use you then toss you aside. I *warned* you.'

'You did so and you were wrong. He is not a stinking gwai lo, he is a fine man. Ah Reven loves me. And I love him in a wonderful way that fills me with joy. Please don't say bad words now, Grandpa.'

She opened some windows to rid the house of smoke. She

set the kettle to boil then went to Grandfather and kneeled next to him. She held his old hand and stroked the gnarled joints of his fingers. 'I am so happy,' she said. 'My life has been changed. Ah Reven wants to marry me. Be happy too, Grandpa. Look here! He gave me a lovely jade bracelet.'

'Wrong. *Wrong!*' He snatched his hand from hers. 'He can't marry you. There is another woman, don't you know? He lied to you. Another woman is carrying his child. He *lied* to you! You are his concubine, no more than that. Hah! *Modern* woman.'

She sprang away from Grandfather. In horror her hands flew to her cheeks. Her stomach twisted. Nausea rushed into her so she thought she would be sick. She shouted, '*You're* the liar!'

But he shook his head to contradict that. He turned his face up to her, and there was not a lying line upon it.

The pain of betrayal of love is a shocking thing, and as quick as a fist. It struck Shen Woo's heart with a terrible blow. Her breath came shuddering; her senses numbed. She had a single thought: It is better to be dead. Then she ran from the house. She ran down the praya and all the way to the tip of the pier. All day she sat there watching the waves break, dull and empty with her thought: It is better to be dead.

That night she came home and she wrote a letter, and the saddest words she knew came to her pen. She told Reven Forrester that he had killed her with his lies. She said that she regretted that she had ever met him, and that he must never come to her again; she did not want to see him again. He was cruel; he had no heart. There lived in him a gwei-demon that would cause him to damage all he touched. She placed her bitter note into the box that held her jade bracelet. She wrapped it all up in white paper, and wrote his name upon it. She did not sleep, and in the morning she went to the house of her closest friend, Wai Han, and had

221

her promise that she would deliver the packet into the hands of Reven Forrester.

She saw Wai Han upon the bus that would take her to Cheung Sha. Then she went home and cried until she could cry no more, and when afternoon turned to evening the late bus brought Wai Han back to Tai O.

'Did you give the box to him?' she asked her friend.

'Yes.'

'In his hands?'

'As I promised, Shen.'

'Did he unwrap it? Did he see my note?'

'It was a lovely jade bracelet. Clear jade; so expensive.'

'But did he read the note?'

'Why did you do that, Shen? I think he loves you.'

'Did he look sad? What did he say?'

'He was sad . . . Yes, I think he was very sad. He just turned and walked away.'

'Did he not say *anything*?'

'I think he loves you, Shen.'

Wai Han looked curiously into the swollen, wet eyes of her dear friend. She said: 'I think Ah Shen loves him too.'

'You have killed me with your lies. How could you have treated me so? What makes you so cruel? I thought you were the kindest man alive – but I see you have no heart . . .'

In the many stabs of that letter those were the lines that hurt him most. He dropped the jade bracelet into the drawer of his desk, and forgot it, but the weight of Shen Woo's injustice bore down on him terribly, and tenaciously. Not true that he had lied to her; he should have told her about Caroline's pregnancy, and had not done so. But Shen's reaction to this error was intolerable. He was not cruel, he was not heartless. These accusations were false, they dispirited him, and they angered him too.

He was angry with Shen for believing the worst – and he was angry with the person who had fed her this poison. That person was certainly Ah Fong. He would deal with her tonight.

At that moment DC Bevan was waiting for him, they were to attend a meeting of the Precious Lotus Monastery, Golden Buddha Committee. They drove there in Bevan's Rover. It was a clear day, and crisp. There were hikers on the road, eager for exercise, all stretch and stride beneath the weight of their backpacks.

The Precious Lotus Monastery was worth the pilgrimage. No shabby, time-worn gods here; no dust, no decay. Great snarling stone lions stood guard at every staircase and arch. Sanguine, gold-skinned Buddhas gazed down from high altars of writhing carved dragons and gilded filigree. And the worshippers came on in their thousands to stand in awe before these awesome images and seek guidance and good fortune in their speculations and business deals. Then if they still had the breath for it, they might climb the thousand steps that led up the hill to the biggest golden Buddha statue in all of South-East Asia. Thirty metres high, the Enlightened One sat cross-legged in perfect meditation with hooded eyes and beatific smile. Now here was a place where a man might profit greatly by a visit. How different was this place to the pathetic little temple at Tai O, with its crumbling walls and single human defender.

The meeting with the committee dragged on with convoluted conversation and endless cups of tea. It was the popularity of this greatest of Buddha statues that had created problems. The roads to the monastery were too winding and too narrow to carry the traffic. A recommendation was required that the PWD do something about the access routes, and a greater police presence was required to deter pick-pockets and rowdies and the like. With true Chinese obliquity the committee took until midday to make their point, and when it was all done he could hardly remember a thing that had been discussed. His anger with Shen had grown, and he was bitter. She should have allowed him the chance to explain – she was immature and headstrong, and to hell with immature, headstrong people. As for Ah Fong, that interfering old shrew, she would get the tongue-lashing of her life . . . To hell with all of them.

That afternoon he retired to the mess at the rear of the police station and drank beer with Bevan and a few junior officers. He drank until his thoughts were sodden and his muscles limp. He should have gone home then, but he did not; his mind was pointed in quite another direction – Tai O. That was where he wanted to go. And that was where he went.

He rode his motorcycle as hard as it could go along the South Lantau Road; he thundered low into the bends and twisted the throttle as though to break it. As it darkened he switched the headlights on but the beam was a poor guide at this speed. It was a mad ride – the roar of the engine and the whip of the wind and the run of the tarmac below. Then came the terminus where he drew the machine up upon its stand.

The alley that led down to the creek he saw only vaguely as he stumbled through the semi-darkness. But there was the pull-ferry with the ferry-man at his rope. He crossed . . . An angry face topped by a red-starred cap. Angry words, angry gestures. They would not let him pass. 'Go back!' A rifle was pointed. '*Go back!*' What could he do but obey?

A slurring, vertiginous, numb, drunk anger rode with him all the way back home . . . his front door . . . Ah Fong . . . a bed that pitched like a dinghy in a storm. Vile nausea and stinking vomit, and the white porcelain well of the toilet bowl into which he hurled his bile. Those were the drunken tatters he collected to his memory the next morning. He could not bear to speak to Ah Fong, and was nauseated by the smell of the breakfast she had cooked.

At Cheung Sha, in the light of the new day, he felt sick and foolish. He sensed that the PCs were tittering at his expense, which was probably true for they were the greatest wits on the island, and what he had done was worth a josh. But they kept their humour private. Whatever the PLA thought about the matter, they made no complaint, for DC Bevan's only comment on seeing Forrester was: 'My God, you've been overdoing it.'

He felt vaguely ill for a few hours but perhaps as a consequence of his stupidity his anger was less intense, and no longer directed outwards. *He* was the author of his own destiny. *He* should have told Shen about Caroline and the circumstances of the baby she was to have. Had he done that in an open-hearted way, then surely she would have understood.

Forrester snatched at the handpiece of his telephone to halt its strident ring. The caller was Chinese – an educated voice: 'So sorry to disturb, Mr Forrester . . .' He became quickly alert. He had heard that voice recently. A few more words and he would be able to put a face to it. The caller gave his name: 'Is Chang San.'

Of course, Eel-eyes Chang. That was the good thing about the nick-names that the Cantonese tagged on to each other: they were as barbed and accurate as arrows. The myopic ugliness of Eel-eyes Chang came to mind.

'So what can I do for you, Mr Chang?'

'Maybe there is something I can do for you . . . Ah, I hear you have been looking for someone that you cannot find.'

Cautiously he said, 'Yes . . . there are things that I'm looking for. Do you have what I want, Mr Chang?'

'To pick the louse off the tiger's nose, Mr Forrester, one must move slowly, and with care. Such answers can only come after the Ging Si and the Incense Master burn yellow paper. So much to talk about; so many things to settle . . . The Celebrated Elegance Restaurant in Tsau Wan, do you know it?'

'I think so, yes.'

'Good seafood, Mr Forrester, I promise. Lunch today hah? A meal you will never forget.'

'One o'clock, Mr Chang.'

So even in Hong Kong's riddle of dark back streets, its looming grey tenements and boat choked waters, there was no place where a man could slide beneath the filth, and stay safe. Chang had found Eddie Woo, and was ready to give him away, if there was gain by such a transaction. And there would be gain. There was no price limit on the murderer of Kit Ling.

In a drawer in the desk there lay a picture. A green sampan bobbed on a sea that was rain-thrashed and churned, and a little girl ran for her life. He took the photograph from the drawer and looked at it for a moment, and wondered as he had so many times before, what thoughts Kit Ling had thought at the end . . . Had she thrown up her arms and let the water demons take her, or had she struggled for the surface, clinging to her breath in the certainty that Uncle would come. What torment she must have suffered. It was right that Eddie Woo should hurt as much as that.

Caroline O'Shea received the news of the termination of Only Son's romance with the fox fairy of Tai O with a pleasure that she was hard put to conceal.

'Really, Ah Fong? Are you sure?'

'Sure,' Ah Fong said from the lounge chair where she sat. The amah was also doing her best to conceal the relish of the bearer of good tidings. She wagged her finger in imitation of her angry master. 'Say Old Mother bad.'

'Oh no, Ah Fong, you weren't bad . . . You did what you thought was right.'

'Thought was right,' echoed Ah Fong.

'He'll see that soon.'

'Very cross.' Ah Fong bulged her eyes. 'Kill me maybe.'

'He won't kill you. He won't even fire you. I know him.'

'Maybe now you make him love you, ah.'

'Can't do that, Ah Fong.'

'Can. Phone him. Tell him come here. Give him good yang food; full brandy.' Ah Fong dipped into the pocket of her sam fu. 'Here, you take this – cost five dollars. Very strong, "Bring love" lucky paper.'

Caroline demurred. 'Ah Fong. No need.'

'Need.'

No question of argument, she took the tissue-thin paper from the amah.

'Paste up.'

Caroline promised that she would. Ah Fong stood and Caroline thought the amah was to depart, but not so. Ah Fong walked about the lounge with her hand to her chin. Dear God, she's checking the Feng Shui of my furniture. Caroline coughed to hide a splutter of laughter. She's going to tell me to rearrange the lounge suite. Wrong again. Ah Fong walked to the bedroom. There she stood for a while, gazing contemplatively at the bed, at the walls, at the angle of the dressing-table mirrors. A decision:

'There,' she pointed to the doorframe. 'Paste lucky paper there, very much.'

'A good place,' agreed Caroline. 'I'll do that.'

Ah Fong said something in dialect that Caroline had no hope of interpreting. But she guessed it was the equivalent of: 'You'd better, my girl!'

Then the amah left.

Caroline sprawled herself upon her long soft couch with the lucky paper in her hand and laughed until her ribs hurt. Then the telephone rang, and it was Reven Forrester – could he come and see her?

'When?'

'Now, if that's OK.'

'Dinner?'

'Yes, I'd like that.'

Caroline taped the flimsy paper charm of Heavenly Master Chang to the frame of her bedroom door.

She rushed to the bathroom and set the taps gushing. She

laid out a shoulderless dress of black silk upon the bed. She ran back to the lounge and sprang the drinks-cabinet doors – champagne – two bottles to the refrigerator. Brandy! yes there was brandy. And if he asked for *that* she was going to convert to Taoism in the morning.

He did not call for brandy, and sipped with pursed lips at the champagne. He had come, not in the pursuit of forgiveness or on the gentle breeze of love. He had come to ask if he could borrow *Dolphin*.

'*Dolphin* . . . I see . . . May I ask why?'

He nodded and chewed and looked thoughtful then finally said, 'I want it to observe a sampan that's tied up at Aberdeen. *Dolphin* is tied up at Aberdeen.'

Why not use a police boat? Intuition touched her shoulder. '*Eddie Woo?*'

'Caroline, I had lunch with a man today . . .'

'It is Eddie Woo on board, isn't it?'

'The man told me that the sampan that I've been searching for is at Aberdeen.'

'And Eddie Woo is on it.'

'I'm not sure . . . He might be.'

'Of course he is.'

'That's what I want to find out.'

'You're lying to me, I know it. I don't trust you, so why should I do it?'

'Because you told me you would hate to see Eddie Woo get away scot-free.'

'I believe you would kill him. You hate him that much don't you? You still have no evidence, but that wouldn't stop you, would it?'

Oh! That made him angry. That made his eyes flash and his cheeks burn. And she was heated too.

'It's called murder, Reven.'

'My God! Caroline, just answer me . . .'

'No. The answer is *no*. Damn you. How can you ask such a thing. You can't fight evil with evil.'

'What I want is *not* evil.' He slapped his hand down and the cutlery jumped. Then they were both up and snarling like two dogs at a fence, senseless and in full-shout with words of spite. And suddenly there was absolute quiet . . . and in the stillness, dry mouthed, they stared at each other, shaken by their savagery. He turned away from her and walked towards the door . . . Let him go.

'Reven, don't go . . . please.'

Crazy! Those were not the words her mind had shaped.

'Don't go.'

You don't need him for God's sake. Please, he didn't come to love you. He came to exploit you. He doesn't love you, babe, can't you see that?

He stood at the door with his hand resting on the half turned handle. He said tiredly: 'I have got evidence, you know.'

'Oh.'

God, look how beaten he looks, he needs your help. She walked towards him and took his hands. Strong, fine hands, how good it feels to hold his hands. The memories of these hands. She pressed his fingers to her cheek and when he stroked her she swelled with love. Is that what you truly want, then?

Oh yes.

She lifted her face to kiss him. Brusquely he touched his lips on hers, then his mouth softened and pressed. His whole warm wonderful body pressed, and it was *so* good.

'I love you, Reven.'

God help you, babe . . .

The harbour waves ran quick and white beneath the spiteful breeze. They rushed and hissed upon the hard block wall of the typhoon shelter and died there. This breakwater was made to contest the mighty seas that lift before winds of the summer monsoon and these splashes were no match for it.

Still, the man who stood at the shoulder of the wall felt the cold spray in the breeze and he shrugged himself, tight-shouldered, deep into his jacket. He could have moved to a drier, less wind-whipped place, but he did not. His position gave him an overview of the harbour before him and that was what he wanted.

Aberdeen Harbour is one of many typhoon shelters that blister Hong Kong's shores. It is home for a vast community of vessels: all sorts and sizes of junks – Hokklo suen, jung dang and gung jai, high-pooped and low-prowed, some ancient timbered, anchorbound and fenced like old men to their cots. While next in row a modern trawler chuffs its engines and strains to be away, to sea. High structures rise up from creaking hulls, bright with hung-out washing and laughing with children. There are food-boats and bars with beach umbrellas sprouting like bright mushrooms from their decks. And hovering everywhere are sampans, some motorized and breathing hard, others gliding in the tide while Mar Mar stands swaying at the stern upon her deep dipped yuloh blade.

There is noise, because the Chinese people approve of noise, and there are so many of them here. 'Packed in like the scales on a fish': that's their description of it. There is a great coming and going, but there is order.

There are water 'streets' and intersections that are kept open to allow the passage of those whose living is made at sea. The Marine Police are rarely seen, and that is the way the boat people of Aberdeen Harbour would have it. They are a mistrusting, proud lot. They squint at the outside world, and don't find much to like about it. Their trust is in the clan, and the gold that they hide deep down in the ribs of their floating homes.

Reven Forrester walked a few paces further along the breakwater and another street opened to his vision. His view of the floating township from this perspective was not ideal as a sampan might lie hidden between larger hulled vessels.

230

He searched that row, and then another, and then he saw it; the replica of the sampan of the photograph; green-hulled; its afterdeck planked up and roofed with a hooped, green oil cloth canopy. A further canopy sheltered the foredeck, and this was new. But he could clearly see the licence number, new white upon the green hull and that dissolved all doubt; this was the sampan of his search. The green sampan was tied up between a Hokklo suen and a smaller sampan. Near it, a big red-painted buoy floated. It was all just as Eel-eyes had described it. Forrester marked the position carefully, then he walked away. His route took him along the edge of the harbour; a long wandering walk, more northerly than any other direction, past boat-builders' yards and godowns, towards the Marina Club's moorings, in the throat of the harbour. Here sleek motor cruisers and high-masted yachts, as white and fresh as virgin brides, lie tied up at their moorings; haughty, stately, all turned to face their grubby, work-a-day bedfellows at the other end of the harbour, sharing the same water but not the same lineage, except for one.

Dolphin lay in the dull green water of Aberdeen Harbour; a jung dang tramp whose obscenity had been polished, but not expunged, by the coming of money. With her overbearing stern and her dumpy deck structures she rubbed shoulders with the well-born, but her accent was Pearl River and she would always be ugly.

This graceless vessel was Reven Forrester's destination. When he reached the east wall of the harbour he climbed down the tide-green slippery steps and called for a sampan water-taxi. *Dolphin* was the easiest vessel to locate in all of Aberdeen.

Ah Tsai – doer of all jobs on board *Dolphin* – appeared soon after Forrester had boarded. Sluggish in his movements, he had been dozing in the warmth of his cabin, which is exactly what Forrester would have been doing in his place. Forrester told him that Caroline had given him full usage of the junk.

'I will be sleeping on board, sometimes. Maybe we'll go to the islands. There are things I want to do. First we must change this mooring. I want to be ready to move.'

'*Tso tak.*' Ah Tsai nodded: 'Can do.'

They cleared away *Dolphin* and took the old jung dang to a mooring at the edge of the pleasure craft buoys, a mooring that positioned him within a stone's throw of the green sampan. And from that position he saw the man who was on board. It was Eddie Woo.

7

THE BITTER MOON

The winter solstice passed and the Bitter Moon arrived – the twelfth moon of the Chinese calendar. The old year was approaching its death and before its demise old debts should be reckoned with, the slate should be wiped clean. It was a time for renewal, for brightening the heart and the house.

Woo Yin-wah purchased a tin of red paint and a brush and set to work upon the old double-door entrance to the house. He painted them with the thoroughness of the fisherman at the hull of his junk, not a crack was left unsealed, and when he had done it once, and they shone like a fire engine, he did it again. Though his bones ached with the cold, he persevered. Red, he told Shen, was the colour of happiness and warmth, and his house needed that. Soon a new year would be born; let everything be shiny bright to welcome it. He had a secret reason for standing there too: to block all access to his house to the gwai lo Ging Si Forrester. While he stood there, brush in hand, his little Lui Lui was safe. For Lui Lui was badly hurt with the pain inflicted by that gwai lo and she must not suffer more. It was a dark world for her and she dragged through it at a widow's pace; slow with her housework, slow at her blackboard at the school, and slow upon the pathway home. Her eyes were ringed and her hair hung unbrushed. She wore her drabbest clothes. She did not comment upon the bright red door that gladdened the house, and said nothing about the coming New Year festivities. Though she laid in a larder of good things to feed those who would soon come to visit, she pecked like a sparrow at her own plate. She became thin and ill-looking, and Woo Yin-wah worried about her a lot.

And he had other problems to contend with. Terrible news had arrived. *Aieya!* The harbour lighter that was on lease to Flourishing Harbour Lighter Company had been attached by the bank. In ninety days, if all the money owed them had not been paid, it was to be auctioned . . . There was a leak beneath the till of the business that Grandson ran on behalf of the family, in fact all the money was gone. It was all too much for an old man to comprehend. He had not participated in business affairs for years; in his day you hid your gold beneath the bilge boards of your junk – that was your bank. What did *he* know about overdrafts and attachment orders and sales of execution? There had to be some explanation for this ruinous storm of ill-fortune that had struck, but who other than Grandson could provide it? *And where was he?* His telephone was disconnected, his office abandoned. His neighbours shrugged and shook their heads when asked his whereabouts.

But there was hope. It was almost New Year, and Grandson would certainly return home soon and account for everything. Then all would be well. There was no doubt in his mind about that. Grandson was the chicken who had swallowed the glow-worm, he would have the explanations. So hurry home, Woo Sung-king; for the burden is breaking old Grandpa's back.

Shen Woo did all tradition demanded of her at that time of mending. She cleaned the house on Shek Tsai Po Street; she washed the curtains and sponged the window panes. She dusted the furniture, seam and cushion. And on the twenty-fourth day of the bitter moon, she sugared the lips of the paper effigy of the Kitchen god, Tsao Wang, that he might report favourably on the house of Woo when he went off on his annual visit to the Jade Emperor. She didn't really care what Tsao Wang said about her, though. No path could lead back to a heart of joy.

As each day came Shen did the things she was expected to do, she toiled in the house and bribed the Kitchen god, and began to prepare the food that would be eaten at the family reunion. And when she had done all that, she climbed to her loft and sat upon her bed with her feet folded beneath her, her hands limp at her side and her face turned to the little window that gave a view clear down the praya and over the roofs of the market buildings to the creek. She watched with dull eyes, dull thoughts.

Reven Forrester lived like a stranger in her mind. Doors opened and closed and he came and went – he smiled his boy smile, he frowned his deep frown. She saw his naked smooth skin and his slim tapering body, so perfectly formed. His chest hair, gathered in a ravine of muscle, fine, not rough and matted like other gwai los', it trickled down his belly to flourish at his groin, his beautiful *yang-wu* . . . And then in uniform, so smart and clean, a Ging Si, whom all could trust . . . *Trust?* What did she know about trust? This man she loved so well on the outside; what did she know of his mind? She did not know him at all. How could she ache so much for someone she did not know at all?

She watched the pathway that led to the market with the small hope that she would see him walk it. But those days were over; the protectors of the land west of the creek now wore red stars upon their caps. There was no need for Grandpa to stand sentry with worried eyes and dripping red paintbrush at the door; her gwai lo could not pass the creek.

A week before the moon of the New Year rose, the fishing junks of Tai O began to come home. Old Woo abandoned his post at the red doors, but so that security would not lapse he pasted a pair of frowning, paper door guards there. In full regalia with halberd and sword they took up post in his place, while he went off to the teahouse of the Lotus Moon and sat where he could best observe the entrance of the bay. There he watched for the first sight of his junks.

His fleet of two sailed in on an evening tide. They came in

line down the centre channel and splashed their anchors home, and was there a lovelier sight in all of China than that? His heart brimmed over with pride. And now there were things to be done. Crew members, those who were not family, had to be paid out for the season and given their annual gratuity so that all could pay off their debts and still have money for New Year. There would be money on the junks for that, and some good fish left over for the table from the trading they had done. What excitement! The Tai O market was as busy as a basket of crabs. He waited upon the wharf for the arrival of the sampans that would carry second and third brothers Man Tat and Tim Hi.

Shen rushed about her work, knowing that she had little time. Soon there would be family seated at Grandfather's table. There were special dishes to be prepared; dainties of ginger and melon seed and litchis to be bargained from sharp-witted merchants. But who could blame her for dawdling at the flower stalls; jonquils and white narcissi, and bowers of butter-yellow peony. She hovered like a sunbird at the nectar of those sweet-scented blossoms. She bought a tub of peach shrubs, nurtured to the last bud to blossom out with good fortune on New Year's Eve. She bought a bright scroll of butterflies and phoenix, and a cardboard cut-out that read: 'May all wishes be fulfilled'. After that her purse was empty. And then she saw the orchid; just a common bamboo orchid in an earthenware pot, its thin reed-like stems bowed sadly down by flowers of white-tinged purple. She went into the stall and lifted it and looked into the yellow-throated blossoms and she thought: They are very lovely children, but they are very quiet. She longed for him then. Oh, she longed for him! Had Reven appeared at that instant, she would have run straight into his arms. But the moment passed.

So firm the jaw, Shen, and rub the mist of soft fiction from your eyes. Put down the quiet children and go home.

*

Eddie Woo had a calendar upon which the passing of every day since the Lion Rock tunnel robbery had been marked off with ballpoint pen. He performed this ritual at every daybreak; he wanted to be reminded of the passing of time. This calendar, being of inferior Western design, and not the usual page-a-day tear-off type that most Cantonese preferred, was not arranged to take into account the *true* New Year – the *lunar* New Year, which fell that year on the tenth of February – so Eddie had penned in an additional block of numbers that terminated then. For that date, and the few days which preceded it, were of vital importance to him.

Hei Shui Triad Society had decided that these hectic days of coming and going, when the streets would be thronged with people and the harbour fussed with junks, was a perfect time to exchange the 130 million Hong Kong dollars of the Lion Rock robbery for gold. How much gold they would come away with in this transaction he did not know. He *did* know how many US dollars those Hong Kong dollars were worth at the current rate of exchange: 17 million. A *one* and a *seven*, and *six noughts*. He had written that figure many times on the back of that same calendar, yet every time he considered that awesome calculation, his hand would quiver; his stomach lurch. Of course, Hei Shui would have to pay a premium in such an exchange. But even allowing for a huge 'commission' charge they should come away with gold bullion somewhere near the value of 15 million US dollars. '*Fifteen million in gold. Aieya!*' And *he* was the one who had been elected to transport it. It was hard to believe sometimes that all this was not a dream. Yet there were the calculations, blue ink upon white paper; as real as the missing finger on his right hand. This was the real thing!

Dreams! His sleep was harrowed with them: confused and seeking, ever seeking for something that he could never find. Always too late, always too slow, always in fear of great loss, he chased through the nights.

The sampan had one very small cabin, no longer than the

foam strip laid out upon its planks on which he slept. The foredeck was about three metres long, its planking tacked over with carpeting in places, which made it easy to sit on. To add to his comfort he had stretched an oil-cloth canopy over its length, and it was in this green-filtered shade that he idled the hours of daylight away; he marked off the days, and he thought about all the money he would get, and all that it would buy him. He kept himself clean with a bucket and a facecloth. He smoked cigarettes, and occasionally when invited to do so, he visited his neighbours to play mahjong, and these activities made it easier to be patient. He did have one small task. It was to ensure that the Yanmar diesel engine that lay bedded beneath the deck was kept in good order, with its batteries fully charged. He ran the engine for an hour each day to ensure that it would be ready when the big day dawned.

And it had dawned.

He was ready. That day he had eaten a breakfast of *conjee*, bought from a sampan vendor. He had stocked up with cigarettes and beer. He had drawn an artistic and obliterating design upon day 10 of his calendar, and even as he did that he felt an apprehensive flutter in his stomach. He started up the engine, which chugged into instant life. The whole sampan shook to its pulse, and while it ran he squatted upon the foredeck in the green-tinged shade. That day there would be no boredom to contend with. Excitement was building in him already, tingling in his bowels, drawing at his testicles.

He lectured himself with words of good sense: 'You have a whole day to wait, calm down, smoke a cigarette, and steady the hand.'

He smoked many cigarettes. He steadied the hand. And then his thoughts raced off ahead again. He saw himself at the tiller of his sampan as he steered it through the harbour; the flash of searchlights of a police launch as it played whitely in his eyes.

238

Senseless to think that way. What if they did shine their searchlight upon him? He would be doing nothing illegal. He would be on his way to Tai O. One of a thousand such travellers upon Hong Kong's waterways that Little New Year's night.

'*Diu lei*,' he swore. '*Diu lei le mo* on all policemen.'

But what if they *did* stop him? His licence was painted on. His permit was in order. His navigation lights worked. They had no reason to stop him . . . unless they knew about his part in the robbery. But it was certain that that was not so. If they had found out Hei Shui would have known, and they would have warned him. He was safe. And yet his apprehension surged on.

What if Grandfather's fishing junks had not as yet returned to Tai O? The whole operation depended upon the availability of one of these Toh Mong Suen. It was in the bilge of one of those junks that he would convey the bullion to the safety of distant Taipei; the easiest of voyages. But what if Grandfather's junks had *both* broken down? Such a thing had never happened before, but what if by some ill-starred, disastrous misfortune this had now occurred?

'*Diu lei*,' he swore again, and lit another cigarette.

Don't think like that; he told himself, then promptly ignored that advice. If neither junk was capable of putting to sea it would be a total disaster, and Hei Shui would not forgive. Without the junk all their careful plotting was as useful as a two-legged stool. Hei Shui would have to find another junk, and another junkmaster, and where would that leave him?

It was an endless day of thoughts such as this, and others equally distressing. His mind ached, his stomach burned with acid, and his throat was scoured raw with the smoke of a hundred cigarettes. He peered endlessly through the slits in his oil-cloth canopy at the vessels all around. But he saw nothing to alarm him. All was as it should be. In the afternoon he lay down, but could not sleep. And when darkness closed he was ready.

He started the Yanmar engine and it did not falter. He cast off the lines that bound him to his fellows and nudged his way out of his mooring. The engine noise came loud, then muted, then loud, as it echoed off dark, still hulls: *tunk tunk tunk*. He was on the move passing fishing junks and pleasure cruisers. Soon he would be rich enough to buy such a cruiser; a US-dollar millionaire. *Aieya! What face!* A motor yacht, and a penthouse apartment in Taipei, from which height and distance he would give the finger to the comrades when they came to Hong Kong . . . Girls, fragrant, soft, and so young that their pubic mounds were hairless. Ah, he would have them! Taipei was the place to be; safe behind the steel-ringed fortress of Free Taiwan. There he would live the good life and never soil his fingernails again . . . In the meantime he would do whatever work had to be done. Let it dirty him; bleed him; alienate him from family – he would do it.

The waves at the harbour mouth were short spaced and sharp. At the flashing red beacon at the breakwater tip they slapped the green sampan in a rude way and shoved at the tiller. Eddie knew that these were the children of open sea waves he would meet later, he had no fear of them. He bore down on the tiller and turned west. West to Lantau Island – west to Tai O Bay. The thought of his destination lightened his mood; fine spray wet his face, and he welcomed it. He cupped a cigarette and lit it with a match flare, and drew in smoke and the tang of sulphur and felt good enough to laugh. He eased the throttle control forward and curled his right hand hard upon the smooth worn spar of the tiller.

Tai O by midnight or a little later, that was his guess. It was hard to be accurate with the shove of this wind to reckon with, but if he arrived by midnight he would have ample time to do all that he had to do that night.

There would be no trouble with those robust old Toh Mong Suen, his doubts were absurd. Those junks had hearts as big as all of China. They would carry him anywhere.

For *Dolphin* it was a slow ride. Forrester set the Lugger diesel engines to 1,000 rpm, and at those low revs they purred like happy kittens. They were sweet-running engines which would have thrust him on to the green sampan in a minute had he asked for such a performance. He did not want that; secrecy was his ally, not haste. The moon was just a scratch, a mingy chink of light in that black sky, but he had no need of its guidance. He had radar: a nine-inch Furuno display ringed like a rifle target, each ring representing a quarter-mile range scale. *Dolphin* was centre target; he stationed the image of the sampan one range ring ahead so that one quarter-mile separated *Dolphin* from the green sampan. Mistrustful of this evidence alone, occasionally he would lift to his eyes binoculars of 6X magnification of infra-red capacity that showed the green sampan wallowing on towards the west as clearly as though it were daylight. This course, if Woo kept to it, would take him through Hong Kong's western shipping lanes and on to eastern Lantau.

Eddie Woo veered north of west soon after that – a course that would bear him towards the Ma Wan channel at the tip of eastern Lantau. Forrester kept station. His compass now gave him a bearing of 320°. He lifted the binoculars and swept the sea for his quarry. The sampan was exactly where he expected it to be, and it stayed on course.

Beyond the Ma Wan channel the sampan turned west again towards a small pair of islands called The Brothers. He wondered how far out to sea Eddie Woo would dare to take his little vessel. The water was deep here – ten fathoms – and the surface was quite furrowed. *Dolphin* rode into it without fuss but it could not have been pleasant on the sampan. When next Forrester put down the binoculars it was to find Ah Tsai at his side; a mug of cocoa was thrust at him.

'*Ho lap haak.*'

He drank it quickly, scalding his throat, wanting its warmth to spread inside him, then he held the hot porcelain tightly in his hands to gain what heat was left. In the green sampan, Eddie Woo would be having a hard time of it. He thought he should feel pleased about his enemy's discomfort; what he felt was that it would be a pity were a chance wave to turn the sampan keel-up and swallow this man. Divine justice would be served: Eddie Woo would go down choking. But it would be too premature and remote an end to this theatre. Let God not intrude tonight; let the sea go hungry and the sampan ride on to its intended harbour. He wondered if that destination could be Tai O. If Eddie Woo took a more southerly course his bearing would be towards Tai O, and even as he thought that, so the image on the radar display screen veered slightly southwards. Forrester adjusted his course to compensate for this shift – Tung Chung Bay or Tai O Bay, one or the other; those were the only logical anchorages for a vessel on that bearing. But perhaps the sampan would put in to neither port, for this whole voyage seemed to lack logic. A dark of night trip in a sampan with the sea kicked up as it was required good motivation. It could be that Eddie Woo was tied to a schedule that was fixed in time, and route, with others equally as synchronized. He thought about that: Yes that could be so; how provident if it were so.

Now the wind swept in from the starboard quarter and both vessels gained from its thrust.

Ahead lay an anchorage for 'dead' ships. Three large ocean liners were anchored there, shut down and rusting, quiet victims of the global shipping recession. The image of the sampan swam into their huge radar reflections, was absorbed, and disappeared from the screen. Forrester pressed forward on *Dolphin*'s throttles in case he lost it . . . But there it was once more, emerging clear from the overbearing images of the big ships, and still on course. He let the gap widen again.

At 10.30 p.m. they passed the Tung Chung anchorage, between the bay and the island that guards it, and the sampan did not turn in. Hugging Lantau's northern shores so closely that sometimes he vanished into the echoes of the land mass and the clutter of breaking surf, Eddie Woo ran on.

So Tai O it was.

This certainty gave Forrester the option of a change in tactics; instead of following on he could now pass the sampan and wait for it at the entrance of Tai O Bay. And that was what he did. Never letting the image of Woo's sampan slip from his radar screen, he rounded Tai O island and patrolled the entrance of the bay. The mountains here broke the north wind and in their lee the waves had no muscle. There were many junks in the bay, the radar screen was blotched with the fluorescence of their echoes. From *Dolphin*'s high poop the binoculars gave him vision right up the throat of the bay to the creek; the praya; along the praya to the houses on Shek Tsai Po Street. People were out, walking, many house lights burned. He thought he found Shen's light.

He counted thirty junks in the bay, but there were more. He could see high masts jutting beyond the roofs of the houses at the creek. There were sampans in the bay too and Hokklo suen. A PLA launch was tied up at the pier; a sailor was standing smoking on the bridge. He took *Dolphin* into the bay half a mile ahead of Woo's approaching sampan. He dropped anchor and shut down the motors and was pleased with the stillness of the place. All the junks, tethered to their anchors, rested quietly in the lisping tide; their crews, ashore, mingling in the excitement of Little New Year.

He stood up from the helmsman's seat and stretched, then took up the binoculars once more. He looked towards the harbour mouth; the sampan had not yet rounded the bluff. He looked towards the creek and then around the bay. He saw the two Toh Mong Suen long-liners that belonged to Woo Yin-wah. There could be no mistake; their white-painted licence numbers glowed neon green in his night-scope.

'Drink. Good.' It was Ah Tsai again, with more cocoa.

Forrester set down the hot mug. He said, 'I want you to launch the dinghy, Ah Tsai. Be quick.'

Ah Tsai hurried away. Within a minute there came the squeak of the launching tackle as the dinghy was swung out; the whirr of rope and the quiet splash of the small boat as it met the water. Ah Tsai rowed standing up with his oars crossed at his chest. As quick and as quiet as a water spider, he transported Forrester to the nearest Toh Mong Suen. Where the big junk's own fishing dories were launched, the deck rail was low enough to grasp. He took a handhold on the rail and hauled himself up. In a moment he was on board and at work. Being such a big vessel, his search was superficial and limited to the small, fast-travelling circle provided by his torch. Still, before he left that junk he had learned its layout well.

The sister ship seemed better kept; the deck was less strewn and where there were plastic drums, they were firmly stowed, and tangled rope did not lie like dropped spaghetti upon the deck planks.

He ducked beneath the afterdeck canopy and briefly shone his torch upon the tiller – as thick as a tree it rose from its housing above the poop. Its long boom was tethered by stout ropes that passed through a system of blocks and tackle to make it easier to manipulate the huge rudder. He followed the progress of these ropes and discovered that they led to a helmsman's cabin high on the poop deck. Here too the engine controls protruded. On the surface this junk seemed as innocent as its sister. Forrester climbed to the high helmsman's cabin and turned his binoculars once more to the harbour mouth. The green sampan had arrived. He saw that it was advancing quickly; so quickly that its engine sound became audible as he stood watching.

He had not expected its progress to be quite so rapid. The wind, of course, had favoured the sampan over the last few miles . . . and now the engine sound was swelling. A light, as white as chalk, reached over the water and paled the deckhouse of the junk, as he rushed towards the dory launching platform where he had boarded. The sampan was so close now that its engine noise was palpable. He jumped for Ah Tsai's dinghy and crouched down on the bottom boards. Ah Tsai rowed, grinning a toothy white grin in the light of the oncoming sampan.

Eddie Woo took his father's junk to sea. He took it to the dead-ship anchorage south of the Brothers Islands. A pleasant, safe and dry voyage when compared to his earlier journey. By 1 a.m. Eddie had drawn close enough to the dead-ship, *Pacific Friendship*, to throw a line to the men who stood waiting on the sea platform at the base of the accommodation ladder. The junk was hauled in and made fast there. Soon after that Eddie Woo crossed over to the *Pacific Friendship*, and climbed the accommodation ladder to the well deck.

Forrester saw all this occur in the pale green tunnel offered by his nightscope. The images were flat and cardlike and distances hard to gauge, but that did not matter. He took *Dolphin* to the lee side of the Brothers, about seven hundred metres off the starboard bow of the *Pacific Friendship* then turned to face the swell and slowed the engines. He gave the controls to Ah Tsai with the instruction: 'Keep us right here.'

Now he watched the radar screen as carefully as he watched the dead-ship. There were many vessels abroad, most of them trawlers heading for Hong Kong. Without lights he could be a danger to them.

A blip emerged from the west, very quick, too quick to be a fishing vessel. A police launch perhaps – one of the Damens from West Division on patrol.

It was not a police launch. At one kilometre he identified it as a sports cruiser. It was throwing up a full bow wave, and it was on a collision course with *Pacific Friendship*. At 100 metres it slowed, the bow settled lower and it curved towards the accommodation ladder of the dead-ship. It was a 60-footer with a fly-bridge and a jaunty stern pennant, and its port of registration was Macau.

He watched as it tied up next to the junk. Men emerged from the deckhouse carrying small, rope-handled wooden crates. More men came down the accommodation ladder carrying black metal cases, and to those cases was stencilled a design: a horseshoe, a bridle and a whip – the logo of the Royal Hong Kong Jockey Club. This was the Sha Tin money . . . And in the wooden crates? Heroin base? Macau was not a heroin route. Gold was Macau's export; five-tael bars, twenty-four to a crate – just like those crates. This was gold.

A further, a more desperate realization was that the sapping lethargy of his sickness had taken grip of him again. He had felt its insidious onset a while ago. He sensed that the first cold rigors would arrive soon, and there was nothing he could do to prevent it.

He watched until the exchange was complete, the cruiser had cast off, and the Toh Mong Suen was turning towards Tai O.

He told Ah Tsai to set course for Tai O then he went below to lie down and wait for the icy hand of fever . . . When it came he would tighten his body and clench his jaw, he would not move or make a sound. He would rob it of its power.

When it came, it came like a mistral wind and his defences were swept away contemptuously. It chilled him so completely that he gasped and his teeth rattled and his limbs convulsed. It was worse than before.

When the junk arrived at Tai O he knew it by the smoothness of their progress. He heard the engine tone lower, and a while later, the splash of the anchor. Then the engine died. The *tunk tunk tunk* of a sampan engine came loud and then soft, then faded into the night. Now all there was to hear was the swish of the bay waves and the squeak of *Dolphin*'s hull, and his own ragged, shivering breathing. He sat up slowly and could not help the groan that escaped him. It took all his strength to climb the steps to *Dolphin*'s cockpit. Ah Tsai came with hot cocoa but he felt too sick to drink it.

Woo's Toh Mong Suen was at anchor next to its sister ship. No guards or sentries were visible on it. There was no requirement for guards. The innocence of this anchored junk was the basis of its defence: as guiltless as one swallow amongst a hundred perched on a high wire. And when the junks once more migrated from the bay this one will fly too, and with it, the gold . . . A simple plan. An ingenious strategy. A light and stylish touch.

And he would crush it.

Ah Tsai held the dinghy steady as Forrester lowered himself into it. Forrester told him to row to the creek: 'To the east side of the creek.'

'Can do,' was all that the taciturn boatman said.

But Ah Tsai was not as reserved of feeling as his vocabulary gave him to be. He sculled to the creek as instructed, and then he exceeded his orders. He walked the long walk to the new police post at Forrester's side. He must have sensed the weakness in him, for Forrester did not ask for help. And though they never touched, he was constantly aware of the strength of arm of the boatman.

He reached the police post; he sat down in a chair and his limbs felt so beaten that he thought he would never rise up from that place again. Inspector Potter came, rubbing the sleep from his eyes, and Forrester told him what he had come to tell him: he gave him the registration number of the Macau sports cruiser with the fly-bridge and the jaunty bow flag. He told Potter that upon that vessel would be found the money from the Lion Rock robbery . . . Stupid Potter kept floating from his vision, in a most elusive and dismaying way, so he had to repeat everything that he had said. But he persevered with the man until he was sure that he had grasped it all. Then he stood up to leave; he heard himself sigh, 'Oh God,' and his legs gave way beneath him.

Ah Fong's most precious photograph had been taken while standing with her back towards the camera, with her head tilted in smiling profile. But it was not this happy image of herself that made the picture so memorable. Upon her back was slung a baby carrier embroidered with the inscription: May you have peace and long duration. Slung within that carrier, one fat cheek pressed against her spine, fat lips wide open in contented sleep, was the baby, Reven Forrester. It was the image of that infant that made the faded old picture so dear to her. It was in a carved peachwood frame, and its place was upon the wall of her bedroom, where she saw it whenever she woke up.

Peace and long duration. Those perfect dual states had always remained her wish for Only Son. And it had seemed until recently that these conditions would be his. Now *this*; this wickedness; this demon fox woman who had arrived to torture him and suck his life essence away. He was growing thinner and paler with every day that passed. He hardly ate, no matter how fine a dish she set before him, he seldom slept in his bed, and wandered, who knew where, in the night. He watched Old Mother with eyes deep with hostility and resentment. What could she do?

She visited the Little People Hitters of Kowloon and gave them Shen Woo's birthdate, and paid those viperous old women to 'burn' the fox fairy of Tai O. This they did, they wrote out 'dark' spells and set them alight and hammered the burning ashes to powder. They cursed the Tai O fairy with a thousand curses . . . and achieved nothing. It was true that Shen Woo had been hurt by their efforts; she no longer walked in beauty, as she had. She too looked sick, and she kept to her house. But these things had not improved the situation. What did it help if Shen Woo was ailing? Her weakness would make her all the more determined to sustain her health with the essence of Only Son.

It was clear to her that the fight for the life of Only Son had reached a crucial point.

This thought was confirmed that very morning by Station Sergeant Wong who phoned from Tai O to tell her that the Ging Si, her son, was at the new Police Station. He had collapsed while talking to Mr Potter and was at that moment prone upon the bed in the living quarters of that same inspector. A doctor had been summoned.

'Useless.' Ah Fong spat. 'This is what you must do. You must lock the door to his room, you must close all the windows. You must stand guard there. No one must pass you before I arrive, understood?'

'The doctor?'

'No *woman* must pass you, understood?'

Wong sounded surprised at her vehemence. He agreed, then hung up.

Ah Fong dropped the receiver upon its cradle. Her hands were trembling; she lifted them, palms upwards, and gazed at them, then drew her fingers in until the knuckles were all that were presented; tight-cudgelled, sharp little knuckles. With forearms tensed she raised these angry fists. She bared her teeth as though to scream, but no screams came. There were no words in her mind, just a thought – an image. It was of hated Shen Woo. And she knew then that it was up to her, and her alone, to save Only Son from the fox fairy of Tai O. She found herself in the kitchen, before the dresser where the big, sharp, bone-handled carving knife was kept. She opened the drawer and took it and tried to find a hiding place for it in the pockets of her black trouser-suit, but, of course, it would not fit. No matter how she tried to secrete it, the knife protruded – the blade was as long as her forearm. She went to the bathroom and took from the medicine chest there a role of surgical tape. She stood before the mirror and opened her jacket until her bare, bony chest was exposed. She peeled off some tape and with it she strapped the blade to her skin. When the buttons were done up the knife could not be seen.

Ah Fong sighed and her shoulders sagged and the stiffness went from her arms. But her will was unbending. She knew what had to be done to save Only Son, and she would do it.

From the bathroom to her bedroom, where the Almanac of T'ung Shu hung on the bedpost. A hundred talismans and charms lay invested within its pages. She copied, with red ink upon a sheet of yellow paper, the charm that was required for Only Son's state.

Now she was ready. A storm wind was coming to Tai O. She carefully locked the house then walked down to the village.

It was New Year's Eve; the day the north star descends to earth to call all families together so that all wrongs may be forgiven, and buried. Thus the roads were full of travellers and every seat upon the Tai O bus was taken. Ah Fong did not mind standing. Her thoughts were so concentrated on her task that she took no heed of her aching ankles. The lumbering, slow-turning wheels fairly flew her to Tai O.

Tai O was dressed in festive garb. The houses shone, wall, window and door. Flag-decked Mun Sun gods and bared-teeth tigers were pasted up, frowning, striking terror at all evil. The market was thronged with customers and a frenzy of trading was going on. With quick pressed dollar and shouted voice the keenest buyers shouldered through.

Those with little money hung back. When time ran out in the early afternoon and evening the bargain hunters would close in to chase down the prices to rock bottom, then scoop the shelves bare. Steel shutters would scrape closed, locks would click, and the merchants in a sweaty sheen would lie back and say: '*That* was a day to remember.'

Ah Fong was as quick as anyone. She bought a cicada husk tea called shan tuei, which would damp down the worst fever, and a faggot of best sandalwood incense sticks. Then she walked to the police post where Station Sergeant Wong was waiting to take her to Only Son.

How sick he was; aflame and washed with sweat. How her heart cried when she saw his pain. Straight away she set about setting a kettle to boil upon the hot plate there.

'The doctor has been,' Wong said. 'He has advised hospital.'

'It will do no good.'

She knew that the remedy for this consuming fever could not be provided by medicine. Even her own best medications were but palliative, and she expected no more from them than that. The defeat of the fox woman of Tai O was the cure, the only cure. Let Old Mother have the strength and spirit to do what must be done to bring this demon down.

The gwai lo called Potter came in while Ah Fong was steeping the shan tuei. He sniffed the air and rolled his eyes and said, 'Jesus.' He looked inquisitively towards Ah Fong.

'The Ging Si's amah,' Wong explained.

'*Ah.*' Potter went to the side of the bed. He spoke in a tone that was calculated to give cheer:

'How are you, *sir*?'

The Ging Si cast Potter a small nod.

'I came to tell you, you were spot-on, sir. The Macau cruiser had the money on board all right; all of it. The Macau Marine Police are holding it . . . Bloody *fantastic*, sir . . .

251

Well, I just couldn't wait to tell you that, sir. The DC wanted you to know.'

'Good.'

The word came without movement of the lips. Potter turned towards Wong and Ah Fong.

'Are you with *her*, Wong? Then will you tell her that she's welcome. Tell her not to worry, we've spoken to the Ging Si's house doctor and everything's organized. We've requisitioned a patrol launch to take him to Hong Kong, and it's on its way. Will you tell her that, Wong? You'd do it better than I could.' Potter smiled at Ah Fong while Wong translated these words of comfort.

'Won't help.' She shook her head – a gesture as sharp as her words. With whispered soothing sounds she mopped at the brow of Only Son. She could feel the heat of his fever rising through the damp towel. Potter's eyes were perplexed, but he kept his smile. Again he said, 'Jesus.' Then he walked away.

Wong left soon after that. Ah Fong was glad to be alone, to get along with the task in hand. She sponged Only Son and dried his chest and face. His dark blue eyes were bright with fever and his hair was tangled wet. But even in his sickness he was beautiful, just a boy, her boy. How many times had she not fought the demons of sickness back from his bed? How many nights had she not sat ready in the shadows to spring to his defence?

When the medicine was drawn and cool enough to drink she held it to his lips until he'd swallowed it all. Then she burned the yellow paper charm and as ashes formed she stirred them into his drinking water. Now she had done all that she could do here. She bent close to his ear and whispered, 'I am going now.'

'Thank you for coming, Old Mother.'

'You will be better now.'

He nodded. 'No more to be said.'

Oh, but there was so much more that *should* be said . . .

When this day is over don't think wrong thoughts of Old Mother. It is written in the Book of Rites that my method is right and honourable. Though I have failed you, I will not fail you now. But what was the use in saying these things? One distant day he would understand with a greater clarity than any words could provide why Old Mother had done what she had done.

She held his brow for a moment in the hope that she might sense some small drop in temperature. But the fever burned on. There was chaos in his body, it was drained, and the touch of a loving hand would not restore order. Ah Fong crept away.

It was midday and the streets were still thronged. Quick feet and sharp elbows gained Ah Fong a place upon the pull-ferry at the creek. Shek Tsai Po Street carried fewer people, so it did not take her long to reach the house of Woo Yin-wah; to advance upon the fresh, red-painted door. There she stopped. There her fear bound her motionless; squeezed her so hard that for a while she could hardly breathe. She raised her arm and knuckled the door.

No one came . . . She rapped again. Her hands, she noticed, were trembling, giving away her secret. She sank them into the pockets of her jacket, but her pockets were high and her elbows thrust out inelegantly like a dressed chicken. Be still, she commanded her hands, then brought them up to rap upon the door again.

But before she could knock, the door opened and a man in vest and shorts with the deep tan of a fisherman stood there enquiringly. She asked for Shen Woo.

Shen Woo was not at home. That was what the fisherman told her. She had gone with Elder Brother to the Toh Mong Suen anchored, there, in the bay. They had gone to paste up New Year mottoes. They should return soon. Auntie was welcome to wait for her at the house.

Ah Fong could not wait, not even for a short while – debts had to be paid, she said. Would he point out the junk upon which she might be found? The fisherman did so.

253

There were two such junks that belonged to Woo Yin-wah, but it was clear which one they had boarded. A green sampan rode at its hull.

Ah Fong hired a water-taxi to take her into the bay, a leaky little yuloh manned by a Hokklo woman with broad straw hat and skin that was as crinkled as old bark. She chatted like a canary on a perch as she worked the yuloh blade, but Ah Fong's throat was too tight for conversation. And now they were closer; close enough to see coiled ropes and buckets, and rigging lines; close enough to see the washing strung out, even the clothes pegs on the line. Green slimed at the waterline where a sampan was tied, the junk rose up plank by plank to a stern that towered over the oncoming yuloh. How would she board it?

The Hokklo woman knew how. She drew her yuloh against the sampan and held it there with her hands. From the yuloh to the sampan then to the junk – easy that way. Ah Fong had been a water woman in her childhood so the prance of the yuloh against the sampan did not spill her, she crossed the divide and the yuloh pulled away. Suddenly alone there her fear returned, her mind pounded and her vision whirled and the thought of calling the yuloh back came strongly.

She spoke to her fear. She said: Oh, you are alone, but no need for more than one to see this done. You have the will, Ah Fong, and your fear is only that you might fail. Be brave, Old Mother. Be strong. Now lift yourself and do it.

The sampan, tied as it was, bobbed awkwardly on the slap and jog of the bay waves. Perhaps it was this motion that was making her so giddy. Her heart was a hammer beating at her breast as though it would burst free. She leaned her body hard down upon the stern rope of the sampan and weighted it until it swung its high transom close to the deck of the junk. Then she scrambled onto the junk.

Shen Woo was at the main mast, a man was standing with her, joking, laughing, as she tacked to the wood a 'Bring Luck' inscription. It read: May this junk bring surpassing advantage. They became aware of Ah Fong's presence simultaneously. Both frowned their eyebrows in surprise. Now Ah Fong was very confused. For here were the two people whom she had thought were one . . . Of course! She was being tricked by the magic of the fox fairy, that was it. No matter if she multiplied herself a hundred times the demon would not stop her.

'Ah Fong?' Shen said. 'What are you doing here?'

'You know this old woman?' said the other. 'I don't want her here. How did you get here, old woman? You must go at once. At *once*!'

He stepped forward and stretched out his arms as though to herd her like a cow that had wandered offendingly off course. She bypassed him. She rushed towards the fox woman. A great calm came upon her over those few paces. Her heart beat evenly and her mind was clear. She felt beneath her jacket where the knife was taped and the good bone handle that she knew so well reached for her closing fingers and settled in her grasp. She tore the blade from her chest and held it out. The fox woman's eyes grew, then she screamed – a shrill, shrill scream that shattered upon Ah Fong. It stopped her for a moment.

Strong hands, rough upon her shoulders and neck, gripped her, staggered her off-balance. The harsh weight of the man fell upon her. She crumpled beneath it and they crashed down together. She could not breathe, she was crushed beneath him. Must not stop her.

He did not stop her. He gasped, deeply, and rolled off her. The knife blade was red and a fountain of blood sprang from his groin.

The screams of the fox woman roared on. Ah Fong raised herself to her knees. She was so hurt and broken that she could go no further. No matter, she was ready to do what she had come to do. With careful control she laid the knife edge upon her own wrist. Her eyes fixed on the fox woman, one arm stretched out, the blade poised, resting lightly where the blue veins rose . . . Be brave, Old Mother. A grim and relentless pressure and the blade sliced in. She felt it burn and saw the blood jet, and from a place deep in her body a slow spreading numbness crept that she hoped was death.

It was death. And as it came it told her that she had done right. Your blood, Old Mother, has stained this woman with a mark that will not wash away – the demon is exposed and disgraced.

And Only Son, will he be freed by it?

He will be free, said Death.

'Ah Fong is dead.'

Reven Forrester dreamed that a hot sun was burning down upon him; a white fireball that seared through skin and skull into his brain. He dreamed there was a bird flying high above him, a single bird, hovering, as though with its wings it could shield him from the furnace above. It died at its task. With folded wings it plunged to earth . . .

'Ah Fong is dead.'

Station Sergeant Wong spoke those words in the flat, ungrieving, impassive way that the Cantonese use to mask their horror of death.

'Ah Fong is dead.'

At last the waking man understood what was being said to him. He frowned at Wong in a disbelieving way. Wong's features stayed inert; his tone apathetic: 'She killed herself on a junk in the bay. She went out there alone and slashed her wrist.'

'My God.'

'Yes.'

'I don't believe it. She was here . . . a moment ago.' Forrester looked at the incense sticks that Ah Fong had lit. None of them still smouldered. 'When?'

'She must have gone straight from here to the junk. We don't know how she reached it.'

'Junk?'

'A Toh Mong Suen. It belongs to a man called Woo Yin-wah.'

'Woo Yin-wah?'

Forrester knew he was echoing Wong but he could not help it. His mind was clogged and sluggish – confronting a towering cliff of grief and dismay that showed no handhold. He was fumbling for meaning, pinning himself to single words that seemed to offer comprehension of this tragedy.

'How do you know this?'

'Old Woo Yin-wah came in to make the report with his granddaughter. We had to send him to the People's Armed Police, because the junk is anchored in their waters. It's not our case.'

'Ah Shen was here?'

'I forgot that you knew her, sir,' Wong lied politely.

'Who was on the junk at the time? Who witnessed the suicide?'

'The old man and his granddaughter were both there. Several other fishermen from neighbouring junks saw the incident too. We've no reason to disbelieve their statement, sir.'

'She did it in front of Shen, didn't she? That's what happened, isn't it, Wong?'

'I believe that's how it was reported.'

Forrester turned his face away from Wong . . . Stupid, stupid Ah Fong. Revenge had moved her to do this ghastly thing; to commit *ji saat*. Ah Fong had died but the wound of it was upon Shen and it would never heal, it would just deepen. Ah Fong was dead and Shen would suffer of an accusation that could never be refuted. For in spirit Ah Fong's power was a hundred times greater than in life. Only the Chinese could perpetrate such everlasting agony.

Wong said, 'Bad thing, Ging Si.'

How would Shen take it? Bewilderment and misery; she would cry for Ah Fong. She would cry for the disgrace that had come upon herself and her family, and her grief would not end there. She would cry for the man who was bereaved of his mother. Sweet, loving Shen, who deserved all that was good, had been served the devil's due. He longed to go to her and tell her that Ah Fong had done wrong. Her act had been an aberration, and no one could bear the blame for it. But Shen had cut herself off from him, so that was not possible. He knew she would not let him near her.

'I'm getting up,' he said. 'I've lain here long enough.'

Firstly he sat up. The room lifted in a vertiginous spin but he firmed his elbows so that they would not give in and lifted his legs from the mattress, one at a time, and lowered them to the floor. His balance held.

Dr Yuen had said that these episodes would be transient. This one was not so transient. He had also warned that they would get more acute if he did not have treatment. He had not had treatment. Yet, he was stronger than he had been earlier; strong enough to think that he could make his way, unaided, to the creek. Wong came forward to help him.

'I'm all right now.' He shrugged off the proffered arm. 'There are some things I must do. I'm going now.'

'The launch will be here any minute now.'

'What launch?'

'Mr Potter called for a launch to take you to Hong Kong, to hospital, sir.'

'I am not going on the launch to Hong Kong, Sergeant. I am certainly not going to hospital. Do I look like I should be in hospital? . . . No I don't, so would you thank Mr Potter for his trouble. As I said, I have things to do.'

It was a long hard road to the creek. He stopped to rest on several occasions. He leaned upon post and wall, and crept on like an old man in the late-afternoon sun. If the villagers noticed his weakness, they showed no sympathy. He was jostled in the crowds near the creek and nearly lost his balance. He came to the wharf and looked out into the bay and saw that *Dolphin* was still riding at anchor there. Ever patient, Ah Tsai was waiting at the wharf, squatting at the bollards, playing tai sui dominoes with some boatmen; all evidence of gambling was swept away by the time Forrester arrived. Just a grinning knot of fishermen having a smoke. Ah Tsai stood up.

'*Hai a.*' He was ready. He led the way to the dinghy. 'Cold wind blowing.'

'The Toh Mong Suen,' said Forrester. 'That one.'

'Can do,' said Ah Tsai. He crossed the oars, he stood at the rowlocks, he hauled smooth and strong, and the dinghy danced out, quick, slow, quick, to the pull of the blades.

Cold wind blowing. Cold right through, Reven Forrester swayed to the glide of the dinghy. The sun was low and blotted by grey cloud; it gilded the choppy bay waves but gave no heat. Miserable in spirit and weak, he watched the Toh Mong Suen grow larger. He thought about many things.

He was sure he would find Eddie Woo upon the junk. There was every reason for him to be there. His business with Eddie was intensely private so he hoped he would be alone. But if he was not, he and Eddie would find privacy on that big junk; both of them would want it. He thought that the investigating officer of the PAP would have left the junk by now. Had he not, there might be complications.

The thought of arming himself occurred as they sculled past *Dolphin*. A shotgun lay in her lockers.

No shotgun. For Shen's sake he would not bring more violence to the Toh Mong Suen. He had a message for Eddie Woo that would shock him as much as the blast of a shotgun, and would kill him in the silence of a whisper – how much more preferable. This story must end today with no further hurt or harm to anyone but Eddie Woo.

The dinghy skipped on, and the spray from Ah Tsai's blades rose to speckle him coldly.

Eddie Woo was alone. He lay prone upon a foam-rubber mattress in the rearmost cabin of the junk. The mattress was thick and his frame sank into it sweetly. His head rested on a pillow that was decorated with a dragon and a gaudy sunset, and if he trailed his fingers to the floor the controls of a portable radio lay within reach. Funky music filled the cabin. If he turned his head he could see a gold-framed picture of a many-pillared temple, a bridge leading to it across a marsh, past trees with pronged black branches. Sellotaped to the glass, positioned so that her feet appeared to be on the bridge, a cut-out of a JAL air hostess paraded. She was proportionately too large. A tinfoil fish, iridescent blue, was stuck to the waters of the marsh. It too was a monster, the whole effect was quite grotesque, but there was nothing else to look at besides some oddments of old Man Tat's winter clothing, and the thick, deep-varnished wooden beams and planks of the inside hull.

There was a porthole in the cabin; an oval aperture cut through the stern planks that provided a view of the bay right up to the creek. But to reach the porthole he had to raise himself from the mattress to a kneeling position. He had done that once and suffered for it – a pain more raw than Ah Fong's knife thrust had jerked up inside him and the bandage that Shen had bound him into, thigh and hip, had seeped red. So he lay still, he looked at Man Tat's gaudy temple picture, he smoked cigarettes, and he thought about luck, and his transient grip upon it. It came to him but it seemed he could never hold it, nor did it leave him in a gradual way. It fell from him like the pearls of a severed necklace. This time it had taken one crazy old woman and a wrongly angled knife blade to do it. *Aieya!* At a time when he needed all his strength and agility, he was flat on his back with a seeping, throbbing wound in him that seared him like a live coal.

Then to learn that Sister Shen had been seeing his deadly enemy, Reven Forrester. What god had he insulted; what evil star had cursed him with such misfortune? *And* the amah with the long knife was Forrester's amah! Let all five noxious animals fall on that gwai lo egg of turtle and his amah. His only luck had been that the PAP had not searched the junk – *ji saat* was a common way to die. They had joked about it, and his wound. 'How lucky she missed your litchis; Ha! Ha! Ha!' . . . What did those fools know about luck!

'*Ah! Aieya!*' Sudden pain wrenched his breath away. It did not seem to matter how remote a part of his anatomy he moved, a forearm, a finger, a cord of pain connected them to his wound. That hellhag, that she-demon.

She had come to kill herself at the feet of Younger Sister because of some supposed wrong, and *he* had impaled himself on her knife. Millions in gold bullion in the bilge beneath him; the wealth of a dynasty which he would share once he had conveyed it to Taiwan. And how was he now to sail this junk to Taiwan?

Hei Shui were benevolent in success and intolerant of failure, and noble purpose did not come into it. They had acknowledged the genius of his strategy, and burned with him the yellow paper of fellowship. But as large as their belief in him had been, frustrated expectation would kill it in a breath. From a smile to an unforgiving scowl – it needed only a small frustration to cause it . . . So he *had* to sail this junk to Taiwan, soon, or it would be the end of him. His life blood leaked from him at every small move; how in hell was he to do it? *Diu lei* on this wound; he had never known such a wound.

Another cigarette. Slowly, he reached for the packet at his side, set a cigarette between his lips and lit it. He sucked in smoothly, deeply, then let the smoke chimney from mouth and nose, and as the thick grey curtain rose, a man's bulk came to fill the cabin door. He saw who it was and yet for a moment he could not accept it, he just gaped. Belief came with a jolt and he moved to defend himself. In a shout of pain, he rose to a seated position; he lifted up his arms, his fingers wide spread. But no attack came.

The gwai lo's eyes were hollow-rimmed, hard and darting,

261

but he made no move of aggression. His shirt was wet and clung to his body, as though he'd walked through rain. His eyes rested on the wide bandage and puzzled at it for a moment. Then he said:

'I've come to talk to you, Woo Sung-king.'

He shrugged past the small space of the cabin door and came into the cabin. 'Sit still and listen,' he said. He reached out and switched off the radio. In the quietness he spoke in a tired, dispirited way. His tone was flat, yet his message struck out as if each word was a fist.

'You killed someone very dear to me,' he said, 'a child. Her name was Kit Ling. She was so innocent and full of love and you raped her, and then you killed her. I despise you for that. How you could have done what you did is beyond my understanding. She was so good, and you destroyed her with your foulness. And so here I am, Eddie, to pay you out.'

Unfair! he wanted to shout, unfair. She was of no consequence, a rag of a child, a refugee. Her death was an accident. If punishment was what Forrester wanted then surely he had achieved that in the destruction of his club, and the beating he had taken. He lifted his right hand with the missing middle finger. *There* was his punishment; you did that to me. Does that not satisfy? . . . It did not satisfy.

'Death would be sufficient punishment,' the gwai lo said. 'Yes, that is how much I hate you. I could do it, Eddie, and I would not feel a thing. But why should I kill you when your suffering is so incomplete? I believe in retribution, and you have not paid yet. One finger – do you think that one finger is worth a life?

'I've been watching you for a long time, Eddie Woo. I was close to you at Aberdeen, I followed you to Tai O. And all that time I was thinking, wondering: what would be the ideal punishment? I was watching you last night when you went out to the dead-ship anchorage; when you boarded the *Pacific Friendship*. And when I saw the cruiser from Macau.

I knew straight away what was happening, and I saw the perfect punishment.'

'What do you want?'

The question was pinned to the bleak hope that something could be saved from this mess; that this talk of deathly punishment was exaggerated. But the eyes of the gwai lo shone in a fevered, frightening way and there was no mercy in them.

'I know what happened on the *Pacific Friendship*,' Forrester said. 'I know about the gold hidden on this junk.'

Eddie did not doubt it. The gwai lo had an ascendancy that was numbing. His security had been a sham. His movements, every step, had been observed as an insect crossing a wide white wall.

'I know about the Lion Rock robbery. I know about all your crimes, Eddie. I want you to realize that these offences don't worry me at all, they were little crimes and I'm glad you committed them. Because of those crimes you are where you are now . . . We've picked up the Macau triads, Eddie, and all the money. Of course, they're wondering which dirty little "twenty-five" boy gave them away.'

Hopeless to argue through this euphoria of vengeance. There was no plea that would touch this man; no bargain to be struck. Helpless, helpless.

'You burned the yellow paper and joined hands with Hei Shui Triad Society to commit the Lion Rock robbery. That is like sleeping in a snake pit, Eddie; one wrong move and the fangs sink in. I made that move for you . . . Just a whisper on the breeze that you were the one who gave away the Macau triads.'

'They'll kill me.'

'Yes, I know. It's the perfect punishment. It's very just.'

'You're a policeman. How could you do this?'

'Eddie, I did it because you killed little Kit Ling and there was no other way of punishing you.'

'It wasn't *me*. She tried to run away and she drowned.'

263

'Yes, and you too may try to escape. How you will die, I don't know. Hei Shui or the Macau triads will catch you in the end, though. The death for "twenty-five" boys is ghastly, I believe. Still, it couldn't possibly be worse than Kit Ling's death.'

'You'll let me go?'

'Yes.'

'I'm wounded. I'm in agony. I bleed if I move . . . look.'

He showed the bandage; the seeping red blotch at his groin. 'Your amah stabbed me. She nearly killed me. What more do you want? I can't move.'

'Kit Ling was wounded,' he said. 'You raped her. She was in agony.'

'I *can't* run.'

'Then they'll kill you here, Eddie.'

Eddie lifted himself to a kneeling position. He flinched and gasped at the pain that movement brought. A trickle of blood ran down his thigh on to the quilt. 'Look.'

Forrester looked. He said impassively, 'It's a bad wound.'

'I'm sorry that Kit Ling drowned. I never meant that to happen.'

'Eddie, your time is running out.'

'*Bastard*, Forrester! *Fuck* you! *Fuck* you!'

'Take some gold. Take all that you can carry.'

'That would make it worse for me with Hei Shui.'

'Yes.'

'You've killed me. You know that.'

'Yes . . . Go get your gold, Eddie. Or leave it. But run now, Eddie, you haven't any more time.'

Eddie had never known such bitterness, and anger and helplessness and pain. 'Bastard,' he cried. 'Bastard!'

'Go,' said Forrester. 'Take the green sampan and run.'

He left a blood spoor. In drips and blotches of moist bright red it led from the cabin into the low dark passageway that served the sleeping quarters and from there to the deck. From the deck to the engine-room hatch, which was open. It marked the rusted, silver-painted ladder that led down into that dark place, and the gwai lo followed on.

There was a neon fixture hanging from the beams. He worked the switch. It flickered, then lit. It washed its milk-white light into the corners of that oil-stained room. He walked on, and so did the gwai lo.

There were two engines, grey painted Perkins 105s mounted upon wide metal girders and bolted to the bottom timbers. Greasy yellow cooling tanks were fixed above them and pipes and wires trailed everywhere. The flooring was of grease-stained metal plate that ran right around the engines.

He kneeled there and blood trickled freely past his knee to puddle on the metal plate. Where the plate met the hull there was a gap through which he hooked his fingers. He knew it would be a hard pull. He took a deep breath and hauled. Pain, as keen and quick as lightning, flashed from his groin right through his abdomen. He gasped and hauled again, and the floor came up . . . There was the gold, glinting, rich butter-yellow brickettes, no larger than choco-late bars, hundreds of them in that space. He lifted a single bar and Forrester came forward and said, 'Aah.'

The strain had done something terrible to the wound. He felt torn in half and blood like hot urine was streaming down his thigh. He pressed his hand to the wound and when he took it away it was thick red from palm to fingertips. His thigh was red, the floor plate was red to its edges.

'*Diu lei*. Can't run. Can't you see? Look; there's my blood. I'm finished, can't you see?'

'Take,' said the man. 'Run.'

He could not do it. He was dying. The Hei Shui triads held no fear for him now, he did not care what happened now. He looked up at his tormentor and hated him with his eyes. He saw the pitiless spite that drove this man and that sent rage burning through in him too – hate and rage enough to set him on his feet. Vertigo came, flickering blue flame rimmed his vision and he knew he would fail soon. He commanded the hand that was heavy with the gold bar and it hit out in a wide angry arc towards the hated face. He thought he would miss, but he did not miss.

At dusk the winter wind from the steppes of central Asia died quietly and a hush of anticipation settled on sky and mountain, and man. The Year of the Cock was close to an end. The Year of the Dog was at hand.

In Tai O the streets were quietening. The bay water, as smooth as silk, was speckled with gulls that rose from the darkening tapestry in ones and twos, crying *kraai kraai*, as they went away to roost. The still, anchored junks rode on their reflections like slippers placed sole to sole.

On the big junk of Woo Yin-wah the family had gathered, but sadly no feast was spread out there to eat. They moved slowly, dully, they spoke quietly, as people do when massive events have struck them, and left them stunned. Prosperity and adversity had come to amaze them; to caress them kindly with the palm, and slap them cruelly with the back hand, all in one action.

Two men lay in the sleeping berths, unconscious: Woo Sung-king and the gwai lo Ging Si. They had fought, *aieya!* The engine-room was red with evidence of their war.

The engine-room bottom boards were tiled with gold; with every floor plate that was lifted, more gold! Glinting, yellow slabs of solid gold. Yes, it was solid – Man Tat had tested it with a hacksaw. He had sawn a bar into quarters and had seen that it was pure gold right through . . . Magic – that was Man Tat's whisper. How else could one explain the conversion of dirty bilge scrapings into the treasure of an emperor? Man Tat pocketed the mutilated gold bar. He had no idea how much those few hacked-up gold pieces were worth, but he intended to find out before the last shops closed.

Woo Yin-wah hardly dared to think of the origin of the

bullion. That such a hoard was aboard *his* Toh Mong Suen was as stunning as a punch to the head. So much money, *so* much money; not even cleverest Grandson could have multiplied the family fortune thus . . . *could* he? One thing was certain: Grandson was the protector of this massive hoard. And so it was a matter of honour that *they* protect it now. The gwai lo had tried to plunder it; Grandson in his weakened, wounded state had defended it with all his strength and almost died in the attempt. But such a lot of money gave men the appetite of wolves, and it would not end there. This gwai lo was a powerful man. Once free, he would summon more wolves to his cause. He was the deadly enemy of their house: that was what Grandfather Woo told Shen.

Shen refused to respond. She bathed and bandaged both gwai lo and Brother and administered healing herbs.

Woo pleaded: 'Look at Elder Brother. The gwai lo did that to him with his amah, and when she failed he came himself. He lied to you, that gwai lo. He used you to get to your brother . . . Listen to me, Lui Lui. That man has no right to the care that you give him. He tried to kill your brother and take his gold.'

She did not listen.

'He's a bad one, that man. He's a thief.'

She did not believe him.

'Care for your brother, not for his enemy.'

She did not obey him.

What could he do? His mind was dull and clouded, yet he was certain of one thing; the very existence of his family was at stake, and it was up to him to safeguard it. If ever before in his life he had needed good counsel, he needed it a hundredfold now.

He went to the port cabin wherein the shrine of Tin Hau, the Queen of Heaven and saviour of those at peril on the sea, was set upon the wall. But his communication with her was brief. Next to her bright red god-box a wooden locker was fastened. It was towards those doors that he reached.

With reverence of body and mind, he stood before the sanctuary of his respected ancestors. For here was the wisdom of three generations past – here stood the ancestral tablets. Carved wooden tablets, each marked with the name of its inhabitant spirit; each painted with the symbol of heaven and earth, and given eyes to see and ears with which to hear, and each tablet was alive, acutely alive . . . He did 'three kneelings and nine knockings'. Then humbly he asked for right guidance in this hour of crisis:

'Forefathers of our house, it is Woo Yin-wah.
Humbly I ask for your protection.
All that we own is your gift.
All that we know is your knowledge imparted:
Of the laws of life, and of death
And of things permissible and forbidden;
Of ways of making the sting of life less painful
Than Nature's way.
And sadness and joy and the error of selfishness;
Of wisdom and kindness and the need to sacrifice
To you, the founders of this house.
I am confused by the things that have happened
And the choices I must make . . .'

He remained in that cabin for a long time. When he emerged it was to a black sky. But his mind was now clear. He was at one with heart and strength and he knew what had to be done.

He called his family together on the deck of the Toh Mong Suen. He told them of his consultation with the ancestors and of the conclusions. Grandson and heir, Woo Sung-king was in mortal danger as long as he remained in Hong Kong, and he must be transported from there at once. He, Woo Yin-wah, would sail on the tide of the new moon, and it was up to each one of them to decide whether they would remain or go with him; each one of them except for Shen:

'You must attend to Elder Brother, Shen. You must come with us.'

'And the gwai lo, the Ging Si?'

'Of course,' said Grandfather, 'he must be put ashore at once.'

'Wrong to do that,' said Shen Woo.

'*Wah!* You argue!'

'No,' she said flatly. 'Can't leave him now.'

'He will go ashore, and you will stay on board. That is my decision!'

'No.'

Now Woo Yin-wah was really perplexed. Never before had he faced such an open and outright revolt by a *woman* of his family. He could not permit such outrageous disrespect. He would put her in her place. He slapped his hand hard down on the timber of the deck housing. He shouted, 'You *will* obey me. *Hm!*'

Quietly she said, 'I will come with you. I will attend to Elder Brother. But the Ging Si must come too . . . Think, Grandfather; remember what you said earlier. Should the Ging Si be set free if he *is* the deadly enemy of Elder Brother? Would it not be wiser . . .'

Old Woo looked tiredly at his granddaughter, and listened, and heard the resolve in her voice and saw the bright spirit of her eyes and he knew he was not a match for her. He took the opportunity to save face that she had offered.

'There might be truth in what you say,' he grumbled. 'But first consideration must go to Elder Brother.'

'No more to be said.' Shen bowed.

'A wise decision, Woo Yin-wah,' commended the others.

'*Hm!*' gruffed Grandfather Woo. 'We are going to a good place, a place of safety. South.' He pointed vaguely. 'We are going south.'

To the distant green islands to the south. To the flat blue-green seas to the south.

'To a place of peace.'

'Have you heard the news? *Wah!* Amazing news.'

Man Tat's quick scamper from poverty to wealth; his prodigal expenditure of pieces of cut gold in the market of Tai O produced a thunderclap rumour that rumbled through street and kitchen and thudded out into the bay . . . One fish scale here, one claw there – there was not a merchant in the whole village who did not have his bit to add to the tale of the fabulous wealth of Woo Yin-wah. It gave new meaning to the New Year greeting, *Kung Hey Fat Choy!* Congratulations, may you get rich quickly!

And where had all that gold come from? Hah?

Well, as many villagers as there were in Tai O were as many as the theories that abounded. Gambling gains! How easy it would be for a man with Woo's divine powers to clean up at the horse races or on the Fan Tan tables of Macau . . . Possible! Possible! Of course it had to happen that someone thought of treasure – and someone else, the lost treasure of Li Ma-hong. Li Ma-hong whose Cantonese war junks had once looted the merchant gold of the South China Sea, from Hong Kong to Luzan. Had Woo the fisherman gained hold of that long-lost treasure? *Aieya! There* was a cat full of fleas!

One man was not impressed by all this flatus and fable. Ah Tsai, the 'master' of *Dolphin*, was not given to romantic conjecture. He was sure that if there was as much gold on board the junk of Woo Yin-wah as was the general opinion, then it had been gained by criminal activity. Why else would the Ging Si Reven Forrester have taken such an interest in that junk? And where was that man now? Miss Caroline might ask that exact question. And what would his answer be if she did? What if Miss Caroline's lover was in bad trouble, or even dead? Who would get the blame? *Aieya!* Who else but Ah Tsai the boatman. He mulled all this over. He observed the activity on the deck of Woo's junk. He considered most carefully what action he should take and what might be the consequence of such action. In the end he decided to report his suspicions to the police . . . Which police? The Hong Kong Police, to whom the Ging Si belonged, or the People's Armed Police, who seemed to rule most of the bay?

He went to the Hong Kong Police Post on the eastern side of the creek. He spoke to a sleepy constable who called a yawning station sergeant, who called a huge gwai lo inspector who came and sat at his desk and said in atrocious Cantonese, 'Bring me some coffee at once . . . Yes, what is it, Mr . . . ?'

'Ah Tsai,' said the Station Sergeant. 'He says he thinks the Ging Si might be in trouble.'

Ah Tsai was asked to tell why he thought so, and as he did the gwai lo drank coffee and listened with a most attentive frown. And then he invited Ah Tsai to indicate on a map the position of the Toh Mong Suen, and he did that too.

'Well, they're in Chinese waters.'

That was the gwai lo Inspector's comment. He drained his cup and stood up. He beckoned to Ah Tsai. 'Come with me. Be quick now.'

He hurried with the huge Inspector to the creek where the pull-ferry lay idle.

'Pull it in.'

Ah Tsai obeyed the big gwai lo. They boarded the ferry, just the two of them.

'Haul us over.'

Ah Tsai hauled on the rope of Dark-boy Poon's pull-ferry and they crossed.

'Comrade Kwong,' the gwai lo instructed the soldier with the red star upon his cap and the rifle in his hands. 'Call Comrade Kwong, urgent need.'

One half-hour stretched into one hour and then twice that

271

time. The gwai lo shouted a lot, and threatened a lot, and eventually Comrade Kwong came with the dawn.

The villagers of Tai O also came down to the praya then and stared out into the bay, and all of them saw that the junk of Woo Yin-wah was no longer there. The treasure ship had sailed from the bay.

'Too late,' said Ah Tsai, and he walked away.

And the villagers too walked away, everyone walked away. And they called to their friends and neighbours, *Kung Hey Fat Choy!* May you too get rich quickly, my friend! For money can make the devil push the millstone; with money you are a dragon, without it you are a worm.

8

STONE BROKEN –
SKY IN TERROR

It was a lonely dawn: a grey morose sky; a ship crewed by hard-faced strangers who would have preferred it had he died during the passage of the last few days. There was Shen, and Shen was not like that, and Shen had seen him through. But now, as his strength returned, even she chose to set herself at a distance, as though he now had no need of her. Dear God! He had such need of her.

On the fourth morning at sea, Reven Forrester came on deck and watched the sun creep out of the South China Sea. The harsh winter monsoon winds blew southwards, kicking up the water into quick waves fringed with white that rushed by with a hiss and a kiss of spray; beating at their stern and pushing them on. The Toh Mong Suen seemed slow in this fussed water but its speed was a steady 8 knots, as it had been for days, as it would be for at least another day.

Without chart and sextant, or advice, he had deduced that they were approaching Philippine territorial waters. If they maintained their present course they would sight land within twenty-four hours. And that land, he reckoned, would be Palawan Island or one of its sister islands, Linapacau perhaps; certainly somewhere near the Cuyo West Pass that led into the Sulu Sea. It was a foolish idea to sail into the Sulu Sea. He had told old Woo Yin-wah that the previous night and he would tell him again.

Forrester climbed the ladder that led to the deck above the poop. Woo was there, crouched in the box-like steering house, his hands clasped, white-knuckled on the ropes that worked the tiller. Woo ignored his presence, and he ignored his advice.

'You had better go back . . . Listen, Woo Yin-wah, you are sailing towards a dangerous place. There are men in this part of the China Sea who make a living from pirating Vietnamese refugee boats. I know what I'm talking about. Please believe me. As you near the Sulu it gets worse.'

Woo's hands did not budge. Like some migrating bird he steered on, fixed to his path by instinct, and the memory of how it was.

'You're an old man, Woo. It doesn't matter for you any more. But what about the others, what about Shen? Do you know what they would do to Shen?'

Woo hawked and spat. He looked at Forrester in cold disbelief then returned his gaze to the horizon ahead.

'As stubborn as a rock,' Forrester said. 'Why won't you listen to me, old man? Do you think I want the gold? Who do you think that belongs to anyway – your grandson? It does not belong to your grandson. But I don't want it.'

Woo glanced at him again. His eyes sparked angrily but he said nothing, and the tiller did not waver.

'I once saw a fishing junk like this one, burned out and adrift with fifty charred bodies littering it. I saw a junk that was caught upon a coral reef; the deck was stained with blood but there wasn't a soul on board. A lot of small vessels just disappear in these waters, pirated and then sunk. Why do you want to come here? It's a bad place, old man, the Sulu is a bad place. Turn back to Hong Kong.'

It was no use. Woo Yin-wah did not trust him and would not take his advice. He set his feet once more upon the ladder; he had dropped a few steps when he heard Woo say, 'Can't go back.'

'Yes you can.'

'Can't go because of you, gwai lo. Because of you, Hei Shui will kill Grandson.'

'Did Eddie tell you that, old man?'

'Yes.'

'Did he tell you the gold belongs to Hei Shui?'

'Yes.'

'Hei Shui believe they have a right to it, that's true, but it doesn't belong to them.'

'You tried to steal it.'

'No. That's a lie. I don't expect you to believe me, but believe this. If you don't turn back soon then you will be in range of the Filipino pirates, and then it will be too late to put about. It won't matter to Eddie or you or me who owns the gold then, because we'll all be dead. You won't be able to outrun them, they use fast outriggers that can travel three times as fast as your best speed. The Hei Shui triads are angels compared to these men; they're merciless. They'll cut you down with machine-guns . . . And Shen . . . Ah, but I forgot, *Shen* is a woman, so what does it matter what happens to her. But think of your grandson, your sole heir, I believe. What a disaster for the House of Woo should he be killed.'

'What *you* care about Ah Shen? Hm!' Woo hawked and spat again and his mucus curved out with the wind. 'What you care about anyone, gwai lo?'

Forrester turned away and stepped down the ladder. Nothing short of violence would bring about a change of course. He'd thought of throwing old Woo clear out of the steeringhouse and taking the helm himself. That would have been an easy task. But then the others would have simply shut down the engines, and he would have achieved nothing. He had no option but to continue on this crazy voyage.

His head was throbbing. If he so much as moved his eyes, the pain increased. He found a sheltered spot on the deck and sat down upon a coil of rope. Man Tat passed by – a younger version of Woo Yin-wah. Forrester greeted him; Man Tat pretended the gwai lo was not there. The fisherman emptied a bucket over the side then went to talk to his wife, a

bonny, fat, suntanned woman who wore a floral trouser-suit
and a bright red scarf to cover her hair. She was fishing with a
scoop net in a metal bath filled with darting, live fish –
breakfast. The youngest of the Woo brothers, Tim Hi,
appeared at the engine-room coaming. He had slow eyes and
the drooping lower lip of the dullard. He bobbed up, saw
Forrester, and bobbed down again in the fashion of a
shooting gallery target. They had obviously all decided that
the presence of this dangerous gwai lo was best ignored.

Shen came to him, though. Small bare feet upon the deck,
in jeans and a cotton blouse with her long, long raven hair
plaited and pulled back. She held out a glass of hot green tea,
pungent with the smell of ginger and ginseng. Perhaps there
was opium in it too, for he had not finished it before the pain
was gone. While he sipped she stood near him, frowning
towards the sun. She would not look towards him, yet she
did not go away. He tried to bridge the gap between them.

'Have I thanked you for all you did for me, for taking care
of me? These last few days have gone in a blur, but you were
at my side all the time, that I do remember. Thank you for
that. Shen . . . I wanted to tell you how sorry I am about
Ah Fong. She must have been mad to do what she did. I had
no idea what was going on in her mind.'

'She hated me so much.'

'I know how you must feel, Shen. I know how hurt you
must be. There are *so* many things that need to be
straightened out. I tried to reach you on Tai O to explain
things to you but you hid yourself away; that was wrong. You
should have given me a chance to tell you the truth.'

'Can I have that glass now?' she said to the sun.

'How can I talk to you if you keep your back turned to me?
Damn it, Shen, do you want to hear the truth or don't
you? . . . It was over with Caroline before I even met you. I
didn't know she was pregnant . . . Shen, don't go now.'

She did go. She turned and walked away without another
word. Forrester and Old Wife of Man Tat remained on deck,

she with her scoop net, chasing wriggling fish, watching from the corner of her eye how the gwai lo pained – good that he should pain.

The morning became midday and the sun burned hot. The engine thumped on, the sea washed by and the hours passed, uncounted. He sought the shade of the deck canopy, and there he rested. He lay there until dusk.

At dusk two things happened to interrupt those vacant hours. A maritime surveillance aircraft of the United States Navy, an Orion P3c, swooped down upon them. Its whistling, hissing engines gave little warning. With its pale grey belly, its drab grey fuselage and its long trailing tail cone, it reminded him of the passage of a skate in an aquarium tank. Round and round it flew, then suddenly in its camouflage it was gone. On patrol for Vietnamese refugees, Forrester thought, so now they were in Philippine territorial waters, God help them.

Eddie Woo came on deck. His skin looked the colour of asbestos. He wore shorts from which a bandage protruded, waist and hem. He crept along, bent forward like a cripple. He saw Forrester and spat sourly on the deck between them. He limped to the rail and glared towards the departing Orion.

Forrester was glad of the sheltering darkness. He went to his cabin and Shen brought him food there; fish and rice. She set down the plate, then would have gone but he grasped her arm and would not let her go. If it was force that was required to halt her long enough to hear his explanation, then here was force. He held her wrists and spoke, and deep-felt words came to his tongue. She did not try to pull away, and so his grip became lax and soon it was her fingers alone that he gently held, and the touch was exquisite. Perhaps she heard him, perhaps not. For after he had spoken her question was:

'What crimes has my brother committed?'

And he was quiet.

He had wondered when she would ask that question, and dreaded it. There were several reasons why the truth should be kept from her and one of them was that as long as Eddie's sins were kept a secret was as long as he held power over the man, and he badly needed that power. It sounded like a lie when he said: 'One day I will tell you, and then you'll understand.'

She frowned. 'Why do you persecute him?'

Not a word came in answer. He did not hold her any longer and she went away.

Perhaps she would never know the truth about the vileness of her brother. God knows, he never *wanted* her to know.

No opium that night. The head pain came, throbbing as pain does at night and he could not sleep.

Perhaps Eddie Woo suffered too – his lamp burned into the deepening night. And the motor throbbed and the timbers squeaked, and the sea rushed by, wave after wave, rising and falling, rising and falling. Tomorrow they would sight Palawan and then what would old Woo do? Forrester knew what *he* would do. He would try to get Shen off this vessel. He would try to convince old Woo that his grand-daughter was a liability to him. He would bite back on his hate for Eddie and bargain with him too. He would do anything to get Shen to leave the Toh Mong Suen. Her safety was the thing that counted now.

His tiredness overcame his pain and he slept. He dreamed that Shen was dead, and that he had killed her.

Palawan island; for the southbound mariner to locate it requires only elementary navigational skill. It is long, 400 kilometres long. It is green, steep mountained and narrow and runs south-west almost all the way between Borneo and the Philippines. On its north coast the great waves of the South China Sea burst passionately on its rocks, but on the south coast there is tranquillity. The Sulu Sea licks at white beaches and coral reefs, and mangrove trees comb the tide. There are passages east of Palawan which lead into the Sulu. They are deep, but narrow, and studded with coral reefs, and they are best negotiated by day.

Palawan greeted them in the grey of dawn. It rose from the southern horizon; a smudge of mist. Then as the sun came up, it cast off its dull cloak and stood out bold green in their path. They came on deck to look at it, all of them, silent, each with his own fears and hopes.

Reven Forrester watched Shen as she steadied herself upon the heavy, smooth-worn timbers that formed at the bow. She stood upon the gunnel there, one arm extended to touch the foremast. Her hair was untied now and it whipped out past her face.

Her brother stood near the engine-room coaming, scowling at the land; tenderly massaging his groin. Forrester went to him. He said to Eddie Woo, 'We must talk.'

'Fuck *you*,' said Eddie Woo.

'You've had a lot to say to your family about how I've been persecuting you. Would you like me to tell them why?'

'No one will listen to you, gwai lo.'

'Shen would listen. She asked me that exact question. Would you like her to know that you're a child-rapist and a child-killer? She wouldn't be able to take it, Eddie. She admires you so much, but I think I could convince her what a bastard you really are.'

'Fuck you, gwai lo.'

'I've nothing to lose.' Forrester turned away.

'Wait,' said Eddie Woo. 'What you want to do that for? What you want to talk to me about, hah?'

'I want to make a deal with you, Eddie.'

'You hate me. You set me up. Why should we deal?'

'It's best for both of us, Eddie. Sure I hate you, but as you can see, things have changed. I've been forced to change too. What can I do but bargain with the devil?'

279

'What's changed? What kind of a deal, hah? What trickery you thinking of now, gwai lo?'

'I'm thinking of Shen; of her safety. Your grandfather is heading for the Sulu it seems. I've tried to get him to turn around and go back to Hong Kong, but his mind's made up. I think he's trying to protect you, Eddie . . . Well, that island there is called Palawan, and on the other side of it is the Sulu Sea. I mean to get off at Palawan, Eddie. There's a port called Puerto Princessa on the north side; I want to be put ashore there. I want you to put Shen off there too.'

'You and Sister, hah?'

'Yes.'

'You go with my sister. So I should trust you because of that. *Mung cha cha!*' He tapped finger to forehead. 'What do you take me for?'

'There's got to be some trust.'

'*Shit* on trust!'

'All right – *shit* on trust. But *there* is Palawan, and I'm going ashore, Eddie, if I have to swim there. If Shen is still on board this junk, then, I'm going to have you stopped by the Philippine Constabulary . . . They're rough, they're very hard. You wouldn't like them at all. What I'm saying, Eddie, is that you have no choice.'

'If Shen goes with you, what then?'

'You will never hear from me again. Your sister will never hear from me about any of your crimes. I don't give a damn about the gold, Eddie. Do as you please with it. I won't interfere. I give you my word.'

'*Shit* on your word.'

'You can take this junk to the Sulu; you can take it to Australia. Go where you like, but *not* with Shen on board.'

'You want my sister, hah?'

'Yes.'

'You want to marry her, or what? Maybe she doesn't want to marry you. What if she doesn't want to go with you? What then?'

'You'll put her ashore, Eddie. You'll order her to do it. That's all you have to worry about. Then you can sail on.'

'And then the pirates of the Sulu will get us; that's what you think, hah, gwai lo? You think we don't have a chance – that's what you told Grandfather. Fuck you, gwai lo. We'll make it. I'll make a deal with the Filipinos. I can buy anything with this gold; *anything!* Do you know what, gwai lo, you did me a favour when you told Hei Shui that I'd snaked on the Macau triads. Fuck Hei Shui, I'll take the lot. I should thank you.'

'That's the spirit, Eddie. Now, go and talk to your grandfather, and tell him what I want. He's the head of your house, and you are his sole heir, so he'll listen to you, and Shen will listen to him. Do it, Eddie, for your own sake.'

'I should have killed you, gwai lo, a long time ago. I could have, you know. I had the chance. You *made* me into a criminal, you chased me to Hell. *You!*'

'Yes. Do as I say now, Eddie. Look . . . see over there that mountain with the flat summit. You see it, Eddie? That's Cabuli Point. It's the easternmost tip of Palawan. There's a passage through there into the Sulu. It's narrow and it's lined with coral reefs, but I think your grandfather is heading for it. You see, there isn't very much time left. By midday we'll be in the Sulu. Go talk to your grandfather, Eddie.'

There was no doubt about it, old Woo was turning towards the Cabuli passage. Forrester watched the mountains of Palawan change shape as the junk came around to the east. More islands came into view. He could not remember the names of all of them but Linapacau was big and steepled with rocky points and he recognized it at once. The wind was pushing them hard now and the current had picked them up too; they were scudding towards the passage at a good speed. Too quick, Forrester thought. Woo had slowed the engines. He would have slowed them further had he been master of that junk.

The Orion found them there once more. It came in low

from the north-east, skimming the spires of Linapacau Island, making no sound at all until it thundered overhead. It topped the tall, green mountains of Palawan and was gone.

Forrester went to the bows and stood where Shen had stood. He watched the bow wave spread out from the hull. He saw the sea swirl where the reefs played up with it, and the wash of breakers upon low rock. He could hear the rumble of distant surf as it broke on land; the death throes of the China Sea, the birthplace of the Sulu . . . A kumpit trading vessel, south-west bound, laden with copra bales crossed the bow of the Toh Mong Suen then sailed on. Brown Malay faces turned to watch the strange junk so far from home, and Forrester watched them. These were Jama Mapun people from Palawan; traders and small-time smugglers. There was little to fear from them. The people to avoid were the Tausug – the People of the Current. They worked the sea in long narrow outriggers, called basnig, that cut the water like a sword edge. He saw no such vessel, but his memories of the Sulu kept him alert. He gazed into each bay that they passed, and beyond each island shore. He saw nothing but beauty: green mountain islands that rose like molars from the sea; sweet coves where the water tint ran turquoise on to white sand; soft-topped palm trees ruffling in the wind. A place of warmth and light, and fear. This was the Sulu.

Eddie Woo came to him that afternoon while he was drinking water from a plastic keg tied to the galley head. He closed the little brass tap at its base and set down the mug. Eddie seemed quite pleased with himself. He said he had spoken to his Grandfather and Uncle Man Tat.

'They both agreed that you are a constipation it would be well to get rid of. I told them you wanted to take Younger Sister with you . . .'

He stopped there, eyebrows raised, a small smile curling his lips; enjoying the manipulation of suspense. Forrester did not respond to the burlesque.

'The old man was against it . . .'

Still Forrester said nothing.

'. . . but I persuaded him it was for the best. There is a condition that must be met: Shen must agree. She must want to do it.'

'Yes,' Forrester said. 'Of course.'

'There is one other thing. We will not take you to Puerto Princessa. No, that would add a hundred miles to our journey; forget it. This is the deal: we must stop for firewood and water soon. At the next village with an anchorage we will stop and you must get off there.'

'That would be hard on Shen.'

Eddie yawned to show how greatly he cared about that. 'Who says she'll go with you? Maybe you find yourself alone, ah.'

'All right.'

'Better hurry then, Mr Forrester, before the *pirates* come.' He laughed and shook his head as he walked away.

He did hurry. He found Shen in the cabin she shared with her grandfather. She was gathering laundry into a plastic bucket.

'Leave that.' Forrester gestured. He took the container from her and set it down. 'I have to talk to you now, *come*.' She did not hesitate; she followed him.

They went together to the deck. Wife of Man Tat was at the fish tank again. On the starboard side Man Tat kneeled at the winch, paintbrush in hand. Forrester needed privacy and there was none here. Then the junk swung to the west, towards Palawan. In the shelter of a wide bay he saw a palm thatch village. He heard the mocking laughter of Eddie Woo. 'Hurry; better hurry, *hah!*'

The bay had two beaches flanked by hilly land that ran out in an embracing atoll. Its approach was teethed with sharp coral but there was a way in; a narrow blue freeway that wandered between swirling shoals. Woo steered a patient course into this passage. Smooth, clean, deep turquoise, the shallows slipped by. The motor throbbed slowly, and Man Tat, leaning head and shoulder over the bow, signalled the helm with palm and fingers held up flat like a rudder. Truly, they were expert seamen. Their skill made that difficult passage look simple.

The bay was not a true atoll. The land that embraced it was broken into islands; two of them quite hilly and wooded, the others as flat as a football pitch. There were passages between these islands through which a Tausug outrigger could easily have sailed. He saw this as they approached. He stood at the rail and Shen stood with him. God, let her believe all he was going to tell her.

Bahang the Bajau sea gypsy was small-boned and had the face of a boy. His skin was deeply tanned and his eyes were large and clear. His hair was dark brown, streaked with sun-bleached gold. There was a myth that the Bajau were born with webbed toes and gills, and to see Bahang swim was to believe that.

Bahang hated being on land. The tree devils, the hantu kayu, were hostile to the Bajau, and he was afraid of them. They would drain him and make him dizzy; even kill him if given the chance. He would rather have ridden out a full storm on his little vinta outrigger than be where he was then: in the shade of the deep forest on the south slopes of Batas Island. He had climbed to that place because he had been ordered to climb there by a man who held even more fear for him than the hantu kayu. He had looked down upon Shark Fin Bay as one might look down upon the palm of one's hand, and he had seen what he had been instructed to see.

The Chinese junk was at anchor in the bay. He had fixed its position in his mind. He would swim the long swim to that junk when the night came, and he would find it through mist or rain or turn of tide. He would find it like a turtle finds its nesting spot five oceans away. He was Bajau.

284

So now he could leave this haunt of the tree devils; this sweating dank slope that reached out to wipe off its sickness on those who passed, and frighten with chatter and scream and maniac laughter . . . Just monkeys, the land-dwellers laughed; just birds, harmless birds. But the Bajau were better informed.

And now as the light softened, a hush closed down upon the jungle, and that was the most dangerous time of all. In the quiet of dusk every evil eye embedded in every tree would open and turn upon the stranger, the Bajau. So go quickly now, Bahang, because soon after hush time with suddenness comes the hate screech of the trees . . . Just insects, said the landfolk, just harmless cicadas. But the Bajau knew better.

Walking in the breath of these demons, then, and frightened by their shout, Bahang began the return trip to the shore. And every tendril was the finger of the hantu and every vine his noose. They touched him in their hate and he shuddered and twisted from their reach, and once he fell. He stood up and in terror he ran, he pushed and thrust and dived headlong through the dark green screaming hell. At last he burst into the shrub line of the beach. Ahead he could see his friend the sea, and he nearly died of fright.

A man stood in his path, a huge, white-skinned, brown-haired Milikan! Bahang stopped dead. With the terror of the jungle behind him and the Milikan blocking his path to the water, he had nowhere to go. He sank down in fear on that spot, his face so close to the sand that every puff of breath blew dust into his eyes. He prayed a quick prayer to Bahar, the god of the great water, to come flooding in and wash him like a crab into the sea . . . but the sea did not raise itself in his aid so he lay quite still and waited to see what would develop.

What happened was that the Milikan walked even closer to his hiding place then sat down facing the sea. It occurred to Bahang then that he had not been spotted. The Milikan began to talk and it was not to Bahang the Bajau that he spoke. A soft and feminine voice came in answer – there were *two* of them there! Bahang raised himself on to his elbows and peered through the foliage of the beach scrub. She was Chinese.

Both of them were seated, not touching but not too far apart. They were talking in a language that he did not understand. He understood the tone of the Milikan, though, and the gestures that he used. The man was in love with the woman. He was earnestly trying to explain something to her. She, it was clear, was keen to hear what he said, and yet she disputed his words. She was angry, or was it hurt? Often she turned stiffly from him and her face was sad and her mouth was bitter. Her words rose up sharply against his pleas. But as time passed by and the sand cooled in the evening shade, her voice grew softer and she sighed a deep mellow sigh and they leaned together.

He watched them make love. She was very beautiful, and he was very strong. It was certain from their movements and their whispers that they loved each other deeply, the Milikan and his woman. Bahang was glad for them, but he turned his face away, shamed by his spying eyes.

When the Milikan had arched in his love spasm and she had sighed her last deep sigh, they walked together, naked, to a tidal pool; a sandy-bottomed pool still warm from the sun. They looked at the bright fish trapped there and plunged into the water. They squatted in the pool cupped to each other, and played and splashed and laughed like children. They washed the sour rind of their argument away, and when the afternoon shadows touched their pool they emerged and dressed. Hand in hand they walked to the little wooden boat they had brought here. It had a single oar and she stood at the stern and set it in its lock. He ran the boat into the water and she made that oar do the work of the tail of a fish. Bahang was enchanted by her grace and he watched until they were out of sight. He wondered where the Milikan had come from and where he was going with his pretty Chinese wife. How lucky they were to share such deep love.

Bahang rose up from the sand and ran for the sea. He bellied like a mud skipper in the shallows, and as the water deepened and gave lightness to his body, he stretched out his limbs and pulled away.

As the night drew in, a light mist lifted from the sea. But he needed no stars to guide him. The feel of the water gave him direction. He was Bajau. He had thought very carefully about the swim ahead. Most of the distance would be tideless, but then the tide would come flooding in from the China Sea and speed through the channels and thrust him quickly towards the junk. If he was off-course at that stage it might sweep him past the junk and towards the reefs on the other side of the bay, and that must not happen.

In his mind Bahang sang a song as he stroked so effortlessly through the water.

> Yes I be far from you,
> My Sitankai bride.
> The smile be gone from me,
> My Narisa.
> But who can see the strong rope
> That ties me to you.
> That no one can break
> Because it be in my heart.
> I will come back to you
> On the strong winds of anger
> That fills the sails of my thoughts
> Every day.
> Every day.
> My Sitankai bride.

The verse came over and over, to the draw of his arm and the flick of his feet. And the strong winds of anger gusted in his gentle Bajau heart:

> Like Kaytan the shark,
> I wait. I wait.
> One day I will tear at him,
> Like Kaytan the shark.
> And the water will redden.
> One day.

Brave words, but words alone would never repair his shattered life. His lovely Narisa had been taken from him by a devil-hearted man.

> He came on a dark night,
> Abdul ul Azam.
> He came and stole you,
> Narisa.
> But I will come
> On the strong winds of anger.
> And the waters will redden
> Around Abdul ul Azam.

But tonight was not that night. For now all he could do was obey the man who had locked away the woman of his soul. So he would swim to the Chinese junk and with his sharp knife he would sever the anchor rope. He would take that rope and swim beneath the drifting junk and tie it to the propellor shafts. He would do everything he had been told to do by Abdul ul Azam, so that Abdul the Tausug sea-raider could take the Chinese junk. And he would be pleased with him, and be kind to sweet Narisa.

> Swim Bahang.
> Swim like a fish.
> Swim with your sharp knife
> Swim.

*

The skill of the fisherman's daughter – the grace of the temple dancer. Small, strong fingers upon the teak yuloh, supple bare feet upon the sternboards of the sampan. Shen Woo propelled them lazily back to the junk. Her eyes looked down at the man she loved and they said: I would carry him like this for a thousand miles and not tire of it. She smiled as she swayed and it was a smile of deep contentment.

This was a place of magical beauty. The tide was still, the waves were lisping trickling ripples that hardly rocked the sampan. Beneath them was a coral forest that set the darkening surface dizzy with colour – red, orange, purple, black. There were underwater meadows of swaying flame seaweed and banks of white, white sand where little fish shoaled, darting this way and that like slivers of glass. As they drew further from the shore and deeper into the bay, a mist rose up just inches from the water that seemed to lift them into the air. Grandpa had not exaggerated when he had described this place, and she would remember it for ever. But as all things must change, so the time had arrived once more for change. She was going to go with Reven Forrester. She was going to leave her family and go with him. She loved him. That was her decision. Tonight would be her last night on the Toh Mong Suen – a night of farewells.

'There.' Forrester pointed. 'There's the junk.'

The mist swirled at its waterline as though it was coddled in cotton wool. They tied the sampan to a post and climbed on board. Shen went immediately to find Grandfather.

At the turn of the tide, the water of the Sulu rose massively, pulling as it did new water through the passages that fed it from the South China Sea. So the current was swift. It swirled past the islands and ripped across the coral reefs. The junk of Woo Yin-wah swung ponderously on its anchor cable to meet the new flow. The junk was old and the timbers well worn, so it creaked with this movement and from the pressure of the tide on the hull. The anchor cable grew taut and as it crept upon its smooth worn track it thrummed and creaked. The noises were part of this vessel at anchor, and were no more notable than the wheezing of an aged relative at his rest. But when the sound ceases it is noticed at once and investigated, and perhaps there is alarm.

Forrester could not sleep. He went on deck and rested on the deck rail looking down into the sea that shimmered like mica through the thin mist. The mist, he noticed, was breaking into patches and dissipating in a mild breeze that the tide had brought with it.

A movement behind him made him turn. Shen pressed herself against him, warm and downy like a bird. He kissed her gently. 'Little sparrow.'

'I've told them,' she whispered. 'It's agreed.'

'Don't be sad. I'll take good care of you, Shen.'

He gathered her small body to him, and as he did so a judder ran through the junk. He felt the deck bob as though a sudden wave had passed. A sound of puzzlement came from Shen. She fetched a torch and shone it into the water, unsure of what she was looking for. He saw a log of driftwood in the water, but it did not pass them by as it should have, it kept station with them. He sprinted for the bow, and there were others running upon the deck. Old Woo came up, and Man Tat, and they worked the spokes of the anchor winch, and the rope came up slack.

'*Diu lei*,' they swore.

They cranked the winch as fast as it would turn, the cable came in for a while, then stopped dead. Forrester threw his weight upon the spokes – the winch would not budge.

Woo shouted. '*Tak che! Tak che!*'

He ran back along the deck. Forrester heard him climbing to the tiller house still shouting for the engines to be started – '*Tak che! Chuen chuk che chin!*' Full ahead.

The starter motors cranked, the engines fired, the prop shafts turned. For a few seconds it seemed they had the

290

better of the tide. The tiller blocks squeaked and the junk began to answer. Then the whole junk juddered and cramped as though a death pang was upon it – then silence. Now Woo Yin-wah rushed out a string of curses; he shouted to his brothers and they scurried to do his instruction.

The anchor cable had snapped and the propellor shafts were fouled, dead. They were adrift in a flood tide that had caught them up like a matchstick in a river.

Cut loose the fouling, restart the engines. Those were the tasks to be done. But they had better be quick, they were in the jaws of the beast, and sharp coral teeth were all around.

Slowly, gracelessly, the Toh Mong Suen slewed without power or will. The thrust and swirl of the current gripped their starboard quarter; swept them beam-on, then stern-on, then it turned them round again. Woo rigged a floodlamp so that its beam brightened the water at the stern. Tim Hi stood naked and bewildered holding a diving mask and knife. A knife would be useless to cut loose such vice-like fouling.

'A hacksaw,' Forrester said. 'Get a hacksaw.' He began to strip – jeans and shirt and gym shoes he discarded on the deck. 'Give me the mask. Damn it, give it to me.'

Tim Hi, his mouth drooping doltishly, looked askance to Eddie Woo. Eddie Woo said, 'Give it to him. *I* can't swim. For fuck's sake, Uncle, do what he says.'

Tim Hi surrendered the mask. Forrester dropped from the deck onto the boards of the sampan that he and Shen had tied up there. Shen came running. She held a hacksaw which she reached out and gave to him. Then she kissed him quickly.

'Be careful, my love.'

No one else said a word. They looked down and watched him swim to the stern into the pool of light.

It was rope that had fouled them. Thick, rigid, fibrous collars of it strangled both prop shafts and trailed off into the green-blue darkness beyond. Forrester inspected the damage and a thousand curious fish inspected him. The current pushed at him and it was massively strong. The junk was ponderous, but he was buoyant – an easy thing to play with. He gripped the rudder and let his legs and abdomen float away, and began to saw. The rudder was slippery with keel-weed and spiked with sharp-shelled barnacles – green-brown blood blossomed from his cuts, and the little fish came tickling and nibbling along. He held on and sawed into the steel-wrung mass. He closed his mind to the plea of his lungs and worked on and on, sawing, sawing. The blade rasped dully upon the rope, hardly cutting it. Bubbles of air trickled from his nose and gurgled past his ears. His throat made heaving, choking sounds. *Air!* He surfaced and gasped, and dived again, and again. Once when he surfaced he shouted, 'It's our own anchor rope.' But he did not think anyone heard him, and he did not call again. Just dive; saw; gasp in air when the surface breaks. His hands and wrists and arms began to burn and cramp and he dropped the hacksaw and was lucky to retrieve it as it snagged the keel-strake. He was tiring, but he did not rest. In the tortuous green gully he sawed and grasped and wrenched and swore with a mind full of fury at this task of no hope.

It came to an end, though, very much as he had predicted it would. Though his mask was flooding, and his eyes were scalding and gave but snippets of vision, he could hear with super clarity; he could hear the hacksaw rasp. He could hear the creak of the hull, and the clank of a hammer being wielded in the engine-room of the junk. Then he heard the loudening thrum, thrum, thrum of approaching propellors and his stomach tightened with fear.

He hauled himself close to his task and saw that the cut he had made was puny – the propellor shafts were still firmly bound. He shoved himself away, and as he floated up he saw a man beneath him.

In the tunnel of green light he saw him, swimming as gracefully as a fish – dark flowing hair, dark flowing limbs.

And the man saw him too. A pearly string of bubbles rose from the fish-man's mouth and passed by. Then he flicked his fin-like legs and his form faded into the dark water.

Forrester broke surface, gasped air, then looked below him again. There was no sign of the man. Above him the bright light shone and the deep-shadowed faces of Shen and her brother peered down. He shouted to them.

'Turn off the light.'

'Have you cut through?'

'Shen, get to the sampan, get away from the junk.'

'Have you cut through?'

They were not listening. 'I saw a man down there. Shen, for God's sake get the light off. Get to the sampan.'

'I can't see you,' Shen called.

The current had swept him a short distance from the junk. 'I heard engines,' he shouted. 'Shen, it's a trap, get off the junk.'

He had not realized how tired he had become or just how strong the current was. He swam as hard as he could towards the junk but his limbs felt lame and disobedient, and the gap widened. He should not have allowed himself to drift away from it. He was swimming in deep darkness now. There was panic in Shen's voice.

'Reven. I can't see you.'

He kicked harder, he fought against the tide, but he came no closer.

'*Reven!*'

He was spent. He had to rest. His leaden legs sank down, small waves slapped his face and breached his open mouth. The row of machinery was loud in his ears. Why could *they* not hear it?

'*Reven!*'

Couldn't she see her danger was greater than his?

He kicked hard, once, to lift himself from the water, then cupped his hands to his lips and shouted, '*They're coming!*'

But they were already there.

The quick, sharp hull of a big Tausug outrigger thrashed past. From its bow a spotlight ranged. It swept the water and found him there and blinded him with its glare, then the light raked on and he could see again. He saw a machine-gunner crouched behind a shielded machine-gun. The bright beam reached out through the darkness, seeking the junk of Woo Yin-wah. And they found it. They made a theatre set of it, and players of those upon its deck. And Forrester was the audience to the tragedy. '*Shen!*' he shouted. '*Shen!*'

The Browning machine-gun crashed out and the junk took the awful shock.

His punished body raised a feeble stroke; he kicked out limply and pulled with his arms but his effort was that of the defeated. They were killing Shen and he was impotent to stop it. He snarled and he raged like a chained dog. The machine-gun fired on and on, and he shuddered at every bullet strike as though it was his own flesh in its path. He shook his fist at the sky and swore, '*Jesus! Jesus! Jesus! Stop! Bastards, stop!*'

The machine-gun stopped.

But for the lap of the water and his sobbing breath he heard no other sound. The death play was far from him now; distant lights on a black sea. He was alone. He let himself drift, let the tide take him where it would. But even that was too great a labour. He did not want to die but he thought the time was near. Much later, in the distance, he saw a light and he struggled towards it, but it came no closer and soon his limbs ceased to work at all; he could not even feel them. The blackness all around him penetrated him; chilled and subjugated him. Shen must be dead and he would be dead soon and it was futile to fight this massive dominance. Let him be it; let it be him. Let the struggle cease. He was slipping under and he did not care.

Something grasped his ribs and the water stirred at his back. He was too feeble to fight off this new enemy. He was lifted to the air.

*

I will come back to you
On the strong winds of anger
That fills the sails of my thoughts
Every day.
Every day.

Had Reven Forrester been able to understand the Bajau-Samal dialect of the singer of that song, then those were the words that would have accompanied his return from a shallow sleep. Had he been conscious of the sentiment of the poet, he would have warmed to him. For here was hope. Here was the enemy of his enemy. But he did not know this.

It was dawn. It was raining. The voice that had been his last memory that night was his first knowledge of the morning. At that moment that was all that he was certain of. He was lying upon the bottom boards of a small boat, humped up with his leg trailing over the transom. Woo's sampan; this was the sampan Shen had ferried him in.

'*Shen.*'

With that name the fullness of his history returned, generous with blame. *Shen was dead*, or if not dead, then in a terrible way, and he had allowed this to happen. He had permitted her to return to the junk – to stay the night and say her farewells . . . He had never felt so sunken and sick with remorse. He made to sit up, a clumsy movement that rocked the sampan. The singing stopped and a boyish, flat-featured face appeared above the stern planks. Sun-bleached, sea-matted dark hair; bronze skin and brown eyes; a finger that pointed to Forrester; a mouth that smiled the words:

'Milikan. You Milikan.' The finger now pointed at himself. 'Bahang. I be Bahang. Be Bajau.'

'Bahang,' said Forrester, and both men nodded.

'Milikan,' said the Bajau and they nodded again.

So the Englishman became Milikan in name and nationality, and here was Bahang the Bajau. Two strangers on a sampan in the Sulu Sea.

295

Bahang had saved him. Bahang had lifted him from the sea when he was drowning and towed his strengthless body to the sampan, and hauled him to its deck. He remembered all that. Bahang, he thought, might also have cut the anchor rope of the Toh Mong Suen and set the junk adrift. Should he praise the Bajau or should he curse him? The man was an enigma.

The rain was good – warm fat drops sufficient to fill his cupped hand and quench his thirst. And while he drank, the Bajau, with legs and hips still trailing in the sea, raised himself upon the transom. A tentative gesture, as though he sought permission to come aboard. Forrester held out his hand; he grasped the Bajau's wrist and hauled him up. Bahang squatted on the bottom boards. He was small but well muscled.

'Milikan,' said the Bajau. 'GI . . . OK . . . Rambo . . . Coca-Cola.'

Forrester pointed to himself; to the sampan; to the surrounding sea, then condensed this gesture into a single word: 'How?'

'Ah.' Bahang nodded, he understood. He too composed a variety of gestures: arms asway, puff-cheeked.

'Swimming?' guessed Forrester. 'Underwater swimming . . . Sawing.'

'*Aho!*' More mime. Rapidly, Bahang glided one palm edge upon the flat of the other – an outrigger at speed.

'Basnig?'

'*Aho!* Basnig . . . Basnig, Abdul ul Azam. *Bam! Bam! Bam! Aho!*'

So Bahang *had* been the swimmer in the water beneath the junk. He had watched while he sawed at the anchor rope. Why had he not helped? He felt angry for a moment, then it faded.

'Who?' He gestured wide. 'Abdul ul Azam?'

Bahang drew tight his little fists, his white teeth bared: '*Nag buno kami* ul Azam.'

'Where? Where is Abdul ul Azam?'

The Bajau capped his brow with his palm and squinted. He pointed into the distance. '*Luwaak.*'

'Far?'

'*Aho.*' One, two, three fingers – three days. 'Jolo.'

'Jolo?' He had heard of Jolo. He drew a mental map and placed it amongst the chain of little islands that dotted the southern Sulu Sea. Three days to Jolo . . . And what does that information gain you, Mr Milikan, lost in a yuloh dinghy in the Sulu? What does it help to pronounce the name 'Abdul ul Azam', and know what he has done, and where he has gone? How do you propose to attack him in your dinghy? Or draw justice to him . . . There would be no justice. ul Azam would be able to ring himself with a hundred witnesses who would swear his basnig had been a hundred miles from that place of butchery.

'Hopeless.' Bahang stared blankly at him. Forrester shrugged. He felt too despondent to say another word.

Bahang spoke: 'Bajau, Milikan, amigos. Father of me, GIs, amigos . . . You, me, amigos . . . OK?'

'Amigos?'

'Amigos.' Bahang seemed pleased with his progress. He drew up his fists again. Again those angry, bitter words: '*Nag buno kami*, ul Azam.' He gestured, frustrated, and desperate to be understood: '*Aho!* Rambo . . . *Ka! Ka! Ka! Boom!*'

'We *fight* him?'

'*Aho.*' Bahang danced up and the dinghy rocked. 'Fight!' he yelled. '*Aho!*' Fight was the word. 'Bajau Milikan, amigos, *fight* ul Azam – *Ka! Ka! Boom!*'

It was an absurd idea, and he shook his head, and smiled at it all at once, as one does when first one considers such magnificent folly. An impossible pursuit – a wooden sword, a straw lance – and they would not survive it . . . and the alternative was to cringe and turn away, beaten, and that thought sickened him. So he shrugged, as though in disbelief of what he was about to say.

'OK, Bahang, let's fight him.'

Two men, naked in a fishing dory with nothing more than resolve with which to arm themselves, joined hands solemnly in that pact. Now how were they to set about this quixotic mission?

Bahang knew how.

A south breeze came to chase the rain away. Green islands emerged from the grey. The Bajau stood upon the stern boards of the sampan and lifted the yuloh blade.

Was it not like the tail of a fish, this long oar? And was there a Bajau who could not imitate the fish? With a sway and a flick and a sway and a flick; with a smile that said look at me. See how clever I am. With a ballad of great hope for his loved one at Jolo:

'I saw him as he swam
The Milikan.
A brave one. As tall as the Salindugu, rainbow.
When ul Azam came
When ul Azam came.

They stole his new bride.
Those Kullo-Kullo pirates.
I save him. I saved Milikan from the deep.
When ul Azam came,
When ul Azam came.
Now I come for you, my Narisa.
Like Kaytan the shark.
The day has come. The day I have hungered for.
Since ul Azam came
Since ul Azam came.'

Bahang the pagan sea gypsy worked the sampan past reef and island, and through the passage that separated the islands that he knew as Maytiguid, and Calabugdong. They came into a bay that was called Shark Fin Bay. Bahang was happy because the days of impotent anger were past. Here

298

was a man of power. Look at the tight-pressed jaw and the deep, sad, angry eyes. Then look past the eyes at the will of this Milikan. Like the gathering monsoon, the will of this man would bring a season of storms into the life of Abdul ul Azam. And Bahang would steer him on to that devil-hearted pirate.

They found the battered junk of Woo Yin-wah. It was lodged upon a coral reef in the bay in but a few feet of water. The planking was smashed and chewed in places as if some sea monster had raked it with his teeth. One mast had fallen and the superstructure was torn apart.

Let Shen not have suffered, he thought as they came on, let her have died swiftly. He took a deep breath and clenched down on his jaw, and came aboard.

Tim Hi had died swiftly. A .50 bullet had entered his chest and blown his spine apart. Man Tat had died as quickly, his head was many paces from his body. Wife of Man Tat had died perhaps not as easily as her husband. He found her body in her cabin; her death wound was in her abdomen and her face told of great pain. He went to Shen's cabin. It was empty; the galley was empty. The engine-room was empty; its metal floor plates had been ripped out and thrown around in the search for gold, but the hull planking looked sound and there was no flooding there. He searched every fish hold and locker, from bulkhead to bulkhead. He pushed aside fuel drums and hauled at fish boxes; waiting for the shock, knowing that he would find her, hoping that he would not.

There were no more dead people on that junk, and that knowledge brought nothing but hideous dread.

He and Bahang cared for the remains of Tim Hi, Man Tat and his wife. They took them to an island, a tiny island where little waves washed up on the whitest sand and green pigeons cooed. With the sun warm on their backs they carried the old folk to the tree line and buried them in that friendliest of worlds.

They returned to the junk. His jeans and shirt and gym shoes lay upon the deck where he had thrown them, soggy with rain. He hung the clothes but put on his shoes, then went back into the water and waded across the sharp coral to the stern. Bahang hung back, not keen to inspect his sabotage. In the shallow water it was easy to see the throttled propellor shafts. Without comment Forrester inspected them. What was the point of a lungful of anger on someone who wouldn't understand a word of it. He scowled blackly instead, and Bahang looked sorry.

Bahang came up with his head hung on his chest in great repentance: '*Ampunun aku,*' then some more words that held greater cheer.

The hull below the waterline was intact; that was Bahang's smile. Look, Milikan; look here, look there; can't you see this junk will float when the tide comes to lift it?

They waded across the pitted coral bed that held the Toh Mong Suen. The junk had run on to the reef bow-on and its heavy blackwood keel had gouged a deep path through the coral trees. The teak hull was scarred but there had been no wave action to lift and dump it and so do serious damage. The planking looked sound. The junk *would* float. He nodded to Bahang, and Bahang beamed. Had he not promised this all along?

In that shallow water it was easy to chop loose the fouling from the propellor shafts. The shafts looked true; if the engines would drive them they would revolve. Let there be no pessimism!

They climbed back to the deck. The damage there looked awful, but looks meant little. They went straight down to the engine-room. He set the clutch to neutral and punched the start button. One engine turned then spluttered and died – then roared into life. The other was as good. He clenched his fist and lifted it and shook it in the face of fate.

'Three days?' He held three fingers to Bahang. 'Three days to Jolo?'

'*Aho,*' shouted Bahang.

The fuel hold stank of spilled diesel. There were fifteen 44-gallon drums standing there, some holed by bullets. He sounded each one and discovered that all but four were empty. The engines were Perkins 105s that used about sixty gallons a day at 800 rpm. At that rate, one engine would drive them at 7 knots on that quiet sea. He reckoned they were two hundred and fifty sea miles from Jolo – thirty-six hours. If the tide would free them they would make it.

'Jolo,' Forrester said. 'You and I . . . amigo.'

'*Aho*, amigo.' Bahang's eyes shone and he bit upon his lip.

They went back to the engine-room and set the floor plates in place. They scrubbed the blood from the woodwork of the deck, then they chopped the main mast loose and heaved it into the sea, and when they had done all that they sat and waited for the tide.

Bahang sang a song then – a *tinis-tinis* of such poignant sound that Forrester was captured by it. It led him to the sad place in the Bajau's heart, and the place of hope. Then it rushed him along in its anger; it rumbled and flashed like a distant night storm. He puzzled at this strange little man who had come from the sea to harm him, then had saved him, and now wished to be his friend; his amigo. The waiting hours were filled, too, with hard thoughts of his own role in the torment of Shen Woo. He blew on the dust of his memories and was dismayed by what emerged. There was a warning that he had given to himself: You dare not love the one who loves your enemy – you cannot hold out one hand in love while the other conceals the dagger. Yet there it was; that was exactly what he had done, and as a consequence, this. He had brought down the man he hated and the woman he loved, all at once. And that was his horror, and his pain.

Bahang sang on, quietly now, his voice sealed in his throat, his lips scarcely moving, as though he had no wish to intrude past the frown on the face of his amigo . . . Forrester thought all he could do now was to chase this thing to an end. Most likely it would end on that little island called Jolo.

The tide came that night and it rocked the junk and bumped its timbers upon the coral, then it lifted it from the coral and set them free.

'*Sihi sigaam,*' Bahang called his thanks to the sea.

9

THE HOUSE OF UL AZAM

It was said that in his youth Datu Abdul ul Azam had been a handsome man. His dark Malay features had shown an Arabic keenness at the bridge of his nose and the brow of his eyes that was likened to the Prophet Muhammad. Indeed if the ancient silk tarsila, upon which the family tree lay clearly inked, was to be believed, then somewhere in the stains of history a drop of the blood of the Prophet had marked his lineage. Abdul believed it to be so.

But now the hair of Abdul ul Azam was wispy and white, his movements had slowed, and his face had changed in a way that he would not have chosen. The likeness of the Prophet had not endured because the truth was that ul Azam was not a godly man. He was proud and ostentatious and wasteful, and so it was that he became marked by these sins. The sun, the wind and the salt spray had tightened his features and pressed them to a skull that was formed by avarice and pride, and now he was ugly.

The only beautiful thing about Abdul ul Azam was his son, his only son, Juhuri.

Juhuri was handsome, but more important than that, he was wise. He understood things in his youth that his father had not learned in a lifetime, and he knew of his father's failures.

> By those that rise
> And those that set
> Let your affairs be directed.

303

That verse of the Koran was the basis of life's meaning. The laws that limited the movement of the stars were the laws that should govern all living things. And his father exceeded those limitations. Man had to live by God's set requirements, just as every other created thing did – as the moon, and the tide, and the crab that crawled across the sand. But man alone of all created things had will, and thus freedom of choice. Man could submit to the hand of God or man could pursue his own passions, as Abdul ul Azam had done. But then he would be punished, as Abdul ul Azam had been punished, and would be further punished. For Abdul had failed and he was marked for Hell.

Juhuri drove his father's Jeep quickly and expertly amongst the pedicabs that run like cockroaches through the market streets of Jolo. It had rained and the streets were puddled, and people jumped from the splash of the tyres. The breeze whipped through the open sides and cooled his skin pleasantly, so he did not slow down until he reached the harbour gates. There he slowed briefly, waved a salute towards the customs building, then accelerated once more. He drove to the very tip of the hook-shaped pier and there he drew up.

Juhuri tightened the knot of the folded kerchief that was bound to his forehead. He took a cigarette from the pocket of his cotton shirt and lit it. He lifted his black nylon pistol-case from the dashboard of the Jeep and hung it on his shoulder, then he stepped on to the concrete surface of the pier and looked out to sea. His father's swift basnig was in sight, curling out a bow wave like a little white moustache. It would be there in ten minutes, he guessed.

Juhuri turned away from the sea and walked the width of the pier. Ahead of him lay the basin in which his father would tie up. From the landing he looked down to the vessels that were docked there now. There were six vessels in harbour, sharp sleek basnigs, all of them, separated widely by the reach of their long bamboo outriggers that stretched out like the legs of great water spiders on each side of their craft. They were beautiful craft, bright painted and clean, they could carry massive loads in the shallowest water. They rode the Sulu like swallows ride the wind, and the lumbering, grey patrol boats of the Filipino Navy did not even try to check them. A bit of trading, a bit of smuggling . . . a bit of random piracy when a likely chance arose. That was the Tausug way of life. Had not the Prophet himself pillaged the caravans of the infidels?

There was the blue-striped basnig of cousin Salihuddin, groaning with crates of Salem cigarettes – bought in Borneo for four pesos a ten-pack, sold in Jolo town by street vendors, one cigarette at a time. There was profit in that. He waved at Salihuddin and his cousin waved back. A rich man was Salihuddin; a Hajj. A man who lived by the five pillars of Islam. Yes, there was a man to admire.

The blue and yellow hulled basnig of his father rounded the pier then, cruising on one engine only. This was truly the finest of all the basnigs of the Sulu. It was long – 80 feet long. Its prow curved up from the water like the blade of a parang. Its mast was tipped like a spear and at its head was fastened a small board that read: *Sug Bituun – Jolo*.

Juhuri saw his father and waved to him, a gentle gesture of wrist and hand that showed nothing of the passion of his contempt. And as the sleek outrigger drew in, he stepped to the edge of the jetty to catch the head rope that a crewman was poised to cast. Expertly, he took the flaying rope and fastened it to a forked, iron bollard. An idler helped him lower a gangway to the foredeck, and when the ladder was secure, he walked down the swaying passage to the deck.

'Assalamu aleikum.' Juhuri placed his hand upon his heart and greeted his father – peace be unto you.

'Unto you be peace,' ul Azam responded. He was smiling. 'Allah has blessed us, my son.'

'He is Al Ghani; the Enricher.'

'Fantastic, fantastic – beyond anything you can imagine.'

305

Abdul almost danced upon deck. Juhuri glanced at his father's crewmen, they were strung with repressed excitement. Not a face turned towards him. They had seen what they had seen and no one would share a glance with him for the fear of it. Their eyes held secrets and they would not give him any of it. Juhuri could not help but become excited too. No cargo of soap or cigarettes today.

'Come on.' Abdul's excited hand beckoned.

He followed his father down the long deck. In the cockpit beneath the central canopy they stopped. There was a hatch there and Abdul's deep eyes gleamed with excitement as he unlocked it.

'Look inside.'

Juhuri looked inside. The hold ran towards the stern of the basnig, it was low and dark and smelt of diesel fuel. He pressed the switch that would light the hold, and stared in amazement.

'*Gold?*'

'Yes.' Abdul laughed. 'Look at it.'

It lay strewn across the floor of the hold in orderless heaps, small bars of glinting yellow gold.

'So much of it.'

'Enough to make me the richest man in Jolo; *no*, the richest man in the Philippines.'

There it lay, from corner to corner, piled against the ribs and planking, dumped upon the bottom boards like so much ballast. Juhuri's throat was taut as he turned to face his father; questioning: 'Where did you get all this?'

Abdul winked and placed his finger to his lips. He whispered, 'There's more.'

Crouched forward they walked the length of that hold, past drums of diesel fuel and provisions, and boxes of ammunition and the big Browning machine-gun, stripped down and wrapped in oiled cloth. Another light switch lit this part of the hold.

Juhuri saw a Chinese man. His ankles and hands were tied

and a blood-stained bandage protruded from his shorts. There was an old Chinese man, he too was tied but there was no need of the bindings. He was so frail, he looked the colour of paper. Crouched over the old man was a woman. She said, 'Mercy, please, mercy. Water for my grandfather or he will die.'

She had long hair that hid her face until she looked up, and then it drew back as if a curtain had parted, a rich black satin curtain. Her eyes lifted up to Juhuri and implored as she spoke.

'Please help us, Grandpa is dying . . . Can't you see he's dying? Why won't you let him have water?'

She touched the heart of Juhuri ul Azam. She was quite the most beautiful woman he had ever seen.

Shen heard the creak of woodwork and the rattle of the lock and knew that the hatch was to be opened. The light came on and she looked up to see the grinning, skull-face of Abdul ul Azam, and next to him a young man whom she had not seen before.

'Please help us,' she said. 'Grandpa is dying . . .'

Ul Azam stayed there. The newcomer withdrew but returned after a while holding an earthenware jug. He came to her and offered her the jug. He bent down and lifted the head of Woo Yin-wah and she propped the water jug to Grandfather's slack-lipped mouth. The water spilled over his chin, and his gullet bobbed weakly as he swallowed.

The young man said, 'He'll be all right . . . Now you drink.'

'First my brother. He's had no water.'

'A lie,' said ul Azam. He turned away. He said some sharp words in his own language as he went away. The newcomer translated.

'He said he saved you and he could have killed you. Be grateful.'

'He's a murderer,' Shen said. 'He's a devil.'

'He's my father . . . You should not have been allowed to suffer like this. This is wrong.'

'Will you let us go? That's all we want.'

'What is your name?'

'Shen Woo.'

'Shen Woo, I can't let you go. That's impossible. But what I can do is see to it that no further harm comes to you. So don't be afraid any more . . . I am Juhuri ul Azam. *I* am a *Datu*. You have the word of a Datu.'

'Is your father a Datu?'

'Whom God has led astray shall find no friend to guide him.'

'Will you help us?'

He nodded. 'I know what you have suffered.'

How could he know what they had suffered, this frothy-worded man. He turned from her then. Crouching, he walked quickly away. The hatch was closed and she heard its bolts rattle home. But Juhuri had left behind him a legacy of hope. Where before there had been darkness a light now burned; the torture of thirst was over.

'May his whole family go to hell! Give me more water, Sister.'

Those were the first words that Elder Brother had spoken since the engine of the basnig had been shut down.

'We must make it last,' she said.

'Are you in charge or what?'

She gave her brother water, and she thought about his question. She thought: Yes, in a way I am in charge. The lives of Brother and Grandfather swayed in a balance which was weighted by her actions. Abdul ul Azam had made that *so* clear . . . She frowned at the thought of those who had died. She shivered and closed her eyes.

Memories: the face of beloved Reven swimming towards the junk. *They're coming*, he'd shouted. The sudden roar of engines, then lights so bright and blinding that they had stood numbed, Man Tat and Tim Hi – all of them quite cataleptic, waiting for the executioner . . . Reven, where was Reven? . . . The crash of guns had shocked them and set them running. Poor Tim Hi had provided the help of a circus clown; staggering on to the deck grasping a bucket before him; he'd tripped and spewed a fortune of gold bars across the planking. He'd stopped to lift them, dropping them as fast as he'd captured them. Tim Hi giving up his life in a fountain of blood as he clutched for his elusive fortune. And everyone screaming, screaming. With the lights so bright and the guns so deafening, and all around them timber splintering, glass exploding. Then with a crashing jolt they had run onto the reef.

Bloody memories. They had come aboard from all sides, and all at once. Dark men with long-bladed krises and flame-spitting rifles. *'Allahu Akbar,'* they had screamed. The head of Man Tat rolling like a ball across the deck. 'Allahu Akbar,' God is the greatest. What god would countenance such carnage in his name?

It was then that she had first seen the skull-faced ugliness of ul Azam. Smiling with huge enjoyment; calling harsh orders; pointing to where she crouched. She had thought they would all die then, and had been surprised with each moment of life permitted. Life had seemed so important, so vivid and desirable in those seconds before it was to end. But it did not end . . . Death looked around, well satisfied with its gain, and the killing stopped; in front of her it stopped. The skull-face had appeared before her and said: 'My name is ul Azam, the Merciful.'

He had paraded the survivors before him, the better that they should perceive his mercy: Grandfather and Elder Brother and her, while the gold from Tim Hi's bucket was picked up with awe and weighed from hand to hand . . . Terrible memories.

Sug Bituun, that was the name she had glimpsed upon a plaque that was fastened to the mast of ul Azam's long basnig. *Sug Bituun* was sleek and sharp and it floated easily above the reef that had snagged the Toh Mong Suen. It had outriggers of bamboo that ran the full length of the hull. A high central mast was rigged with cables that led out to support the outrigger spars. Because of these outriggers they had boarded the basnig at the bow. Then *Sug Bituun* had sped as quick as an eel across the quiet-waved Sulu. Three engines drove it at a pace that raised a stinging spray and caught her hair out like a flag. She had never known such speed; or such a nightmare voyage.

Grandfather and Eddie had been taken to a hold that she had only visited for a short spell. It was dark and it was hot and so close to the engines that the roar of them fell upon her like a physical beating; a darkness so filled with din that nothing else was left – no air – no voice – no sight. Stunned, she had felt as though madness was just a scream away.

But ul Azam, 'the Merciful' had taken her from that place. He had had her brought to him. Sprawled upon a mat beneath the flapping canvas canopy he had wagged his hand at her, a curious dropped-wrist gesture that she had not understood. Come, said the hand, quick to impatience – come, come, come. Sit, sit, sit. There, right there, within reach of me, pretty thing.

She had sat within his reach, but he had not touched her, nor had he spoken to her. From sockets deep and blighted his eyes had studied her. Their message: I spared you, you are mine. You live or you die at my whim, as does your brother, as does your grandfather. You will do as I say, woman, you are mine. Know it.

She had tried to converse with him. She had told him of the hell beneath that deck. She had begged him to bring Grandfather, at least, up to the air. Ul Azam had not so much as acknowledged that he had heard her. He had not blinked. And the basnig had sped on, the sea had hissed, the rigging had sung, and the outriggers had sprayed as they skied over the flat blue Sulu.

In the afternoon ul Azam had nodded to sleep. His men

had taken her back to the hold where Grandfather and Elder Brother lay. She fought the strident darkness and held Grandfather's limp neck upon her lap and stroked his forehead, and wondered if he was dead. That had been the hardest time of all to endure . . . But it had ended. The engines had slowed and quietened and the basnig had come to rest.

And then, as though lifted from the passages of the Koran, had come Juhuri, giving kind words and promises of compassion. But to what purpose? The eyes of Juhuri were as fanatical as his father's were cruel. He had seen the captive woman and had liked what he had seen, but father and son, either man would break her like a toy when the game was ended. And that would be the death of Grandfather and Elder Brother too.

Shen shuddered where she lay and had no hold upon the sigh that came with it. Yes, she *was* in charge. What happened to all of them depended on *her*, and she was weak with fear.

The sleep of Juhuri ul Azam was usually easy and sound and patterned with the images of good things from first to last. The dawn would come pleasantly and he would smile at it and stretch and fall down to his prayers in a most thankful state.

That night was different. Sleep came quickly enough, but with it came galloping in a dark horse that took him on a wild ride. He dashed into a dreamscape peopled with unhappy faces – themeless but for one consistency. The Chinese girl, Shen, was constantly there in one form or another.

They stood on the high tower of a minaret, he and she, looking down to the dome of a mosque. There was a creature upon the dome, it had the wings of an eagle, but was more man than eagle, and it held a sword; a burnished Moro kris. The creature flew up with the kris outheld but now it was he

311

who held the kris, and he threatened her with it. Aroused, he wanted to bury his strength in her, and he tried. Urgently he pushed and thrust for he knew he was close to orgasm and she had to take his seed, but he could not penetrate her. Anger swept through him. He raised the kris and stabbed her with it, deep, deep. And thus he was in her, exploding in orgasm.

He awoke with a stream of semen issuing from him, but there was no easing of his lust. She who had been the vessel of his seed had shattered into atoms, gone, yet refusing to go. The dream was so potent. He gathered the mists of it to relive it for a while longer, and with these thoughts came shame.

It was true that he had not wished that dream upon himself. Such things were impossible – the night mind of man had no gatekeeper . . . But now the dream had passed and still he lusted for the person of it. *This* was his shame. For the Chinese woman was a heathen, and in mind and flesh she was totally forbidden.

At his side his wife Fatima slept, snoring peacefully. He knew what he had to do to rid himself of this prurience. Moving slowly so as not to wake Fatima he stood up. At the washstand he lathered his groin and washed clean, and as he did that he prayed silently: 'Oh! Allah protect the chastity of my private parts and purify my heart . . . Free my neck of the burden of my sins . . . Ameen.'

When that was done he crept back on to the mattress and began to knead the fleshy wide hips of the woman who was his property, his field. And he went into his field and he tilled it thoroughly, as was expected of him, and was right. And though his seed was placed properly that time, it did not help. The effort of it had tired his body, but the mind of Juhuri still called upon the dream. Like a rock that has been heated in a fire pit, the mind of him would not cool.

In the morning it was not cool.

The house of ul Azam was built so that the dawn's first yellow rays would brighten its face and come into its windows and front door. It was a very big house, a fine

312

house. It reflected an aura of wealth that surpassed the richest of houses within the heart of Jolo. God hates a spendthrift, but a miser is even more despised, and Abdul ul Azam had taken pains to ensure that those who passed that place would know he was no miser; that those who passed by would look upon his double-storeyed residence with its green-shuttered windows and terracotta tiled roof and say: 'There lives the Datu Abdul ul Azam the Third, a shrewd man, a powerful man. Look at the casa he has built. Look at the high wall; look at the armed guards.'

The wall that defended the casa of ul Azam marched all the way around it, shouldering severely at the poor, split bamboo and sani-palm shacks that neighboured it. But that wall had not always been so forbidding and grand. It had grown over the years. As a barometer of the coming of wealth and power, and enemies, it had kept pace with the fortunes of the house of ul Azam, and now it was tall. Now it had grid-iron gates and two bright brass coachlamps that burned all night long, and it was complete.

Now stationed at the gate, within the yellow pool of light a guard lounged, dressed in green fatigues and cap, he carried an automatic rifle. Shen could see him through the shutter slats on her window. She watched as he leaned there; one shoulder to the wall, a drooping cigarette at his lips. A skinny brown puppy with sickly legs and noduled tail appeared out of the shadows. It stretched wide and almost did not have the strength to regain its posture. The guard waited until the pup had come close to him, then stamped down hard upon the ground. The pup ran squealing with fright. A cock crowed. She turned away from the window, glad of the approach of dawn.

Shen knew little about the house she was imprisoned in. The rooms were many, the walls were thick. The floors were of wood planking, the passages were long and gloomy and joined by stairs and steps wherever they intersected. It seemed to her as if the house had been added to over a long period in an unplanned and disjointed way. It had doors that were heavy with long iron hinges and decorative bolts, made for the untrusting. These things she had been able to glimpse during the quick and hard-pressed walk she had taken last night, from the Jeep to the interior of the casa.

She knew her room very well. It gave a night view of a courtyard where some palm trees grew; a big wrought-iron gate, and a guard who was bored to the point of sadism. If she turned from this window she faced a wall that held a colourful and most intricate tapestry. On the floor lay a mattress and a heap of kapok cushions, all richly embroidered too. A low table, adjacent to the mattress, supported a beaten brass urn, which held fresh water. A light burned behind a filigreed copper shade, casting ravelled shadows, and adding to the perplexity of the tapestry.

She watched the tapestry now. A most illusive pattern, it gave an impression of depth that needed to be touched to be detected as a lie. She touched it. She traced her finger upon its geometry; harsh triangles and squares that quite baffled her eyes and led her hand into a tunnel of flame red, yellow and blue, that drew her inwards and led . . . to nothing. Curiously, it seemed that there before her lay the essay of her predicament. Whoever had woven that composition had known something of suffering.

She was so tired, so sad and swollen with guilt. She lay upon the mattress and worried at the pattern upon the wall. Her eyelids blinked and drooped, weighted with exhaustion, and her mind begged for sleep, but she would not grant it sleep. Chastisement was the requirement and so she administered it; weal upon weal, with accuracy and pain. She had killed Reven with her love. She had defied the wisdom of Grandfather; how could she have been that perverse? Oh, but she had loved him! . . . Yes, you loved him, Shen, in a wilful, obdurate way, like a possessive child. He would have lived but for your selfishness.

Yet she slept. Her exhausted body had its way. The

tapestry of guilt swirled away, her eyelids flickered shut and the little death of sleep took her soul.

She slept so soundly that she did not hear the solemn wail of the Muezzin from the minaret of the mosque:

> 'Come,' called the voice of the Muezzin.
> 'Come to receive salvation.
> For prayer is better than sleep.
> Prayer is much better than sleep.'

The mosque was nearby and the call reached clear through window and wall and door in the house of Abdul ul Azam. Yet she slumbered on.

She did not hear the bolt of her door scrape back, or the creak of the hinges as it opened in admittance.

Juhuri heard the cry of the Muezzin and he responded to it with the speed and piety of spirit of a candidate on the day of resurrection.

He dressed and tied on his headband. He shouldered his black pistol bag and hurried to the mosque. At the water trough before the great doors he stopped, he rolled up his shirt sleeve and began Wudu. He washed his hands and splashed water on his lips and nostrils and said, 'Oh Allah! allow me the aroma of paradise, and forbid me the stench of Hell fire.'

He splashed his cheeks. For the day would come when some faces (such as his) would shine and some – he thought now of his father – would be blackened and turned away from paradise. He washed his right forearm, saying, 'Oh Allah! give me the record of my deeds in my right hand.' He thought of those who would receive with their left hand – 'a difficult reckoning'. He testified:

'There is no God but Allah and Muhammad is his Prophet.'

Then he admitted himself to the mosque, and with his face turned to Mecca, he entered into prayer. He bowed and straightened, and prostrated as was prescribed and was right. He repented his wrong thought and promised never to return to the same. He asked for protection from the mischief of evil.

Juhuri did not rush his prayers, nor did he let his mind wander. For prayer that was not of full measure counted for nothing in the eyes of God. By the time he had finished and turned away it was quite light.

He was most surprised to find his ambu – his mother – waiting at the gates outside the mosque. Halima who had borne him as the first wife of Abdul ul Azam; had fed him of her womb and brought him forth, a small and fragile thing; she who had protected him from the devil-eyed Tilik as he grew; he looked at her and saw that she had been crying.

'I am not crying.'

'But you were crying. You can't hide that from me. And why are you on the streets even before the market is open?'

'I came to find you.'

'Well here I am.' Juhuri took her arm and walked towards the coffee shop that he preferred. But Halima would not go in.

'I won't be seen like this.'

She was a handsome woman; always well dressed in clean loose sawal trousers and sublay blouse that came down to her hips, and was buttoned with real gold dublum. Juhuri would have scoffed at her objection on any other day. That morning, however, he did not press her further. His mother's eyes were red and puffed with tears, and her jaw was aquiver with emotion. He led her steadily away.

'We'll walk together back to the house,' he told her. 'There you can tell me what all this is about.'

They had hardly taken a pace, though, before the tears spilled over, and with them, the story.

'The Chinese woman . . . Oh! It's cruel, Juhuri . . . Your

316

father . . . you know I get up as early as anyone . . . I wasn't spying, I heard a door open in the passage . . . You know I wouldn't spy don't you, anak?'

'Go on,' was all that Juhuri cared to say.

'I watched your father come out of his room. I was about to call out to him to ask him if I could bring coffee, I did not though. He was treading so carefully upon the floor boards; like a thief. Why should he walk like a thief in his own house? I did nothing. I stood at my door and watched for a while, until he had turned the corner. Then I followed him . . .'

Juhuri cut short a further burst of sobbing by jerking sternly at his mother's elbow. 'Go on.'

'I followed him, anak. It was disrespectful of me but I did it, God forgive me. I am sorry that I did . . . no I am *glad* that I did. He went into the room of the Chinese girl.'

Neither stern gestures, nor kind words, could halt the sobs that racked Halima then, her bosom shook and her throat choked, and Juhuri had to wait for her to recover. His heart beat fast and his head felt very full. The house came in sight before Halima could go on.

'I stood there at the closed door. Of course I could see nothing, but I could hear. *Oh!* Juhuri . . . I heard the woman sobbing. I thought he might have beaten her, but it wasn't that kind of sound. I knew what was happening then and I nearly turned away and ran. But I stood there, listening, and the sobbing of that poor woman went on and on. It was more than I could endure. I did not care what would happen to me.' Halima's eyes sought out the approval of her son. 'I had to stop him, didn't I, Juhuri?'

'Yes.'

'Whatever he was doing?'

'Yes. *Yes.*'

'I thought the door would be locked. A part of me hoped that it *was* locked. But it was not locked. I pushed it and it opened . . . God forgive him! There was your father. He was stripped, naked but for his shirt. He was fondling the

Chinese woman. I wanted to be sick. He saw me. He screamed at me – terrible words. He cursed me. He said he would kill me.'

'What of the Chinese girl?'

'You wouldn't let him kill me, Juhuri?'

'What of the Chinese girl?'

'I ran from the house then, to find you. Help me, Juhuri. *Help* me.'

Halima wept again, but Juhuri's strong arm no longer supported her.

'What will you do?' she called. But that question was not answered, neither was the plea: 'Do something to stop him, Juhuri . . . *Juhuri!*'

He did not hear her, or if he did, he did not show it. There were others on the street who heard her plainly. They turned their faces away as people do who feign disinterest. And when they were past her their heads came together and their lips lied in sympathy.

Halima's dignity was destroyed but she was past caring. She sobbed quite openly.

Juhuri ran towards the house of the adulterer Abdul ul Azam and his thoughts were savage.

Scourge him with a hundred stripes, and let not pity withhold you from obedience to Allah, if you truly believe in Allah and the judgement day!

He believed in all that, and the verse came in cadence with his quick feet. Over the last stretch his mind seethed blankly and blind fury was his companion. Juhuri had never known the company of jealousy, so how was he to recognize it now?

What he saw was his father's guilt. Sin – foul sin, and the need for God's stipulated punishment. He would flog this false Muslim a hundred times, and each stroke would be sweeter than the last.

He ran into the house and up the stairs. The door to Shen Woo's room burst open with a cyclone violence and crashed against the wall. But Abdul ul Azam was not there.

Shen Woo was there, her head bowed forward, and once more as she lifted it her beauty touched him to the heart. She was stripped of her clothing. She quickly gathered her bed sheet around her up to her shoulders. Juhuri approached with the care of one who wishes to capture the broken-winged dove. He kneeled next to her. Her eyes were red and her cheeks were shining wet. After a while he spoke.

'My mother told me.'

She turned her face away.

He said, 'I'm so sorry.' She did not respond in any way. He went on, 'I suffer with you. I want to help you.'

Shen wanted no one to suffer with her. She wanted no help.

'Did he hurt you?' Juhuri said.

She shook her head. She had been hurt, but what had been done to her was irrelevant.

'Talk to me,' Juhuri pleaded.

'Go away,' she said.

There was nothing that this man could do. There was nothing that anyone could do, she wanted no kindness, no good things.

'What did he do to you?' Juhuri whispered.

'Nothing,' she said.

And in a physical sense that was the truth. Abdul ul Azam had come and crouched next to her in his semi-nakedness, flaccid and impotent – pathetic. And yet the power he had over her was total, and demanding of subservience. So she had been subservient. While he had groped at her buttons and her waistband and come seeking with his foul lips she had been pliant. When his harsh knees had pressed in between hers, and he had fallen on her with hips heaving like a dog, she had not resisted . . . She had cried. Oh she had cried, but she had done nothing to hinder him.

'Nothing, he did nothing,' she said.

He had been too feeble to penetrate her. He had kneeled

back and stared at her sex. He had stroked ineffectually at his limpness as though betrayed by it.

'Please go now,' she said to Juhuri.

He rose up. 'I'm going,' he said. 'I don't believe what you've told me. No. But I understand. I blame myself for not protecting you. I promised you my protection and I failed. But by God this will not happen again.'

'What will not happen again?' Abdul ul Azam stood at the door. He asked: 'What will not happen again?'

How long he had been standing there; how much he had overheard, Juhuri did not know. His violent anger towards his father had gone, but with all his heart he hated him now.

'Ha!' Abdul gestured towards Shen Woo. 'Do you think I would harm this little bird? I would not harm her . . . Tell him, little bird, if I harmed you.'

'A shameful deed,' Juhuri said. 'An evil road to follow.'

'So you say, Juhuri.' Abdul stepped into the room. 'Now tell me the cause of all this righteousness.'

'Your sin. Your adultery, Datu ul Azam. Your destruction of the honour of this family.'

'Did *she* say that? Did *she* make such an accusation?'

'You know who your accuser is.'

'Yes, I know who said it. The point is: is it the truth? The punishment for slander is equal to the punishment for adultery, Juhuri. The curse of God is just as applicable to slanderers . . . So go ahead now; while I'm here to hear her; call your mother and let her swear four times that I committed zina with this woman. And I will swear four times that it's a lie. Ask *her*!' Abdul pointed.

'I have asked her.'

'Well then?'

'She and I and Halima all know the truth. And Allah knows it. Allah is as close as the jugular vein and he knows it.'

'So let Allah be my judge then, Juhuri. Not you.'

Abdul ul Azam bent down to Shen. He took her chin in his hand and pinched her cheeks and tilted up her face.

'She's beautiful, isn't she, Juhuri? Look at her hair – those eyes, like the gazelle of Batin is she not? She's mine, Juhuri. Yes, I've decided, I'm going to marry her.'

Juhuri gasped.

'You should see your face, Juhuri . . . Ah! I see now what has lit your fire.'

'She's a pagan.'

'Yes . . . Would it not please Allah if she was admitted upon the right path?'

'You have all the wives that one is allowed.'

'I'm going to divorce Halima, who lied about me. I have already pronounced Talaq upon her . . . I am going to see that the feet of my little gazelle here, soon take the path of Islam. And then I will marry her.'

'*Marry* her!'

'I want her, so I shall marry her. The Prophet Muhammad revealed this allowance for the needs of man. I have a need.'

Juhuri was stunned by his father's defamation: such *kafirun* excretion of the pure food of the table of God. Words would not come to him.

Abdul ul Azam walked from the room then, as calmly as he had entered it, his bearing unaffected by Juhuri's sudden exclamation: '*Heir of Hell!*'

It was the worst thing he could think of to say. 'Heir of Hell. You've perverted the message of Allah and you know it.' Juhuri shook with unspent fury; his jaw muscles ached with tension and his breathing was shallow.

'He wants to marry you.' Juhuri spoke on in Tausug; too angry to perceive his error. 'God! May this devil be stopped.'

Shen stared at him impassively, but she understood well enough. Abdul wanted her and Abdul was as resourceful and cunning as a monkey on a chain. Ultimately he would get hold of what he wanted . . . Let it happen. Die, and die again; what did it matter? She felt nothing. She would not do a thing to escape the groping monkey at the limit of the chain. Juhuri spoke on in English now.

321

'Marriage of a Muslim to a disbeliever is forbidden. He cannot marry you unless you permit it; unless you become halal.'

Go away, Shen thought. Just go away.

At last he did go. He closed the door behind him, and after some time, as though he had given thought to it, the lock turned slowly, apologetically.

She lay down and chased once more at the enigma of the tapestry, and marvelled at man's ability to endure the bare nerve of sin, as long as it is a private sin. But let it be revealed and there was no knowing which way he would jump. Marry her? Abdul ul Azam merely wanted her to satisfy his flesh, but with the pain of damnation being shouted he must look to his everlasting soul. So she must be halal. And Juhuri was in conflict with his father. Carelessly, she wondered at the consequences of all of this.

Shen thought about Grandfather and Elder Brother then. She doubted that she would see them again. She told herself that she had reached the depths of her misery, and was now used to it, and could be hurt no further. But that was not so. Again she saw the face of Reven and cried until she slept. She thought she was still dreaming when she heard the voice of Elder Brother.

'Ah Shen, Ah Shen.'

He was squatting at the foot of her mattress. Before the image could slip away, Shen rushed upon him and hugged his neck. 'Wah! What's all this!'

Eddie shrugged himself from the embrace. He had come, he said, to take her to Grandfather. She sprang a hundred questions upon him, and his answer to all of them was: 'Come and see for yourself.'

The room that held Woo Yin-wah was almost a mirror image of her own prison; there were two mattresses and more pillows, and the tapestry was of a different design.

Grandfather looked deathly pale and shrunken, laid out upon his mattress like some ancient ivory figurine, too fragile to touch. A sparse white stubble upon his chin gave him a neglected look. Shen kneeled down and took his frail wrist. 'Has he eaten?' she asked softly. 'Has he had anything to drink, anything at all?' The pulse of a butterfly fluttered beneath her fingertips. A whisper as brittle as a fallen leaf came from him.

'Lui Lui?'

He opened his eyes and turned his face as if to ensure that his senses had not misled him. A smile for the truth of it.

'My little Lui Lui.'

'Yes, Grandpa, I'm here.'

'He eats a bit,' Eddie said. 'He had some water earlier.'

She held a glass of water to his lips. He pursed his lips and sipped, but the effort seemed too great for him. He closed his eyes and she lowered his head.

'He must have medicine,' she said.

'Some coincidence. ul Azam's exact words. The Datu says there is a clever Chinese healer in Jolo town. Says he will have him called if you wish it.'

'ul Azam . . . *Abdul* ul Azam said that?'

'He wants to help. He's not the devil we thought he was.'

'I can't believe my ears. How can you say that!'

'It's true. He said that if *you* wish it he will send for this healer.'

'Of course I wish it. Of course, of course!'

'Wait then.'

More an order than a request; Shen complied without question while Eddie went away. Yet she did think a lot about Elder Brother's new-found faith in the virtue of Abdul ul Azam. She knew of the rottenness of this Datu, she had encountered him as no man would ever encounter him. So now he had withdrawn beneath a cover of kind words and compassion. That this poor camouflage should fool Elder Brother was a wonder. The man was a murderer, they all knew that, and if a reminder was required, then there lay Grandfather. ul Azam 'the Merciful' had done that.

323

But here was purpose once more, and a reason to fight for life. Grandpa needed her and there was no room for any thought other than that. She stroked his wispy white hair and Grandfather smiled his weak smile, and he whispered, 'My Lui Lui, what has happened to us?'

'It will be all right.'

She held his feeble hand and swore that it would be so. And almost believed it. Elder Brother came back then.

'He's sent for the healer,' he announced as he came into the room. 'His name is Pang Ho.'

'That's good.'

'You don't sound pleased.'

'I can't help remembering that if it wasn't for ul Azam there would be no need for this healer. You seem to have forgotten that, but I haven't. He's a murderer; *have* you forgotten that?'

'I forget nothing, Ah Shen.' He walked to the window and peered into the yard below. 'See that guard down there? Yes, well there are two more guards inside this house. We are prisoners here, Sister. I'm trying to make things easier for all of us. That's something you might try to do as well. Understand, Sister – this is a different world and so, different rules for us to follow. Abdul ul Azam is Tai lo of this whole island. You'd better get that straight . . . Respect him.'

'*Respect* . . . did I hear you say that? Elder Brother, are we talking about the same man?'

'Try and see things this way. He holds the power of life and death over us. And if you can't see that then you're a fool.'

'I hate him.'

'And you showed it.'

'I showed it? Of course I showed it.'

'Yes. Don't do it again.'

'Again?' Shen took the word and tested its implication. 'Again . . . What must I not do *again*? What did ul Azam tell you about me, Elder Brother?'

'He told me he went to your room . . .'

'Go on.'

'What does it matter? I'm sure that now you'll be more understanding, ah? . . . Don't look at me like that, Sister, you must know there is no option for us.'

As though she had discovered a dead rat in the drinking urn, Shen Woo looked at her brother in utter dismay. Drink up; all is well. That was the message.

'It will be all right, Sister, if you don't make problems.'

Shen had to wait for a long while before she felt calm enough to speak again. Then her voice quavered. 'I suppose Abdul ul Azam has told you that it would please him if I became a Muslim?'

Eddie nodded. He knew.

Shen said, 'Do you know why he wants this?'

'Does it matter why?'

'It matters that you should know why.'

Eddie took a while to reply. He said, 'I'm sorry,' and those words seemed genuine. Then in breezy contradiction he went on, 'It won't be so bad, for God's sake.'

'He tried to rape me, does that not make you hate him too? He tried to rape *me*, your sister . . . But I can see that you know that. Then you must also know that that is why he wishes me to become Muslim; so that he can continue his rape . . . legally. Do you still approve of my conversion to Islam? Is that what you want for me?'

'He said he would care for you.' Eddie sulked his words.

'And you, Elder Brother; did he say he would care for you too, if only Younger Sister would do as told?'

'Don't you care what happens to the old man? Look there . . . Yes, look there, Sister. Do you think he's got a chance without the help of ul Azam? No, no chance. So you hate ul Azam; so Grandpa must die. Is that how *you* see it?'

She could summon no quick defence against this flail of rhetoric. 'Don't talk like that, Elder Brother. You know that's not true. You know I'd do anything for Grandpa.'

'You're not a virgin. Your flower was hacked by the *yang*

tsat of the gwai lo cop. He plucked your lute strings, ha! We all know that. You lay with the gwai lo.'

'So I'll lie with anyone? Is that what you're trying to say? I'm a whore; a green-lantern girl, is that it?' She was so angry she could not guard her words. 'You hated him, Brother, not because he was a gwai lo, but because he was a better man than you are. You care for no one but yourself. I'm loyal to the family but I'm not blind. I see you as he must have seen you, and I don't like what I see. Don't talk to me of saving Grandpa. The only person you are interested in saving is yourself. Go and tell Abdul, your friend, that you've convinced me to become Muslim. Tell him anything you like. I'm sure he'll reward you well . . . What did he promise you? Gold? Go get your gold. I'll do what I have to do for Grandpa. But don't expect me to believe your lies. From this day on, I'll never trust you or respect you again.'

She thought that her brother was going to hit her. He came up to her. His body was rigid and his eyes furious. He stood there for a moment, but he did not touch her. He walked past her to the door and there he stopped again, in search for words to lash her with. But no words came and he just stared, and then he turned and went away.

Shen felt amazingly calm and light – unburdened of the cold stone weight of her depression. Not at all how she would have expected to feel after such an angry encounter. Thank you, Brother, at least for that. You came to take from me in a cruel way, but the gain was greater than the loss. For opposites are the spawn of their own reformation, and, as everything must change, so once more I must change. She had had to experience darkness in order to know the light.

Yes, there was light. There was the promise of the healer who would come and strengthen Grandpa.

A soft and feminine knock upon the door brought into the room the sweetest featured girl that Shen had ever seen. A dimple-cheeked smile, brown skin and dark brown hair gilded at the crown; she advanced on Shen holding out a tray. The smell of coffee reached Shen, and confectionery. There was a brass urn on the tray, and glasses and a plate of cakes.

'What is your name?' Shen asked. '*Your . . . name?*'

'Be Narisa.'

Shen took the tray from her and set it down. She smiled and took Narisa's hand and squeezed it. The squeeze and the smile were returned and Shen thought, here is a friend.

'Grandpa.' Shen pointed. 'Sick.'

'Grandpa, sick,' echoed Narisa.

'Stay with me,' Shen said. She poured coffee into a cup. It was black and tasted like caramel. She blew at the rim of the glass and when she looked up again Narisa was gone.

From Grandfather came the faintest of whispers; the feeblest of gestures, beckoning. 'Lui Lui . . .'

'Grandpa.'

'I heard . . . Yes I heard it all. No mistake, Lui Lui. What you said is right. Elder Brother has been poisoned by the gold. He has done awful things . . . Great wrong . . . Do you hear me?'

'Yes, I hear you, Grandfather.'

'I feel so weak . . . I'm so tired. It's hard to know if my words pass my throat or are just in my mind. I'm an old man, Lui Lui . . . The sun has reached the western hill.'

'A doctor is coming, a Chinese doctor . . .'

Woo Yin-wah waved weakly and impatiently for her to keep quiet. 'Listen to me, Lui Lui . . . Though Elder Brother has gone wrong he is the only one who can take my place and see to the memory of our respected ancestors . . . You are the strong one, even though just a girl. You must stand by Elder Brother until he finds his own worth . . . Can you hear me?'

'Can hear you, Grandpa.'

'Yes . . . You must do as I say. He must never know what I have said. You must be like good soil is to the bamboo . . . He needs this, Lui Lui. He will grow.'

'Will try, Grandpa.'

'Our family must regain face. While Grandson is shamed we all are shamed, the living and the dead, ah.'

'Yes.'

'I can no longer see to it. You must see to it.'

'Grandpa . . . You will get well.'

'*Tsha!* You are the strong one, Ah Shen. No more to be said.'

┥ 10 ┝

THE SWORD OF AL MUMIT

Southwards. The engine throbbed and the junk of Woo Yin-wah crept into the peaceful Sulu. The north wind wavered, then died. The hours were sheathed in kind deep skies and placid water. There was little for the two men to do but stare to the horizon and wait. Succulent fish clung to their line; they ate well, they rested, and they spoke. Bahang told his story. He made of his hands the collaborators of his tongue. He mixed in with his cupful of English a multitude of gestures, and told of a love as high as the sun and as wide as the sky for his beautiful Narisa. His words flashed fire and his fingers clawed out the agony of his loss; the terror of ul Azam . . . But now there was hope. Milikan had brought hope, and strength – like Kaytan the shark.

'Yes,' said Forrester. He understood about love.

Few ships came their way. There was a smoky funnelled, rust-hulled freighter that came close enough for them to feel the heave of its wake. Its skipper, with binoculars upheld, observed them as he passed. Some kumpit boats from Palawan came by, their crews, lazed out upon the decks, passed curious eyes over the battered Toh Mong Suen. Bright-sailed Bajau vintas skimmed the green shallows off the Tubbataha reefs like butterflies in the wind – the boats of the sea gypsies. Their only concern was the 'breath of heaven' that blew them there, and would blow them home again . . . This was the Sulu; the place in the memory of Woo Yin-wah that had called so sweetly, but hid a savage heart.

At midday on the second day there lifted from the horizon an edging of land. Distance bleached the colour from it, but as the afternoon wore on, high-clouded blue mountains rode up. This was the sombre beauty of Jolo. A hundred green islets were set upon the sea to guard Jolo's approaches; and they guarded them well. Where the sea slipped between the islands there were tide rips, eddies and whirlpools of monstrous strength. The junk ran on straining engines and Bahang sweated at the tiller ropes. He did not sing. His white teeth bit upon his lip and his eyes frowned with worry. The Toh Mong Suen was not made for this water, it answered obstinately and lumbered from one danger to the next like some obese drunkard, while basnig outriggers and vintas danced lightly past.

They anchored in a sheltered bay in the cusp of three small islands. Bahang named them: 'Cabucan, Pangasinan, Marunngas.' He pointed to the south: 'Be Jolo.'

A five-mile stretch of lake-flat water was all that remained to be crossed. Beyond that steep mountains rose from the sea. There was a stubble of green palm trees on the shore, and a sprawl of buildings upon which hung a haze of smoke. 'Jolo Town,' Forrester guessed.

Towering over the town the peaks were caught in a gloom of grey clouds; a bit like Hong Kong, Forrester thought, but then he changed his mind. Hong Kong was a neon-bright whore, shouting to be bought. This city lay low and sombre and did not speak in a welcoming way. This place was bearded and frowning with religion, and he did not like its looks. He felt deep apprehension as he and Bahang stood at the rail. They watched as cloud and water and vinta outriggers, full-sailed in the whispering breeze, took on the fading complexion of the sunset; first gold, then pink that dusted the mountaintops and clouds, then grey that melted mountain and sea and vinta and cloud into darkness.

It was easy to see Jolo now. It glistened like night dew in the moonlight. And somewhere there amongst the pinprick glimmer was a light that belonged to the Tausug killer ul Azam, and if Shen was alive, perhaps she too stood in that glow. Tomorrow he would go to Jolo. Tomorrow he would discover how far audacity would take him in his invasion of this Muslim keep. But he thought he had a chance. Bahang had friends on the island of Jolo.

Bahang the sea gypsy slipped into the water soon after it was dark. He made no splash, no sound at all as he swam towards the island he called Pangasinan. He had said he would return at dawn; that he would come sailing back in a vinta. Forrester believed him.

And when the dawn came there was a vinta with a bright striped sail of yellow, red, blue and green, and Bahang was its master. Another Bajau man sat in the bows. They came alongside.

'*Owa!*' waved Bahang.

'*Owa!*' Forrester returned.

'*Sung na kita.*' Bahang beckoned him down.

The vinta was small – a shoulder-wide hull, as sharp as a javelin. A bamboo, tripod mast held up the bright lug sail. The breeze was light, but so was the vinta, it picked them up like a kite and dashed them away.

Brown, well-muscled; Bahang bent, tight as a jockey on a horse – two rigging lines for reins. The boat skipped over the water with a snare drum whirr as rippled waves smacked past, and whippy, long-reaching outriggers slashed at the smooth sea.

Quickly past the islands, Forrester looked back and saw that the junk was just a small thing now. Ahead lay Jolo, expanding even as he watched it. A shoreline beach of whitest sand was drawing them. Behind the beach grew a forest of leaning, grey-trunked, green-crowned coconut palms.

'Bu Dahu,' Bahang pointed to the mist-covered mountain. Forrester ducked low beneath the sail and gained a clear view of it. The crying mountain, he remembered, and looking at the rainclouds smudging it he could see why it was so named.

Beneath the crying mountain a city of nipa palm and bamboo sprawled down to the tide mark, but did not stop there. On stilts, the houses marched out into the shallows. Basnigs and vintas were tied up there, graceful and bright-hulled amongst the grey piles . . . Inland, a mosque came into view; green domes and minarets as sharp as pencils grew out of Jolo's compost of dwellings.

There was a harbour, a long pier of bleached wooden piles which ended at a lighthouse. But it was not towards the harbour that Bahang's quick vinta sailed . . . Far beyond the easternmost dwellings, he saw a long white beach that curved into a bay. The water was shallow there, green, patched darkly where rocks and reefs lurked just beneath the surface.

The vinta sped straight into this bay and skipped across reefs and shallows. Then the keel hissed on sand and the sail could carry them no further. They were beached in ankle-deep water. Bahang chatted to his companion as Forrester waded ashore. The vinta was turned around and Bahang's friend sailed it from the bay.

Forrester was to wait in the coconut plantation; those were Bahang's instructions. No one would find him there.

'Damn good,' Bahang reassured. 'OK. OK.'

But Bahang was wrong.

Forrester watched his little friend depart. It was the first time that he had watched him walk any distance on land. He kept to the shallows where the water wetted his ankles. He was graceless on his feet, unhappy on land – awkward, like a turtle out of water. He observed the Bajau until he was out of sight beyond the bend of the cove.

When Bahang had gone, he lolled down upon the soft grassed sand and squinted past the shifting palm tufts into the sky, a slow, cloudy sky that drifted whitely past. As the sun climbed, so the clouds shrivelled and he was forced to move with the drifting shade of the palms. The sand scorched where it was not shaded and flies came to drink his salty sweat. The wavelets whispered of their coolness but he did not go there. He was to stay hidden; that was agreed and it was a wise decision. A basnig skirted the mouth of the bay. Its motor thumped lazily and its bow wave was small, still the outrigger ran like the cut of a scissor through silk. This vessel was similar to the one he had seen on the night of the attack. As it passed from east to west across his line of vision there were memories of searchlights and gunfire, then it was gone. He leaned his spine against a palm trunk and whisked at the flies. Then he dozed.

The sound that awoke him contradicted the sanguine expectations of Bahang. There were people close at hand, they were running. He could hear, he could feel the thud of feet upon the sand. They were coming in his direction and they would almost certainly see him in a few seconds.

They did find him. They were young boys, six of them wearing shorts and sandals with nothing more upon their minds than being first to reach the sea. Then they saw his tracks leading from the water and they followed them. Forrester did not even bother to hide. He sat there, propped up by the palm trunk, and waited for their curious young eyes.

'*Dain di'in kaw?*'

It seemed he was being asked a question of sorts – '*Dain di'in kaw?*'

Yes, a definite question. He smiled. He shrugged. He tapped his chest and said, 'Milikan.'

'Milikan? Ah! Milikan . . . yes?'

'Yes,' said Forrester.

'Good morning.' They tested him.

'Good morning,' said Forrester.

'Good afternoon.'

'Good afternoon,' said Forrester.

'Milikan.' They nodded. Yes, this was the real thing.

'John Wayne,' said Forrester.

'*John Wayeen!*' they shrieked, delighted with the drift of this cultural exchange. But nothing more came from the visitor from distant shores. They stared at him a while longer, then the cool sea beckoned. They turned from the Milikan and rushed for the water; all of them but one. The smallest kid had something more to offer. He hawked to his lips a great blob of throat mucus, then dribbled it loose. He gazed at Forrester, then, satisfied that he had impressed with this massive display of glandular function, he too turned and ran for the waves.

Bahang returned at dusk. He clucked his distress at Forrester's story. He bent over the tracks of the little boys and bit his knuckles with anxiety. He had said that this place was safe and it had proved unsafe; *his* fault.

'Tausug kid, bad.'

But Bahang had news to burst upon him that was poignant with joy: your tanung – your sweetheart – don't you know, she be alive. Yes, let disbelief leave your eyes. Yes, look at me and see the truth: your *tanung be alive*. Be happy, amigo, be happy!

God, he was dizzy with happiness! But all he could say was, 'Are you sure? Are you sure?'

Bahang was sure. He wanted his amigo to be sure – but where were the words?

'She OK. She OK.'

That wasn't enough to lift the frown of worry for long.

Slung across Bahang's shoulders were two rough-wove raffia baskets. At his hip he wore a parang machete with a worn teak hilt and brass-bound wooden scabbard. He showed his amigo what he had in the baskets: two plump coconuts, still buried in their thick green husks. He fetched them from their raffia bindings and laid them on the sand. With the parang blade he lopped off their crowns, and he offered Forrester an opened fruit.

No beverage in the world could have tasted better. Forrester lifted the heavy fruit to his mouth and poured, and the fresh cool milk ran down his gullet, cleansing, filling him with its richness. He knew of the qualities of fresh coconut milk; it was so pure that it could be passed straight into the veins as a substitute glucose drip, and the Japanese invaders had used it that way. He drained the coconut completely. He had not realized his thirst until that moment.

The parang was wielded again. This time to fashion a small spoon from the coconut husk. With this Forrester scraped the butter-soft flesh from the inside of the shell, and passed it to his mouth. The tree of life, that was what the Malays called it, and that was what it was for him that sunset.

'OK, amigo,' said Bahang. 'OK. OK. Go Jolo.'

Bahang beckoned, and he came on; pleased to be on the move again. He was sure that the Tausug kids would have reported to their parents about the amazing Milikan they had discovered washed up on the beach, but there was nothing that could be done about that. He felt strong and light: Shen was alive.

They kept to the beaches where they could. Beside him Bahang walked happily in the wavelets. But they could not stick to the shore; they came upon a barrio of nipa huts that crept upon piled stilts right out over the water. There were lighted windows here and silhouetted human shapes; the smell of cooking; the barking dog and the chuckle of guitars and split-cane xylophones. They turned inland to avoid discovery. Bahang crept craven-spirited through the woods. They passed through groves of shadowy rustling trees, a bad place for the Bajau, for here dwelled the spirits of those who had lived and died in an ugly way.

'Lutao,' whispered Bahang. They were everywhere!

Through these dark places Bahang dogged Forrester's footsteps. At times the jungle grew so thick that large detours were necessary, and he suspected that Bahang, in his fear, had lost them, so he navigated as best he could. Eventually he found a road. Two concrete strips shining whitely in the moonlight.

It was not a good thing that they should follow this road. The Philippine Constabulary would surely patrol it or maintain checkpoints along it. And he did not trust the PC; they had a shocking reputation. The alternative was to plunge back into the shadows of the jungle, and Bahang was just not up to it. He was in a funk; his wide eyes shone and rolled towards the jungle as though he would die if he was compelled to go back. He plucked at Milikan's arm and gestured towards the road.

'OK . . . Damn good. *Tabangau aku.*'

'OK,' said Forrester.

He compromised. He walked along the verge of the road; in the shadows of the big trees but not quite in the jungle, and they made good progress like that.

The Philippine Constabulary *were* on the road. They were deployed in a guard house – a little fort built up of stone and logs, with a blazing searchlight that cut the jungle at two hundred metres into patterns of white, black and dark green. Behind this cyclop-eyed fort the city lay in the forced and melancholy slumber of the PC curfew.

They bellied like monitor lizards through the slick under-growth until they had passed the searchlight, then onwards at a crouch for a few hundred metres, and when they rested again it was within a muddy alleyway that separated a crush of slat-walled homes. The fungus odour of earth drains hung heavily in the air and the flicker of television escaped to the dark street. Dogs sniffed and snuffed behind the bamboo fences, and some barked at the two strangers who flitted by like thieves in the night.

The alleys were narrow and dark as tunnels, and one gave on to the next so it was easy not to be seen. There were others in that warren of lanes, daring the curfew like them; quick-moving people who did not spare a word or a glance as they passed.

The alleys became wider. They became roads, tarred and paved, and bordered with buildings of brick and glass and shops with signs hung out to advertise their trade. A plaza

336

opened before them, a place of trees and benches – but no people. Here there was a great mosque. It stood up all minarets and domes, quite senior to everything around it. High white walls kept it safe, and apart.

Bahang led on. They skirted the mosque and entered a further street of shops and stalls with billboards outside that invited them to enter. But they could not enter because the doors were locked and the windows were dark.

Pang Ho – Yeuk Choi Po

They stopped at the door beneath that sign. That door, too, appeared to be locked, but it was not. Bahang knew its secret; he twisted the padlock and worked the handle . . . Made welcome by the tinkle of wind chimes, and the aroma of incense and herbs, they entered what seemed a friendly place. The floorboards squeaked, the lights were dim; Bahang knew the way to the rearmost room.

The god of healing, Yee Pak Kung, gazed down from a wall shrine lit with little red lamps. There was Pang Ho's stove, a kettle hissed upon its surface. There was a sink that was stacked with dirty dishes and bottles and tins of herbs and Pang Ho's porcelain mortar and pestle. A wooden table stood in the centre of the room with four chairs around it and Pang Ho's mahjong set fully laid out at its centre . . . Pang Ho sat there. Pang Ho was a cripple, his spine was buckled forward so deeply that his head hardly showed above the white mahjong tiles. He wore only a singlet and shorts and clearly did not care one bit that his warped and grotesque body was so openly displayed. He rose a little way from his seat and bowed the smallest of bows.

'You give me great face by coming. Please sit down.' He spoke good English. 'Of course you would like something to refresh you. Tea, coffee if you like. Not American coffee, I'm afraid, but island coffee. Quite good, I assure you.'

'Tea,' said Forrester, 'would be perfect.'

'Ah yes.' Pang slid from the chair. He had to reach up and stretch to fetch the kettle. 'Unusual for an American to prefer tea. You don't sound American; are you? Forgive my rude question, ah. You see, all Whites are called "Milikan" here; that, or "Joe". A legacy from the war years. We have fond memories of the Americans.' He had a foot stool upon which he stood to pour water from the kettle to the teapot. He peered into the rising steam, then added a dash more. 'Never let the water boil for too long,' he advised. 'Water is a living thing, too much heat saps the vitality from it.'

Pang Ho set the teapot down upon the table and climbed painfully back upon his chair. He lit a cigarette and coughed a bit. He wheezed as he spoke.

'My friend Bahang has told me about your adventures . . . most hectic. I hope since you landed on Jolo that all has gone well.'

'Thank you for seeing me,' Forrester said. 'My name is Reven Forrester. I'm British. I'm from Hong Kong.'

Pang Ho bowed again, and said, 'Humble name is Pang. You are welcome to my house.'

They exchanged small talk for a while. Pang had studied botany at the University of Hawaii, hence his excellent English. He had a sharp mind and bitter, quick eyes. Forrester quickly liked him. He said, 'It's good of you to see me.'

'Bahang is my friend or you would not be here now. All the Bajau are my friends. Do you know about the Bajau, Mr Forrester?'

'Very little, I'm afraid.'

'Let me tell you a little more. The Bajau are the most gentle and compassionate of people. When there is trouble, they will run from it. They are the nomads of the sea. They farm it as you might farm the land. They know of every reef and gully, and every underwater mountain, and have names for them all. They know their way in the deep sea as you must know your way in the streets of Hong Kong. That is why you are alive today. I am telling you this because you should know about the man who brought you to me.'

'I have learned to admire him, Mr Pang.'

'Ah! And he admires you . . . *too* much, I'm afraid. Pardon my directness. It's not your fault, Mr Forrester. He sees you as a conqueror – a champion. Which I am sure is not the impression you intended; but there it is. Do you know about Narisa, Mr Forrester? Did he tell you about her?' Pang Ho lifted the lid of the teapot and studied the condensation that had collected there. 'May I pour for you?'

The tea was of excellent quality. He was being treated royally.

'A fine tea, Mr Pang . . . Yes I know a bit about Narisa. I know that Abdul ul Azam holds her in virtual slavery.'

'Complete slavery,' Pang Ho corrected. 'Absolute submission. For as gentle as the Bajau are, the Tausug are warlike and cruel. They despise the Bajau, they call them *Luwaan*. That means spit-outs. The Tausug treat the Bajau like dogs . . . *worse* than dogs. The Bajau are terrified of the Tausug. It's easy for them to be made slaves, do you see? They believe themselves to be inferior to the Tausug. They dare not run from the Tausug. Bahang thinks that you have the strength to take on Abdul ul Azam. He's given you almost a supernatural status, Mr Forrester. Don't blame him for that. I will delicately explain the impossibility of this to him. Leave it to me.'

Bahang said something to Pang then. The cripple frowned and concentrated as the Bajau spoke. 'A difficult language,' he explained to Forrester. 'He wants you to know that he is not afraid of Abdul ul Azam . . . That's not word for word, but that's the gist of it. You mustn't believe that. But it is what he wanted me to tell you.'

Bahang spoke on in a language that ran like swift burbling water. Pang Ho was hard pressed to keep up with him.

'He says ul Azam is powerful . . . but you are more powerful. I'm just translating, you understand. He says that your wife is at the casa of ul Azam. The Bajau at the harbour saw her being taken to a Jeep and then to the house . . . He says that Narisa will look after her. He has got word to her to look after her. He says his Bajau friends know how to steal guns, if you want guns.'

Bahang fell silent. Pang Ho said, 'Don't think of such a course of action, Mr Forrester.'

'Why?'

'Because, that would achieve nothing but your certain death . . . Is the Chinese girl really your wife, Mr Forrester?'

'We will still marry, I hope. ul Azam has stolen from me as much as he has stolen from Bahang.'

'I see. I understand your anger. Yes, ul Azam takes what he likes. He has the strength to do it. No one opposes him here.'

'That's why I'm here, Mr Pang. I want her back.'

'A big knife and a wide axe. You can't take him on like that.'

Pang took a cigarette and offered it to Forrester. When his guest declined he set it in his own mouth and hobbled to the stove to light it. He coughed as though his lungs would burst from him as bits of mince. His face reddened and his poor, crooked body bent to breaking point in the spasm. He gulped a cup of water and patted his chest.

'My lungs are wrecked, ah . . . But what would life be without cigarettes? I was saying that you will not succeed with guns; no, no chance with guns. You must believe the power of the Datu Abdul ul Azam. He is a man of the blood of the tree of the Quarish. That means that he claims to be of the blood of the Prophet Muhammad. And whether that's true or not, that is what is believed in the Sulu. He has followers; and guns. He owns land and he has money, and in real terms he is probably more powerful than even the Sultan of Sulu. A shot fired at him would bring a thousand in return. A shot fired by you, an infidel, would cause not only your death, but the death of everyone connected to you; a Jihad would be declared against you. Do you understand?'

'What sort of help could I expect from the Philippine Constabulary?'

Pang laughed on a lungful of smoke, and that set off a further chain-explosion of coughing. 'The PC,' Pang wheezed. '*Ha!* The biggest villains of them all. They're in on all the killings on the island one way or another. No one trusts them and everyone fears them. ul Azam pays them well, don't you worry. Do you have more money than the Datu, Mr Forrester? No? Then forget the PC. They're rotten to the core . . . Ah, I see your despondency. Don't be despondent. Perhaps you have allies more powerful than the PC that you don't know about yet.'

'That's good news, Mr Pang.'

'I said, *perhaps* . . . Tell me, did Woo Yin-wah really have so much gold on board his junk? Are the stories true?'

'There was a fortune on board. How did you know?'

'Treasure; where there's a whisper of it, the newspapers will poke their noses. If it's the treasure of Li Ma-hong then the Manila newspapers are bound to print it. They say it's buried on the islands off Manila. Did Woo really find it, ah?'

'No. It wasn't buried treasure. It's triad gold.'

'I'm intrigued, deeply intrigued. You're no triad brother, Mr Forrester.'

'You wonder what I was doing on the junk.'

'Forgive my impertinence.'

'I have no interest in that gold. No claim upon it. I'm a rich man in my own right. I did not come here to retrieve that gold.'

'Amazing . . . Yes, I believe you. So it would not concern you if *I* had an interest in that triad gold.'

'It would surprise me if you didn't.'

'*Wah!*' Pang feigned wide-eyed surprise. 'You are most direct. Straight talk; all right. What if I had thought of a way of helping you get what you want, and in my turn gained in the transaction?'

'It would delight me, Mr Pang.'

'Our enemy's strength is his weakness too.' Pang Ho crawled off his chair. He stoked his stove and set the kettle upon it. He lit a cigarette, this time without choking on its smoke, and while he did this, he spoke on. 'The Tausug are the fiercest of peoples. They love a fight. They're always spoiling for a good fight; looking for a cause. Arguments are not too hard to find, there are vendettas on this island that go back to the turn of the century . . . Yes, it's true. They have family and kinship bonds that are practically unbreakable. The honour of the family comes before life. Friendship is a sacred thing. A man, if called upon to do so in the name of friendship, will lay down his life. *Bagay Magtay manghud* – my friends, we are brothers. That's how it's described, and only the most terrible of betrayals can sever such kinship or friendship bonds. But, when that does happen, and friends or kin become enemies, only death can end it. I want you to appreciate your enemy. Bahang says you are brave. You had better be brave. The Tausug wear amulets – *anting-anting* they call it. It gives them magical strength. Ten bullets will not drop a man who wears the *anting-anting*. It's true. I've seen it . . . But as I said: our enemy's strength is his weakness too.'

Pang brought the fresh tea to the table. He raised himself back on his chair, clearly he had pain.

'Do you see what you're up against here, Mr Forrester? Well perhaps I have seen the soft underbelly of Abdul. I say again, *perhaps* . . . Tea, Mr Forrester? . . . Yes, Abdul has a son named Juhuri. A firebrand of a man; he has the hot blood of the Tausug and a head full of Islam – a most explosive mixture. Juhuri is the son of Abdul's first wife, who should thus be his most senior and respected wife, ah? But old Abdul and Halima have never got on. Her family, too, claims Datu blood, but Abdul disputes it. So the resentment

342

is strong. He has tried to divorce her – has pronounced talaq upon her several times in the past. But for the sake of Juhuri, she has fought it. But things have come to a head . . . The reason why I know all these things is because when there is doctoring to be done at the casa, then I am the one who is sent for.' Pang seemed hesitant to go on. He stared across the table at his guest, frowning in deep assessment. Then he said, 'I cannot continue without relating an incident that is bound to upset you. Please be calm.'

'Go on.'

'See, this is a small town, and gossip here lifts like dust on the wind. A lot of it lands on my doorstep. A healer is in a position of trust, not so? People like to tell me things . . .'

'Mr Pang,' Forrester said. 'It's been a long night. I'm tired. Please be direct.'

'Of course. You do look tired. That is most understandable . . . I'll tell you this as it was told to me. Halima was seen waiting for her son, Juhuri, outside the mosque. Apparently she had been crying; she seemed most distressed. When Juhuri came out he tried to comfort his mother, but she would not stop crying. Well, if you want the whole of Jolo to know your problems, just whisper them on the street . . . She was crying about some terrible thing that Abdul had done. It had to do with the Chinese girl.'

'Go on.' He really did not need Pang to go on. He knew that Pang was going to tell him that Shen had been raped by Abdul ul Azam.

'And Halima walked in on it . . .' Then she had run to summon her son. 'Juhuri was furious. He rushed off to the house . . .' And Shen could not hope to escape the wrath of the insulted first wife of Abdul ul Azam. 'She's right in the middle of a potential feud of terrible proportions. Now, Halima's family will not allow this insult to her to go unavenged. It could turn out to be a very bloody thing.'

Forrester felt suddenly drained of energy. His mind was

coping cumbersomely with this new atrocity. He swore quietly – just a puff of air: 'Bastard.'

'Indeed.' Pang had heard him. 'My sympathy.'

'Where does Juhuri stand now? Does he blame his father or Shen? And even if his father is guilty, might he not try to shift the blame for the sake of his family honour?'

'You see the complexity of it.' Pang coughed rawly again. 'But I see Juhuri as our man.'

'Would he turn against his own father?'

'I can't be sure. Halima's influence on Juhuri is very strong. She might provoke a blood feud, but I think Juhuri would try to prevent that – there would be no end to the bloodshed. God knows, Mr Forrester, anything could come of this. But I *think* Juhuri will see the release of Shen as a way of defusing things – an honourable thing to do. I have access to the casa, to Shen, and to Juhuri. I have a plan. When you have heard it I'm sure you will agree that it is a good plan.'

It was not a good plan. Forrester heard it and as keen as he was to find merit in it, he could not. It had flaws and ambiguities, and it relied totally on the emotions of the firebrand mind of Juhuri ul Azam. It was too complicated a plan, with too little adhesion and too many steps. But it was all there was.

'It can work,' Pang Ho added, 'with luck. Let's drink to luck.' He fetched a bottle of brandy from the cupboard beneath the sink and poured three cupfuls.

'*Yamsing!*' cried Pang and downed his liquor in one gulp.

Drink to victory: that was the toast. He echoed it, and drank. The liquor spread its fire from stomach to spine, but the hopes of Reven Forrester still wintered.

By all that was just, and proper, and holy, it would be wrong for the marriage of Shen Woo and Abdul ul Azam to occur. It would have to be stopped.

344

These were the convictions of Juhuri. But being of reverent mind, and thus humbly aware of the fallibility of human judgement, he took his predicament to the prayer mat.

Was he, Juhuri ul Azam, right-minded in his objections? That was the question. Of course he did not phrase it so bluntly. God knew of the problems that beset His true servants, there was no need for words. He fasted. He recited the Koran; great passages of it, with due attention and humility. He turned his face to Mecca and opened his heart and mind and waited for the flame of enlightenment to ignite him.

For two full days, and almost as many nights, Juhuri stayed steadfast. He ignored his hunger until he was no longer hungry, and wet his mouth with a rag to drive out the thirst. When the drug of tiredness came to numb him to sleep he slapped his cheeks until his eyes ran and his thoughts sharpened. When the face of Shen Woo shimmered into his consciousness he banished the lovely phantom, held firm to the rope of right prayer and refused to allow his anger at his father to touch him. But despite all this, on the second night at some time beyond midnight, in the depths of a prostration, with forehead to floor and knees drawn up beneath him, his eyes closed and he fell asleep.

For man is weak and forever distracted from the true path of the Sharia. How is it that God even hears him? . . . Juhuri awoke in the dawn light. Oh, ashamed and filled with repentant prayer! And yet, amid that spiritual drone rose up a peal of elation as clean and clear as the horn of Israfeel. This was the sound of victory. He knew it. He recognized it in an instant. He had been granted enlightenment. The marriage was wrong, and forbidden, and would now most certainly fail to take place. If a thousand angels had come down to reinforce him in this conviction, he could not have been more sure. The sweet warm glow of righteousness was alive in him. Juhuri fell down in praise of Allah – the Patron of the faithful.

345

It was a comfort to know that he had been right, and even more so to know that infinite omnipotent powers were on his side. He was not certain how it would be prevented from occurring – but all that would be explained. Juhuri felt moved to go at that very moment to the room of Shen Woo, to reassure her that his absence had been in her cause and that she was not forgotten. He would tell her that she was in the safest of safe hands.

'God is the Greatest!'

Her lamp was still lit but Shen was asleep. Her long hair streamed like spilled ink across her pillows, a lock of it close to her mouth whisked lightly in her breath. A single sheet covered her, expressing exquisitely the form of her hips and breasts. His eyes became her prisoner. How lovely she was, how innocent.

He did not wake her. He poured from her decanter a glass of water for his thirst, then he further explored her room. Both sound and scent drew him to a far corner, where, atop a small spirit flame, a saucepan simmered and steamed. Medication for her grandfather, no doubt. A not unpleasant pine-like odour rose in the vapour.

She stirred and muttered something in her sleep, and Juhuri felt suddenly ashamed of his intrusion. In her torpid movement one hand had reached beyond her sheet. That hand, he noticed, held a folded slip of paper. As gently as one might remove a bedtime toy from the grip of a sleeping child, with no other motive beyond the comfort of the slumberer, Juhuri reached down and withdrew that slip of paper . . . It was the stationery of Pang Ho the herbalist. Upon one side was written four columns of Chinese characters that made no sense to him. The other side was similarly unintelligible. Ah, but, behold, beneath the mess of Chinese script was written one single word in a most Caucasian hand: 'Reven.'

Juhuri had no trouble in reading this. English was the language of education in the Sulu, and no one was better educated in Jolo than he. His problem was one of comprehension. What could this single word possibly mean?

'Reven . . . *Reven?*'

He rolled the word around his pallet as if in oral treatment the meaning might speak out. It did not. There was a pleasant and almost Arabic roundness in the issue of the sound, but that was all.

'Reven?'

Could it be that this single, unusual word concealed a vital message? He examined the invoice, turned it this way and that and held it to the light. Just a piece of cheap paper upon which had been stamped in purple ink the name of the originator:

Pang Ho – Yeuk Choi Po
Herbalist

He looked at the intriguing document again, but nothing crystallized in explanation of that single word, Reven.

The woman stirred then, as though she was about to waken. Juhuri held his breath. He set down the note upon her breast. In haste he left the room.

Juhuri returned to his own bedroom, undressed, lay down and eased himself against the soft flesh of his second wife Fatima. What a blessing were his women. Truly, they became more beautiful every day.

That was what he told himself. It was an excellent thought; a worthy, bright and proper thought. Alas, it was not a pervasive thought – its ampleness did not fill him up sufficiently to exclude the picture of the Chinese girl who lay beneath the thin white sheet in the adjacent room.

Sweet torment! The image of Shen's perfect form defied all efforts to see it off. It would not depart. No matter how tightly he held to the good buttocks, and ravaged the full lips of Fatima, the Chinese girl drew between them. She was with him at orgasm. *Allah is forgiving!*

347

Had he not followed the Prophet's own example, exactly? He had seen another woman and become aroused by her, but had hurried to his own wife. Did purity not lie in such slavish imitation?

Allah is merciful. He would pray for greater endurance when he awoke. He was sure he would receive it. He would have slept immediately if it was not for Fatima's startling question.

'Do you love the Chinese girl? Do you love her, Juhuri?'

He did not answer her, but the question provoked a lengthy and tense debate within his own mind, which required a good deal of attention before it was put to rest. But when he did sleep it was a good and peaceful sleep. He awoke with bright sunlight in his eyes, feeling rested and free of doubt. He did not arise at once, it was too late for the dawn prayer. He lay there, comfortable in body and mind, while Fatima brought him some well browned rice and coconut cakes and a glass of sweet kahawa, coffee. He ate and he drank and he felt marvellous. He dragged Fatima down next to him and she came, giggling. What a treasure was this woman – neither chaste nor lewd. She bared her hips for her husband and he was a stallion at the rump of her.

He washed and dressed, he slung his pistol-case on his shoulder and walked with a wide pace into the streets of Jolo, towards the market. A bustling, shouting place of a hundred sari-sari stalls, and barbers and sword makers, and money lenders, and kadday houses that smell of coffee and hot peppered meat. As many people are at the market as there are flies on a week-old carcass, and all of them as busy. A thousand pedicab drivers sweat their customers from shop to shop, dodging roaring buses and Jeeps with hooters and radios ablare.

Juhuri paused at a sari-sari stall to buy a Pepsi and a cigarette which he lit with a spill from the vendor's stove and while he drank, he listened to the gossip. A Milikan had washed up on the beach: that was the story of the day. Some kids had seen him rise out of the water. It was said that they had even spoken to him. But no one had seen the Milikan since that day. Was that not an amazement? Juhuri agreed; it was a fantastic story, but *just* a story. He walked on to his destination.

Pang Ho – Yeuk Choi Po

Yellow lettering on a red board; the sign was suspended above a doorway which was well set back from the street. Juhuri advanced to the door and tried the handle . . . Too early for the Chinaman. He cupped his hands and peered through the window. He could see glass counters, shelves, and a mess of bottles, packets and boxes, but Pang Ho the Chinaman was not in sight. Juhuri stood back, he knuckled his hand and rapped upon the door frame – a most authoritative knock. And Pang must have conceded it to be so for he hastily appeared. He looked up from the lower pane of the glass door, saw Juhuri and looked somewhat startled. He immediately drew back the bolts.

Pang Ho bowed as best he could bow with his back so horribly welded, and said, 'Welcome to my humble premises.'

Juhuri crossed the threshold of the humble premises. Though Pang Ho had been to his house on many occasions to do his doctoring, this was his first venture into the herbalist's shop. It was rather a dusty, dismal place and reeked of herbs. The floor was of wood and gave as he trod upon it causing the merchandise in the glass counters to rattle. Its shabbiness gave Juhuri confidence, for truthfully he was a bit apprehensive about this visit. Although he knew exactly what information he wanted from Pang Ho, he did not know how to go about asking for it.

Pang disappeared behind a counter and when he came into view again he was propelling a rattan chair before him which he nudged into the bend of Juhuri's knees. Juhuri sat upon it.

'Honoured by your visit,' said Pang. 'In what way can I be of service to respected Datu, Juhuri ul Azam?'

'I'm quite healthy,' Juhuri assured. 'I haven't come about my health.'

Pang set a patient smile upon his face and rested his arms upon the counter, and waited for Juhuri to go on.

'I've come about an invoice that you sent to the house. An invoice for some medication, I'm sure.'

'I hope the charges did not upset you. The price of good imported herbs goes up by the day.'

'No, nothing to do with the charge. You see, there is some lettering on it: Chinese characters.'

'I see,' said Pang, as though he did not see. What could be more natural upon a note from one Chinese person to another than Chinese characters? 'It was an instruction to the woman . . . Shen, is that her name?'

'Shen, yes . . . It's not the Chinese writing that I'm here about. There was a single word amongst them that was not written in Chinese – "Reven".'

Pang said nothing.

'*Reven?*' Juhuri said again, as though that single word might prompt the little cripple into effuse explanation.

Pang Ho did not stir.

'I want to know what the word means.'

'Ah,' said Pang. 'Your father is my most esteemed customer. I have supplied his household with medicine for years. Anything I can do for him I will do.'

'What does it mean then?'

'Reven?'

'Yes.'

'I don't know what it means.'

'It was on your paper.'

Pang shrugged his grotesque shoulders and opened his arms in a wide gesture of honesty. 'I don't know what it means.'

He was lying. If Pang had owned the stature of half a man,

Juhuri would have beaten him then. He would have reached across the counter and thrashed the man until his lying tongue came to the truth. But here opposing him was a cripple, a bent and feeble thing that would not survive one strike. Yet he had to get the truth from Pang. Now more than ever he was sure that this word 'Reven' had true significance. Juhuri breathed hard for a while, then let his anger subside in a long sigh. From nowhere surfaced the magic words:

'I'll pay.'

Pang Ho, too, expended a deep breath; as though his tension had been as great as Juhuri's. He said, 'Reven . . . I don't know what the word means, that's the truth. But, if how it came to be written on my invoice interests you, then you only have to ask.'

So Juhuri asked. And to ensure that the cunning China-man omitted no detail in the telling, he produced a substantial roll of hundred-peso bills, which Pang Ho captured in a movement that was quicker than the eye. Even before Pang's hand reappeared he was telling Juhuri about the man called Reven.

Pang Ho spoke for a long time. He spoke slowly and credibly and no detail was omitted. He told an amazing story about a man whom Abdul ul Azam had left for drowned, who had returned to life; who had come across that whole wide ocean to find his loved one. And as Pang spoke on so the mystery of pure revelation moved in Juhuri once more . . . A man who had drowned at sea, had arisen from the sea; upon the very shores of Jolo. Was not the power of Allah quite measureless? He could not help but interrupt the Chinaman to express it.

'Allah is the Greatest.'

'Indeed.'

Here was a miracle: Reven was a man; the man was in Jolo. He had been carried there in the hand of God, in service of God. The wonder of it!

'Allah is the Greatest.'

His prayers had been answered as only Allah could answer them. Here was the means to put an end to the sin of Abdul and save the honour of the house of ul Azam. Here was the means to cut loose the hand of Saitan from his father. Now, his instruction was obvious: Deliver the Chinese girl to this man Reven. For this reason he is provided.

And where was this Reven now? That was the next question addressed to Pang.

'I don't know,' was Pang's reply.

Would he lie again, this loathsome little wretch? Juhuri forbade himself the intemperance of anger. He wondered how God could have invested in this obtuse and mercenary cripple such awesome responsibility. But there it was. This was the man who had been chosen to link him with Reven, so this was the man he had to deal with. He would pay any price.

Pang named a figure that staggered him. Then Juhuri saw God's hand at work again. That Abdul, his father, should pay so dearly in order to repair his own depredations was perfect retribution.

'You shall have your gold,' he said to Pang.

When Juhuri finally left it was with a dull tread. His piety had been rewarded, and that was a most wonderful and humbling thought. He would obey. He would unite Shen with this Reven, and he would see to their deliverance. That was the punishment of Abdul, but the son of Abdul would die a little too. For the question of his wife, Fatima: 'Do you love the Chinese girl?' was now clearly answerable. He did love Shen Woo. Yes, yes, he loved her and he did not want her to go.

Juhuri's melancholic pace brought him at last to the east side of the town: the barrio of Busbus, the most antique barrio in all of Jolo. The humble timber houses of Busbus had been there to shelter the first Conquistadores when they came there. Of course such perishable woodwork had not endured the stress of centuries. It had been torched by the Spaniards, and built again, and blown down by rogue winds, and blown up by the Milikan. But always it had been built again. The inhabitants of Busbus had an ant-like temperament for reconstruction, and a firm belief in the virtue of *adat tabiyat* – what the father did, let the son do also. Busbus stood now in appearance much as it had at the beginning of its history.

The house that was Juhuri's destination was the house that he had been born in. It stood close to the beach at the eastern edge of the barrio. A cool house, its grey sago-frond roof was dappled by the shade of tall leaning coconut palms, its floor planks were raised a bit above the ground to permit the passage of air. Wild hibiscus and Indian coral shrubs flamed with flowers all over the yard, and the bright-blue vinta of Uncle Ibrahim was dragged up next to the steps. As a child this house had been a place of peace for Juhuri; a place of games and laughter. As he mounted the steps then, the adult felt no joy.

'Bapu. *Uwa*,' he called. 'Uncle, I am here.'

'Come inside.' Uncle Ibrahim came to the door. 'Peace, Juhuri, I'm glad you have come.' A big man, thick-shouldered, swarthy and passionate. 'These are bad times, Juhuri. We must know who our friends are.'

'Ambu?'

'She is expecting you.'

'How is she, Bapu?'

'See for yourself.'

She was seated, leaning upon a heap of cushions. In her lap rested the heavy old Arabic Koran that in his youth he had studied. The light that came from the open window was filtered by foliage, and cosmetically kind. But his mother's age was more apparent to him then than ever it had been.

'Ambu.'

She looked up while her lips still moved in silent recitation. Juhuri looked into the Koran and saw that the sura she was engaged with was Al-Anam. She closed the heavy book.

353

'Juhuri, how pleased I am . . . come, come.' She patted a cushion in invitation. 'You're not too old to sit with your Ambu.'

He did not take that cushion. He drew another from the wall and sat upon it facing her.

'I have so much to tell you, Ambu, I hardly know where to begin.' But he knew where to begin . . . 'That sura you have just read. Is it not revealed therein that just as Allah splits the seed of the fruitstone and brings forth the tree, so he can bring forth the living from the dead?'

Halima paged into the Koran again, but Juhuri had no need of confirmation. He went on: 'If a man is drowned in a sea full of sharks, and he goes under never to be seen again, then is that not proof enough that he is dead?'

'Of course he would be dead.'

'So if that same man were to be seen again, then it would be a miracle such as only Allah could perform.'

'It might be a balbalan – the ghost of the man. I've heard of that. The daughter of Hadji Arastam saw such a balbalan one night in the plantation behind their house.'

'The daughter of Hadji Arastam has an ugly face and a fine imagination.' Juhuri was annoyed with Halima for muddling such fiction with his solemn treatise. 'I am talking about a miracle.'

Halima looked impressed. 'You saw this man? You touched this man?'

Juhuri felt compelled to tell a small lie: 'Yes.'

'A miracle,' agreed Halima. 'Who is he? How did he come to you?'

'His name is Reven . . . I have been fasting and praying as you know . . .'

'If ever there was a time for praying!'

'It was revealed to me that this man had come to Jolo. It was revealed to me that this man had been left in the currents of Palawan by Abdul when he attacked the Chinese junk. But most importantly it was revealed to me that

354

this Reven and the Chinese woman are *tanung*, they are sweethearts.'

'The wrongdoing of your father.'

'Yes.'

'How could he have done such an evil thing?'

'Saitan is everywhere, Ambu. We must defeat him where we can.'

'God willing.'

'Yes. Where God provides the weapon, we must cut his hand from our shoulder.'

'Yes. Cut him! *Cut* him!' Halima's little fists came up, tight and trembling with anger. 'Let Abdul bleed double what I have bled.'

'Saitan; it's *Saitan* whose grip must be severed.'

'*No*. Your father; he is the one who should bleed.'

'Bleed?' Juhuri was unsure of his mother's interpretation of the word. 'He will bleed, don't you see? With shame and humiliation, when he is brought down . . . Yes, *double* what you bled.'

That was not what Halima meant: 'Blood, he must bleed blood. He must be whipped.' She tapped the open Koran. 'That is the punishment prescribed.'

'He would not survive it.'

'Better that he should not,' boomed Uncle Ibrahim.

He had come into the room silently, but now he was full voiced and roaring for retribution. 'Let his hand be severed, let him be crucified. Let him be shot down like a dog.' That was his most lenient suggestion. 'Abdul ul Azam has committed his final outrage against the family of Ibrahim. How can there be honour while he lives on?'

Juhuri stood up. 'It has been shown to me how honour can be preserved. Do you think I admire what he has done, Uncle? A few days ago I might have scourged him for it, but I didn't and I'm glad I didn't. I prayed, and I fasted, and . . .'

'He witnessed a miracle. Tell him about the miracle,' Halima said. Then she told Uncle Ibrahim herself . . . Bapu

Ibrahim stroked his bearded chin and agreed that something extraordinary had happened. But did it prove what Juhuri believed it to prove?

'Yes,' Juhuri insisted. 'It proves that Allah wants only one thing: the release of the Chinese girl into the custody of this man Reven. If Allah so wishes it then it would be a sin of Jinn and Saitan to disobey. A sure path to Hell!'

'If Allah wishes this,' said Abrahim. '*If? If?*'

'It was revealed to me.'

'A man walked out of the sea: a miracle,' Halima said.

'There's no proof of that,' said Ibrahim. 'I too heard the rumours in the marketplace about the man who had walked a thousand miles across the sea to reach Jolo. I went to the beach where he was supposed to have emerged. I spoke to some children who had seen this man . . . Yes, they had seen a man; a Milikan. I believe that. But did he walk out of the sea or was he brought to the beach on the Chinese junk that's anchored off Cabucan Island?'

'It makes no difference *how* he came,' Juhuri said. 'It does not alter a thing. It was revealed to me that he would come . . . and he *came. That* is the miracle of it. How do you suppose he survived the currents and sharks of Palawan? How do you suppose he knew just where to come? You talk about proof, bapu Ibrahim; what further proof do you want that God's hand guides this man?'

'Ameen,' said Uncle Ibrahim. 'I have no argument with that. A man was returned from the dead. Now that *is* a miracle that only Allah could be capable of. But God's intended usage for this man could be in quite another way.'

'I tell you it's not,' said Juhuri. 'What God intends for him was shown to me.'

'No, no, you are confused.' Uncle Ibrahim made fussy gestures and looked embarrassed. Again he said, 'Confused . . . Perhaps you are not in a position to really judge what God intends. Tell him, Halima. Tell him.'

Halima spoke. 'Juhuri, you see the release of this girl as a

356

most terrible punishment. But who would it be terrible for? And who would suffer? You are confusing your father's guilt with your own; your father's punishment with your own . . .'

'What guilt? What are you talking about?'

'Don't be angry, Juhuri. You've committed no sin, and your guilt is apparent to no one but yourself. You love the Chinese girl . . . *No*, don't deny it. Your wife Fatima told me. But I didn't need her to tell me that . . . Oh, she is very beautiful, but beautiful women are easy to find. It's more than that, I know, I've watched her. She burns with that special fire that so few women have, and that all men, all *strong* men, want.'

Juhuri felt the heat of embarrassment rise to his face. Halima was famous for her straight talk. Even Uncle Ibrahim had found a distant spot upon which to fix his gaze.

Halima went on undeterred: 'No, there is no sin, and I am not your accuser. *You* are your own accuser. Yes you are; and *she* is your confusion. But don't be confused. The whip that you would lay upon your own back would in no way hurt your father.'

'It would hurt him if she was gone.'

'No. Not at all. He would be relieved if she was gone. He is caught in his own trap and is desperate for a way out . . . No. No. A great punishment is needed to restore honour.'

'*Honour!*' thundered Ibrahim. 'Abdul ul Azam has cut the palm branch. He is now *taohansipak* – he is on the other side. The question is: where do you stand, Juhuri?'

Halima spoke before Juhuri could do so. 'He stands at God's shoulder, that is where he stands. And he has brought to us the most wonderful news.'

'Ameen,' said Ibrahim.

'Here is the answer,' Halima held up the heavy Koran. 'God's answer! That son should not turn upon father, nor wife upon husband, nor family upon family. *Here* is the answer: this Reven has come as Juhuri saw that he would

357

come. And he has come as God's weapon for us: *Al-Mumit* – The Death Giver! God's deliverance of us all from the blood of Abdul ul Azam. Bring Reven to me and *I* will thrust him upon Abdul ul Azam, for this is clearly the will of Allah . . .

> 'Give courage to the faithful and
> strike terror into the hearts of sinners,
> Cut head from shoulder,
> and maim them to the finger!'

'Ameen!' cried Uncle Ibrahim. He opened wide his arms and pulled Juhuri to his bosom, and there Juhuri was anointed with pious tears: 'Ameen.'

In that moment of deep emotion, with heartbeat shared and face pressed hard to the wet, bristly jowl of Uncle Ibrahim, it came to Juhuri that his dear Ambu could be right. He could have misinterpreted God's message, and His intention. And the more he thought about it, the more certain he became: Reven was more than just the punisher of ul Azam; he was the sword of Al-Mumit – The Death Giver. Abdul ul Azam was consigned to Hell. Reven had come to accelerate his passage.

'*Ameen,*' he swore himself with the others to that end.

So where was this Reven, this man on whom so much depended? That was Halima's question.

'He will be delivered to me. It's arranged.'

'Protect him,' said Halima. 'That is your duty. Take him to a safe place and see to him well. Keep him close at hand until the moment comes for him to be thrust upon the Datu ul Azam.'

'I will.'

Halima stood up from her couch of cushions. '*I* will return to the casa. *I* will watch Abdul, and I will judge when the moment is right to end it. Be ready, Juhuri.'

'The blessings of Allah . . .' Uncle Ibrahim squeezed Juhuri tightly once more, then stood away. 'Your task will be most difficult.'

It would not really be difficult. There had been confusion but that was over now. Like the night sky when the rain has passed, now he could see for ever.

Eddie Woo was satisfied that he was not a coward. Big winds and steep waves did not frighten him at sea. Dark nights and dark alleyways had never kept him from a journey upon land. And when his anger was up he would fight anyone.

What frightened him was the thought of poverty. That was his phobia. That was the dread that turned his gut to jelly and brought sweat to his palms. He had never been poor, so this fear had not been born out of the pain of hunger. He had never had to lick the empty rice bowl, or shiver with bare feet on a winter cold floor. There had always been fuel, and tea, and rice and fish at the stove of the house of Woo. There had always been clothes to wear and a good thick quilt to creep beneath at night. Even when Father and Mother and Daai lo and Ga je had all perished before the power of typhoon Rose he had not gone lacking. Grandfather had arrived to take Younger Sister and him back to his warm junk and the pulse of life had not skipped one fine beat.

So his young days had been without want. But that which fulfils all the needs of the child does not place a smile on the face of the man. The standards by which Eddie Woo judged life had somehow undergone radical change. *Money*: that was what was needed to calm the dragon in the temple of the adult, and how that dragon had got there was irrelevant. *Money*, and in large sums – as much as he had recently had within his grasp; that was the food of the dreams of Eddie Woo. He had worked and he had suffered the risk of death in order to get that money. It had been stolen from him, and he wanted it back; he *needed* it back. If ever he got to Taiwan it would have to be as a very rich man. Forgiveness was a scarce commodity within the triad brotherhood, a most expensive commodity; and he needed forgiveness in abundance. He wanted his gold.

Eddie wanted his gold back so fervently that almost every conscious thought was connected to that aim. From morning to night he worried at his plans for its recovery, and his dreams were bleak for the want of it. He knew where the gold was kept. There was a cellar beneath the house, thick doored and guarded; that was where it was. ul Azam had said that it was there, and one glimpse down those steep stone steps had convinced him that this was so . . . But how to liberate that gold, and of course himself from the keep of ul Azam? *That* was the question that threatened to stir his brain to *congee*.

When Abdul ul Azam summoned him to his presence that afternoon, Eddie complied immediately. The call to the great man's chamber did not cause a moment's qualm. His whole mind was occupied with his problem. There was curiosity, but no dread.

He had been to ul Azam's office before. He did not need the guard to prod him down the passage like an abattoir ox. It was a most luxurious room, dressed with drapes and cushions and tapestries of masterful design. One whole wall was decorated with old bladed weapons; krises and boarding spears, and long bamboo lances with barbed metal tips, all set out like spokes around the focus of the display – a pair of heavy, curved scimitars with pommels that were luxuriantly tasselled (he believed) with tresses of human hair. A stub-legged table squatted centre-floor, littered with papers and ledgers and newspapers from Manila. An ancient brass inkstand weighted down some papers. Abdul's desk was the perfect height for one so partial to the horizontal.

ul Azam, it seemed, was always lying down. He was lying down as Eddie was brought into his room. He was propped up on to his shoulders by three huge kapok cushions, reading a newspaper. The man looked sick, even consumptive. Did he suffer from some fatal disease that kept him prone? Eddie wondered. Perhaps he too would spend half his day on his back if he possessed the kind of wealth that ul Azam had.

Without taking his face from the newspaper ul Azam commanded: 'Sit.'

Eddie sat upon a cushion and drew in his legs, and thought: Go screw your own mother.

'Do you fear death, Eddie Woo?'

Eddie jolted. Had this man detected his curse? ul Azam folded the newspaper and set it aside. 'I don't think about it,' said Eddie.

'I'm talking about the Chinese as a race. They have no stomach for a fight. Is it because they fear death?'

'They're realists,' said Eddie. 'They don't fight unless they have to.'

'We Tausug, we're different. We love a fight; any time, any place. There is no race on earth that lives with greater zest. We know how to live and how to love, and when it is time to die –' he waved towards the wall full of weapons – 'we know how to die. If you were a Muslim you would not fear death, you would look forward to it. Paradise awaits me when I die. What awaits you when *you* die?'

'I don't know,' Eddie said.

'That's it! *That's* it! *That's* why you live such miserable lives, you Chinese – the thought of your inevitable end is such a burden to carry. How different for me. Why don't you become a Muslim, Eddie Woo? Your sister is learning. You must encourage her, you understand. It would please me greatly if you did that.'

'I have. I already have. I've spoken most strongly to her.'

'She must not falter. It's a wonderful thing, you know, to be a Muslim.' ul Azam turned and punched the cushion at his spine to make it more pliant. 'Surrender to Allah, Eddie Woo – Allahu Akbar! There is nothing else as good, in life or in death. The good things in life are given to all Muslims to enjoy – food, drink, sleep, sex, they are the gifts of Allah. And in death the Muslim need not change . . . In Heaven I will be mounted by jewel-eyed virgins, face to face, *yes*, and each moment of pleasure will last for twenty-four years. Imagine that.'

Eddie imagined.

'What do you think of that?'

Eddie thought that it sounded a fine place. He said with reverence: 'Virgins? Does the Koran really promise virgins?'

'In a hundred places.'

'Do you believe it?'

'Of course. It's God's word: "There will be streams of clear water and fruit of any choice within reach, and wine that does not cloud the head, no matter how much is drunk."'

'And virgins?'

'Dark-eyed *houris*, lying at your side.'

'What do the women get; the women who die as Muslims?'

'It's slightly different for women. God made these promises mainly for men.'

'Most reasonable . . . and sensible. What *does* God have for the women, ah?'

'They are returned to their husbands, remade as virgins.'

'Aah!' So Heaven was filled with virgins, waiting to be mounted. But the news was not all good. These benefits were reserved for the faithful. For those who rejected the faith a torrid time awaited.

'Pitch black smoke for them to breathe. To drink: seething water, and festering blood. I shouldn't be surprised if that was your destiny, Eddie Woo.'

'But I'm not a Muslim.'

'There is only *one* God, Eddie Woo, *one* Judgement Day; *one* Heaven and *one* Hell . . . See what help your idols are able to provide when Allah points you to the gates of Hell.'

The finger that came up to accompany this dire warning was long and knotted at the joints like dry bamboo cane. It was the perfect accompaniment for the message: 'Allah brings up the sun from the East, and lowers it in the West.

Challenge your false gods to rearrange its path. See *then* who the true God is. Allahu Akbar!'

That was more of an argument than Eddie was prepared to contest. He waited there, wondering if this lesson in Islamic privilege was the sole purpose of today's audience. It was not. ul Azam relaxed with the contentment of the righteous. He dropped his hand, sank back into the cushions and favoured Eddie with a final message of hope.

'Allah is forgiving.' Eddie presented his credit-worthy expression. 'Even you, Eddie Woo, could be forgiven.'

ul Azam then stared at him with his dark sunken eyes in deep contemplation . . . A servant came in bearing a tray and ul Azam's gaze wandered. Eddie watched her too.

She was as pretty as a flower, and as fresh. He had seen her before at her duties around the house, but never in such proximity; never bending before him so low that her blouse gaped open. She had small, schoolgirl breasts, firm, nut brown. He could see them to the nipple and he stared, and he felt his gut go taut.

'Bajau.' ul Azam curled his mouth as though the word gave a bad taste. 'Luwaan, that's what we Tausug call them. It means "spit-outs", vomit, that's what they are. I own the woman.'

Abdul waved the servant away.

'You *own* the woman?'

'Her husband owed me "reef tax" and couldn't pay.'

'She's married? She's *very* young.'

'Do you like her?' ul Azam bit into a cake. 'Tell me if you like her. Her husband's dead.'

'So young . . . pretty.'

'They marry at the second menstruation, those Luwaan. Perhaps she's twelve.'

'*Twelve.*' Eddie's gullet throttled upon the word so that it could hardly pass.

'Her husband's dead,' ul Azam said again. 'Couldn't be helped. They say you can't drown a Bajau. They say they can stay submerged for hours and can walk along the ocean floor.

In very rough seas they sink their vintas then walk along the bottom until they reach dry land. It's nonsense of course, *her* husband drowned.'

'Ah.'

'Stories,' said ul Azam, 'fables . . . Do you know that the junk of your grandfather is anchored five miles off Jolo?'

'*Wah!*'

'Yes, it's there. I went out and I saw it. There's no one on board.'

'The Toh Mong Suen . . .'

'A ghost didn't sail it here, although that's the gossip in the marketplace. Then there is another story; it's about a Milikan who came out of the sea like a nesting turtle; he was seen at Patikul beach. I wonder if these two stories have a connection. What do you think, Eddie Woo?'

'The junk is here, off Jolo?'

'That's the truth.'

What Eddie thought was: Here is a vessel that I know, and I can handle. How can I reach it?

'Do you think there is a connection?' ul Azam asked.

'The man who walked out of the sea?'

'Yes, and the abandoned junk.'

'Difficult . . . most difficult,' Eddie said vaguely. His mind was employed with a far more interesting problem: how to connect Eddie Woo to the junk, and how to transport a fortune in gold with him. He answered the Datu: 'Can't see the connection . . . No.'

The strangest thing was that ul Azam seemed relieved to hear him say that. He smiled his skull-smile and poured more coffee. 'Just market gossip,' he said. 'The Bajau probably salvaged the junk. They're the scavengers of the sea, those Luwaan . . . I'm pleased with you, Eddie Woo. I'm happy that your sister obeys you. It's good, it's good. I'm going to reward you for your effort. Yes, I saw how you looked at the Bajau. Is that what you would like? . . . I see it is . . . Well then.' ul Azam waved Eddie off as the father

364

waves the child out to play: an indulgent, amused little gesture. 'Go on. Go on now. Oh, you will find that you have your room to yourself now. I have had your grandfather moved. So much better to have a room of your own.'

It was as Abdul ul Azam had promised. The room was his alone, and he had no sooner entered it than the Bajau girl came in bearing a water urn. By the time she had set it down he had locked the door. When she turned to go he blocked her path. As she tried to slip past him he caught her and drew her down upon the mattress. And his *yang tsat* lifted, rock hard.

The half-grown beauty of the spring bud; he reached for it and grasped the tender thing. He pushed at her sprig limbs and wrenched at the child-slim hips. There was thunder in his mind. A storm raged from him and tore like a typhoon at the youth of her. Tears; they only drove him harder, lifted him higher. There was ecstasy in such destruction.

ul Azam was wrong; Paradise was not the prerogative of the souls of the faithful. Paradise was *his*; and it was *now*.

DRAGON CROUCHING,
TIGER CIRCLING

It had rained all afternoon, but with the dusk the storm lifted and puffy, copper-toned clouds flossed the steep green mountaintops. In the jungle the last light melted sombrely away. The trees, all wetted and heavy, leaned down their wide arms and wept upon the mossy, mouldy floor. The day creatures grew quiet and those that loved the night burst into evening song. Frogs and cicadas croaked and screeched to burst the eardrums in a see-saw sound that swelled and faded, and swelled again. Where man had cut his trails, rivulets of water now gushed, rutting the earth, then fattening into warm muddy pools that filled the shoes and sucked at the heels of those who walked them.

Reven Forrester found the rain forest a dismal place. He felt wrung out there; deprived of breath; drowned in its cloying, humid greenness. In places his vision was so dull that progress was made in the slow outreaching way of the sloth; then to slip and curse and clutch out left and right or crash down into the wet undergrowth. They followed a ravine for a while then climbed a steep slope, and Reven's thigh muscles burned with the effort. Sweat stung his eyes and mosquitoes his arms and neck, and his legs were hosting a community of leeches. But every step taken was a step closer to the end, and so he walked on, imitating the actions of his guide, knowing that the man ahead was suffering equal discomfort.

All he knew of his guide was his name, Nurasid, and his source – 'Pang Ho send me.' All other questions had been referred, by pointed finger, to the note that he carried: 'This man will lead you to Juhuri. Go with him.'

Pang Ho's *chop* authenticated the brief message.

When Forrester had received that note he had humbly thanked the gentle Bajau people of the houseboat community at Pangasinan Island for their shelter and their food, and had promised to come back one day when there was peace in his heart. Bahang had translated as best he could, and his people they had nodded and smiled and told him in turn that he had made a place in their hearts, and his sorrow was their sorrow, and they hoped he would find his peace. But their eyes had said that his peace might be that of the dead if he went against Abdul ul Azam. The *tinis-tinis* they sang to him as the vinta sailed away was as sad a sound as he had ever heard. The mournful tinkle of their gabbang – bamboo xylophones – had followed him far out into the bay.

This man will lead you to Juhuri. Go with him.

Two terse and single statements. Pang Ho had done what he had said he would do, and that was all that the message conveyed. Forrester was to meet Juhuri ul Azam, the son of the Datu Abdul ul Azam, he did not know where or exactly when. He did not know how strong his position was, or how weak. He did not know what Juhuri expected from him, or what to expect from Juhuri. Would there be violence or would he be received in peace? Even Pang Ho might not be able to answer that. He wondered if he would see Pang Ho before he met Juhuri. He doubted it. Pang had made his deal. He would wish to distance himself from its consequences.

As he walked, he thought of Shen. He called upon his favourite memory of her. Her hair was wringing wet and hung in rat tails on her forehead and shoulders, and her lips tasted of salt. She was so vibrant and bursting with bright joy and throaty laughter. They had played like kids in the rock pool on that island of love. He remembered how her lips had softened and widened as tenderness had become passion, and they had come together in a bonding that had stunned them with its power . . . Pictures of amazing clarity provoked him then; and this was *his* woman. With vicious suddenness the thought of what ul Azam had done to *his* woman kicked in him and he was furious. Hate sprang up – a bleak blank insanity that would not go, and walked with him for hours.

A jungle-trapped village came suddenly. There were no searchlights here, or fortifications. Where the thick trees stopped the bamboo walled houses began. A single street ran the length of the village with houses crowding it on both sides. A white moon lit the rooftops and cast black shade to the ground, the odour of wood smoke and cattle dung lingered in the damp air. Now he could place his feet firmly on the ground and he could hear, no longer did the cicadas rev up in concert, it was very quiet. He could see right down the length of the street and no one was in sight. But as well as he could see he could be seen, and there were eyes upon him, he could sense it, and the hair on his neck tingled and rose. He cast around but saw no one, and in that moment Nurasid ran. He heard the acceleration of his guide's footsteps, he saw the white of his shirt as he chased into the shadows. But before he could react Pang's man had vanished. Here was the trap. He tensed, and he pressed his back against a bamboo fence.

Four men emerged, no, there were five of them, with five rifles that glinted metallically in the moonlight. And to prevent any thought of flight, the click of that many safety catches sounded to warn against such folly. And the rifles were raised so there could be no doubt: he could be dead in a second if he wished it. He could feel the ache of his jaw muscles, his lips were wrung back – Christ, was he snarling then, with bared teeth like a dog? He raised his hands slowly and with palms exposed and fingers stretched wide. In his mind a voice said, Let these be Juhuri's men. And they were.

'Reven, Tuwan?'

A man came forward and asked that, and Forrester breathed, 'Yes.'

368

The house they entered had bamboo floors and walls and a steep high roof thatched with palm. It had a large central hall that was lit with kerosene lamps. Juhuri ul Azam stood there.

The Datu Juhuri ul Azam was shorter than he, but his bearing gave him stature. His neck was straight and strong and he held his chin proudly. His eyes were black as coal and they smouldered like coal, and a vein throbbed at his temples. His gestures were commanding and quick and conveyed energy. He gestured then – Forrester was to sit. A hard kapok cushion was brought and laid down for his comfort. Juhuri sat facing him, silently.

Food was brought and placed between them on wide banana leaves. They ate with their fingers a stew of beef and coconut meat, high with garlic, and brown rice wrapped in teak leaves. Then a scented damp towel was offered to him, and he wiped his hands. Only when that was done did Juhuri speak to him.

'If Allah punished all men for their sins, then hardly a person would be alive. He allows them to go on to their appointed day, but when the hour has come they shall not outlast it for a second . . . nor can they go before that moment. Do you believe that, Tuwan?'

'You've quoted from the Koran.'

Juhuri's smile came pleasantly. With enquiring eyes he said, 'Allah's guidance is wonderful and he bestows it on his true servants as he sees fit.'

'Yes.' Forrester knew he was being tested by Juhuri. But his theological knowledge was scant and he was afraid of the answer that would burst like a bomb amid this fanatical company.

'Yes,' Juhuri said. 'You seem quite calm at finding yourself here tonight, Reven, Tuwan. I think I should be less calm if I were you.'

'Inside me there is a lot of fear, Juhuri. I've come for a purpose: I've come for Shen. I believe that you will help me,

369

and that is my hope. But I haven't heard your word on the matter, so I fear.'

'One man against an island. You have a lot of courage, Tuwan. I admire that . . . I tell you you'll need it. We Tausug have a saying: "Better the white of the bone than the white of the heel." It means better to die than to run away – it seems you believe that too.'

'There is no running away for me, Juhuri. I'm here of my own will.'

'A will to do good or a will to do bad, that is how we differ from animals. Is your will for the good, Tuwan?'

'I've been moved in many ways by my will – to anger, to love, and to hate. I've done many things because of it. Some I regret deeply; not because they were wrong, but because of the consequences of my actions. Shen is where she is now because of my will. I have made mistakes in judgement . . . But here I am, Juhuri; in fear; in the hands of a stranger. There is no doubt in *my* mind that my cause is right.'

'So you've come for Shen, Tuwan. You've chosen a hard path. But then the path of good is usually hard, and sometimes bloody too. Shen is protected well. It may happen that you are unable to free her. It may happen that you don't survive it. It would not be cowardice to think again.'

'I've done nothing but think, for days. I've done my thinking. I'm here. I've come to you for help.'

'I'm not your brother, Tuwan – your bagay. If I was your bagay then I would be obliged to help you. This is *your* fight. Go and fight it . . . but wait, let me think. If you fight my father then you must be my enemy. Except that my father has sinned a terrible sin – an offence against the sacred law of the Shariah. So where does that place me? You have made great complications, Tuwan. Why don't you go away? . . . Listen, there is *so* much money; gold. Even before my father pirated the treasure junk of Woo Yin-wah he was the richest man in Sulu. Let me soften your great will; let me pave the pathway of your retreat with so much gold that you'll skip along it. How much would it take to make you go away?'

'Would that solve your problem, Juhuri?'

'Yes, I've paid Pang richly to have you brought to me. I'll pay you more. I'll pay you anything to go away.'

'I've come for Shen, Juhuri, and for no other reason. You've misjudged me.'

'I could kill you and end it now.'

'I don't wish to die, but it's not my greatest fear. And if I was dead how would it improve your state, Juhuri? I hear you're a man of honour.'

'I *am*.'

'So am I. I couldn't run away.'

Juhuri ul Azam nodded gravely, then his quick smile came again. He said, 'I think you see through me. Eh? I'm happy that you cannot run away. I like the words you use. Yes, I believe your will is for the good.'

'I stand against your father, Juhuri. Does that mean I'm without a friend amongst the Tausug?'

'Listen.' Juhuri leaned forward and his face came so close he could feel the heat of his breath. 'It is how you stand in the eyes of God that concerns me. And I think you stand well in His sight. God has pledged to us, in the Gospel and the Koran alike, that if we fight in His cause we may slay, or be slain, and the Garden will be our reward. You see, my wilful Christian, you have made a fine bargain with your life. So take the frown from your brows; be content . . . *Yes* you have a friend. Allahu Akbar!' Juhuri spread his arms and opened wide his hands. 'Allahu Akbar.' Twenty voices supported that truth.

He had noticed them lining the wall; listening intently to the conversation between Juhuri and him, strong, dark, Malaysian-featured men. Mostly they wore jeans and T-shirts, and were shod with sandals. All of them bore Colt Armalite rifles with barrels that shone with wear. Now, at a gesture from Juhuri, these men drew in into a close circle and sat down, their weapons upon their laps. Coffee came, brought by a pretty Tausug girl. She set down a filigreed brass tray with a tall brass decanter and glasses for everyone. A box of cigarettes was offered. 'Smuggled from Borneo,' Juhuri laughed; they all laughed.

Forrester took one and smoked it, and enjoyed the headiness that it caused. He singed a fat leech that was hanging from his calf muscle and it dropped away.

'Reven,' Juhuri said, 'don't be afraid of the consequences of your will. Your will, like all events in nature, only exerts its power at a time of choice. Like a root that comes to a boulder; only then does it begin to work a new path. Do you see, you're not as free to act as you may think, but you are never helpless either. Like the root, if you are determined to do good, then, in your moment of choice you will act correctly.'

Juhuri translated what he had said to his disciples and their heads nodded gravely and they murmured in agreement. He again turned to Forrester.

'You see *this* does not happen because of this or that act; God alone can make preconditions. He sees every event, then lets man make his choice. And sometimes, *sometimes*, He intervenes . . . The Datu Abdul saw your face in the water, *his* choice was to leave you to the sharks. But Al-Baith – the raiser of the dead – saw your face and brought you up. And so it was, and so it is . . . And now you are here, Reven. So we go on. I make my choice and so do you.'

'And maybe, just maybe God will intervene . . . What is your choice as it concerns me, Juhuri?'

'I'll bring you to the casa of my father, where Shen is.'

'I'll need more help than that.'

'One decision at a time, Tuwan. God has you in his hand. He helps with the doing of good. Be satisfied.'

He would have to be satisfied. This was Juhuri's world; he was obliged to adhere to Juhuri's rules. Yet as he sat there in the flicker of the kerosene lamps and looked into the fervent black eyes of Juhuri ul Azam, he knew he was being told less than the whole truth. This Tausug Datu was not totally bound to the simplistic route he paid lip-service to. Juhuri's decisions were far advanced, and it was no comfort to know that it would be considered an act of friendship to see that he reached the Garden of Paradise. He would fight the good fight, but he would do everything that he could to survive it . . . A cock crowed from the yard and then, distantly, another. Dawn was near. He drank his coffee and stubbed out his cigarette. He said, 'Will we go to Jolo, to the casa, this morning?'

They would not go that morning. That morning there was to be sport in the village.

'It is legal to hold cockfights only on a Sunday. Today is not Sunday but we do not care. It is the pleasure of my men to watch the cockfight, Reven. We call it takbi. It's our passion; our sport. You will see why . . . Come, Tuwan, let me show you great beauty, great nobleness. And courage, my friend; come with me and learn about courage.'

The morning was bright; the trees were dripping and the earth was patched with puddles. The rough grass in the yard sparkled with dew that left green footprints in their passage. The game cock of Juhuri strutted the perimeter of a diamond-mesh coop beneath some Lanson trees. 'Look at him, Tuwan. His neck plumage is like beaten silver, is it not? Look at his crest, see how it flames.'

Forrester's eyes burnt for the want of sleep. He saw no more than an ordinary, if somewhat large, rooster before him. He said, 'It's big.'

'Ah, he says you are big.' Juhuri bent before the coop and serenaded its occupant. 'But you are so much more than big, my Bulik. You are strong and you are *loyal*, and you are the gamest fighter on this whole earth . . . Watch, Tuwan.' Juhuri scraped his finger on the mesh and at once the big bird crouched with hackles raised in anger. 'He knows he's to fight today, my Bulik. He cannot wait. You will see something today.'

They went back to the house and ate breakfast and rested for a while on the kapok cushions in the hall. And then it was time for the takbi.

The cockpit was a waist-high square of bamboo stakes around which the fans clustered and milled. But the Milikan's arrival turned them from their sport. They stared. They stood back respectfully for Juhuri and his Bulik, then they closed in again and the Milikan became part of them. Two cocks were fighting when they arrived, scrawny birds when compared to the great Bulik that Juhuri carried wrapped so tenderly to his chest.

'Hacks,' Juhuri nodded derisively towards the fight in progress. 'Not worth watching . . . You wait.'

Forrester watched anyway. These two birds scooted around the ring, flapping and kicking out their spurred legs. Spots of blood speckled the earth floor of the pit. When one bird would fight no longer, the other pecked it a few times and was declared the winner, and that raised a mild cheer. Juhuri was right; the spectacle had not been worth the walk. And the next fight was just as tame . . . But an air of expectancy hung over this crowd. They knew there were better things to come.

The Bulik of Juhuri ul Azam had been matched to fight a big red, a Pula with a deadly reputation that had been brought all the way from the island of Siasi. The Bulik was in the pit in the hands of Juhuri's second. He held him by the tail feathers and the big cock looked sharp with excitement. Now a roar went up. The Pula had been brought into the pit. The cocks strained out to reach each other, their hackles raised, their eyes red, wicked with viciousness. The betting was on, and Juhuri's Bulik was favourite – Llamado. But the Siasi contingent had brought a lot of cash. One thousand pesos was the shout from their side of the ring. Juhuri's followers improved on that amount. They jeered and taunted the Siasians and yelled their bets at a gravel-throated kristo who held the bets.

'*Sinko!*' shouted the kristo – five against four. His fingers flicked busily to signal the odds. The sun shone brightly, and the gamecocks crouched, and people roared and rollicked and waved their pesos in the air – it was fiesta time.

Then suddenly there was quiet; not a total lack of sound, for the crowd still murmured. But he could hear the song of the jungle birds now, and the lowing of a carabao buffalo . . . and the low gear whine of a truck engine ascending a steep slope. And that was the sound that had hushed them to fear.

The jungle track did not lead right into the village so the Philippine Constabulary had to dismount and walk the last stretch. And that gave Juhuri time to conceal the Milikan and close big Bulik in his coop. It gave the villagers time to gather their families and their goats and their Siasian friends and run into the sheltering green jungle. It gave the bodyguard of Juhuri ul Azam time to lift the thick kapok cushions from the hall and barricade them against the inner wall of the big house; to cock their weapons and point them to the street. It was not a good ambush for only a very foolish enemy would walk straight down the village street.

Forrester, if he pressed his forehead hard to the bamboo wall, could gain a fine view of the street.

The PC came on in single file. Ten men in forage caps and sweated green jungle fatigues. They carried Armalite rifles at their chests . . . And they did walk straight down the village street. They walked so close to the big house that he could hear the thud of their jungle boots in the soft soil and the murmur of their conversation. And there stood the village headman at the gate of his house, with his cheeks twitching as he tried to smile but couldn't. On they came, all ten of them, so close he could smell the smoke of their cigarettes. A big fellow who wore dark glasses led them on. His rifle had been modified with the addition of a long, handmade magazine trimmed with brass that would take triple the quantity of bullets of a standard magazine. Stuck to the forestock of his rifle was a decal that read: *Exterminator*. He stood before the village elder now, so casual and loose. He asked a question and jestured to the jungle as he spoke. Forrester looked away from his peephole to see how Juhuri's men were reacting. There was not a man who did not have his rifle raised and his eyes squinted over his sights. Juhuri caught his glance.

'They've come for you, Tuwan,' he whispered. 'They're looking for you, those PC dogs.'

The village elder spread his arms, his palms wide with innocence. He was not a good liar, though; his features were drawn in fear and his eyes darted constantly to the big house where his saviours lay concealed in ambush.

Such a blissful place of grey thatch and bamboo with washing on the lines and stove smoke curling in the still air. Broad green banana plants and lanky papaya trees grew in the yards where wandering fowls pecked at the quiet earth. And the crash of rifle fire and the fountaining of life blood was only the pull of a trigger away.

Go away: he willed that of the big man who led the PC section. Believe the old man and live. Go away. It was not to be.

He was disbelieving, the big man, and he was violent. He slapped the village elder so hard that the sound clapped like a pistol shot. The old man staggered and fell back, then he cursed and he spat straight into the face of the constable. The 'Exterminator' came up. Juhuri's rifles roared shockingly and the bullets punched through uniform and skin and flesh and spun the PC this way and that. And then there was quiet . . . such a deep, deep quiet.

The smell of cordite went, but the smell of blood would not lift. The grass stalks prickled red with blood and the soil was pooled with it. The foolish enemy were all dead; all sprawled and splintered and splashed with the fluid of their own veins. How suddenly it had ended for them.

Juhuri's men took the PC bodies and carried them to the truck. Forrester heard the starter motor turn and the engine rev into life. Then the engine sound faded and the men came back and washed the blood from their hands and arms and kicked earth over the stained ground. But the blood smell had permeated that village and it would not go away. The sun shone and wood smoke lazed in the air, and the men gathered in the street and laughed too loudly and spoke too softly, and hid their shaking hands. For violent death has a touch that leaves no one as he was before.

Juhuri knew what to do. He came into the street with the Bulik in his arms and marched straight to the cockpit, and the people fell in behind him. The kristo appeared and swallowed hard and gruffed through his shrunken throat: '*Sinko!*'

The Bulik faced the Pula, and the referee commanded: '*Bihaun!*'

The crowd roared out and the gamecocks shot like rockets into the air. And in the air they collided in a storm of feathers, a flurry of beating wings. First Bulik was uppermost, then Pula. They whirled and soared, locked to each other in a frenzy of ginger and red. And as the sharp spurs kicked and slashed they fell; they tumbled on to the ground and separated for a moment. Then they brawled on the earth floor, tumbling and flapping and kicking and pecking. And the crowd roared louder than ever.

Forrester watched the people; their faces – widemouthed, then biting down, then wincing as if a spur had punctured their own skins, and their own blood spattered the cockpit floor. He watched them laugh and he watched them frown, and point and push and throw up their arms. What excitement! What bravery! The Bulik and the Pula fought furiously and they forgot all else . . . And what did he feel? He felt remote from all this; this shoving, widemouthed crowd, this strangest of entertainments, as though he was some irrelevant and unaffected observer. But it was a mind trick. He was a part of this massive violence. Ten men had come down the jungle track in search of *him*, and every one of them had died for it . . . He glanced to where Juhuri stood and saw that Juhuri was not watching the cockfight either. The Tausug's pitch-black, impassioned eyes were fixed on him. And in that moment he knew that more death was planned.

The Bajau girl had been a delight; her skin so smooth, the hair of her black rose so juvenile and fine. Her breasts – *aieya!* No larger than young peaches; to suck in whole from lip to gullet. How she had fought! He had exploded inside her in a thunderclap orgasm that had left him rigid and gasping. As he thought these thoughts, the drums of yang began to hammer and throb again in a most intrusive way . . . Forget her, he told himself. There are important matters that need your closest attention. Relax; lie back and consider how you are going to win back your gold.

There were the implications of the arrival of the Toh Mong Suen to be considered. Someone, perhaps the Bajau sea gypsies, had brought it to Jolo, and anchored it five miles out. Five miles in which direction? Was the junk still in working condition? Those were essential facts to acquire. He might get that information from Pang Ho the herbalist. Pang Ho, who dragged himself up the stairs of the casa every day to administer to Grandfather, was Cantonese, like himself. That hideous little dwarf might be just the ally he needed. He would see.

He thought about the gold. In his mind's eye he saw himself travelling the steep steps that led down to the vault beneath the casa; he inserted a key and turned a handle and a thick, studded plank door swung open. There before him lay the gold, gleaming yellow in neat square piles upon the floor; *his* gold! That was the bitterest memory. His whole mind centred on it. Then the face of the thief, Abdul ul Azam, came before him and he hit it till it was pulp, and he cursed it for a bastard egg of a turtle. Such was his passion that he sat up sharply and his temples throbbed and he had consciously to draw slow, even breaths. No more thoughts of Abdul ul Azam; that was his mind's instruction. Do not consider the insertion of the key until you have established how you can obtain the key. Do not consider passing the door until you have worked out how you will do away with the guard who always stands there. Lie back now, and reflect on these realities.

And so he did. He plotted and schemed and worried like a dog at the bone of his predicament. He thought of cunning ways, and daring ways, and ways of pure violence, and he discarded them all – none of them offered the slightest hope of success in the present circumstances. Frustration bore down on him so massively that he pounded his mattress with his fists and cursed out loud. And his headache expanded from his temples to his cheeks, to the nape of his neck. The pain became so crushing that he could think no longer. He closed his eyes and hoped that the blackness would blank out the pain. It did not.

He was further distressed by the bad manners of Younger Sister, who flung open the door to his room and addressed him most rudely:

'So I've found you.'

'Go away, Ah Shen.'

'How could you do what you did? How could you do such a terrible, *filthy* thing?'

'Like what?'

'Don't pretend. Don't lie.'

'I'm tired. I don't feel well. Go away.'

She strode into the room and her anger made him uneasy – it was in her eyes; they shone with it. Her hands trembled as she pointed to him: 'What have you done!'

'What's this about, ah?'

'You raped Narisa!'

'I didn't *rape* her. Did she say that? Do you believe that! The little chicken came in here and . . . did she say that I *raped* her?'

'You did. I see it on you.'

'No. By God, it wasn't like that.'

'I don't believe you.'

'Believe me . . . bring her here. How can she accuse me behind my back, that little chicken-whore. She won't get away with this. Do you know what she is? Do you know what the Tausug call those Bajau? Luwaan, that's what they call them. It means vomit. It's because they're so deceitful and dirty that they call them that. Don't believe her.'

'I believe her. She's just a child. You raped a child. Oh no! *Oh no!*'

'You believe her? Do you know what Abdul ul Azam says? He says that you encouraged him into wrong deeds. How about that, ah?' That got to her. That hit her like a slap in the face. He said, 'You see what it's like to be wrongly accused?'

'He's so evil.'

'Yes. I didn't believe him, though.'

'Both of you are evil. Both liars. What's happened to you, Elder Brother? I look at you and I don't know you any more. There's no remorse in your eyes or your words, yet I know you did this thing. It's as though you can't see the wrongness; like some animal or something. You lie, and you know that I know it's a lie but you don't care, and no shame. Can't you see the agony you have caused? If you stabbed her in her child heart you couldn't have hurt her more. What madness has come over you? What have you become?'

'She's nothing – a Luwaan.'

'She's a beautiful, innocent child.'

'She was married. Her husband is dead. She's not a child, and she's not innocent . . .'

'Your honour is gone. All of it. If Grandfather heard of this he would die of shame.'

'Then you would have killed him, Sister, not me. You are

380

the one who brought shame to our door. You're the whore. From the moment you took that stinking gwai lo lover of yours you began to kill the old man; and not just him, everyone else around you, too. First the amah, then your uncles and aunt. Then, thank God, it was the gwai lo's turn. *You* killed him . . . yes *you*. He's dead because of you. You made us bring him, that's why he's dead. And that's the only good thing about it.'

'*Not true!*'

'Shout that as much as you like. But I know it's true, so do you. Would he be dead if it wasn't for you? You killed your own lover.'

'He's *not* dead.'

'He's shark meat.'

'*Wrong*. Reven is alive.'

He shook his head; pleased with the punishment he had given. Shen deserved it. She did not mean he was alive; not in a literal sense.

'Reven is alive,' she said, in the face of his disbelief.

'What do you take me for?' He studied her, sure that the lie would become apparent. 'How could he be alive? Explain.'

'He's here at Jolo.'

'You dreamed it.'

'No more dreams, Elder Brother. Everything is clear to me now. I understand why Reven was so set against you. It wasn't mindless persecution, as you told us all it was. He did not want "your" gold. I never fully believed those stories and now I don't believe a word of it. I've seen the rottenness of your soul and I know that you must have done something terrible in Hong Kong. It must have been an awful crime. What was it? . . . No, you'd just lie again. Believe me when I tell you that Reven *is* alive. So don't make a wrong move. Because I would not lift a finger to shield you from him.'

He would not listen to this. He closed his mind to his sister's disloyalty and thought back to a most recent remark by ul Azam: 'A ghost did not sail it here . . . Then there is another story; it's about a Milikan who came out of the sea like a nesting

381

turtle' – Reven Forrester. It had to be that bastard gwai lo. The awful thought came as a whisper: He is alive then.

Shen spoke on as though she had not heard. 'You see why you cannot hurt me any longer. I have no respect for you. You call me a whore. I don't feel the insult. You blame me for Grandpa's condition. It's you who caused it. Listening to you is hearing the sound of a yapping dog. It means nothing.'

'I did all I did for the family.'

'You did it for yourself. And you dragged your family on to your muck-heap. Madness.'

'Is it madness to strive to be rich and respected?'

'Do you think you can weigh out respect and pay for it like a catty of rice? Poor Grandpa. He knows there is no hope for you and yet he still hopes. He knows there is no other heir; no one else but a snake-heart to take succession and "remember" the ancestors. He thought that one day you would find your worth. But I know that there is no worth in you to find. Disgrace is all you have to offer.'

'Shen . . . little sister.'

'Too late for that. I'm not "little sister" to you any more. You're lost to me . . . Now I'm going but I warn you if you touch Narisa again I will make life hell for you with ul Azam. You know I can do it.'

'It was he who said I could have her.'

'Sounds like the truth at last.'

'I wouldn't have done it otherwise . . . Yes I *did* do it. It's the way I am. Different flowers have a way with different eyes. It's not my fault. Abdul said she was once married, so there was no harm in it.'

'So much harm. So much . . . you will never know.'

'I didn't mean to hurt her. Don't go, Shen.'

She did not go away. She stood at the door and watched him with cold eyes. He lowered his gaze and he hated her silently. But what was to be done? For if Reven Forrester was coming then let him not come as an enemy . . . Had a hundred people been there to witness his humiliation he

382

could not have felt it more. Very quietly he said, 'Abdul ul Azam knows that Forrester has come. He said some things to me today about a Milikan that made no sense until now . . . Has Forrester come to help us, Shen?'

'Yes.'

'When will he come?'

'He will get a message to me.'

'Will you tell me then, so I can be ready? We must be ready. How will he get his message to you? Shen, I'll help him if I can. Yes, he'll need all the help he can get.'

'I don't think Reven will be relying on you, Elder Brother. I wouldn't if I were him.'

'Shen, if I get out of here it will be different; I promise. I'll be all that the old man wants. I want the same things he does . . . same things. Can't you see how hard it's been for me, hah? Forrester made seven hells for me. If I told you . . .'

She cut him short. 'Tell me what ul Azam spoke to you about. What's this about the Milikan?'

'He told me about some marketplace gossip. Some kids saw a Milikan – they call all white men "Milikan" here – coming out of the sea. The Toh Mong Suen is anchored off Jolo, and Abdul knows that. Forrester must have somehow sailed it here, *he's* the Milikan that the kids saw. That's what I make of it, and Abdul will work that out soon too, if he hasn't done so already.'

The worry in her eyes was heartening. He wanted to see more of it. 'He'll kill him if he finds him. He's ruthless. Yes, we both know that. Jolo is a small island . . . Difficult for him; difficult. He should get all the help we can give him. I could help him, for sure. But if you doubt me, and you turn on me, and you want to make an enemy of me . . .'

'Liar! Not a word of truth, even in prayer.'

'All right, I've lied in the past, but I should get another chance. This small thing with the Bajau girl has blinded you. Don't let it blind you. We're children of the same womb,

Shen; you and I. What do you think? Do you think *all* this is my fault; that I worked against my own family? I've always wanted the family to be proud of me, honest truth. *Tsha!* I've made mistakes, but I would never go against the family. There's blame on all of us. Yes, the old man too. He brought us here, didn't he? He remembered a heaven but this is a hell. So who's to blame for that?'

'I don't know . . .'

'I could help him. I've studied the layout of the casa. I've watched the guards; I know their routines. And I've made plans . . . Tell me; when will he come?'

She would not answer that vital question. Anger dried his mouth; his fists were knotted so tightly that his arms trembled. He wanted to lash out and hit her then, right upon the point of her obdurate up-tilted jaw. He forced himself to breathe evenly; to relax – smile. Show her, Eddie, that she hasn't hurt you.

The phlegmy, sick cough of Pang Ho barked from somewhere in the house . . . Pang was ascending the stairs; he heard the wood creak as it took his weight. Shen heard it too. 'I'm going to Grandpa,' she said. 'I'll tell you this: it will be very soon.'

'Soon? Is that all you'll tell me? And how will he get in here? Do you think that that guard down there with the machine-gun on his arm will throw a stiff salute and wave the great Ging Si through? Madness, the whole fucking thing! This time you'll *see* him die, Sister.'

'I'm going now.' She walked away.

'How do you know these things? Hah?'

But there was no need for her to reply to that question. How dull he had been not to realize it earlier; Pang Ho was the courier for Reven Forrester. There was no other possibility. How easy it would be now to gain every scrap of information that he sought. He waited until he was sure that Shen and the cripple had both entered Grandfather's room, then he too went there.

They were kneeling at the mattress and neither of them saw him at the door. He walked with great stealth; he knew which floorboards would give him away and which could be trodden in silence, so they did not hear him approach. He rested his back against the wall and he watched them. They shared an understanding, these two, that was obvious from the aggregate of their conversation.

'For Juhuri it is a matter of honour, Shen.'

'I know we must trust, but it's hard to trust.'

'He wants to see it over and done with . . . I don't know . . . I don't know. I've done all I can.'

'So many possibilities . . . I have such fear.'

Pang Ho was clearly the master of his art. He gathered Grandfather's wrists, first one, and then the other. He held them delicately and did not speak as he detected the whispered messages of the pulses. He sniffed at old Woo's breath as delicately as a cat. Then he said, 'Too much anger. Too much sadness. That's what's brought him to this; that's what's emptied this old man.'

'Sadness, yes. He was wronged a thousand ways by strangers and family alike.'

'Yet he's stronger than he was, Shen.'

'Shall I wake him?'

'No need. Has he been drinking his herb soup?'

'And eating too; better every day.'

'*Mcho.*' He nodded, pleased. 'You see it has nourished his heart; given him more energy. Let him sleep. Keep him warm. That's all we can do.'

'Yes. Yesterday he walked; just to there . . .' Shen turned her face as she gestured, and she saw her brother. Her eyes widened and her mouth fell open.

'Elder Brother!'

He walked towards them. 'What good friends you two have become. I'm really most, most jealous.'

'Mr Pang says Grandpa is improving.'

'Yes, I heard what Mr Pang had to say about Grandpa . . .

385

and other things too; secrets I think. Do you believe it's proper that there should be secrets between brother and sister in such circumstances? All this lack of faith. I'm bitter. I'm very bitter. Don't worry, I won't betray you. I have no reason to . . . or have I? But you and I must talk now, ah? . . . Come, Mr Pang. Yes, lift your miserable arse and come with me.'

'I cured your grandfather.' Pang whinged and shrank. 'I've been a good friend.'

To be ascendant again; ah, the scales of fortune had been so slow to tilt. 'Come, wipe the tears from the opera mask, Mr Pang. Let's talk of relevant matters.'

At last he had the facts he needed to give him the basis for a plan. Pang Ho had quivered and snivelled and his and Shen's secrets had fallen from him like ripe fruit in a typhoon – amazing secrets! Reven Forrester was in the hands of Juhuri ul Azam. Juhuri himself would bring him to the casa, and then into the presence of his father Abdul, *whom he hated!* Yes, that was what the cripple had given him, and it was the truth, he was sure it was the truth. There were two valid keys to the vault of the casa; one was in the possession of Juhuri, the other lay within a pocket of the sabitan belt that was buckled to the scrawny waist of Abdul ul Azam . . . Pang Ho had known all this and Shen some of it. She had certainly known of the locality of the Toh Mong Suen, and that the Bajau had possession of it. She had kept all that from him; from her *elder brother*. That really burned him . . . But this was not a time for anger. What Shen did *not* know was that there was a third key that would turn the lock of the vault, and this key was in the hands, the cunning, quick little hands of Pang Ho, the healer. And she also did not know that Pang was to give him the third key. That was Pang's promise. And thus Eddie had devised his strategy.

As a flame is to gunpowder, there would be violence when the gwai lo Forrester, and old ul Azam came together, that was natural. How much violence? Enough to roar through the casa and suck in all Abdul's bodyguards, that was his hope. Then he would utilize the chaos in the casa to go unnoticed and do what he had to do. That was his plan. It was not a plan that appealed to his Chinese sense of tidiness, it was nowhere near as good as the plan conceived for the Lion Rock robbery, but there it was; he could take it or leave it. And he decided to take it. There might never be a better chance, or even another chance. Having decided that, there was nothing more to do than wait and watch. So he positioned himself at the window of his room and gazed out at the casa's big black wrought-iron gates, and beyond the high white wall to the bustling street; up the street and down the street and into the shadowed alleyways that fed it. He watched for Juhuri and Reven Forrester. Timing; that would be critical to the success of his plan and the starting point was to be the moment of Forrester's arrival at the gates below.

He waited and he watched and smoked cigarettes, tip to tip, until the air was grey and acrid. The hours limped slowly by. His feet tired and began to throb, his headache worsened and the recently healed wound in his crotch burned dully, deeply from his groin right into his scrotum. But he was steadfast at his post. Of course, he had much time to think. He thought about Hong Kong; how perfect life had been there before that gwai lo cop had come crashing down like the thunderbolt of Lei Kung, to destroy everything; to send the rival Luen Ying triads in to break up his club and chop him . . . And why? He had never been able to work out how Forrester had justified such mad and insensible action . . . Kit Ling? That rag of a child, the Dog Star of ill-fortune shone on that girl. Look where it all had ended. Look where your revenge has brought us all, Reven Forrester. Madness, madness.

And now he was waiting for Forrester, that amazing survivor, that ingenious and frightening enemy. He had luck, that gwai lo, there was no denying that. And he was tough. His folly was that he loved Shen, and so he would shift even the gates of hell to free her. But the gates that Forrester would open would provide an exit for the brother of Shen, and the wealth of the brother of Shen, too.

He thought about the gold that was locked in the vault of the casa, and he thought about the man who had undertaken to help him recover it. Pang Ho was the greediest man he had ever come across. He had never seen anyone become so fired up with lust for money as that little cripple. Pang's eyes had lit up like a pig at a trough when he had learned about the treasure in ul Azam's vault! 'How much will be mine? How much will you give me if I provide the key?' It had been child's play to manipulate such greed. He had promised Pang a mountain; perhaps he would give him a grain . . . perhaps he would give him nothing. He would see.

He thought: Be alert and do not falter. When the time comes, move like a ghost. It will be soon, both Pang and Sister Shen said it will be soon.

The house stood on stilts that rose up in an old and arthritic way from the seabed. The floor was made from slatted bamboo nailed to jati wood beams. The walls were bamboo too, and had glassless windows that drew the sea breeze. The roof was palm-frond thatch.

If Forrester peered downwards between the cracks of the floor slats, he could see the ripple-free surface of the new tide, as transparent as a glass aquarium, and as alive. Its pebbly bottom was seeded with quick little fish that flashed as bright as new minted coins. They flitted and spangled, this way and that, and nibbled the green algaed pylons.

His forward vision gave him an open doorway, part of a veranda and some more bamboo-walled dwellings like the one that sheltered him. A labyrinth of footbridges straggled and wandered in a dislocated arrangement of bamboo and plank and other rickety, swaying things to connect the inhabitants of the stilt houses to one another, and ultimately to dry land and the streets of the city of Jolo. The casa of ul Azam was but a short walk from there. Its terracotta tiled roof was visible from the window of the little stilt hut; it stood out bold and vain amongst the litter of weathered grey thatch that roofed the majority of the houses in the barrio. And that was the view that drew Forrester most often as he waited for the arrival of Juhuri ul Azam.

Salihuddin was an inhabitant of the stilt-house village; Salihuddin was his guard. The man sat on a portion of the veranda that was out of view, but Forrester knew he was there. He could see the barrel tip of the Armalite rifle that Salihuddin owned, and he could hear the creak of bamboo as the man shifted his buttocks in search of greater comfort upon the split slat floor. He could hear the shriek and splash of children as they played in the shallows beneath the stilt houses. He could hear the thrum of a guitar and the voice of its owner in mellow, repetitive harmony. The throb of a basnig engine grew louder, and then faded away. A washerwoman called to her neighbour.

These sounds were familiar to him because for two days he had listened to them. For two days he had sat upon that bamboo floor; had paced upon it and trailed his sweat upon it, and lain down and slept upon it while waiting for the arrival of Juhuri ul Azam. But Juhuri had not come. And now he wished that he would not come . . . God, it was hot. The sun had ridden above Jolo that day as though it had halted in the heavens. A hazy, heavy sky had wrapped the little island and the heat had no escape. But the sweat that drenched his body was not the sweat of health. A short while ago the first stealthy, false cold chill of malaria had expanded like a ripple of ice water from his entrails. Now he was gaping with nausea and his whole body was aquiver.

He fought it. He would not let his body lie down and curl and shiver like a swatted fly. He pressed his spine hard to the bamboo wall to give him support. He turned his face towards the window that gave the view of the casa and he listened to the noise of the kids at play in the water. He heard the sound of the basnig and the washerwomen and the strum of the guitar. He fastened to these things because they were here and now, and might defend him from the cold and constant midnight that this fever possessed, where nothing moved or lived. But if Juhuri came now he would find an impotent ally. Two days more. Yes, two days and he would be strong again . . . If only he was allowed this delay.

Juhuri came that afternoon. He had closed his eyes, and when he opened them again the Tausug was there. He saw his frowning face and he heard his words, but it was a struggle to respond to the urgency in his voice.

'It's time, Reven, Tuwan. It's time . . . You must come now.'

You must come now, came the echo of the mind. Yes, he knew he must come. He must rise up and go with Juhuri. He rose up and a chasm of vertigo yawned open to accept him. But for Salihuddin's quick strong grip it would have taken him. But now he was upright and enduring the swim of vertigo . . . They walked into the hot bright sunlight. There stood Juhuri's men, hard-faced with rifles slung. He vomited right there at their feet and saw the bilious muck splash from the planking into the water, and the little fish close in upon the stain. More bile roared up from his gut and choked his nose and throat, and through this acrid wretchedness came his voice: 'Two days and I'll be strong.'

'Allah is at your shoulder,' said Juhuri. 'So, have no fear. You are his sword. I am his arm. Together we will end the hours of evil. Now is the time.'

To go to Shen; to take her from the prison of ul Azam. That was his commission. And it *was* time.

'For the term of every life is ordained, and no evil shall continue for a moment longer than Allah wills it. And Allah is with the righteous, and his strength is their strength. He guides them and he supports them . . .'

Strength; where was it? He found himself embraced to a pole and he knew that if he released it he would spill from the footbridge into the water below. Yet he did let go, and he did not fall. He walked, and he kept on walking with Juhuri's words bouncing like a shout in a cavern in the hollowness of his head.

'If there are twenty true men, and in faith they go up against a hundred, they will rout them . . . Be faithful, Tuwan. You are a man of the book, be strong. Allahu Akbar.'

The footbridge narrowed further to become a swaying gabbang of bamboo slats that gave like slack rope as he trod it; and had him clutching like a drunkard for support. 'Be strong, Tuwan; go forward.' Damn the man. Damn his advice . . . He set his feet wide and he commanded them to go on, and go on they did. With Salihuddin before him and the high passion of Juhuri driving madly at his back, he went on.

'Every grief and every bad time and sickness is ordained beforehand. That is a simple matter for Allah. I see you are fevered, Reven, Tuwan. Allah knows it. Al Muquit, The Strengthener; even now he helps you on.'

Then they reached dry land. There were alleyways here that slotted and jigged past slanted bamboo walls. They entered. Juhuri's men closed about him, and so narrow were the passages that shoulders and elbows jogged and a rifle butt pressed hard against his hip. He would have shoved these men from him had he the strength to spare. They walked the alleyways and idlers, flipping coins to pass the time, sprang from their games and stood back. Shaded faces peered out from dark windows, dogs sniffed their scent and were frightened and cowed, and small children with fingers sucked and docile eyes watched the passage of these hard men. Forrester, who had little faith in prayer, prayed in a fashion: 'Let Shen be untouched by what is to come. Let her be safe.' But he doubted if the Great Hearer of such supplications would hear him and come to his aid. He had never done so before.

'And those who are right, fight in the way of Allah; they fight against the friends of Saitan. Reven, you were brought here in the hand of Allah; the sword of Allah. Expect to do His will.'

There was the casa, high walls and green shutters; he glimpsed that, then the alley turned and it was lost. How close it was, though, the passage of seconds would bring them to it. He drew a full chest of air; they turned a corner and emerged upon the pavement of a wide street where shade trees grew and pedicab taxi drivers pedalled along. Beyond that stood the wrought-iron gates of the casa of ul Azam. The gates were tall and they were locked and behind the filigreed metal work stood a guard with an Ingram machine pistol slung carelessly underarm. He watched them as they walked across the road.

'Here is the house of my father. That is where your tanung, Shen, is held . . .' He pointed to a first-floor window, then to a window beyond the gate. 'That is the room of Abdul, my father. We are going there.'

To Abdul ul Azam, the rapist of Shen Woo. He looked towards that window and in that moment the maniac power of wild anger that had stood so close to him for so long, so well controlled, leapt loose. Its energy matched his fever. It thrust out iron strength into his limbs and quickened his mind . . . As he walked he might have glimpsed a face at a far window. He wiped the sweat from his eyes and looked again and saw he was mistaken.

Now they were at the gate.

The hours of pain and patience were rewarded: Forrester had come – there he stood with Juhuri ul Azam and a group of armed men at the gate of the casa. The gwai lo looked drained

392

of life, dragged out and limp as a piece of old rope. His eyes stared, purple-rimmed and sunken. But when those eyes glanced up to the window where Eddie stood, he quickly withdrew. He had seen Forrester look equally as beaten on a previous occasion, and then he had been as dangerous as a snake. He would not underestimate him now.

With the curtain to conceal him, Eddie continued to observe the events at the gate. It seemed that an argument was in progress. Juhuri's gestures were urgent, wide and threatening and he spoke with a frown but in a tone that did not carry as far as Eddie's window. The guard, intimidated, inserted his key and turned it in the lock, then he drew the gate slightly open; just wide enough to permit the entrance of Forrester and Juhuri. He forbade the bodyguards to follow and they retreated to the alleyway from where they had come.

Eddie's pounding heart was violent in his chest. His stomach was in a whirl and his armpits were trickling sweat. Where the hell was Pang? By now the cripple should have arrived at the gate. That was the arrangement; that was his promise: *In Forrester's shadow*, those had been Pang's exact words. Forrester and Juhuri were in the courtyard and walking towards the casa. *But where the hell was Pang?*

Pang was not coming. Pang had doublecrossed him. The third key was a myth. The impact of those shocking revelations staggered him as if he had been physically struck. What if Pang had gone to Abdul with his story? The strength drained from his legs and his mind grasped drunkenly with the consequences of such a betrayal . . . What was to be done? He thought he knew.

Eddie ran from his room and into the passageway. He pivoted upon the top banister post and scampered down the stairs – three at a stride. And even before he had reached the bottom rise, his new plan had matured. A demon's pat on the back of the head: an inspiration that was pure genius! He was surprised to find Abdul's first wife Halima in the passageway that led to Abdul's office, and Shen was with her, sobbing as though her heart was broken, being propelled forward by Halima at a quick rate. She called out to him:

'Elder Brother! . . . It's Grandpa . . .'

He did not so much as turn. He ran past them and up to the door of Abdul's office. The guard was so surprised he made no move to stop him. Eddie flung Abdul's door open.

Abdul ul Azam lay reclining upon his cushions. A cigarette was in his mouth from which a lazy drift of smoke rose up. Eddie knew just what to say.

'Forgiveness, Datu. Urgent, *urgent* news. Life and death news, Datu . . .'

The fingers of the guard closed upon the back of his neck and he was jerked up as a chicken about to be wrung of its life.

'Urgent news?' Abdul sat up. 'Life and death news?'

'*Aieya!* So urgent.'

'What is it then?'

Abdul waved; that delicate, small gesture, and his neck was freed from the terrible grip.

'Ah! You remember you spoke to me about a rumour. A Milikan who had come from the sea?'

'Yes.'

'It was no rumour. He sailed the junk of my grandfather to Jolo. A minute ago he was at your gate.'

'*No!*' Shen's shout. 'No! Don't tell him!'

'Yes.' He turned on her. '*Yes!*' He shouted too. 'I came to warn you, Datu.'

Did Abdul look grateful? He should look grateful. His future depended on Abdul's flow of gratitude.

'*Nagbuno Kami!*' Abdul shouted and sprang up.

Halima screamed and shoved Shen forward with such spite that she sprawled into the old man.

'*Bunuou!*' Abdul shouted. There came the metallic clash of a cocking handle being sprung. '*Bunuou!*' Abdul pointed straight at him – the rifle swung straight at him and he had no doubt that Abdul's command meant death . . . Shen screamed. He shouted.

'*M hai!*' He flinched his eyes tight. An explosion shocked him. He shouted again. He expected great pain but there was no pain. He thought: So this is how I am to die, so unfair, so unfair.

Another explosion; so *hard* and *loud*. It all seemed so impossible, yet inevitable, and he felt certain that he had experienced all this before . . . But it was not he who was dying. He saw that as soon as he opened his eyes. It was the guard who lay bleeding with his hands clamped at the red wound in his chest. But there was no stopping the flow. It was Juhuri who had shot him.

Eddie began to crawl towards the door. He was sure that if he stood he would be targeted again. There stood Juhuri with his big black pistol in his fist; a passion of words came from his mouth. 'By my heart and by my tongue I tried to change you . . . now *here* is the sword.'

Gunsmoke and sermons and the blood of a dead man; there was a madness filling this room. He must get away from it. His whole body was trembling, ringing filled his ears. He saw Reven Forrester, dripping with sweat, and Forrester looked down upon him with those fever-quick eyes, so filled with hate, but he made no move to impede him. Juhuri stepped back to give him space. He heard his sister sobbing, her voice crying, 'Reven, Reven.'

He did not stop. He did not look. The dark stormy words of Juhuri rumbled like a drum. He did not want to hear them.

'It is Allah who has brought him here. Allah who splits the peach stone, who brings forth the living from the dead and the dead from the living. He has brought him here.'

He crept into the passageway, away from the room of madness, and of shame. He wanted above all to be away from that place. But what did distance help when the mind would not follow? He saw himself as Forrester had seen him:

cringing with shock upon the floor. He had been utterly humiliated and all face was irretrievably lost. He shoved his knuckles painfully tight against his jaw and the inky taste of blood filled up his mouth. No matter; in anguish he pressed even harder. He hated those who had witnessed his abasement. The sound of another shot boomed in the passage; the scream of a woman. A man bearing a rifle ran past him towards the office. He did not care who had been shot: Shen, Juhuri, ul Azam, Forrester, he hated them all equally at that moment.

He raised himself from the floor; he took his hands from his mouth and leaned against the wall and stood. Then he walked up the stairs.

Narisa, the Bajau girl, stood upon the landing. She made no move to retreat from him. She stared at him, without fear; and beyond him, questioningly, into the hall. It was as if she too had seen him crawl, and despised him. Well, he hated her too. He came up to her, drew back his arm and struck her with his open palm so hard upon her cheek that she staggered and fell back. Then she ran down the passage away from him.

The minor violence of that single slap brought no improvement to his mood. What it did was to cause an awakening of his need for retaliation; the want of it burst frantically in him: *retaliation*, immediate and vast. He thought he knew exactly what to do to achieve it.

Upon the landing there was a plywood cupboard that held the paraffin lamps that were brought out on the nights when the generators of the Jolo Light and Power Company failed, which was two nights out of three. A wire hasp and a cheap lock were all that protected it. He pushed the door inwards at the top, and a gap appeared at the base of the door through which he anchored his fingers. That was all the leverage he needed. He tugged and the lock burst open. There were lamps inside, some cleaning cloths and a full bottle of paraffin, and *that* was what he wanted. He took the bottle to his room, uncorked it and splashed most of it on the mattress. He wet the pretty embroidery that hung upon the wall, then he flicked a lighted match on to the pyre. It caught fire with a *whoof*, and yellow-blue flames danced up. It blazed well for a while but then died down. He watched it and wondered whether it required more paraffin. There were the lamps in the cupboard, he could easily empty them on the mattress. Now he could see no flame at all but thick black smoke rose from the scorched kapok, it caught at his lungs and smarted his eyes . . . More paraffin was needed.

He closed the door of his room behind him, went to the cupboard and gathered all the wick-lamps there. He was sure he could raise a good fire now.

He could not get back into his room. As he opened the door, thick choking smoke burgeoned out. He hurled the lamps into the room and slammed the door. Fingers of smoke squeezed their way through the crack at the top of the door. He ran back along the passage and on to the staircase. Then with self-preservation on his mind he descended prudently, slowly, watching for Abdul's bodyguards as he went.

The guard post at the door of the vault stood abandoned! Eddie could scarcely believe his eyes. He took two paces down those steep stone stairs, halted then peered down again. There was definitely no one there. Here was luck at last. He ran to the bottom of the stairwell.

There were two doors, not one as he had imagined. Both doors were constructed identically of thick teak planks, riveted and studded and hung upon wide, ornate metal hinges. *And one of these doors was ajar!*

Eddie could scarcely breathe, such was his excitement. What if the guard stood behind that door? What if the gold was behind that door? *Aieya!* What if Pang had beaten him to it, and had looted the vault?

Neither guard, nor gold, nor Pang stood there. On the other side of the door was an armoury. The walls were chiselled stone. A single paraffin lamp burned upon a table giving a sombre light. Serpentine-bladed krises were pegged to the wall. A gun cabinet had every slot occupied with Armalite rifles and AK47s. A heavy machine-gun mounted upon a tripod stood centre floor. There were even some old circular leather shields and lances of bamboo with jagged barbed tips. As Eddie looked around he saw more: an open metal crate, its topmost tray filled with handgrenades nestling neatly in an indented plastic mould like so many green apples in a fruit box. He lifted one of the grenades – spherical, heavier than he had thought it would be. It was stencilled with yellow letters: GRENADE, HAND, FRAG. M67.

This was the first grenade he had ever seen other than those that were tossed about with such fearsome effect in the Vietnam movies. It was certainly the first grenade he had ever held in his own hands. He knew that here was a very, very potent weapon; more than a weapon. He thought: Here is the key to the locked door, if only I can use it.

Of course you can use it. There is the safety pin, see, pull that out and it will be live. That's how it's done. Place it against the locked door, pull out the pin, then rush back here. When it explodes it will blow the door into a thousand pieces and you can enter the vault, *and help yourself to the gold!*

Eddie carried the grenade, cupped in both hands, to the stairwell. He placed the thing at the base of the door. He held it firmly and tugged at the safety pin – it would not come loose! His chopped hand gave insufficient purchase on the grenade so he changed his grip. He pulled more vigorously and now it did come out. *Wah!* The grenade, being round, rolled away from the door and followed him as he ran. He dived into the armoury and clapped his hands to his ears, and waited . . . and waited. No explosion. His face relaxed, he looked around the corner of the door. There was the grenade, as good as new. He picked it up again. Of course the thing had not gone off; there was a second safety clip

398

attached to it, a bent wire spring that obviously prevented its detonation even if the safety pin was out. This needed to be removed before it would work . . . So he had made a mistake, but he had learned a valuable lesson at the same time. The grenade would somehow have to be fastened to the door, or it would waddle of its own accord down the slope of the stairwell in pursuit of him, and cause him grief.

He searched around and found another box. This box contained blocks of greyish, malleable substance wrapped up in cellophane. He sniffed it; he peeled back the edge of the cellophane. He read: Plastique RDX-80.

It felt tacky, like new putty – just what he needed to stick the grenade to the door. He took two blocks of the stuff from the container and stripped off the cellophane as he walked. A volley of firing thudded through the house. No time to think about that; he moulded the 'plastique' blocks to the door and implanted the grenade in it. It stayed in place; he was ready. He pinched the little bent wire and it sprang away. The handle of the grenade flew off and spanged off the wall. There was a small crisp crack, like the sound of a one-cent squib; a wisp of smoke rose from the grenade. Eddie ran. He pushed past the door of the armoury and clapped his hands to his ears and waited.

Reven Forrester knew that the strength he had found was fed by the power of his rage, but had no endurance beyond that, no muscle of its own. It took no effort to walk from the big gates to the door of the casa, and through the long passageways to the room of Abdul ul Azam.

He heard a shout; a woman's shout. Shen's shout; and then the raised voice of her brother. They sounded so close. Juhuri strode on and he followed. From the nylon satchel slung upon his shoulder Juhuri drew a big Colt pistol. He cocked the hammer.

Juhuri reached the door ahead of him; he had the pistol raised. More shouting came, then the blast of the big pistol and Juhuri's arm rose up with the recoil.

Then he could see right into the room and an overload of sighs and shouts assailed him. He saw the skull-ugliness of Abdul ul Azam, strident with anger. A guard in khaki jungle fatigues was dying, Juhuri's bullet had struck his chest to blood, but even so he was trying to raise his rifle. Juhuri shot him in the head and the rifle clattered to the floor. Forrester was aware of Eddie Woo, shrunken with fear, on hands and knees, scraping towards the door. He didn't care where Eddie crawled to, he hardly looked at Eddie Woo; his presence was irrelevant. Juhuri was talking. He heard him but the words passed him by. Where was Shen?

Old Abdul arose, all yells and spittle, gesturing with hands that were clawed with fury. Forrester walked into the room, and he saw Shen. She stared at him as one does who sees yet does not believe; incredulous eyes, they watched him approach. Her lips worked and mouthed silently the word: Reven. Then she believed and she called out aloud: 'Reven! *Reven!*'

Juhuri said, 'This is the man you left for dead in the rip tides of Palawan.'

Abdul frowned, and stared as though seeking some previous memory of Forrester. When he spoke again it was with a voice that hissed with passion: 'This is the Milikan? This is the man who was spat out by the sea? You brought him here, Juhuri, Halima? What shallow treachery.'

'God brought him to your house,' the old woman called Halima spoke out.

'You're mad . . . you too, Juhuri.' Abdul turned to Forrester. 'Tell us all: are you an angel? Did you walk beneath the sea from Palawan to Jolo?'

'I sailed here in the junk of Woo Yin-wah . . .'

'God's will,' shrilled Halima.

'I came for Shen and for that reason alone.'

'What disappointing news . . . He came for Shen,' Abdul mocked. 'For *no* other reason than the love of this woman. A noble cause, perhaps, but hardly a divine cause.'

Juhuri pointed. 'This man raped your sweetheart.'

Abdul's sniggering stopped at once. Straight out he said: 'No. That's a lie.'

'He *did!*' Juhuri's words rode over his father's. 'Ask Halima.'

'He did,' said Halima, unasked.

'Is it true?' Forrester said to Shen. 'Is what Juhuri says the truth?'

'No!' Abdul shouted out. 'No! *No! No!*' As though by the weight of repetition his denial would overmaster his accusers: 'No! No! . . .'

Shen's voice was small and wretched with sorrow yet it carried over Abdul's drubbing: 'What does it matter what happened to me. Grandfather is dead, and that is your crime. Your great crime. You killed him . . .'

'No! No! He was old.'

'You are a murderer.'

'How can you talk like that? I tried to help him. I am a Muslim. I live by faith. I do Salat. I've made the Haj. Don't listen to her kafirum lies, Juhuri.'

'Oh, he tried to rape me. He came into my room while I was asleep and when I woke up he was there . . . But he was too weak to do anything. I don't care about that.'

'I care,' Juhuri pointed at his father. 'It is written in Ya Sin, in the Holy Koran, that those who strive with might and main to do evil shall be slain or crucified, or have their hands and feet cut off on opposite sides. *That* is the Law of Punishment.'

'And who are you to stand against me as a witness? We all know that you love the Chinese girl.'

'Don't try and turn the sword with your half-truths. You are the wrongdoer. Your heart has hardened towards Allah.

Your deeds will be a snake in your tomb . . . So, now it is time, judge him, Reven. That is your duty to God.'

'Your duty,' echoed Halima.

'How can I judge him? I hate him too.'

'*Judge* him.'

Juhuri's pistol arm was straight at the elbow. The big Colt pointed dead at Abdul's chest and the knuckles upon the grip were bloodless with tension. Abdul was one single word from death; the word was 'guilty'. And he *was* guilty. That was the judgement of Forrester, and it would have thrilled him to see the big pistol explode to rupture the heart of Abdul ul Azam; and all in God's name. But he knew what he must say.

'No matter what this man has done, you cannot kill him like this. Don't shoot him, Juhuri. How would that help?'

'Don't do it.' Shen's small voice. 'He is your blood.'

Abdul did not flinch in the face of his son's aim. He stared ahead straight at the pistol and there was not a tremor of fear about him as he raised his hands to his throat and undid the buttons of his blouse. He said quietly: 'God will be my judge, Juhuri . . . and yours too. Shoot me then, Juhuri, here, and feel the torment of Hellfire on the day of reckoning. God is my only judge!'

'Blood?' Juhuri held to Shen's word. 'Blood; yes . . .' His shoulders unstiffened, his pistol arm sagged. 'How right of you to remind me of that, Shen. I am no more than this man's blood. I have no right . . . no right at all to interfere in these events. Don't you see, Mother? Here is the man . . . Reven, you must take the pistol. Here, take it. It is for you to use it.'

'God didn't lift me from the sea, Juhuri.'

'You must do what must be done.'

'Listen, Juhuri. A Bajau sea gypsy saved me. He showed me how to get here. We sailed here together.'

'Allah's hand. Who are we to doubt it? He works in wonderful ways: *As Sami*.'

'Allah the Life Giver,' said Halima. 'Take the gun, Reven, it is His will.'

'Give me the gun then.'

The metal was hot from the shots expelled from it. He took it by the barrel from Juhuri's hand. It was fully cocked and set to fire. He said:

'You see me as something that I am not. I am the last man on earth that God would choose to do his work. I'm full of bitterness and hate. I judged your father long ago according to those emotions; don't you think I found him guilty? But tell me, Juhuri, would Allah select a man as angry as I am as his executioner? . . . No. And yet, if shooting him would change a thing, I'd do it. But it won't. So I hold the pistol and I choose not to use it. I will *not* use it.'

'Wrong,' Halima cried. 'Wrong.' In deep emotion she spoke on in Tausug to her son. And Juhuri answered her in that language.

'Shen, come.' Forrester took up the small hand of the woman he loved and held it tightly. Now his anger had burned out, and with it, his strength. He swayed as he walked, seeking balance with the concentration of the tightrope walker.

'Narisa, Bahang's wife. She must come with us.' Shen's voice sounded distant.

'Yes.' He had not forgotten his promise to his little friend. The power of the fever was raging in his body, but he remembered that. His vision shimmered and swam as though in a mirage of heat. And in this visual fallacy a man with a rifle appeared, coming towards him at great speed. The rifleman was going to shoot them, that was certain; the rabid voice of Abdul filled up the room and this was Abdul's man . . . The kick of the big Colt and its roar was startling, as though it was not his hand that held the weapon, and his finger that had stroked the trigger. As red as sun-red hibiscus a flower blossomed in the man's chest, its petals flooded out. He shot him once more; this time with deliberate aim.

403

Then he shot Abdul ul Azam. He shot him again, and again. He fired until there was not another round to shoot. But Abdul's kris had swung, and from its jewelled handle to lustrous blue blade, it was wet with blood. Shen's blood. Her back was slashed to the bone.

'*The will of Allah!*' Halima shrieked. 'See, it's done! You've *done* the will of Allah.'

There was a voice and it was saying: '*She's dying.*' Over and over; that single phrase: '*She's dying. She's dying.*' He could not concede it, even though the words came from his own mouth, and they were true. Shen's breathing was shallow and quick and her face was grey. He groped with the wound and tried to halt the blood, but the slash was long and deep and the blood kept coming. '*She's dying. She's dying.*' So he held her in his arms in his helplessness and cradled her head and kissed her. He heard her whisper, 'I love you, Reven.'

'Oh I love you. I love you.' Her eyes were dulling. 'I love you, Shen.'

'There is no pain.'

'No pain; that's good, my love, my precious love.'

'You came . . .'

'Of course.'

'I knew you would come.'

'Oh, Shen, Shen . . .'

He went on calling to her though he knew she was dead. He held her sweet body and his misery spilled from him in deep tearless sobs.

An explosion shuddered the floor and walls and buffeted the air. A quick gust of wind brought the harsh smell of Nitro and hot smoke began billowing through the open door. He rose up and carried Shen from that room.

The blast was monstrous. It was savage. It was raw. There was heat, white light and a percussion that stunned Eddie, shocked him and punched the air from his lungs.

He had been squatting against the wall, now he lay sprawled wide upon his stomach. His head pained hollowly as though he had been struck a massive blow. He was in darkness. He raised himself up, brought out his matchbox and struck a match. Rifles and ammunition clips and krises and lances lay strewn upon the floor. The gun cabinet had fallen forward across the big machine-gun. The paraffin lamp lacked glass, but the body was intact, so he lit the wick and carried it to the stairwell.

Grey smoke, and the stench of explosive, much stronger than it had been at Lion Rock, it rasped his nostrils and throat like raw ammonia and bent him double, coughing. He blinked and slitted his eyes, and through the tears he saw that the door to the vault was destroyed.

There were the metal hinges, and attached to them some splintered wood remained, that was all. He stepped past that into the vault.

Gold, *his* gold, there it was. It lay in disorder in little heaps and single slabs, all covered in dust and debris. He went upon his knees and began to scrabble for it.

Eyes streaming, lungs tearing; Eddie crammed his pockets with 9-ounce slabs of gold. And when they were full he looked around for a container, and found amongst the debris a leather satchel filled with papers. Out went the papers and in went the gold slabs. He stuffed its wide pouches until they bulged, then tried to lift it – a ponderous weight but he could manage it. He clasped it to his chest and staggered up the stairs.

The house was on fire. He saw that the moment he arrived at ground level. He didn't think this could be his fire, his midget arson could never have amounted to this roaring monster. The wood planks of the ceiling were burning, thick smoke bundled through the cracks and the heat beat painfully at his skin. He wondered which direction to take and before he had decided, the topmost banisters of the staircase burst into flame and down skipped the fire along step and post, as quick as blazing matches. He fled towards the front door, and found that he was not the only one running from the fury of that heat.

Juhuri was there with his swooning, fat hag of a mother in tow, screaming, flailing her untethered arm . . . Reven Forrester was closest to the door, which position was unearned for he was the slowest of them all. His posture and pace was that of an old man. He walked bent forward as though his burden was more than his spine could bear. His burden was Shen. Her arms swayed limply, her head lolled back and her hair trailed to the floor. She looked terrible. He elbowed past them and was first out through the door.

He was the first into the garden and he did not slow down until he had reached the gate. There his progress was checked, the gate was locked, the sentry was absent. Breathless, clutching the satchel as tightly as ever, he turned to look towards the casa. Black smoke tongued with bright fire billowed up from the roof and flame leapt in a wild dance from the windows. He saw Grandfather . . . just an instant, just a face – a hand raised up, then nothing but swirling flame. He hoped it was not his fire . . . He hoped that what he had seen had been an illusion and that Grandfather would emerge soon with the others through the door. They had said he could walk, hadn't they? Sure, he would walk out any second, ah?

Shen was dead. He saw that as Forrester staggered out of the house. The back of her white blouse was slashed and ribboned with blood. Forrester's face showed stark grief. Juhuri emerged then still pulling Halima. Then came the Bajau girl, Narisa, retching and coughing. No one else came out; no one at all.

He turned away from the casa. Beyond the gate the street was crowded. Faces of strangers; he tried not to embarrass them with the sorrow of his great loss. Grandfather and Shen were dead and the grief of it was choking his throat and blinding with tears. Especially let Forrester not see his sorrow. The wail of an oncoming fire engine grew louder and louder, but they were too late, and he hated them for their tardiness. He clutched the leather satchel even tighter to his chest, that was all he had now. That was all that was left.

The Toh Mong Suen rode the dull water of a grey sunset, and from the shore it looked tired but at peace. If only Younger Sister could have seen it. With her poet's eyes she would have sprinkled silver dust upon that leaden sight and delighted them with her words. And Grandfather would have listened in silent awe to the brilliance of his descendant daughter and grunted 'Hm!' in an imperious way to hide his pride: 'Hm!'

But Shen was dead, and Grandfather too, and so the view was his alone, and for him it was a bringer of a bitter cup of memories . . . The gwai lo Forrester sat near him, but they had nothing to share, not even that most shareable of conditions, misery. The man sat with his buttocks in the sand, his knees drawn up and his face pushed into his hands, and occasionally he would raise his head and stare out to sea. He looked as though he might die too. He was as sick as any man Eddie had ever seen. He would not be mourned.

Yet Forrester had done one right thing. He had told him that Grandfather had not been alive at the time of the fire. 'Thank God,' the gwai lo said, 'he was dead.' Yes, thank God, they could both agree on that. So now he could mourn Grandfather with a clean heart. He could mourn him as a grandson should mourn, and he would see to his eternal soul. The ceremony of thrice-times-seven would be a no-expense-spared affair and Grandfather's journey through the Ten Hells would receive every human aid that could be given. Now he was rich, and Grandfather would travel first-class. The King of the Dead would be strongly petitioned to ensure it . . . And he would attend to Shen's funeral too in a way that would ease her path. He had forgiven her her

407

wrong accusations, for after all she was just a woman. Both would be buried well.

The crunch of feet on sand caused him to turn. One of Juhuri's soldiers had emerged from the coconut plantation where they had taken position. He walked towards Forrester and touched him on the shoulder. When Forrester looked up the man pointed out to sea.

A Bajau vinta with a bright-striped lug sail of yellow, red, blue and green was scudding towards the beach. Forrester saw it, and nodded, but did not move more than that, and the soldier walked away.

On came the vinta, as delicate as a kite this little craft. A single man crewed it, plying the rigging ropes from the stern. Neither slowing nor swerving he ran his frail craft right into the shallows and keeled it on the sand. The boatman was a little fellow; hard-muscled with sun-bleached hair and sun-brown skin, he wore only a loincloth. He leapt from the vinta and ran to Forrester and dropped to his knees and embraced the gwai lo. Forrester tiredly ruffled the man's hair. They spoke for a while then Forrester stood and walked towards Eddie. His voice ached with tiredness.

'Woo Sung-king, I won't be returning with you. I think you knew that . . . There's your grandfather's junk. It works. It's yours. Take it.'

'I won't go back to Hong Kong.'

'Go where you like . . . I don't care. I don't want to see you again. That's all.'

'Nor I.'

'Juhuri knows that you started the fire. I wanted you to know that. He's glad you did it . . . in a way. You wouldn't understand, but your last rotten deed might result in some good.'

'Will he come after me?'

'I doubt it . . . Go now. Bahang will take you out.'

Bahang held the vinta for him and gestured for him to sit in the bows. He sat with the satchel between his knees. The

Bajau turned the craft and ran with it until the water churned at his thighs, then he hauled himself aboard. The sail filled up and swept them from the bay. He looked back once; Forrester was still there, seated again upon the sand. Jolo looked dull and grey beneath its sullen high mountains. But now he was leaving all that behind him. A shiver ran through him and it was in that instant that his gloom lifted away. His luck had changed, he felt bold and strong, and he knew he could make it now. A chuckle that was hovering in his ribs built up into a laugh that he could not hold back.

The little Bajau sung a song while they sailed. It seemed it was a sad song; the tone was mournful and the words repetitive, and it took them from the bay right to the side of the Toh Mong Suen – *his* Toh Mong Suen. It was terribly scarred with bullet holes and one mast was gone, but the joy of the touch of the hull planking on his outstretched hands was the joy of the child come home.

The Bajau nosed his vinta close to the low mid-deck, close enough for a fingertip touch upon the deck rails. He bent down and lifted the heavy satchel and reached out again. One hand to grasp the deck rail, one hand to hold the satchel, he stretched out and as he did so the vinta slid back. His feet stood in the vinta, his body hung over the water, his fingers clutched the rail; and this was his weak hand, his chopped hand; three fingers only to hold him. The fool Bajau could see the peril of it; if the man did not draw in immediately he would fall into the water.

Bahang did not draw in.

Bahang stopped singing as the Chinaman screamed and fell into the water, but the words of his *tinis-tinis* still turned in his mind. He dived into the sea after the man who had raped his dear Narisa. It was not abnormally deep there, but the sky was gloomy so the middle depth was dark and the water did not lighten until he reached the reflective white bottom sands. There he saw the man again. His mouth was pinched and his cheeks puffed out. His eyes bulged and turned towards the surface and he kicked and thrust in a frenzy to propel himself there. He had landed upon a meadow of black, branching akar bahar coral. A rainbowed shoal of parrot fish rode the current there and stayed to watch the strange sight.

The Chinaman would not release the case and it held him down like a diving stone. He struggled and thrashed to raise himself; he might as well have tried to jump to the moon. He held that case as though it was part of him; as though separation from it was unthinkable. He held it until the pressure to breathe cramped his lungs and his breath burst from him in a plume of silver bubbles. Then he dropped it. Still he was weighted down – his pockets were filled with pieces of heavy gold metal. He wrenched and he fumbled to be rid of them . . . then his movements slowed, and slowed further, then he was still.

The weight in his pockets drew the drowned man to his knees and his arms relaxed and rested out upon the akar bahar in a peaceful pose. Bahang swam right up to him then and touched him, he worked loose a piece of the gold from his pocket and admired its glow, then he let it fall and watched the sand swirl up and take it. He peered into the face of the dead man and he spoke to him with the mind; he asked:

What made you so bad?